PRAISE FOR
SEAFIRE

"One of the most spell-binding adventures of the year. This is female piracy at its best."—*SAN FRANCISCO CHRONICLE*

"The best kind of fantasy. . . . Impossible to put down."—*PASTE*

"This is *Mad Max* by way of Davy Jones, a high-energy, breathless adventure."—*BOOKLIST*

"The pace of the book is fast and relentless, and the action sequences tense and believable, but the best moments are the ones in which the female relationships shine."—*NPR*

"Absolutely enthralling. *Seafire* is a relentless adventure about friendship and found family, trust and betrayal, and a vow for vengeance as unstoppable as the sea."
—**HEIDI HEILIG,** author of *THE GIRL FROM EVERYWHERE* and *THE SHIP BEYOND TIME*

"Parker has crafted a thrilling, empowering tale of doing what is right, not what is easy. Any reader who's dreamed of the high seas, adventure, and freedom will be clamoring to join the crew of the *Mors Navis*. An emotional and pulse-pounding read."
—**TESS SHARPE,** author of *FAR FROM YOU* and *BARBED WIRE HEART*

"A stunning and powerful book about choosing to fight in the face of vicious odds. *Seafire* will stay with you long after you finish reading."—**BRENDAN REICHS,** *New York Times* bestselling author of *NEMESIS*

"A brilliant story that shows the strength and bravery of girls against the world. Natalie C. Parker has given me a book I wish I'd had when I was younger."
—**ZORAIDA CÓRDOVA,** award-winning author of the **BROOKLYN BRUJAS** series

STEEL TIDE

STEELTIDE

NATALIE C. PARKER

RAZORBILL

RAZORBILL

An imprint of Penguin Random House LLC, New York.

alloyentertainment

Produced by Alloy Entertainment
30 Hudson Yards, 22nd floor
New York, NY 10001

First published in the United States of America by Razorbill,
an imprint of Penguin Random House LLC, 2019

Visit us online at penguinrandomhouse.com

LIBRARY OF CONGRESS CATALOGING-IN-PUBLICATION DATA
Names: Parker, Natalie C., author.
Title: Steel tide / by Natalie C. Parker.
Description: New York, NY : Razorbill, 2019. | "A Seafire novel." |
Summary: Rescued by the Blades, a nomadic crew hiding from Aric Athair, Caledonia seeks
their help to find the *Mors Navis* and her sisters, defeat Aric's fleet, and take back the Bullet seas.
Identifiers: LCCN 2019016804 | ISBN 9780451478832 (hardback)
Subjects: | CYAC: Ship captains—Fiction. | Sex role–Fiction. | Seafaring life–Fiction. |
Adventure and adventurers–Fiction.
Classification: LCC PZ7.P2275 Ste 2019 | DDC [Fic]–dc23 LC record available
at https://lccn.loc.gov/2019016804

Printed in the United States of America
1 3 5 7 9 10 8 6 4 2

Interior design by Corina Lupp
Text set in Elysium

For Sean & Maureen
and
Travis & Carly,
my siblings before the law had anything to do with it

BEFORE

The stars felt close tonight. From his place cradled in the nest, far up the mainmast on a night as dark as this one, Donnally felt they were especially near, almost within reach. He loved that illusive, unsettling feeling of suspension. If he held still, breathed just right, he could convince his mind that it was as possible to sink upward into the sky as it was to slip into the sea. For a split second, his body was as light as air, and the entire universe was at his fingertips. When he reached up to pluck a single star from the glittering array, the illusion broke. In a flash of disorienting dizziness, he was part of the earth again, with feet firmly planted on the floor of the nest and head tipped up.

"Would you quit picking at the sky?" Ares slumped against one side of the protective bowl that encircled them both, bored and tired. The combination made him irritable. Like his older sister, he was destined to be tall with broad shoulders and long arms. His skin was the same sunny brown as Pisces's, and his hair was long and black.

"Why does it bother you?" Donnally asked, tipping his head backward over the lip of the nest so that the ocean became the sky.

He heard Ares sigh and crack his knuckles. The truth was it probably didn't bother him. What bothered him was being awake at this hour and the way the nest tipped back and forth like a pendulum. At twelve turns each, the boys had been friends long enough for Donnally to recognize when Ares's irritation was an arrow in need of a target. And he'd been the target frequently enough to know he'd rather avoid it, so when Ares didn't answer, Donnally didn't press.

They'd been posted as lookout for nearly an hour, long enough for Caledonia and Pisces to reach the nearby island called the Gem and start foraging, but not quite long enough to expect them to return anytime soon. Donnally leaned even farther over the edge of the nest, letting his arms hook around the railing and the blood rush to his head. The ocean was all gentle black chop. It lapped against the hull of the *Ghost* as the tide swept in, pushing them back and forth.

Suddenly, Donnally felt a foot hook beneath his own and kick upward. The force lifted his whole body, and he began to slip over the edge of the basket. He shrieked, arms flailing. Then hands gripped his knees and tugged him right back into the nest, where Ares was hooting with laughter.

"You know you're strapped in, right? You can't actually fall?"

Ares laughed all the harder, bending over to brace his hands against his knees.

Donnally didn't find it funny in the least. He lunged for Ares, aiming a fist for his face. But Ares was taller and stronger. He deflected Donnally's blow easily, snatching the arm of his gray jacket and whipping it off him in one smooth motion. The jacket flew into the air and fluttered toward the ground, where it landed in a heap.

Now Donnally was mad. He felt his temper burning in his cheeks and in the curl of his fists. He roared and dove for Ares again.

"Boys!" The voice belonged to Donnally's dad, and it stopped them dead in their tracks. They'd both be in trouble for this. It didn't matter that Ares had started it. There was no roughhousing in the nest. "Sounds like you need something else to keep you occupied."

Donnally peered over the edge, sure to keep a firm grip on the railing this time. He spotted his dad standing near the port rail, chin tipped up to watch the boys, a gray coat pulled over his shoulders.

"Found your coat," he called to Donnally.

Ares laughed again while Donnally fumed. "Thanks."

They were definitely in trouble. Donnally could see it in his father's expression. They were going to be on kitchen duty for weeks, peeling and canning whatever fruits and vegetables the girls brought back, forced to endure Cook Orr's protracted stories about the way things used to be. It was going to be hot and boring and tedious, and it was all Ares's fault.

"Hey," Ares said, voice capped with humor. "Donnally, I'd never let you fall. I was just playing."

Donnally was preemptively plotting his revenge when three gunshots pierced the night sky.

The entire ship went still as a stone. Donnally met Ares's eyes for one brief second, then the two of them turned to search the waters around the Gem. They looked for anything—light, movement, their sisters—but there was nothing for them to find.

On the deck below, the crew vaulted into silent action. They moved in all directions, readying the ship for sail. The laundry lines came down, the goats were taken below, the box gardens were carted away, and it was all done without a word, every single command given without making a sound. It was a familiar sight. Rhona ran this drill regularly, kept the ship parts seamlessly oiled and cushioned. They would be ready to go in moments.

The stretch of ocean between the *Ghost* and the Gem gave no indication of the little boat that carried Caledonia and Pisces. Donnally watched the choreography unfolding below him in a sort of suspension, stuck between the comfort of routine and the fear of knowing this time it was real. They were preparing to flee.

Ares gripped Donnally's shoulder, alarm making his eyes wide. He whispered, "We won't leave them, will we?"

Donnally wanted to deny it, but there was a coil of dread in his stomach, writhing like a snake. "Never be seen," he said, citing the first rule of the ship.

The strength leached out of Ares's grasp. He looked horrified and then suddenly angry. "No."

Before Donnally could stop him, Ares had unsnapped his harness and climbed out of the nest. Without taking the time to hook on to the safety line, he began to climb down. Donnally followed. He detached his own harness and moved down the mainmast as quickly as his shaking hands would allow.

They reached the deck to find their world unraveling. Their parents stood near the bridge with their shoulders together, engaged in tense conversation.

The boys made straight for them, pushing into the circle just in time to hear Ares's mother say, "And what if it's nothing? What if they fired at an animal and we abandon them?"

"If that's the case, they'll survive two days." Rhona Styx stood with her arms crossed and a rifle slung over her shoulder. "I don't like this any better than you do, Agnes, but our girls know what they're doing. They'll wait for us."

"But *we* should be the ones waiting for *them*." Agnes planted her hands on the round curve of her hips.

"Boys!" Donnally's father cried in alarm. "Who's on watch?"

Whatever happened on Donnally's face was answer enough. His father cursed and raced toward the mainmast, but it wasn't soon enough.

"Captain," a young man named Bandi called from the bridge tower. "We've got trouble. An assault ship. They're close, and they're on course to box us in."

"Damn." Rhona's jaw fixed in place as she swiveled to search the ocean.

Each and every time the *Ghost* had encountered a Bullet ship, they'd taken a single course of action: run. While Donnally was too young to remember any of their more narrow escapes, he'd been raised to believe that running was the only way to ensure they survived.

Right now, running was the furthest thing from his mind.

All he could think about was his sister. Had she fired those shots? Or had those shots been fired at her?

Would he ever see her again?

"Rhona?" Donnally's father asked, coming to stand at her side. "Captain, your orders?"

Rhona's eyes fell on Donnally. Her gaze was as powerful as the sun, and he felt warmed and emboldened at the same time. He feared for his sister almost more than he could stand, but he smiled for his mother, to show her he was afraid and also brave.

Rhona nodded and swallowed hard. "I'm afraid we have no choice," she said. "Weigh the anchor and grab your guns. We're going to fight."

In the wake of those words, the ship seemed to transform. Commands were shouted in all directions, the anchor clanked in its channel, even the sea seemed to slap at the hull with more vigor than just a moment ago. Rhona swept forward, gathering her son into her arms and holding him tightly. She kissed his head and released him, saying, "Do as your father says. I love you, my brave boy."

"I love you, too," Donnally said, and then she was gone, climbing toward the bridge and disappearing inside it.

"Let's move." Donnally's father caught his hand and pulled him toward the quarterdeck, where the rest of the children were being herded by a few tight-mouthed adults. Agnes was there, helping each of them over the side railing and into the remaining bow boat on the water below.

"I don't want to go," Donnally protested, fear spiking through him. "I want to stay with you."

But Donnally's father pulled him along, stopping only when they reached the railing. "You must go. We'll come back for you, but for now, you need to get as far from this ship as you can. Head for the Gem. Find your sister."

In the distance, a deathly crooning pushed through the air, growing closer and louder. The crew of the *Ghost* had lost all pretense of quiet now. They'd become a different kind of machine right before Donnally's eyes, one that sounded like bullets snapping into chambers.

"Tagg!" called Agnes. "We're out of time."

Suddenly, Donnally was pressed against his father's chest. "Find your sister," he repeated, squeezing the boy more tightly than ever before. "Find your sister and live."

Before he knew it, Donnally was over the side of the ship

and tucked into the boat waiting below. There were eight children already aboard. Astra, Derry, Lucero, and Jam sat silently, their eyes pinned to the hull of the *Ghost*, while the others searched the darkness for the approaching ship. Ares and Lucero, oldest and strongest of the small group, took up oars, and soon their small boat was cutting a shallow path through the water, heading for the same small island as Caledonia and Pisces.

For a few precious moments, there was nothing but that steady wail of the ghost funnel and Astra's sniffles. Time felt like a vise around their little vessel. Donnally kept his eyes on the dark outline of the island just ahead, wishing they could stay locked in this moment indefinitely. Then, a flare of light. The terrible cry turned into a deafening roar.

Donnally couldn't help himself. He turned to watch as the Bullet ship closed in on the *Ghost*.

Red dripped down the nose of the Bullet ship like a bloody gash. Men swung in harnesses, armed with magnetic bombs and roaring with fury. Spikes studded the ship's perimeter like thorns, bodies in many stages of decay impaled on each one.

Every muscle in Donnally's body clenched. The little boat was moving faster now, assisted by the wake of the Bullet ship. Behind him, Donnally could hear Ares calling a rhythm to Lucero, keeping their oars synchronized.

In the next minute, the *Ghost* was in flames, and the children knew speed would not save them.

There was a small but bright part of Donnally's mind that was as calm and distant as a star. It was the part of him that marveled at how quickly the Bullet ship subdued the *Ghost*. The seeming chaos of their fury was only an illusion. In reality, they were an expertly conducted choir, striking the deadliest of notes at precisely the right moment. After their magnetic bombs weakened the *Ghost* and forced half the crew belowdecks, the attacking Bullets easily bested those who remained topside. Donnally watched the battle unfurl with sense and strategy, and slowly, his body began to still.

"Stroke!" cried Ares.

But Lucero's oar slowed. One thing Bullets knew how to do was find running children, and a bow boat was already in the water, racing toward them.

"Stroke!" Ares cried again, panic making his voice thin. The approaching Bullets pulled alongside, and still Ares kept rowing. He didn't stop until the Bullets circled them twice, then fired a single shot into the nose of the small boat.

Ares's fingers tightened around his oar as though he were considering whether or not to fight. His rebellious thoughts were clear: if they were going to die, they might as well take a Bullet or two down with them.

"Two choices, recruit." The Bullet who spoke had fresh blood smeared across his cheek.

Choices. Live or die.

"Ares," Lucero whispered from the rear of the boat. In a few short moments, they'd become their own small crew, and every child on this boat now turned to Ares to lead them. Donnally put a hand on Ares's back, and the older boy's grip loosened. He shook his head and lowered the oar.

The Bullet smiled. "Good choice."

The Bullets lashed the children's boat to theirs and sped across the water toward the ship with the red stripe across its nose. The *Ghost* slumped awkwardly in the water, smoke curling away from the deck, a hole ripped into one side. The closer they got, the more Donnally's mind clung to that distant star. He smelled the smoke, heard the screams, and when the gentle thump of a body against the side of the boat made the other children cry, he thought only that whoever it was would probably prefer their watery grave to what awaited the rest of them.

His gaze drifted toward the steel pikes studded around the perimeter of the Bullet ship. One by one, they were plucked from their brackets, like the petals of a flower, and placed on the deck where he could not see. He held his eyes wide as the stakes were lifted once more, this time with the skewered forms of people he loved put on display for them and for any others who might dare evade the Father's arm.

His heart fluttered in his chest, signaling a great swell of something hard and unfamiliar pushing up from the bottom of his lungs. But in his mind, that star cast a cool, soothing light, and he remained still.

It wasn't until he saw a gray coat flapping loosely around a familiar shape that his first tears fell. As the Bullets lifted the boys and girls onto a ladder and told them to climb, he saw them impale his father's body on a pike near the front of the ship. That distant star in his mind crashed to the ground, and in a single disorienting moment, Donnally was on his feet and running toward his father.

"Don't touch him!" he was shouting, he hardly knew what. "I'll hang you! I'll drive your bodies on spits and roast you!"

The Bullets abusing his father's body ceased their work long enough to watch his approach with bemused expressions on their faces.

Donnally stood before them, angry that they touched his father, angrier still that they didn't think him more worthy of respect than amusement. His mind spun until all that was left was perfect fury.

He drew a deep breath, and he roared.

The sound filled him up. It was raw and ugly and loud. It was like a fever racing through every part of him, changing every part of him.

"Now, *that* is a battle cry." An older boy came to stand before Donnally. He had a crown of blond hair and a face like a collection of knives. He met Donnally's glare with piercing blue eyes of his own.

"That kind of rage will serve you well," the boy said. "What's your name?"

Donnally raised his chin and sharpened his eyes.

The boy was suddenly very close. He gripped Donnally's jaw and tilted his head back, exposing the tattoo at his temple. Recognition lit the boy's eyes, and he released Donnally.

"Your sister was very brave."

At first, the words didn't make sense. Donnally assumed he was speaking to someone else. Then a new, horrible reality ripped through his mind like a wind scouring everything in its path.

"Will you come with me, little brother?" the boy asked, not unkindly. "Come with me, and I will teach you to be just as brave as she."

An image of Caledonia appeared in Donnally's memory. She was laughing and proud and her hair tossed behind her in a friendly wind. How had she died? The boy standing before him wanted him to ask. Wanted to tell him. He was sure of it.

"Don't you want to be brave?" the boy asked. "Tell me your name."

Tears slipped down Donnally's cheeks. He felt them on his skin, but not in his heart when he answered, "Donnally."

The knife-faced boy smiled again. "Hello, Donnally. I'm Lir," he said extending a hand. "Your new brother."

CHAPTER ONE

Four Years Later

C aledonia dreamed of fire and of drowning.

The sea was glassy and cold. It surrounded her in a way that was almost loving, pushing at her fingers and toes, swirling at the nape of her neck. The current nudged her gently back and forth as though she were a piece of kelp, relaxed, yet not quite adrift. Directly above, the surface blazed. Fire danced along the water as far as Caledonia could see. And somewhere beyond those flames a voice called her name.

She reached up, and her fingers met something soft and dry.

"I think she's coming around." A hand wrapped around her own. "I've got you."

She blinked and was surprised to find she was not underwater but in a room. Her eyes refused to focus on the broad dark outline of the person holding her hand.

"Try to relax," he said.

Her eyelids felt heavy. She let them fall closed, and the fiery ocean folded over her once more. Exhaustion urged her to stay there. Yet a quiet voice inside her insisted she open her eyes again. She'd left something undone. She'd left people unprotected. She'd left before she meant to, and on the other side of those flames were people she loved.

Pisces.

Amina.

Redtooth.

Hime.

Donnally.

Now she was burning. The room was hot. So hot. Her skin was burning, and she could barely draw a full breath. She tried a second time, and for a second time felt her lungs constrict. So she tried harder and harder still, but it was as if she were trapped, by water and by fire.

"Oh, hell. Someone get Triple!" the boy holding her hand called.

"She'll kill herself if she keeps this up." This was a new voice. And not a kind one. "Good riddance."

"You're not helping, Pine." A third voice. This time a girl. "Move over. I'm going to put her under."

The cool glass of the sea returned. Caledonia drifted. Her lungs heavy and shallow, but she didn't mind. The sea had her. And she always trusted the sea.

» «

When she woke next it was dark. The air smelled like damp cloth, and the only light came from a small pile of dying embers cradled in a ceramic bowl. It cast its ruddy glow over the wall nearest Caledonia's feet. Fabric, not steel. Her eyes struggled to focus, and her mouth felt like it had been filled with tar. A soft pain throbbed in her back.

A breeze pressed against one wall of the tent. The fabric rippled, and just on the other side of that thin layer pine needles whispered. *This is not the* Mors Navis.

Her mind was suddenly very alert, her memories returning in a flash. Her crew had sailed into these cold northern waters for a chance to save her and Pisces's brothers. They'd fought *Electra* and won; they'd found Ares. But not Donnally. And when Lir's ship appeared on the horizon, she'd left the *Mors Navis* for the chance to take revenge on the boy who'd killed her family and stolen her brother. She'd faced him on the deck of his own ship, and for a second time Lir had left her to die.

That explained the pain shooting from her lower back to her stomach, but not the tent in which she now found herself. Not the loose-fitting shirt and pants in which she was dressed.

She curled her fingers and toes, carefully testing each one. They burned and protested at first, then movement came more easily. Encouraged by their progress, she drew a breath of air that tasted like smoke and attempted to sit up. Pain—hot, lancing, angry—blossomed from a point in her back. It sliced through her like a spear through water, seeming to cleave her in two. A noise escaped her mouth, and suddenly the tent flap was pulled aside.

There was a disorienting swirl of dust and daylight, then the flap was closed, returning the room to smoky darkness. Only this time, there was someone else inside. Hands landed on her shoulders, holding her firmly against the bed.

"Lie back, would you?" The boy's voice was gruff and distantly familiar.

Caledonia's eyes settled on his arms, on the old scar running across one bicep. In this light, everything was washed in a colorless shadow, but she knew what hue she'd find there—a dense, violent orange.

A moment ago, her body had been full of so much pain it threatened to overwhelm her. Now she was alert. Her heartbeat quickened, energy surged through her, and suddenly all that pain was a faded memory.

She twisted beneath the boy's hands and leapt to her feet. He stumbled back with a look of keen irritation. He was bigger than she was, and his muscles left no doubt in Caledonia's mind that he would best her with barely a thought. So she wouldn't give him time to think.

While he climbed to his feet again, she was through the tent flap and running. She found herself in a ring of tents beyond which tall trees stretched toward the sky. The air was fresh and cold, tinged with woodsmoke and pine. And everywhere she looked there were more of them.

Bullets.

Even if she couldn't see their bandoliers, she could sense it in their walk, their gaze, their sudden focus on her. There were dozens of them. She was in a camp of Bullets.

She quashed her instinct to head toward the horizon and instead turned toward the woods. The trees would be harder to navigate in her current state, but they would provide cover. The Bullet from inside the tent emerged with a scowl, his eyes finding her immediately. Now that they were in daylight, she could see that his skin was a pale, smoky brown, and stubble darkened the strong line of his jaw. He was not quite as large as she'd thought at first. Still, he was uninjured and unimpressed.

Caledonia broke for the woods, running as hard as her legs allowed. She spotted a narrow trail that slipped between the tall trees and avoided it. Her only hope was to become invisible as quickly as possible.

The woods were a combination of lofted evergreens, waist-high ferns, and tangled undergrowth. Her steps were uncertain and her balance worse. Behind her, the confident stride of her pursuer pounded steadily. She pushed to beat it, to be faster and lighter on her bare feet, but her body was slower than her will. The trees blotted out all sense of direction, and the undergrowth obliterated the ground beneath. Where she was unsteady on this terrain, her pursuer was at home. With each step, the muscles in her back twisted harder, screamed louder, and warmth began to seep toward her waist.

She pushed faster, trusting that the ground that supported this endless sea of ferns might also support her. For a short while, her luck held, then her foot landed in a small rut and she rolled over a twisted ankle. Her pursuer was on her in a second.

She tumbled and he pounced, grabbing her around the shoulders. Caledonia slipped his grip and spun to face him, lashing out with her fist. She caught him squarely across the jaw. The hit took more from her than it did from him, and she landed firmly on her knees. Spent.

"That was never going to work." The boy's hands landed heavily on her shoulders, applying enough pressure to hold her in place. "I suggest you return to bed before I have to do it for you."

Now that she'd stopped moving, pain surged through her back. Her head spun, her lungs twisted, nausea left her mouth viciously hot, and her ankle throbbed with the fresh injury. It wasn't going to be long before her legs gave out completely.

"I *can* carry you," he said, sweeping his eyes along her body. "Though I'd prefer not to."

"That makes two of us," Caledonia sneered, still breathing hard as she climbed slowly to her feet. She had no option but to do as he said and he knew it.

The boy crossed his arms and waited for Caledonia to precede him back to camp. The trip seemed to take so much longer than her haphazard flight through the unfamiliar wood. Each step sent a fresh wave of pain singing through her bones, and exhaustion caused her to tremble constantly. She desperately wanted to stop and rest, but if she stopped, that Bullet would make good on his threat to carry her. She willed her legs to hold her up until they reached the tent again and the cot within.

The Bullet stopped just inside the open tent flap as Caledonia settled against the thin mattress. The move cost her in both pain and dignity. She cried out, shivering as the wound in her back wept fresh blood.

"Stupid ideas. Stupid rewards." The Bullet's voice was unconcerned and still surprisingly judgmental.

"It's never a stupid idea to run from a Bullet." The words came out rough, pressed through the sieve of her pain.

The Bullet grunted. "Don't run again."

It was a command, but he didn't move forward to bind her, and for the first time she marked how strange it was that she hadn't been bound to begin with. Either they thought she wasn't capable of escape on her own or they were confident she wouldn't want to. Though she'd certainly proved the first to be true, it was the latter that left her unnerved. Where was she?

"You'd be dead if it wasn't for us," the Bullet offered, still watching her with that mixture of indifference and judgment. "You'd be one more carcass for the birds to finish off. Maybe that's what you'd prefer? Wouldn't break my heart."

He was a dark outline in a bright doorway. It made him difficult to see clearly. Caledonia didn't want to look at him anyway. She closed her eyes and turned her face away.

"That's what I thought," he said gruffly.

And then he left. For several long moments, it was just Caledonia and the stuffy dark air of the tent. She drew careful breaths, counting to four on each until her heartbeat began to slow. She couldn't move again if her life depended on it. And it might; she wasn't entirely sure. She focused instead on the things she did know. She was in danger. She was in the custody of Bullets far from her crew. And she was alive.

She let the pain remind her of all she'd done to get here and that this was not the end of Caledonia Styx. Where there was pain, there was promise.

Tomorrow, she would be stronger.

CHAPTER TWO

When Caledonia next woke, there was someone else watching her.

He stood in the center of the tent, but he occupied the entire space. His figure was towering, and each of his limbs was reminiscent of a ship's mast. Broad was the only word that could possibly describe him: broad shoulders, broad chest, broad stance, even the frown he wore seemed broad. He was dressed in layers of old-world fabrics—a shiny black shirt with short sleeves peeking out beneath a sturdy green vest and black pants tucked into boots. On his back was a single sword, and sheathed against his thigh was a smaller blade. He studied Caledonia from his great height, as though he'd come across a fallen tree in his path and was deciding how best to cut through it.

"You're bigger than the other guy," she said, giving her fingers a test squeeze.

The boy smiled, and nothing could have surprised Caledonia more. He crouched down so that he was as close to her eye level as his hulking form allowed, giving Caledonia a clear look at his face. Rusty-brown eyes shone against the faint bronze blush of his skin, and a few tendrils from the long brown braid down his back curled around wide cheekbones. Like the other boy, a single orange scar bisected the tan skin of his upper arm.

"You mean Pine. Yes. I'm bigger than Pine. And everyone here." He flashed another smile. "How are you feeling?"

She felt worse than when she'd first opened her eyes. Her body was on fire, and every breath added fuel to the flames. She felt utterly weak. But he didn't need to know any of that. "I'll live," she said.

He nodded. "That was our conclusion as well. Triple patched your wound after you tore your stiches with your little jog yesterday. You slept straight through. A normal person? We would have assumed you were done for. But we were pretty sure you'd pull through the night. She wrapped your ankle as well. It's a little less serious than the stab wound."

Caledonia cataloged each new piece of information. He was a Bullet, but he wasn't talking like one. And they'd worked hard to keep her alive. She wasn't exactly ready to be dead, but what motivation could they possibly have for saving her life?

"Keep still." He swept one hand over her legs without touching them. She hadn't even realized that she'd been moving them. "I get the sense that's hard for you. Soon I think we'll have something to speed your healing along. Otherwise, you'll be cot-bound for a long while yet."

He spoke with command, the kind that came with the confidence of leadership, and he had yet to threaten her overtly. Even his physical presence, while anything but subtle, was somehow nonaggressive. It left Caledonia uneasy, unbalanced.

"How long have I been here?"

"Eight days," he said apologetically. "Like I said, you've had a fever, and medtech isn't exactly easy to keep around."

Caledonia barely heard his words. Eight days? Without thinking, she heaved her body up. "My ship," she said. "What happened to my—"

The fire that sliced her body left her speechless, and her vision went white for several long seconds. Strong hands caught her just beneath her shoulder blades and gently lowered her onto the cot.

"We don't know," he said, in a tone that promised more answers. "They left the bay before the Fiveson's fleet arrived, and that was the last we saw of them." He released her and sat back on his heels with a heavy sigh. "We found you and your tow and that's it. Damned if you haven't been fighting since we hauled you in, Red."

The name hit her like a cold wind, bringing with it a spear of memory: the gunshot snapping the air, the wide-eyed look of love on Redtooth's face, the gentle way her hands fell on Amina's shoulders, and the moment her light went out.

She clenched her jaw, hoping this boy didn't see the tears that now leaked into her hair.

"Don't call me that," she said when she'd regained her composure.

"What should we call you instead? You have a name, I assume."

"Why are you helping me?" she countered, eyes straying to the scar on his arm. "Are you healing me so you can hand me over to Aric?"

The shadow of a frown flickered across his features. "We saw what you did out there. When that conscription ship came into the bay, we were watching, and we saw you. We saw your crew destroy that ship, and we thought that was the end of it. But then we saw something truly unbelievable: a girl sneaking aboard a Bullet ship. We saw everything. The fight. The explosion. And when your tow pulled you to our shores, we decided that a girl willing to do all that was not a girl we could let die."

"So you're doing all of this because you like how I fight?"

"Something like that." The boy's smile returned, and he rose to his full height. "Does that earn me a name?"

"Depends. What are you going to do with me?"

"We're going to see you healed. I thought I'd made that clear already. We want to help you."

"And after that?" Caledonia couldn't help but look again at the scar on his arm. It was old, the color slightly dulled, but there was no doubt as to its origin.

The boy gave a wounded sigh. "We're not what you think.

We aren't going to hand you over to Aric or sell you to the next Ballistic who drives his ship into the bay."

"Why not? You're a Bullet, and Bullets serve Aric."

"We're *not* Bullets." The boy clenched his fists, frustration chiseled into every flexed muscle. "Once we were, but none of us chose to be. We are here because we choose a different kind of life. Where we do everything we can to ensure none of us has to return to Aric. That includes you. You're welcome here. The only thing I ask is that you do not try to run again. When you run, you put us all in danger." He paused, a heavy regret slipping into his expression. "I need you to trust that I will do whatever it takes to keep my people safe."

Suddenly, it was Pisces's voice in Caledonia's mind begging her to give her the gift of trust, urging her to stay with their crew. She pictured the close-crop of her sister's hair, the soft, uneven bend of her smile, the salt drying on her sunny brown skin, and she missed her so desperately that for a moment she couldn't breathe. She pressed her eyes shut against the renewed threat of tears. Pisces would tell her to trust this boy.

When he spoke again, it was with an edge of concern. "Get your rest, friend. There will be time for questions later."

"No, wait." Caledonia struggled to prop herself with her elbows. "My name is Caledonia."

She braced herself for the moment recognition brightened the boy's eyes and betrayed him as a Bullet. But it didn't come. Instead, he said, "It is good to meet you, Caledonia. You can call me Sledge."

"Sledge." Caledonia nearly laughed. "Did you give that name to yourself?"

Sledge's smile was full-toothed when he answered, "No. But my friends did."

"It's subtle."

"About as subtle as I am."

Caledonia returned his smile, easing herself off her elbows and back to the cot. "One more question, Sledge."

"Yes?"

"Am I your prisoner?"

Sledge crossed his arms and considered her with a crease between his thick eyebrows. "Are you planning to run?"

In fact, it was her most immediate plan, yet Caledonia didn't feel like she could lie to him outright. She held his gaze and didn't speak.

"I see." That crease appeared between his brows again as he considered his next words. "You look at me and you see a Bullet. You have no reason to trust me. But I hope that when you're well enough to get up and see the rest of this camp, you'll understand that no one here wishes you harm. My people are recovering from everything Aric put them through, and I will do anything to defend them. We brought you into our sanctuary. We put ourselves at risk to help you. So the answer to your question is that I would strongly prefer it if you chose to stay of your own volition."

"And if I don't?"

When Sledge paused, it was as though the small tent leaned toward him. He studied Caledonia with a gaze so long and impervious that she found it difficult to draw a full breath.

"I will do *anything* to defend them," he repeated, each word a low rumble of thunder.

The threat slid over Caledonia's shoulders and skimmed down her arms to loop around her wrists like manacles. If she ran, if she was caught, she was certain Sledge wouldn't give her a third chance.

"Prisoner, then," she said.

Sledge remained impassive, but he pulled something small from his waistband and held it out to her. In his hand, engulfed by his massive palm, was a small black blade with a wooden handle.

"I wouldn't arm a prisoner."

Caledonia was suddenly dizzy. Her ears buzzed lightly, her fingers tingled. It was the blade Lir had stabbed her with four long years ago, the night he killed her family and destroyed their ship. She kept it with her as a reminder—of what she had lost and why she needed to fight. She drew a slow breath and took the blade.

"Thank you," she said, her voice unnaturally distant.

Sledge stepped back and moved to the doorway, opening it to reveal a sky filled with a dusky-blue glow and a boy seated just outside. She recognized him by his scowl and his shadowed jaw, and thanks to Sledge she had a name for him: Pine. His attention was focused on the blade in his hand and the whetstone he used to sharpen its long edge.

Before leaving, Sledge turned to meet her eyes once more. "It's a true pleasure to have you in our camp, Caledonia. I do hope you'll consent to stay."

CHAPTER THREE

C aledonia spent hours watching the color of her tent change
from a very dark khaki to shadowed khaki to smudged khaki
to khaki with a hint of sunlight behind it. She went from thinking
khaki was a beautiful, subtle color full of unexpected variations and
depth, to thinking it was an insult to all other colors to call it such.
She'd traced the patterns of dirt stains and followed each seam
from beginning to end more times than she could count, and she
still couldn't move a muscle without setting off a chain reaction of
pain that reduced her to shivers.

Most of all, she focused on the color of her tent to keep from
thinking about how she was trapped inside it. Again and again
she steered her mind away from whatever distant waters now carried her crew. But no matter how hard she worked to drown her
thoughts in the khaki threads around her, she discovered herself
far away.

She imagined the sleek hull of the *Mors Navis* cutting through
the warm waters of the Bone Mouth as the crew made for the Net.

Pisces would scowl at the wide ocean plane not because she was afraid, but because she was still angry with Caledonia. And because being captain would keep her on deck more often than she'd like. Amina would see Pisces's struggle and step in close, challenging and encouraging the new captain as needed. Hime would stand beside them, ready to keep the ship healthy in body and spirit. They were the perfect trio—compassion, strategy, and fortitude—to lead the crew into brighter seas. It wasn't the future they'd planned, but it was a future they couldn't have had if she'd remained on board.

Nettle would become a fixture at the helm if she hadn't already. Tin would eventually figure out that the work she did managing the duty roster was essential and valuable. Pippa and Folly would turn their fighting style into an art form that each of the girls would one day master. And Oran—oh, seas, the last thing she'd done was to take the kiss he'd offered. Just thinking of it now made her heartbeat tap erratically in her chest. It had been a reckless act and she wasn't sorry, but it felt unfinished in a way that thrummed under her skin.

She pressed her lips together. Meeting Oran had changed everything. He'd saved Pisces's life and defected from his Bullet clip, coming aboard the *Mors Navis* at great risk to himself. She'd tried to kill him, but Pisces convinced her to wait, to show compassion and mercy, and in return, he gave them information they'd never hoped to have. Their little brothers were alive, and he knew how to find them. They'd rescued Ares. And Donnally—

Her stomach twisted violently. Before she could follow that thought too far, she plunged her mind back into the colorless cloth above her head. There was a patch where the threads were thicker, as though they'd grown stronger as they were spun and now they were knotted together forever. Immediately, her mind returned to Pisces. She had always been the strongest thread of their fabric, holding both Caledonia and their crew together with a kind of strategic caring Caledonia could never quite reach. Pisces may not have believed she'd be a good captain, but she was wrong. She was just as strong as Caledonia and just as clever. And with Amina and Hime at her side, she'd struggle that much less.

They would all be fine.

"They'll be fine," Caledonia repeated to herself. Yet even as she said the words, she knew no one was fine in this world. She might never know what became of her girls. She'd traded her place in that family, and she'd failed to kill Lir in the process. She'd given up everything, and for nothing.

When at last the tent flap opened, Caledonia was so tired of her own thoughts, she almost hoped it was Sledge or even sullen, heavy-handed Pine come to scowl at her. Instead, a girl with strands of hair ranging from honey gold to reddish brown passed into the tent with a small bag in her hands and a sense of purpose in her step.

"Awake, I see," she said, voice warm yet as deliberate as her stride. "I'm Triple, and I've got a surprise for you. Can you sit up? Here, let me help you."

She moved to Caledonia's side, settling herself on the edge of the cot as Caledonia slowly moved into a sitting position. Triple was small and sturdy with muscled curves that reminded Caledonia of Redtooth, except where Redtooth had been as white as lilies, this girl was tanned in a way that suggested the sun would never burn her. She was dressed in clothes reminiscent of Sledge's—black top over green pants with a woven sash of silver knotted at her waist, long tails fluttering by her knee. An empty sheath hung from one hip, and Caledonia suspected the blade had been removed specifically for her benefit.

The girl rummaged around in her bag and produced a square patch that was so gray it was almost metallic. "A nanopatch," she said proudly. "It'll fix that wound on your back better and faster than anything else we've tried."

Caledonia knew about nanopatches. They were old-world medtech. They were rare. And they were incredibly valuable. She didn't like the thought of being indebted to these people any more than she already was, but she also didn't like the idea of sitting around here for weeks while her body slowly knit itself back together.

"With your permission, of course," Triple said, holding up her free hand with her palm facing Caledonia. When Caledonia shook her head in confusion, Triple added, "With your consent."

Caledonia lifted her hand as Triple had, placing her own palm against the girl's. At that, Triple gave a satisfied smile and turned again to her work. The gesture was there and gone, but the meaning was clear: Triple would only touch Caledonia if she agreed to be touched.

"I'll need to get under your shirt, and this will definitely hurt, but it shouldn't last too long."

With gentle hands, Triple lifted Caledonia's shirt and carefully began to remove the old bandage. She gave a series of displeased hums as she worked that were clearly, if not overtly, directed at her patient. Hime would have chided Caledonia harshly for ruining her stitches and making things worse than they needed to be. She could imagine just how Hime's delicate features would draw to a point as she addressed Caledonia.

Captain, I do not put stitches in your skin for my enjoyment! Do not make me do it again. I may choose not *to!* she'd sign, placing precise stitches before her even as her shoulders hunched with irritation.

The thought brought a sad smile to Caledonia's lips.

"I'm sorry I ripped your stitches," Caledonia said over her shoulder.

Triple responded with a disapproving "Hmmm." And then added, "It hurt you more than it did me, but apology accepted. I'll apply the patch on three. Ready?"

Caledonia almost stopped her to ask what it would feel like, then thought better of it. She nodded. "Ready."

"One, two, three."

The patch went on with a cooling vibration, like cold silk

humming against her skin. It was such a soothing sensation that Caledonia relaxed. Just as she was beginning to breathe easier, the sensation turned sharp and prodding, as though a hundred needles had stabbed her at once. She cried out.

"I'm here." Triple's voice was confident and calming. "It won't last too long. Here's my hand. Breathe."

Caledonia did her best to follow these instructions as the needles pierced her again and again for several long minutes until finally the cooling vibration returned. She drew a deeper breath and opened her eyes.

Triple sat on the cot facing her, Caledonia's hand still clenched in her own. Her wide eyes were a hazel green, and for the first time, Caledonia saw that one side of her head was shaved nearly down to the skin while the rest of her hair moved in and out of braids that cascaded over one shoulder.

"There. Not too bad, right?"

"Bad enough." Caledonia's voice sounded hoarse. She was still weak, but she could already feel the difference in her body. Though far from comfortable, the patch had done its work well, inducing her body to move through the healing process at an accelerated rate.

"In another hour, your ankle will be worse than that stab wound. I don't have anything for that except continued compression and rest."

"Thank you," Caledonia said, voice genuine. "I know how rare nanopatches are. I appreciate you spending one on me."

"Thank Sledge." Triple scooted around to check Caledonia's wound before helping her sit back against the pillow. "He risked a lot to get that patch. I just know how to use it."

Caledonia reached for the glass of water by her cot and took a long drink. She shouldn't care what he risked getting the patch. She hadn't asked him to, after all. But she couldn't help herself. "What do you mean he risked a lot?" she asked.

"Anytime we need something like that we have to go to the colonies." Triple watched her shrewdly as she spoke. "And anytime we go into the colonies, we risk our safety."

"Why?"

"Because." She hesitated. "Because even though most of us were born there, the colonists fear Aric more than they want us back. If they even want us back."

"What do you mean?" She couldn't imagine being so close to her family and not being with them. She would—and had—done everything in her power to try to free her brother from Aric's army.

"I mean we're already lost to them. In their minds, the damage is done. If they thought they could save a few of their children by returning us to the Father, then that's what they'd do. So we keep our distance. Only go near one of the colonies when we have no other choice."

"So you aren't trading with them."

Triple regarded her coolly.

"No," she said. "We aren't trading with the people who would likely take us prisoner and return us to the life we've just escaped."

"You stole it."

"We stole it." Triple's answer was unashamed.

The colonists lost more than nanopatches on a regular basis. Between conscriptions, they shouldn't have to worry about this kind of thievery. Yet these Bullets were still taking from them. Whatever they needed. And in this instance, it had been what *she* needed.

"Once a Bullet . . ." she said, guilt and resentment turning in her gut.

Triple stood abruptly, slinging her bag over her shoulder, and turned a cutting glare on Caledonia.

"We're *not* Bullets. We're Blades. We belong to ourselves and ourselves alone. We're sharp and flexible and nothing like the things Aric Athair forced us to be. You can judge us all you want, Caledonia, but if you refuse to see that we are more than these scars on our bodies, then you're more like Aric than we are. That's on you."

Triple's eyes were alight, her cheeks flushed. She was fully alive, fully rooted in her own strength and convictions, and Caledonia knew immediately that she'd spoken carelessly. In spite of having two defected Bullets on her own crew—Hime and Oran—she continued to make this mistake. She had reacted to the idea of Triple as a Bullet rather than the complicated, compassionate girl before her.

"And for what it's worth, we give back to them when we can. Here and there. They might not know where it comes from, but meat cooks the same on any fire."

With some effort, Caledonia swung her legs off the cot and lowered her feet to the floor, then very carefully stood on her own. Triple watched.

"You're right," Caledonia said sincerely. "I apologize. You've spent a good deal of time saving my life, and I have no business showing you disrespect."

They stood eye-to-eye. Triple's breathing was quick, her posture defensive after Caledonia's remark, but she nodded.

Before either of them could speak again, the tent flap was pulled aside and replaced with a mountain. Sledge stood in the entryway with a plate of food in his hands.

One eyebrow lifted at the sight of the two girls standing so close in the middle of the room. "I can come back?"

Triple's eyes never left Caledonia's face. "I was just leaving."

Caledonia almost protested as Triple moved to the door. She didn't want the girl to leave her so soon. In spite of their brief argument, Triple gave Caledonia the sense of security she'd been craving. But she held her tongue and her pride and said nothing as the girl ducked beneath Sledge's tree trunk of an arm and out of sight.

CHAPTER FOUR

"I wasn't expecting to find you on your feet so soon. That patch is something of a miracle," Sledge said.

In truth, Caledonia wasn't sure how much longer she'd be on her feet. She braced her hands on her hips. "Triple says you risked a lot to get it, and I don't mean to sound ungrateful, but why? I'm just a stranger to you."

"The old world left us all strangers." Sledge's voice was as solid as he was. "And anyone who goes after the Damned Athair the way you did deserves to be treated as more than a stranger."

He stood just inside the tent flap, plate balanced in one hand. It was piled high and steaming and it smelled beautiful. There were rows of flaky pink fish, roasted greens, and seed cake. Caledonia's stomach made a noise like a storm.

"I thought you'd be exhausted from the tech, but if you're not, maybe you'd like some fresh air while you eat?"

The patch had certainly left her exhausted, and a thin layer of cold sweat now covered her body, but the invitation to leave this khaki-colored wasteland was too good to pass up. She nodded, and they went outside.

The guard perch next to her tent was empty for once. Sledge led her past it and a short row of tents to a felled tree trunk that served as a bench. When they were settled, he offered her the plate, and Caledonia wasted no time on politeness. She dug in, shoveling tangy fish and savory greens into her mouth at once. Something about the nanopatch had left her ravenous, and she didn't stop until the entire plate was clean.

"Food never lasts long around here, but you may have just set a new record," Sledge said with humor.

Caledonia licked the sticky paste of the seed cake from her fingers, savoring its sweet flavor. With a full stomach and her body on the mend, she turned her attention to the camp around them. It was laid out with precision, each tent spaced evenly from the next. In the center, the ground had been cleared and the grass tramped down from frequent use. Beyond the camp, the woods crowded in on three sides. The fourth sloped gently upward, bearing only low, scrubby plants and patches of wiry grass. Caledonia suspected on the other side of that rise she'd find her beloved ocean.

Milling between the tents and darting in and out of the woods were dozens of people. They were not only Bullets as she'd assumed, but Bullets and Scythes. There were boys and girls here, and they weren't polishing guns or preparing ammo, they were purifying water and weaving and cooking and laughing together.

"There are a lot of girls here," she said, watching two young girls stoking the flames of a fire beneath a small pot of water.

Sledge followed her gaze. "Seems a normal amount to me."

"Not for a group of defected Bullets."

He raised an eyebrow, regarding her with a curious air. "And Bullets aren't girls?"

"No. I mean, I've never seen any," she said. "Only Scythes. And they don't fight."

Sledge gave a lazy shake of his head. "I promise you, Aric makes use of any willing body. Women occupy all kinds of roles in Bullet society. If girls want to fight, they fight. They're there, even if you don't see them."

As if that settled the matter, he leaned back and stretched his legs out in front to bask in the late afternoon sun. It was strange for someone so large to remind Caledonia of a cat, but there was something undeniably catlike about the way Sledge moved and watched her through narrowed eyes.

After a long moment, he added, "You can ask me questions about our camp if you trust me to answer them."

She didn't. Not about his defenses and supplies. He would deflect any question he deemed to be a threat to his people. She knew it because she would do the same thing. She *had* done the same thing, only she hadn't been so kind. When Oran defected from his Bullet ship and asked for mercy from her crew, Caledonia had ordered him thrown overboard. Even after Oran promised to help find their brothers, she'd locked him away, mistrusted every word that came out of his mouth, and only slowly, reluctantly come to trust him. Now she was in the very same position: taken in by Bullets—Blades—just when she'd needed help the most, and the first thing they'd given her after ensuring she wouldn't die was their trust.

"What about Silt?" she asked.

Sledge's fists tightened. "What about it?"

"You don't use it, that's obvious. But you did." She gestured to the camp. "How'd you get everyone to make that choice?"

"It wasn't easy," Sledge answered tightly, clearly unhappy to be sharing anything that felt intimate.

"I've seen it." Caledonia's voice carried the raw weave of recent memories. "More than once."

This seemed to smooth the waters between them, and Sledge sat up with a sigh. "Silt is something that happened to us. It is Aric's way of exerting complete control over his people. It is force, and soon it becomes compulsion. When we break the cycle, it also happens by force, by compulsion. But after that, everything we do, we do by choice." He paused, everything about him becoming calm and stoic. When he next spoke, it was with the kind of gravity that created a steady orbit. "Consent is our most sacred possession."

Caledonia understood what he was unwilling to say. He'd forced some, if not all, of the people in this camp to purge the Silt from their blood, and after that, they'd chosen to stay. These Blades weren't just rejecting what Aric had turned them into; they were rebuilding themselves, creating a version of themselves that was better than anything Aric could have promised.

"When you're more recovered, you'll meet them," Sledge continued. "They're all excited to welcome the girl who attacked a Fiveson on his own ship."

"What happened to that ship? The Fiveson's vessel and his fleet?" she asked.

"They stayed in the bay for a day. Searching for you or your body, no doubt." He smiled, lifting his eyebrows conspiratorially. "Obviously, they did not find you."

She shuddered to think what Lir would have done if his men had been the ones to recover her. His delight in seeing her again, his dark joy at the thought of killing her again had been nothing short of terrifying. To be entirely vulnerable in his hands was an unbearable thought.

And yet, even in her weakened state, the thought of driving her blade into his heart was dangerously alluring.

"You must be quite the catch if they were willing to spend so much time on you," Sledge continued, lightly probing for additional information. "That, or Fiveson Lir feared the Steelhand's punishment for losing you."

A dark expression rose out of whatever memories were tethered to that name: the Steelhand. Caledonia wanted to ask, but that wasn't the information she needed right now.

"Your bomb left a nice spot of damage in their tower, but I doubt it slowed them down any," Sledge continued. "They got *Electra* back on her keel and tugged her carcass with them when they left. Leave no scrap behind, you know. Her parts'll be transformed and back on the water inside a one-moon."

Lir had been the first to tell her of Aric's propensity for reclaiming destroyed vessels, and she found that she understood something more about the man who called himself the Father. Aric didn't use ships, guns, or people without a thought about what he would need tomorrow or ten moons from now. He used them knowing he would need them in the future. Bullets were fed and cared for and, if they survived, eventually they would return to the Holster or one of the other eastern towns. They'd settle into a slower kind of violence and raise children for the Bullet fleet. Before, she'd only understood this as an oppressive manipulation—after all, they had no choice in the matter—but it was so much more than that. Aric's power wasn't the furious burning fire she'd once taken it for, but a garden like the ones he kept in his AgriFleet. Aric's power had roots.

"You said you found my tow. Where is it?" Caledonia asked.

Sledge shook his head in wonder. "You've been on your feet for two minutes, and already you're thinking about getting back out there? On a tow?"

"I'd take a boat if you had one to offer," she replied.

It took him a moment to respond. His lips pressed tight together and he shifted to face her, eyes narrowed and studious.

"No boat," he said finally. "But your tow is moored in a cave low on the cliffs. Hidden at high tide. It's not an easy climb. We'll take you when you can stand up without breaking a sweat." A frown appeared. "Or sit for any length of time."

She could ignore the words, but they didn't change the fact that over the course of their conversation her body had weakened considerably. She was still upright, but there was a faint tremble in her sides that indicated it wouldn't last much longer.

"Good. Thank you."

Sledge climbed to his feet with a shake of his head. Stooping to gather her discarded plate, he said, "Get some rest, Caledonia. Tides know you'll need it."

For a second, it looked as though he wanted to help her back to her tent. If he'd offered, she might have accepted, but then he nodded in parting and left her there to make her own way back.

Caledonia tipped her head back to study the dimming sky. She pulled a deep breath into her lungs, willing her body to hold steady. A thin spray of stars pushed their light between skimming clouds. Somewhere far from here, her girls were studying those stars and using them to guide their course. A small piece of her heart hoped they would follow those stars back to her. They shouldn't. They should make for the Net and find a better life on the other side of it. But oh, how she wanted them to return for her. She wanted it so keenly that a spark of hope wedged between her ribs like one of those stars, glimmering against all reason.

With a frustrated growl, Caledonia climbed to her feet. Her body trembled with the effort. It was a visceral reminder that she was stuck here until her strength returned. She turned her eyes toward the ocean, one thought holding space in her mind: her crew. In spite of everything—distance, time, injury—they would be fine, and she would find her way back to them.

CHAPTER FIVE

The first time Caledonia left her tent without invitation and without guard, she was certain it was a trap. At the very least, a test.

Since receiving the nanopatch, she'd slept hard and long, awakening each morning to find herself covered in a slick of sweat. After three days of this, her ankle no longer ached, and she finally felt like her body had enough energy for more than the few exercises she could accomplish in her tent.

In spite of being assured she was not a prisoner, she was surprised to find the guard post next to her tent empty. It was midmorning, and the camp buzzed with activity. Nearly everyone was gathered in the central open space, sparring and cheering one another on. The clashing sounds of wooden staves punctuated their shouts and laughter. And on the other side of the group of sparring Blades, a single figure stood with arms crossed. His eyes planted on her.

Pine. She'd recognize those coiled muscles anywhere. There

was nothing like being pursued and slammed into the ground by a person to learn all the ways their body was also a weapon. He watched her now with perfect focus, the way a bird of prey might watch a mouse in an open field. It made her skin crawl, but it would be foolish to assume she wasn't being watched. At least Pine made it obvious.

Though she'd been in camp for nearly two weeks, it was still very much a mystery to her. And the only way to unlock a mystery was to start.

Avoiding the gathering in the center and Pine's intense gaze, Caledonia directed her steps toward the treeless rise along the fourth side of camp. Her body was stronger than it had been, but even so it was challenging to walk at a moderate pace. The last time she'd suffered such an injury—also at Lir's hands—she'd been alone with Pisces, and while the girl had salvaged a few of the medical essentials from the husk of the *Ghost*, she'd healed without the benefit of a nanopatch. By comparison, this was practically painless. Still, she needed her body to recover quickly. Every day that passed here was another day between herself and her crew.

The air was brisk and clear, the sun stood boldly in a bright blue sky, and she thought if only she could find the ocean, she wouldn't feel so trapped. Just as she reached the base of the sloping hill, a figure appeared at the edge of her vision, stalking her every step. Without turning, she knew it was Pine. Even his silhouette had a brooding air about it.

She might not be a prisoner, but neither was she trusted. She ground her teeth and pushed onward, climbing the hill while Pine remained at the edges of her awareness, matching her step for step. It didn't matter if she picked up her pace or slowed down, Pine stayed level with her. What did he think she was going to do? Run? Light a signal fire for the next passing ship?

Mid-stride, Caledonia pivoted and charted a path across the field directly toward him. If he was going to irritate her, she was going to return the favor.

At her approach, Pine paused. He turned to face her but made no move to meet her halfway. He waited until she came to him.

Caledonia knew it was a power play, and she didn't care. She closed the distance between them and announced, "If you're going to follow me, Pine, you might as well be useful."

Pine remained infuriatingly still. He was as unconcerned with Caledonia as she was concerned with him. He held his arms behind his back, confident and assured, and he took a single step toward her. That step put him closer to her than an arm's reach. Though not as broad or tall as Sledge, he held himself in a way that bristled with a quiet kind of power.

"I am not interested in being useful to you, Caledonia."

Caledonia forced herself not to back away, but to tilt her head and look directly into his eyes. "Sledge gave me permission to roam," she stated.

"Indeed," he said, holding a hand out toward the rise of the hill. "I won't stand in the way of any order Sledge gives. Only ensure they're followed as intended."

The sounds of sparring filtered between them, though Caledonia was sure their meeting had not gone unnoticed.

"So, if it were up to you, I would be confined to my tent."

Pine's eyes narrowed and he leaned in even closer, so close that she could see a scatter of old orange scars hidden along his shadowed jaw. "If it were up to me, we'd have left you in the bay to drown with your mistakes."

"Then I'm lucky it wasn't up to you."

He leaned away with a nod. "This time."

The truth of the statement rang as clear as a bell. Though Caledonia had every reason to fear Pine's strength, and his dislike of her, he was loyal to his leader, and that would always guide his actions. Even if he didn't agree with them. In a strange way, she found this comforting. She might not know precisely where she stood with Sledge, but she would always know with Pine.

She smiled. "I'm afraid I like you, Pine."

He frowned, finally taking a small step back. "You'll get over it."

This time, Pine let her go, perhaps satisfied that she wasn't going to light a signal fire after all. It was a small relief. Caledonia preferred to greet her ocean alone.

Though the hill was gentle and sloping, her body demanded she take it slow. She focused on pushing one foot in front of the other and not the small feeling of frustration that wanted speed.

The grass underfoot was sparse and weedy, thick stalks growing in powdery soil. Not unlike the Blades themselves.

The wind picked up as she neared the crest of the hill, bringing with it the smell of salt and the distant sound of rushing water. She pushed herself to move a little faster, to reach the peak where wind whipped at her cheeks and toyed with her curls and the ocean glittered in the sun. It danced along the coast, playful and teasing as it rolled in and out of coves, licking at cliffs and laughing in tide pools.

Caledonia let her eyes trace it in all directions, and for the first time in days she felt like she knew where she was.

CHAPTER SIX

T he twenty-first time Caledonia left her tent, it was to fight. Caledonia braced for attack, holding the wooden staff across her body. Her muscles strained, and she relished the sensation. Four paces away, Sledge crouched and bared his teeth. He held his own staff in one hand, gripped just behind his body so it lay along the back of his arm and shoulder.

"Think we can step up the pace?" Sledge asked.

"I'm waiting on you." Caledonia grinned, knowing her words promised more than she could possibly deliver.

A small laugh. "You should never let optimism cloud your good reason."

Increasingly desperate to return to fighting condition, Caledonia had pushed her body a little further each day. Before she could even attempt to find her sisters, she had to know she was strong enough to survive the sea. She'd found Sledge to be a patient and ready partner, appearing outside her tent every dawn to ask the same question: "Will you consent to spar with me, Caledonia?"

Days passed before she could do more than stretch her weak limbs and move through a few basic exercises. No matter how little she accomplished, Sledge continued to show up, continued to ask the question, and one day she'd surprised even herself by slowly mimicking his routine with the unfamiliar staff.

Others had joined them, gently goading her toward recovery, and she'd come to know the Blades as she rediscovered her range of motion. There was Harwell, who was tall and lean with a nose made brown by freckles and eyes that caught everything; Glimmer, who was as pale as anyone Caledonia had ever encountered and built like a boulder; Shale, who was just as pale and slender in all the ways Glimmer was broad; and Mint, who told Caledonia she'd picked the name because the plant was impossible to kill.

Now she felt her strength as she moved in careful steps to circle Sledge. "I still seem to be waiting."

Laughter sounded around her. Not from Sledge, but from the many Blades who'd cut their own routines short to watch her spar with their leader.

"There is no waiting in a spar. There is action and there is reaction. If you're waiting it's because I have you exactly where I want you."

Caledonia faltered. He was right. She'd let her minimal experience make her hesitant, moving only as his movements dictated. That alone didn't bother her; what bothered her was that Sledge had seen it and she hadn't.

Sledge used her moment of doubt against her. In a single, gliding step, he was upon her, stepping her through their practiced routine at full speed. She scrambled to block his first strike, and barely managed to meet his second. For someone who resembled a mountain, Sledge moved with enormous grace. In that way, he reminded her of Redtooth.

Caledonia settled into her rhythm, letting the rapid pace sing through her body. It was exhilarating, but she wanted more. She followed Sledge's lead until she found an opening, then she drove forward with a strike to his torso. Sledge released a surprised laugh, stepping back to absorb the blow.

"A challenge!" he cried, gripping his staff with renewed energy. "Caledonia has issued a challenge!"

A sudden thrill zipped through the crowd at the prospect of a real fight. Cheers and whistles rose into the chilled morning air, and a circle tightened around them. Harwell's eyes widened with concern. An appraising smile flitted across Mint's face. Pine just smirked, clearly eager for her defeat.

A spike of adrenaline raced through Caledonia's blood, making her feel light and grounded. This was the thrill she craved—the moment a fight moved from controlled to uncontrolled, the line between study and practice. She'd studied Sledge enough to know that when he fought, he wasted nothing—no movement, no breath, no thought. He would force any opponent to come to him and then overwhelm them with brute strength. In theory, that meant she need to stay agile, keep him moving. She was ready to test that theory.

"I claim the challenge!" A new voice rang out. "Do you consent, Caledonia?"

Disappointment landed briefly in Caledonia's chest. She'd been so eager to fight Sledge that she hadn't stopped to consider how her challenge would be received. But as the crowd grew louder and Triple stepped into the center of the ring with a staff braced against the ground, her disappointment twisted into excitement.

"Caledonia." Sledge spoke softly at her shoulder. "You have pushed yourself already today."

Caledonia turned to meet his eyes. Her breath still came quickly and her lungs ached with each expansion. It hurt. But it hurt like living. "I made the challenge," she reminded him.

Sledge sighed. "Not every challenge must be met."

"Seagirl!" Triple called.

Triple had been to check on Caledonia a handful of times since giving her the patch, but she never stayed longer than necessary. An uneasy tension stretching back to their first conversation rested between the two girls. Every time Triple came near, Caledonia burned with the desire to win her trust and her friendship. Now here she was, standing confidently in the center of the ring. Her hair was woven in a sequence of tight braids down one side of her head, the gold strands shining in the morning sun. Her gaze landed on Caledonia and in it was something so much more than a fight.

The girls of the *Mors Navis* had often sparred with one another, in the long days at sea to stave off boredom or when tensions boiled over. And if there was a fight, Redtooth always found herself in the center of it. Once, as she and Pisces watched Hime do battle with Redtooth, Pisces said to her, "I've finally figured out why Red loves to spar with us all so much. For her, it's an act of love."

Caledonia had winced as Redtooth's elbow connected with Hime's jaw. The girl kept her feet, but barely. "That doesn't look like love to me, Pi."

"What does it look like, then?"

She'd thought for a moment. Redtooth and Hime squared off again. In the crowd that clustered around them, Amina stood like a rock, bristling but unwilling to step in where Hime had not asked for help. It was the first time Caledonia remembered seeing the bonds that connected the two girls, the way Amina always knew where Hime was. That looked like love.

Hime ducked, avoiding the next blow, and Redtooth beamed.

"It looks like survival," Caledonia said.

This brought the slip of a smile to Pisces's lips. "Exactly my point. For Redtooth, teaching any of us to survive is the most intimate thing she can do. That is how she loves."

Caledonia was sure Redtooth had shared a more pleasurable kind of love with several of the girls, but she understood what Pisces was saying. Redtooth hit them hard in practice because she loved them all too much not to.

Triple wasn't only offering Caledonia a spar, but she was also offering the first slender branch of friendship. She could not turn it away.

"I consent!" Caledonia called, using the preferred phrasing of the Blades.

The crowd cheered and closed in once more.

Caledonia spun her staff, letting the wood slip easily around her hands, giving her muscles a moment to reconnect to the fight. Triple, however, didn't give her that time. She sprang forward, attacking Caledonia with a series of quick strikes, forcing Caledonia to block and give ground. It was the jolt she needed, and the second Triple gave her an opening, Caledonia pushed back with a dangerous jab of her own.

There was no time to feel satisfied in her actions. Triple was far superior with her weapon. Better even than Sledge. Triple moved as though the staff were an extension of her body. She was dexterous and strategic, making up for anything she lacked in strength with agility and speed. It was a skill set Caledonia had seen many times among her girls.

Triple's attacks were faster than Sledge's had been. Varied and sharp. But—there! Caledonia felt herself slip into a defensive pattern, a pattern that pointed to a weakness in her opponent's strategy: Triple attacked in sets of three.

A fierce grin split Caledonia's face. An opponent she could predict was an opponent she could beat. The next time Triple moved into a pattern of three, she would slip the third strike and surprise Triple with an attack of her own.

One! Caledonia lifted her staff to absorb the blow. Two! She met the strike again. Three!

But just as she began to swivel, Triple's staff arched around to catch Caledonia across the throat, stopping an inch away from impact.

Caledonia froze in place. Triple's staff brushed the tip of her chin, smooth and dangerous. She plunked the butt of her own staff against the ground, beat.

"Surprise," said Triple, satisfied and glowing.

Caledonia couldn't help the smile that bloomed on her face. Triple had set a trap. She'd convinced Caledonia that her pattern of three was unbreakable, and when Caledonia believed it, she'd taken her out. It was beautiful.

Hands clapped Triple's back and Caledonia's, too, as all around them the crowd reveled in the energy of a good fight. The rest of the Blades had seen Triple do this before, and seeing Caledonia beat in this way seemed to raise her in their esteem rather than diminish her.

"You see how she got her name," Sledge said with admiring amusement. "She's taken every single one of us with that ruse."

"Some of us more than once, right, Sledge?" Shale called from the crowd.

"Hm," Sledge answered through tight lips.

He ushered Caledonia and Triple away from the sparring ground to an open tent where water hung in solar sacks. The Blades hadn't left the Bullet Seas empty-handed, and the few items they'd escaped with were both portable and critical. Like solar sacks. Their durable skins transformed from transparent to opaque depending on the state of the water within. Once purified, the sack turned dark blue. Sledge pulled one down for each of them.

"It's not a ruse," Triple protested in a way that suggested this was an old argument. "'Ruse' implies that I'm cheating, which I'm not. It's a tactic."

"A good one," Caledonia added, pausing after for a drink. "You'd be welcome among my crew with moves like those."

"The crew you left?" Pine, her constant shadow, stepped into the tent, which seemed so much smaller with the addition of a fourth person. He stepped close to her, ostensibly to retrieve a water sack hanging over her shoulder, but she knew it was more than that. Caledonia hadn't spent a moment in this camp without Pine hovering somewhere in her periphery.

With the water in hand, he stepped away and continued. "Or was it the crew that left you behind? Which way did that go?"

"Pine," Sledge warned.

Anger, resentment, and guilt gripped her throat with cold fingers. Pine was flinging barbs, hoping they'd strike a sensitive target, and they'd hit their mark. She'd left her crew. Forced them to leave her. Forced them to sail on without her, and now all she could do was hope the sea would keep them safe.

They'll be fine, she thought. *They are fine, and I will find them.*

"Why does it matter?" Triple asked. "We all saw her fight Fiveson Lir. I think that's everything we need to know."

"Is it?" Pine turned his attention from Triple to Sledge. His stance was aggressive yet tempered. When it came to Sledge, he made sure his posture showed deference even as he inched toward a challenge. Keeping his voice low, he said, "Don't you think we should be asking *why* she took a shot at Lir? Alone?"

"We all have reasons to want to go after a Fiveson," Sledge answered meaningfully. "I'm content to let her keep hers if that is her wish."

"We can't afford to let her! Tides only know how many of Lir's clip saw her face." Pine cast a dark look toward Caledonia. "She's a marked girl, and she's been here long enough."

Caledonia couldn't disagree with him, and even as she felt her position growing more precarious by the second, she had to admit that if their positions were reversed, she'd make the same argument.

"They think she's dead," Triple stated.

Pine clenched his fists and his jaw in the same frustrated motion. "They searched for her and didn't find her. What makes you think they won't come back and try again?"

"For one girl?" Triple asked, disbelief in the press of her lips. "This is Lir we're talking about. He—"

"Holds a grudge," Pine finished.

A pause settled among the four of them. Triple's brow was furrowed in doubt, Pine remained expectant, and Sledge was folded into an internal deliberation. Caledonia kept her face stony. These were not her friends, and it was dangerous to forget that. This was where she should have been all along: in turbulent, unfamiliar waters.

"Keeping her here puts us at risk," Pine pressed, holding Caledonia's gaze.

That was the crux of his argument and one Sledge was likely to respond to. And while Caledonia had no intention of staying here any longer than necessary, she needed their support for a little while longer.

"You're already at risk," Caledonia answered smoothly. "You're already marked. Or are you going to tell me that thirty-two Bullets escaped without attracting attention?" Caledonia drove the point of her argument forward like a dagger. "I don't think you did. I think you had to do something incredible to get everyone out, and they've been looking for you ever since."

The rigid bend of Pine's mouth told her she'd hit very close to home.

"What exactly did you do? Mutiny? Steal a ship? How did so many of you just disappear?"

She could see the irritation expanding in Pine's chest. He was still a formidable figure, taller than her with hawkish features and smoky-brown eyes. The muscles in his arms flexed as he tightened his fists, wrestling with the desire to set her right. Caledonia hoped he would. At least then she'd know something more about these Blades than their habits.

"You're defected Bullets. If Lir or any of the others got their hands on us, our fates would be the same. The only difference is that I'm out there doing something about it."

"*Were.* You *were* out there," Pine corrected her. "Now you're here, doing nothing but bringing your troubles to our shores."

Her teeth crashed together. Her temper was rising in a way it so rarely did, but there was something about Pine and his shadowed jaw that made her want to hit it.

"You aren't *safe.* You never were." She fought to keep her voice low, directing her next words to Sledge. "Why do you stay here? The only way to evade Aric is to *keep moving.*"

"If you'd like to keep moving, be our guest." Pine cast an arm out wide.

She ignored him, holding her focus on Sledge. "You must know this village is an illusion. And it won't last."

"Enough." Sledge commanded the space with a single word. "We aren't going anywhere," he said to Caledonia, and turning to Pine, he added, "and she stays."

That was the end of it. Sledge turned on his heel and left the tent with Triple following in his wake. Caledonia's head buzzed faintly, and looking at Pine made it worse. She shouldn't care so much. She was grateful to the Blades, but the instant she found an opportunity to get back on the water, she intended to do so. She would find her crew. It didn't matter to her what the Blades did or didn't do.

Pine took a small step toward her, coming close enough that she could feel heat radiating from his body. He didn't speak, didn't touch her, didn't do anything but look into her eyes, and there she saw Pine the Bullet lurking just beneath the surface. The violence in his past was within easy reach, and he wanted her to know it.

"I see you," she whispered.

He blinked, and for a second his features were kissed by sadness. Then he nodded almost imperceptibly and left.

CHAPTER SEVEN

"Wake up, Caledonia." The voice was hushed and very near her shoulder.

Caledonia opened her eyes to a dark tent lit by a small, hand-held sun pip. Triple crouched near, the blue light giving her tawny skin a cool glow.

"What's wrong?" Caledonia kicked her blanket away, senses skimming quickly toward battle. "Colonists? Bullets?"

"Neither." Triple paused. "Or both. There's something I need to show you. Get up." She dropped her sun pip on the cot and left the tent.

Caledonia did as instructed, dressing quickly in the near dark as cold nipped at her bare skin. She added a second shirt to cut the chill, laced her boots, slid her fingers into thin gloves of old-world clothtech, and she was ready to go. She joined Triple just outside, expecting to see the camp in motion after her hasty summons, but everything was still. Quiet. No one else was yet awake.

"What—?"

Triple raised a finger to cut her off, then led her toward the dark woods behind the camp.

A trap. That's what this was. Pine's arguments had swayed Triple, and he was waiting for them some distance away. They would kill her or somehow compel her to leave and tell Sledge she'd done something terrible or run off to join the colonists.

No, she told herself. *That's a Bullet move.*

These were Blades, and she could trust they would do nothing without her consent.

A quarter moon lit their way over the frost-covered ground, the only sound the delicate crunch of fern fronds beneath their boots. Caledonia had spent very little time in the woods since her flight from Pine, and she found the experience of walking within them both stifling and disorienting, not unlike being underwater. Except here she kept only a vague sense of direction, and in the water she always knew she could travel up and find the sun again.

When they'd gone some distance from camp, she finally broke the silence. "What is it you need to show me?"

Triple paused long enough to toss a curious smile over her shoulder. "Everything," she said simply.

The land was rocky and soon turned steep and difficult to navigate. At least, Caledonia found it difficult. Her thighs burned, her feet slipped over moss-covered rocks, and she was sure each breath she took was more shallow than the last. She could focus only on the next step and on nothing beyond. If this was part of the "everything" Triple wanted her to see, she was missing most of it.

When at last they broke free of the cover of trees, the sun was high, throwing honeyed rays over a small meadow. On the other side of that meadow, a steep protrusion of rock towered over them.

"More climbing?"

"C'mon, seagirl," Triple answered with amusement. "You haven't come all this way to give up now."

They began the climb, and Caledonia found she had to reconsider her definition of steep. This required hands and feet and promised a treacherous fall if you trusted your weight to the wrong perch. That danger was exhilarating, reminding her of the feeling of climbing one of the four masts of her ship, racing toward the sun with the wind at her back.

Soon, they'd reached the peak, and Caledonia's heart caught on the sight of the ocean opening before her. It was sparkling and full of vigor, it was limitless and free, it was at once a point of origin and a destination. Looking on it filled Caledonia with a sense of purpose. When she was near the ocean, she always knew where she was.

"This is why we can't leave," Triple said, voice heavy.

The girl faced north, her back to the ocean. Caledonia followed her gaze, and in spite of the sun, a chill washed over her like a sudden rain.

For a short distance beyond where they stood now, the land tumbled through valleys dappled by pine forests, sweet meadows of golden grasses, and rocky rises, places where people might find enough to support a slender way of life; then, suddenly, it stopped. There was land, but it was stripped of life and color. To the east, it was as if a once great mountain range had shattered like a mirror, leaving behind a senseless patchwork of half mountains and waterways. To the west, the land was bare and white, bleached entirely to a poisonous, endless stretch of rubble.

The coast was a narrow strip of green between the sea and the destroyed legacy of the old world.

Caledonia stared, thoughts twisting over the mystery of their collective past. She wanted to know how and what and who, but more than that, she wanted to know why. Why had this happened to what must have once been a beautiful world? Maybe those questions had answers. But they'd been destroyed along with everything else. All that remained was a future continually threatened by a past they would never know.

"What's the point of leaving here when the rest of the world is dead?" Triple asked.

Caledonia had heard tales—everyone had—of how much land had gone to waste, leaving only a few wisps of green behind. But it was one thing to hear about it and another to see it. It was like an ocean, miles of poisoned soil that stretched mercilessly toward the horizon.

"What could do that?" Caledonia asked, squinting. The soil was so white, it reflected sunlight as vibrantly as the ocean.

"One theory? They did it on purpose. The old worlders were trying to correct all the damage they'd done. I think they actually thought this would help. Maybe it did." She sighed, twisting toward the green hills between them and the sea. "We think they left the coasts alone on purpose so they had a place to wait while the rest of the world recovered. But who knows? Maybe it was all one long mistake. Maybe by the time they did anything about it, the only options were bad ones."

"No good options." Caledonia released a long breath.

"The same is true for us now. This is the home we have. It's not perfect, and I would give anything for greens you didn't have to boil for a year before they were edible, but it's better than where we were."

"And it's where you came from," Caledonia added, understanding why they'd been drawn back to the Northwater. "How long have you been here?"

"Nearly a full turn. Eleven moons," she answered quickly. There was a stiffness to her now as she turned away from the wasted lands to the north.

Eleven moons ago Caledonia had been with her sisters on the *Mors Navis* menacing Aric's bale barges outside of the Bone Mouth. She'd had no idea that her brother was still alive, that Pisces's brother was still alive. She'd been angry and driven and cautious. And if someone had told her that in less than a turn's time, she'd find herself trapped in the Northwater away from her girls, she'd have laughed in their face.

"I had—have a sister," Triple said, breaking into her thoughts. "You remind me a little of her. Stubborn and a little self-righteous. You'd have either been perfect allies or terrible enemies."

"Is she still here somewhere?" Caledonia traced the forested coastline west until it faded into the horizon. The colonists had hidden themselves well here, using the dense cover of trees and unfriendly terrain to mask their numbers from Aric's Bullets.

"I don't know. Possibly. But more than likely she was conscripted soon after me."

"Did you ever try to find your parents?" Caledonia asked.

"I wanted to." Triple gave a wavering smile. "But then I realized that if I knew where they were, nothing in this world would stop me from going to them. And that would end badly for everyone."

Caledonia nearly laughed. "As someone who has made that choice, I have to admit you have more restraint than I."

"Caledonia, I suspect even the Perpetual Storm has more restraint than you."

The girls laughed together, finding common ground in the similar threads of their pasts. It must be maddening and painful to be so close to home and unable to rejoin it. Still, maybe it was better to be near enough to leave gifts of meat and know they had what they needed to survive. If Caledonia were in their position, she could imagine making the same choice. The Blades were as close to home as they could possibly get.

"I understand," she said. "What you're trying to show me. I understand."

Triple smiled as a cold wind pushed strands of sunset hair across her cheeks. "I thought you might."

They were halfway down the hillside when a horn sounded in the distance. Caledonia froze, senses on alert.

Triple, however, was unconcerned. "It's a colonist horn. They spotted a conscription ship." She kicked at a pebble on the trail. "Took them longer to come back than I expected. They must not be too hard-pressed for—"

A quiet boom pulsed through the air. The sound was as familiar to her as the beating of her own heart.

An explosion.

Triple turned, wide-eyed, to Caledonia, who nodded grimly back.

A *bomb.*

CHAPTER EIGHT

The girls didn't move—they barely breathed as they waited for what they feared would follow.

A minute passed. Then two. And before either of them could entertain the hope that they'd been mistaken, a second explosion sounded.

"That one was closer," Caledonia said, wishing they hadn't abandoned the high ground so soon. Was it a single ship? Two? Or had the Father sent a fleet this time?

"We have to go!" Triple turned and pelted down the trail.

The two girls ran hard, each explosion spurring them onward. Bombs fell with increasing speed, one bursting on the heels of another, growing louder as the girls descended the hillside.

Then, as suddenly as they began, the bombs stopped. A deafening silence flooded the woods. Triple turned to Caledonia, both girls bracing for the attack to resume. But nothing followed.

The girls rushed onward, and when they finally spilled into camp, they found it in an uproar. The entire western edge was in splinters, more than half of their tents were missing or reduced to singed scraps of fabric. The ground was scorched, the trees smeared with webs of fire caught within the bark, the air dusky with smoke and ash. And it was loud. Shouts and cries, cracking trees, the snap of fires still chewing up their camp, all contributed to the cacophony. Caledonia let it wash over her, settling into a kind of order.

In the center of camp stood two groups of people in opposition to one another. Shouting. It took Caledonia a moment to understand that not everyone in that small circle belonged here.

There was Sledge, standing tall in the middle, the picture of calm strength, and there was Pine behind him. Pine had his hands planted on his hips, and by his posture alone Caledonia knew he was ready to attack the stranger currently yelling at Sledge.

The man was tall and thin, and even at this distance Caledonia marked the guns holstered to his hips and thighs. Behind him were three others, two men and one woman, all dressed in simple clothtech.

"Who are they?" Caledonia asked.

It took Triple a few seconds to answer. When she did, her voice was thinned with something like pain. "Colonists," she said.

The man's voice climbed once more, and this time they heard him clear across camp. "We want you gone! NOW!"

All of camp paused. They were raw and injured, and in this moment it might not matter that these colonists were their family. They would fight if Sledge asked it of them. But Sledge only shook his head, answering in a voice that carried without shouting.

"We did not do this."

"Didn't do this?!" the man answered. "You show up, a conscription ship is destroyed in our bay, and now this? Nothing like this ever happened before you arrived. And it will *never* happen again."

Sledge drew a deep breath, quelling his answer and considering his response. "Good father, I promise you my people are not the reason for this."

Pine's eyes cut toward the ground. Anger simmered across his shoulders, and Caledonia knew he was thinking of her. The Blades had been here for eleven moons without incident. She was the thing that had changed. She was the reason for this attack. Sledge was protecting her.

"It doesn't matter. That conscription ship is still in the bay, a holo counting down to tomorrow morning when they expect our children. It doesn't matter that they've just murdered a dozen of our boys and girls, they want more. Those twelve only died because something changed here. I believe that was you," the man stated, cold fury vibrating on his lips. "Leave or we tell them you're here."

This was how Aric maintained his rule. This was his power in action. He had bent the colonists to his will so perfectly that even when he attacked them, they would not blame him. Violence from Aric didn't create resentment against him, but against those who opposed him.

She strode forward. Pine glowered at her approach, Sledge shifted uncomfortably, but neither moved to intercept her. The man's anger was a weapon and that was something she knew how to face.

"I am Caledonia Styx," she announced, raising her voice so that all might hear her. "My brother was taken by the Father many turns ago, and you have been attacked today because I tried to get him back. I am the one who challenged *Electra*. I am what has changed here. Not these people." She glanced at Sledge, finding his eyes wide with alarm. "They are peaceful and do not deserve your anger. Don't turn them over. Don't do Aric's work for him."

The man turned to her. He pulled one hand down a bearded chin and answered her, "We all do Aric's work whether we want to or not. This is his world."

"Only if we let it happen," Caledonia argued. "Stop letting it happen."

Now he laughed, and it was a tired sound. He raised an arm, gesturing to the destruction surrounding them. "My girl, if I had the power to stop this from happening, don't you think I'd have done it?"

His anger faded, and for a brief second Caledonia glimpsed what lay behind it: fear, sadness, and an overwhelming sense of futility. Surrender had become such a way of life for these people that it was possible they didn't remember any other way.

"Would you have?" she asked.

The man's anger returned in a flash. "The only way to survive in this world is to play by his rules. And we are here to survive."

"I'm made for more than surviving."

"And what's that?" he snapped.

It was Oran's voice she heard when she answered, "Fighting back."

The man grimaced. Nodded. Let his lips fall into a strangled smile. "That's a good way to die, young one. I'd prefer not to be the reason it happens, but I'll choose our children over everything."

The man gestured to his people, and they vanished inside the smoldering wood. His message was clear: if the Blades stayed here, they were dead.

Camp was finally quiet.

In the hours following the departure of the colonists, they'd catalogued the extent of the damage. Three of their number had died in the attack, and many of their supplies were destroyed. The mood was somber as the Blades tended to their wounded, dismantled what remained of camp, and swept away all traces of their home. Caledonia helped where she was welcome, but it was hard for anyone to ignore the fact that her actions had led to this moment.

She played her conversation with the colonist over and over

again in her mind. Her initial shock was long gone, and now she was just angry. It was the kind of anger that felt good, or at least better than whatever waited just beneath. She was angry that the colonists were so thoroughly subdued they would turn on the Blades a second time, angry that they were so committed to keeping Aric happy, and angry at what it all meant. After all this, her mother had been right. The only chance they had at a life not spent running was on the other side of the Net. For now, though, the Blades simply had to move.

As soon as the wounded were on their feet, they would head into the hills and regroup where the colonists didn't have an immediate read on their location. It was a temporary solution to a very permanent problem, and Caledonia couldn't shake the feeling that it was ultimately a mistake.

Caledonia waited until Sledge was alone. He crouched by his own pack, testing the bindings and weight one last time. Across his back the black scabbard of his sheathed sword caught the fiery glow of the late afternoon sun.

"Sledge." Caledonia noted the new tension in his jaw at the sound of her voice. "May I speak with you?"

"We need to move, Caledonia." He was tired, sad even. And still so desperate to get his people to safety.

"I know. That's why I need to speak with you." She braced herself for resistance. "There's an opportunity here that you should consider."

His sigh was sharp as a knife. "Caledonia."

"You can't stay here. Not anymore. Going into the hills only buys you time, not peace. And there's a ship in that bay waiting to fill its gut with children."

Sledge held his arms crossed over his chest and his feet planted wide. It made him even more mountainous than usual, and Caledonia made sure she stood so that she could look him in the eye without craning her head.

"I can take the ship," Caledonia stated, confident and sure. "With your help, *we* can take that ship and sail right out of here."

"To where?"

She smiled. "You don't want to know how or why I'm so sure I can take the ship?"

"If there's one thing I've learned about you, it's that you can pull off the impossible. A few weeks ago, I'd have said taking any Bullet ship was impossible. But then I met you, so I ask again, sail to where?"

His response was so unexpected that for a second, she had no answer. "The Net," she said, an image of the *Mors Navis* appearing in her mind. "We sail to the Net, and we punch it."

A frown appeared on his face, carving deep lines of displeasure upon his brow. "The Net," he repeated in disbelief.

Caledonia nodded once.

"That's the terrain of Fiveson Tassos," he stated as though he expected her to understand.

"And knowing your opponent is the first step in besting them, or, in this case, avoiding them."

"Ignoring for a moment the sheer absurdity of thinking we can get through his ships intact," he said after a long pause, "the Net is on the opposite side of the Bullet Seas. There are plenty of opportunities to die between here and there."

"I know. But if you stay here, you'll be looking over your shoulders until the day those colonists decide they have more to gain from turning you in than letting you live. The way things are going, that will be tomorrow. At least if you aim for the Net, there's something to fight for."

"The Net," Sledge said again, his disbelief carrying him into silence.

Caledonia needed him to make this choice on his own. If he didn't, there was no way she'd sway the rest of the Blades to join her.

"You came here looking for your brother. Isn't that what you told the colonists?" Pine took them both by surprise. He stood a few feet away, guarding and listening. And, now, talking. "Did you find him?"

"No," she answered sharply, confused by the change in topic.

Pine studied her as though seeing her for the first time, or as though he'd just learned the first true thing about her. His lips hinted at a smile without committing fully. Then he nod-ded, tucked that true thing away, and asked, "I thought you were made for fighting back? What you're talking about sounds a lot like running."

"We fight for each other," she said. "You help me get that ship, and I'll fight like hell to get your people through the Net."

The sun was reaching for the horizon, its light burning against charred tree trunks. It seemed days ago that she and Triple had climbed to the top of that lookout and gazed over the bleached soil of the north. This morning she had sat perched on the edge of an illusion. And now it was shattered around her feet.

"She's right." Pine stepped toward Sledge. "We can't stay here."

A quiet, intense look passed between the two of them. It was a look flooded with meaning Caledonia couldn't decipher, and so private she nearly looked away.

Finally, Pine added, "She's the best chance we have right now."

Caledonia's eyes widened in surprise. If anything, she expected the events of this morning would have locked her in the cold embrace of Pine's distrust, yet here he was speaking in her favor. It was easily the last thing she'd expected of him, but now wasn't the time to question such a gift.

"What about the colonists?" Sledge asked. "What if we do this and the Damned Athair sends another attack like this one? What happens to them then?"

Even after the colonists' demands, Sledge still cared about them. Enough to consider how his actions might impact them in the future. If the colonists knew what an ally they were losing in this boy, they might have thought twice before evicting him. It was one more twist in the tragedy unfolding here.

"If it's me those Bullets are flushing out, then this won't be the last attack no matter what we do." Caledonia had to search for an echo of the compassion Sledge felt for the colonists. "Now that the colonists have seen you, we're a danger to them whether we stay or go. At least if we go, they can't be abused for neglecting to turn you in."

Silence fell between them as Sledge considered her words. He lifted his chin and regarded her through cat-narrowed eyes for a long minute. Then, finally, he spoke.

"All right, Caledonia," he said. "Let's take that ship."

CHAPTER NINE

The ship sat in the glittering bay, an orange holo projected into the sky and counting down the minutes beneath the barest sliver of a new moon.

"It's the Youth Moon," Pine whispered to Caledonia, crouched next to her in the tall ferns that spilled out of the forest toward the pebbled beach. "An unpredictable moon, full of fickle desires and high passions."

"That doesn't sound good," Caledonia answered.

"Could go either way. It's just superstition, of course," he said, but his eyes flicked again to the moon and his lips pressed together in a thin line.

Once Sledge had agreed to take the ship, Pine had glued himself to her side. His usual surly demeanor was gone, replaced by ready attention that was unnervingly agreeable. Sledge may have been the leader, but the minute a fight was promised, it was Pine who pushed him in the right direction. He'd been solid as stone until the appearance of the Youth Moon.

"Stay steely, Pine," Caledonia soothed with a firm tone. "The moon is slim and will conceal us exactly as we need to be concealed."

The Bullet ship was a sweeper class ship, so named for the periodic pulse it emitted in order to trigger any mines waiting in the surrounding waters. Its primary purpose was to clear the way for more deadly ships that followed. Sledge had explained that the colonists were once so adept at setting traps for Aric's ships that sweepers became the first choice for conscription runs. It had been years since the colonists fought back, but the ships were still used because in addition to their pulse, they also had large bellies.

Pine fidgeted next to her, eyes pinned to the orange glow of the countdown holo. It hung in the air above the deck of the ship, clearly visible from the shore.

"It was a ship like this one that collected you?" she asked.

"Of course." His eyes flicked to her, suspicious and confused. "If you're about to ask if that makes me nervous, I'll be disappointed."

In fact, she had been trying to determine exactly how to ask that question. Pisces would have known. Pisces would have asked it before they were crouched in a thick of ferns waiting for the signal to advance. And she'd have done it so seamlessly, Pine might not have noticed. But Caledonia had never been good with the human side of commanding a crew.

Irritated at having been so obvious, she changed course. It was always better to be direct. "Why did you support my plan?"

This time his glare was annoyed. "Because it was the best option."

"You might have traded me to the colonists," she pointed out. "You'd have bought yourself some time and been rid of me all at once."

"The thought occurred to me," he said, turning his dark eyes fully on her. "But I don't have to like you to agree with you. It was a temporary solution at best."

She smiled. "And I'm a permanent solution?"

When he grinned, his teeth gleamed in the moonlight. He'd smeared his skin in rich gray mud and it made his teeth especially bright. Caledonia had done the same, coating her ivory skin and fiery locks so the moon wouldn't reveal her too soon.

"Hardly," he said. "You're just better than the alternative."

Fighting the urge to laugh, Caledonia tipped her eyes skyward where stars arranged themselves against a black curtain. Without meaning to, she traced the patterns Donnally had taught her to see. She found the crab and the two fish, the tragic young girl and her hero. She found the great whale and the notes of his song.

As though reading her thoughts, Pine said, "Punching the Net will mean leaving him behind for good."

Her eyes snapped back to his. Without saying it, she knew he meant her brother.

"You did all you could," he added with the tired resignation of someone who'd been left and who also understood the choice to leave.

Regret pinched at the back of her throat. She clenched her jaw, fighting against a gentle swell of tears.

"Pine?"

He turned, expectant.

"How did you come back from being a Bullet?"

The faint laughter of waves slapping at the shore slid between them. A look of pain blossomed on Pine's face. He knew why she was asking. And even if he didn't care about hurting her, he didn't want to be the one to give her this answer. He grimaced, turning his face toward the ferns at their backs where thirteen additional faces waited silently for their signal.

With a reluctant sigh, he faced her again. "None of us comes back, Caledonia. It's not possible."

"But—"

"None of us," he repeated. "If we had, we wouldn't be here right now, ready to dive into a gunfight without guns of our own." His expression was hard, but not unkind. "Think of us like individual ships. We've been through battle, taken damage to the hull, and even if you can pound it back into shape again, it will never be the same. It's been changed on an essential level. We didn't come back from being Bullets. We just got out of the chamber."

It was what she needed to hear, but not what she wanted. Triple would have told her that it was possible under the right circumstances. Sledge would have told her it was a process. But Pine. He knew what she was really asking.

She tipped her head once more to the sky and swallowed a lump of sorrow. She spotted the crab, Donnally's favorite collection of stars, and for the first time she acknowledged with all her heart that he was out of reach. There would be no second chance to find him. He was alive and out there, and that was going to have to be enough.

I'm sorry, Donnally.

"There it is," Pine whispered.

Out on the water, very close to the eastern edge of the bay, a sun pip flashed three times. Triple was in place. While Sledge led a second team farther down the shoreline, Triple had gone down the cliff face to untether their catboat.

"So you *do* have a boat," Caledonia had teased, as Sledge laid out every resource they had to offer.

Triple had taken the small boat and drifted as near to the Bullet ship as she could without risking detection. The next steps were up to Caledonia's team and Sledge's. With five wounded and out of commission, they were twenty-five in all. Caledonia hoped it was enough.

Pine passed Triple's signal down the beach, and when Sledge returned it with three brief flashes of his own, Caledonia waved her team into the singing waves.

The water was like ice. It stole away her breath in an instant, and several Blades hissed as their skin burned before sinking into a pleasant numbness. They would not be able to stay in this water for long, but if all went well, they wouldn't need long.

Together, they swam toward the ship, taking care to disturb

STEEL TIDE

the water as little as possible and to keep a good distance between each of their bodies. Across the bay, Sledge's team did the same. Caledonia could just make out their heads bobbing up and down in the dark water.

Before them, the ship grew larger and more detailed. The hull was deep and hung low in the water with a solid nose. The rear of the ship sloped downward, bulging slightly where the propellers dipped below the waterline. Around the deck a spiked railing protruded in all directions, dripping with leathery bones and tattered clothing. Caledonia shuddered against the memory of her last encounter with such a railing on Lir's ship. She'd get a lot closer before this was over, and it wouldn't do to be precious about it. She gritted her teeth and kept swimming.

Banishing all thoughts of Lir or Aric from her mind, she focused on the task ahead. The ship was a gift, but only if she could orchestrate its taking. The Blades had exactly zero guns between them, which meant that while their first challenge was to board the ship without being detected, their second was to arm themselves. Fast.

She reached the hull three strokes behind Pine. He was already unhitching his bow, fitting it with the grappling hook Harwell had designed earlier in the day. They would have one shot, which was why the bow was in Pine's hands and not anyone else's. He steadied himself with his strong legs, treading water with only the muscles of his thighs and core. Beside him, Harwell's thin arms

85

lifted the length of rope from the water and held the coil in open palms. Pine raised his bow.

Caledonia turned slowly in the water. She counted all fourteen of her team and tracked the last of Sledge's toward the propellers where they would gain entry. They were ready.

"Go," she whispered.

Pine loosed the arrow with a wet snap. It flew upward, dragging the rope like a snake's tail. It landed with a *thunk*, and they all held their breath as Pine gave the rope a sharp tug. It held, latched in place where the tines of the grapple had found a home among those terrible spikes.

"After you," Pine said with a satisfied smile, holding the rope for Caledonia.

Caledonia gripped the rope with numb fingers and hauled herself out of the water. She climbed, forcing her frigid limbs to move faster with each pull and ignoring the burn in her palms. Every muscle in her arms and legs strained as she methodically heaved herself up the rough rope. By the time the spikes of the railing were within reach, she was no longer frozen, and beads of sweat itched beneath the mud at her temples.

The spikes were bracketed against the railing at irregular intervals, some of them pointed outward while others turned their dangerous tips inward.

Caledonia hung just below the lip of the railing for a moment, forcing her breath and heart to calm as she listened for a sign that their grapple had been spotted. She shifted her grip away from the rope to the spike directly overhead. And that's when she heard it.

Footsteps. The clearing of a throat. A soft curse against the cold. A sentry.

Cold metal burned beneath her fingers, but she didn't dare return her grip to the rope. Caledonia hung, an open target dangling off the side of a Bullet ship. She focused on the sound of the guard's footsteps. If he was sharp enough to pick her hands out from between the detritus decorating the spikes, her only option would be to drop. Their attack would end before it had ever begun.

A shuffling sounded directly above her head. Sweat slipped down her spine, the muscles in her arms trembled, and she feared her fingers would soon be too numb to hold on.

Breathe, she reminded herself, drawing a controlled breath deep inside her lungs.

Below her, she could sense the Blades' tension. They knew why she paused. She could almost hear Pine's nervous thoughts about the Youth Moon.

Silence.

The guard had stopped, but had he seen her?

Her arms trembled and now her fingers were slipping from the cold metal. She was out of time.

In a single motion, she swung her body forward, catching a second spike beneath her knees. Here, her size was her advantage.

Trusting her legs to catch her, she released the spike she'd been holding and curled her body forward to catch the next. She pulled herself into a seated position, and in another second she was over the railing.

The guard was a few paces beyond her. At the sound of her feet on the deck, he turned. But she had the advantage. She rushed him, delivering a pristine blow to his jaw before he could call out. He was too slow, too surprised to counter her next attack. A jab to the throat followed by a kick to his knee, bringing him low enough that she could deliver the blow that would render him unconscious. It was a sequence she'd learned from Redtooth, and using it now felt as much like a prayer as anything Caledonia ever did.

Working quickly, she shifted the grappling hook to the widest possible entry point, securing it in place before whistling to Pine. The rope snapped taut under the weight of a body, and Caledonia lugged the unconscious guard into the shadow of the command tower, stealing his weapons and surveying the deck for any other signs of danger.

One by one, the Blades appeared over the edge of the railing, maneuvering carefully over the spikes. Sledge and his team would be through the propeller shaft by now, gaining access in the most dangerous way possible. If the Ballistic of this ship decided to spin up the engines and set sail, Sledge's team would be slashed to ribbons. Silence was their best indication that Sledge's team was alive and on target.

The plan was coming together. The last of Caledonia's team landed quietly on the deck and joined them against the wall. They were fists clenched around knife hilts, eyes that snagged on every movement, and nerves like scattered marbles. It had been so long since they'd engaged in any kind of fight. For most of them, they'd never done so without the heightening effect of Silt, and the near-ness of battle was plain in their eyes. Caledonia met them with her own calm gaze, forcing them to see her, to feel the ship beneath their feet, and to sink into this moment.

It was time for Triple. Caledonia took the sun pip from Pine and held it aloft, facing the cliff. She flashed the little light three times, paused, then three more.

Now they waited.

The night pressed close around them, gripping them in a cold breeze. It carried with it the smoky scent of the colonists' fires, burning where they couldn't be seen from shore.

After a few minutes, Pine nudged Caledonia. A spark had started out on the water, catching slowly at first, then climbing up the catboat's sail until the entire length of it was engulfed.

For just a second, there was no reaction. Then a cry of alarm from the tower echoed throughout the ship. Bullets raced from be-lowdecks, each of them turning toward the sight of the burning boat.

Caledonia smiled, lifting a hand to hold her team steady. And when twenty Bullets stood with their faces held toward the flames and backs unguarded, she gave the signal.

They moved, flanking the unsuspecting Bullets. Then she raised her voice, unleashing a tremendous battle cry. Fourteen Blades took up the call and rushed forward, using their advantage to tremendous effect. The Bullets were caught completely off guard, relinquishing immediate control of the battle to the Blades.

Caledonia's blood sang as she fired her stolen gun into the crowd, then dove forward to slash her opponent across the ribs. Blood smeared across the steel of her blade, glinting in the grim orange light of that countdown. In the midst of it all, a comforting warmth spread through Caledonia's limbs. This was where her footing was most secure, on the deck of a ship, in the midst of battle. She could see it unspooling around her as it had in her mind. This was the first wave. The second would come from behind.

Just as she thought it, gunshots ignited behind her as Bullets raced from belowdecks. The twenty Bullets before them had dwindled to half that number, but even so, they were a match for her own team. They were outnumbered, and now they were surrounded.

Where was Sledge?

He should have been here by now. For one heart-stopping moment, Caledonia feared that he'd been caught in the belly of the ship, his team quelled while Caledonia allowed her own to be flanked. She cleared the thought as soon as it landed. He was coming. They simply needed to hold their ground a little longer.

If she had her sisters—again, she cleared the thought.

"To me!" she called, raising her voice above the clamor. "Let them come to us," she ground out, knowing their only chance now was to stick together, to form as dense and as vicious a knot as possible.

Pine found her at once, expression grim as he understood her orders. "To Caledonia!" he shouted.

The Blades did as commanded, maneuvering toward Caledonia to concentrate their efforts and protect their backs. But it was a temporary measure and one that wouldn't last for long.

Bullets circled around them, raising guns and blades as they prepared to carve a path straight through the band of Blades.

The Blades were going to lose dearly in the next moment.

Then from the shore came an explosion. A missile burst on the nose of the ship, tossing a handful of Bullets to the ground. For a brief second, the fight stopped and all eyes turned to the darkened shore. Colonists. It could only be colonists.

Caledonia's mind whirled. Either the colonists were fighting back or helping the Blades. Both were potentially dangerous. Especially if they damaged her ship before she had a chance to take it!

Before she could process that thought any further, a shout sounded from within the belly of the ship, climbing closer and closer until it spilled onto the deck. Bullets came first, followed by Blades. At the lead was Sledge, roaring and brilliant.

Another explosion landed against the ship's hull, throwing

them all to the ground. When they'd regained their feet, the fight had lost its center. Blades and Bullets darted in every direction. The melee spun around her with chaotic frenzy. This fight would kill them all if she didn't do something about it.

"To me!" she shouted again. "Blades! To me!"

The response was instantaneous. Pine spun, the bliss of battle dancing in his eyes. The Blades formed a circle around Caledonia, giving them the ability to concentrate their attack where the Bullets could not.

Caledonia took a moment to study the scene. The Bullets no longer held the upper hand, yet they showed no sign of ceding the fight. She surveyed the faces before her, stopping the instant she found the person she wanted. Their Ballistic.

She darted forward, eyes locked on her target.

An elbow crashed into her cheek, and she was on her knees beneath a Bullet twice her size. He loomed over her, shoulders like boulders and a thin orange scar stretching from the corner of his mouth up to his ear. An eerie, painful kind of smile. He swung an arm back, and Caledonia caught the glint of sword gilded with blood. She rolled into him, thrusting her back into his chest as she rose and throwing him off balance. Before he recovered, she drove her own knife beneath his ribs, pulling away again as he slumped to the ground before her.

She had no time to wait. Their Ballistic rushed her and she fired, hitting him square in the chest. It was over that quickly.

Their leader was down. Caledonia held her ground, giving the clip a moment to submit. But not one of them gave a sign of surrender. They shouted, and together the Bullet clip drove forward.

Caledonia stumbled back in angry confusion. There was no question who would win this fight. The Bullets were outnumbered and entirely surrounded, but they continued to fight. Violent cries rose from their throats as they dove toward their opponents. They slashed viciously, vibrantly even, seeming to welcome each killing blow.

With a small shock, Caledonia realized that's exactly what they were doing. They would not surrender here, but fight until every last one of them fell.

Body after body thudded to the deck or splashed overboard until, with a sickening quiet that ballooned around them, the ship was theirs.

CHAPTER TEN

S ilt had an odor like a flower that had been plucked and laid too long in the sun. It was the sort of sweet that smelled wrong, cloying and so thick it was almost a taste. It was present in every room of the sweeper, threading the hallways with its sticky promise, teasing and tempting in every breath. As soon as they'd swept the ship for stragglers, the Blades promptly returned topside and stayed there.

In the med bay, the scent was smothering. Sledge stood in the doorway, every muscle in his large body rigid and unmoving. His arms were crossed, his lips pressed so tight, Caledonia questioned whether he breathed at all. But he watched her, eyes trained on every movement.

"You don't have to be here," she offered. "I can do this on my own."

Sledge only nodded and remained where he stood. A great, unhappy mountain.

The Silt was neatly packaged in crates and portioned for daily distribution. The bright orange pills were a beacon in their clear plastic sacks, piles of deadly seedlings ready to take root. There was enough here to supply the crew for a few months if need be, though not any longer. Aric kept the leash short.

Sledge wanted it gone, and Caledonia didn't disagree, but she couldn't simply dump it. Packaged as it was, it would float and wash up on the bay where anyone might find it. In order to destroy it properly, Caledonia would have to release each pill from the waterproof sacks. And Sledge, apparently, was going to watch her do it.

"It's a good ship," she said, continuing the tedious work. "Thank you."

For a moment, Caledonia worried that Sledge was going to stand there, unable to converse for however long it took her to do this. Then he drew a shallow breath and answered, "If it's going to get us through the Net, it needs to be better than 'good.'"

She nodded, thoughtful. "The strength of any ship is in its crew. You all fight well."

"Fighting isn't a problem for us," Sledge answered solemnly. "It's what happens after that we struggle with."

None of us comes back, Pine's voice whispered.

The little pills slipped one by one through her fingers, leaving a powdery orange stain on her skin. It would wash away with little effort. It was what it did inside the body that left more than a stain. This simple pill had scoured the Blades from the inside, leaving enough of itself behind that it would always cry out for more.

It's like a song, Hime had told her once. *The most beautiful song you've ever known. So strong that the instant you hear those first notes, you're singing along in your mind before you've even processed what's happening.*

She'd thought she understood what Hime meant. But after the events of last night, she was certain she'd underestimated the power of this drug once again.

"They kept fighting," she said, directing her words to the pills at her feet. "Why did they keep fighting?"

She sensed Sledge's frown in the pause before his next words. "It is never good to fail, but it's worse to fail a second time. Returning after a defeat like this one? Well, they knew their options. They took the better of the two."

Caledonia sat up suddenly. "But they were so far from his reach out here! They could have surrendered! They could have run! Why wouldn't they choose that?"

Sledge didn't answer.

Caledonia dismantled packages of Silt until she thought she'd never get the scent of it out of her nose and lungs. It was so strong that for a moment, she imagined she felt its altering effects. She paused, careful not to touch her face with her smudged fingers, and Sledge moved in close, placing a light yet steadying hand at her elbow and helping her toward the open porthole. After a few breaths of salty air, her mind cleared and she returned to her task with renewed speed.

Finally, every last pill had been freed from its packaging and tied inside a cloth bag. Sledge stayed at her shoulder as she carried it topside. In their absence, Triple had come aboard and the Blades had worked to clean the deck, preparing bodies for burial and washing away the blood. And while half of them watched her every step, the rest made an effort to look away, to busy themselves with some other work as she and Sledge hurried to stern.

It was as though dumping the Silt released the Blades from a spell, and they began to move freely from above to belowdecks. In moments, three Blades returned to Caledonia with sheets of crinkled paper in their hands. On each was drawn a blunt-tipped arrow, one half filled in with black ink.

"They're in every room." Glimmer sounded apologetic as he spoke, broad shoulders drooping. "Want us to take them down?"

Caledonia collected the pages, eyes tracing the familiar lines of the family sigil tattooed on her temple. So Lir hadn't assumed she was dead. And he was still after her. It was almost a compliment.

"Leave them," she said. It was a good reminder—to her and the rest of the crew—that no matter where they sailed, someone was looking for them.

Glimmer bobbed his head and followed the other two belowdecks. Soon, they had the contents and capabilities of the ship catalogued, and it was beginning to sink in that this sweeper was theirs now.

The ship was well stocked, which came as no surprise. The

galley was packed with protein bricks and seed cake, canned vegetables of every color and even barrels of firm, crisp apples. Caledonia had never seen such a wealthy pantry. If Far were here, the
woman might even smile at the prospect of feeding the crew of
the *Mors Navis* so well. Beyond that, the bunks were clean, the
med bay stocked with everything from fresh gauze to antibios,
and the weapons lockers were flush with any weapon Caledonia
could dream of needing. This was a ship ready for combat; all it
needed was a willing crew.

Night rolled on, and Caledonia took her time walking the passageways, getting a sense of where this sweeper carried her heft, how
low her hull dipped beneath the waterline. It was broad compared
to the *Mors Navis*, but shorter, her hull denser. Even before they'd
revved her engines, Caledonia knew the ship would gather speed
slowly but cruise with steady power when they were away from the
capricious currents of the coastline. She could already anticipate
how she'd cut through the sea, how her engines would thunder, how
the propellers would churn a frothy path through the ocean. Soon,
she would feel the spray of ocean waves against her cheeks.

She turned her steps toward the bridge just as the sun nosed
above the horizon, sending streaks of early light through thin
clouds hanging low in the sky. It was a slow explosion of purple
and gray and finally a burning orange that bled along the sea, beck-
oning to her.

The bridge was a small, low-ceilinged room with long windows overlooking the command deck. She surveyed the room with a practiced eye, running through a checklist in her head as she found each command station.

"You look like you're already out there." Sledge spoke from a few feet away, having followed her into the bridge.

"I am," she answered without turning around. "I'm always out there."

A crackling noise sounded from one of the control stations, like a receding wave, then it became a voice. *"Beacon, Beacon,* this is *Lighthouse Three,* come in, over."

Radios were Bullet tech; she knew the mechanism, but not the practice. Slowly, she turned to meet Sledge's eyes.

"They'll want a status report. Doesn't sound like the previous crew had time to send a distress signal," he said.

"We should keep it that way," she answered, a plan already forming where a moment ago she had had only questions.

Sledge frowned and took a step toward the radio. Next to it, a paper with her sigil was tacked in place. He brought the receiver to his mouth and pressed the button on its side. *"Lighthouse Three,* this is *Beacon,* preparing to collect the taxes, over."

"Taxes?" Caledonia asked when she was sure he'd released the button again. But Sledge only offered an apologetic shrug.

"Update from the Holster: the Father wants them doubled." The answer was fractured by static. "Make sure they know the cost of rebellion."

"They didn't rebel!" Caledonia's heart raced. Anger expanded inside her like smoke rising from a flame. It didn't matter that not a single colonist had defied him, Aric would make sure they took the blame. And in the process, they would be validated in their mistrust of anyone who dared to stand against him. It was brilliant. Brilliant and terrible.

Sledge raised a hand to quiet her as he responded. "Received, we'll double it and then some." Sledge answered so easily, Caledonia might have believed he meant it.

A dark laugh punctuated the air. "Keep to your tides."

"Keep to your tides," Sledge responded automatically, his eyes focused on some distant point. Caledonia realized with a start that it was a valediction, a parting wish passed from one Bullet to another.

"Sledge," she said eagerly when he'd released the receiver. "Can you ask him if there've been any sightings of the *Mors Navis*?"

Sledge nodded, giving himself a moment to think through his approach. *"Lighthouse Three*, come back, over."

It was several seconds before the radio crackled to life. "Miss me, *Beacon*?"

"Tremendously," Sledge answered with a wry tone. "We've got eyes on a ship that matches the description of the one Fiveson Lir was tracking. Does that match recent reports?"

Again, the radio released only static. Caledonia balled her fists and forced herself to draw even breaths while they waited. It was difficult to find the place to pin her hope. If her crew had been spotted, then they were being pursued. If they hadn't, then she'd have no idea what had become of them. She wanted to know that they'd punched the Net and were safe on the other side. But most of all she just wanted confirmation that the Bullets didn't know where they were. That they were safe.

Finally, the radio clicked, and static was replaced by that same Bullet's voice.

"Negative, *Beacon*; that ship and her crew were captured two days ago. Except for that red-haired captain of theirs. The rest have been taken to Slipmark for processing. Whatever you're seeing out there, it isn't that ship."

Caledonia saw Sledge's mouth move. She knew he answered the person on the other end of that terrible radio. But she didn't hear anything. All she heard was the furious roar of her mind.

CHAPTER ELEVEN

*C*aptured.

The word was a bomb in Caledonia's chest. Her crew had been taken into Bullet custody. Slipmark, Aric's northernmost stronghold, was notorious for being the first part of the Bullet empire recruits saw and the last rebels did. It was a prison. It was the place crews like hers went to die. But they wouldn't simply be executed. They'd be interrogated, tortured, and only finally killed in some cruel, brutal way.

Caledonia held on to the only piece of hopeful information that Bullet had given her: two days. For now, her crew was alive. And if she could get to them soon, they'd stay that way.

If she could get to them.

She let her legs carry her outside where the sun shone and the air was fresh, down the ladder to the busy deck, but she sensed none of it. The tide that surged away from her heart filled her lungs and her head until she was sure she would drown.

"Caledonia," Sledge said from behind her.

She didn't turn. She needed time for this to settle before she could deal with sympathy or judgment or whatever it was he had in store for her. She needed to cast her thoughts out over the ocean until she understood herself again. But there were too many people on this ship. Too many *strangers*. And she couldn't let her guard down even for a minute.

Caledonia took a steadying breath. Her crew had been taken. And she was going to do something about it no matter what it cost her.

"I'm sorry about your crew," Sledge continued. His voice was gentle, almost tentative with understanding and deep, painful regret. It was not the voice of someone preparing to offer aid. "I wish I could tell you they wouldn't suffer. And I wish there was something I could do to help."

Caledonia turned to face him, her determination as fresh as the sunrise. "Come with me."

"Cale—"

"Come with me and you *can* do something, Sledge. You're an army, and a good one. If you came with me, if you *fought* with me, we could get them back. I know we could!" Her fingers trembled with the effort of holding back the full light of her passion. Sledge opened his mouth to protest, but she pressed on. "You've seen what I can do. We just took this ship out from beneath the noses of a crew twice our size. I can do so much with so little—it's how I've survived my entire life. And it's how I've kept my crew alive. Help me keep them alive now. Please."

The frown appeared first in Sledge's eyes before slowly bending his lips. "You're talking about breaking into a Bullet fortress."

"Yes." She nodded with confidence. "You broke out of one, didn't you?"

"Caledonia, this is different. This isn't a ship we're talking about. I'm very sorry for your crew, but if they're on the other side of Slipmark's walls, then they might as well be dead."

"Slipmark?" The name was repeated quietly and with awe. The Blades on deck stopped whatever they were doing at the sound of it, their faces turning toward Sledge with wary and terrified expressions.

Without meaning to, she let the iron grip on her thoughts slip. The current of her own fears was both swift and strong, and her mind flooded with thoughts of her sisters. In Slipmark. Where they would receive no mercy. Where, very soon, they would meet with terrible punishments for defying the Father. Why, why, why had she assumed they were safe?

"I need your help," she said simply.

"Seems like that's all we've been doing, seagirl." Pine pushed to the front of the crowd, planting himself before her. "We got you this ship so you could return the favor and help us."

"And I will, but—"

"But you want us to put everything at risk and sail into a place none of us should ever set foot again? Do you have any idea what you're asking us to do?" Anger pinched at Pine's eyes, but it was overwhelmed by fear. Even he was afraid of this place.

Each of them had been taken from their families, forced into the belly of a ship just like this one, and taken to Slipmark, where children were whittled into soldiers. Except, they hadn't been taken, had they? They'd been offered up. Traded or tithed. Given away by the people who should have held on to them the tightest.

It was the way things were. She'd known this her entire life, but with Pine's defensive gaze fixed on her, a sudden clarity swept through her mind. The true power of Aric Athair was rooted in mistrust. He'd succeeded in making every person under his thumb feel completely and utterly alone. Even her.

"Caledonia." Sledge was on her opposite side, placing her in the center of a growing cluster of very nervous Blades. "I understand your impulse, but this simply isn't possible."

"I don't believe that," she answered.

"It isn't that we don't want to help, Caledonia. Slipmark is a fortress. Even if we could get inside, the chances of us making it out again are . . . well, they aren't good." Triple was speaking now.

"And what about Sister?" Shale spoke in a thin voice, hands clasped before her.

"Who is Sister?" Caledonia asked.

Shale slipped back into the crowd, unwilling to say more. It was Pine who finally answered. "She runs Slipmark. She's the first face recruits see when we arrive. And the last before we leave. If we were unlucky or stupid, we'd see her in between those two times. She—" Pine stopped suddenly, choosing his next words carefully.

"She makes sure we choose the Father's family over any other."

His horror was so palpable, it sent the echo of a shiver across Caledonia's skin.

"It isn't possible." Pine spat the words, angry and bleak.

"But it is." She planted her feet, resisting the fear Aric had rooted so well in all of them. She raised her voice. "It was impossible that a group of Bullets could defect and create a new way of life for themselves. But you did it. It was impossible that a single girl could sneak aboard a Bullet ship to attack a Fiveson and survive. But I did it. It was impossible that without anything more than bows and fists we could take a Bullet ship as our own. But we did it." She cast her gaze around the circle from Pine to Triple, Harwell to Mint, Glimmer to Shale. They were afraid, but they were listening.

"I will help you exactly as I promised I would. *After* I find my crew. And I'm asking for your help. No one knows better what is happening to them in Slipmark. No one knows better the challenges of getting in and out of that place." Her eyes found Pine once more. Instead of the glare she'd expected, his brow carried a brooding expression. He understood loyalty. "I could tell you that saving my crew and my ship will be worth it because it will make our chances of punching the Net that much stronger. But that's not why I'm asking you to help me. I'm asking because they are my family and they did not consent to this."

A shiver of anticipation had settled in Caledonia's hands.

Though the sun was warm on her skin, she felt cold and alert, like the edge of a knife. The Blades watched her with an air of solemnity.

"This is no small request," Sledge said into the quiet.

Caledonia nodded. "I know."

Sledge drew a deep breath and walked a slow circle, passing each Blade. When he'd completed his circuit, he stood in their midst, quiet and contemplative.

"Friends," Sledge's voice boomed. "All our lives we've been asked to fight for reasons not our own. Every one of us has used our strength and skill to accomplish things we didn't believe in, done things we didn't want to do. This is not one of those things, and I do not relish the thought of placing any of you in danger. However, I've only ever fought for one thing I believed in: you. We may not know them, but this is the same fight." Sledge moved to stand by her side. "You choose. All in favor of going after her crew, stand to starboard. All in favor of sailing for the Net, stand to port. We sail with the majority."

Caledonia made her expression one of fierce determination. Her stomach clenched and her mind raced, but she let none of it show. She would be as steely and steady as the deep ocean.

Triple was the first to move. She strode across the deck to stand in front of Caledonia and paused there. "Before today, I'd have sworn nothing in the world could compel me to voluntarily go to Slipmark."

Caledonia didn't dare to smile.

"But I'd rather fight at your side than anywhere else," she added with a small nod. The girl stepped behind Caledonia.

The choice spurred others to do the same. One by one, the Blades moved to stand on opposite sides of the deck. Some were quick to decide, while others took their time. They stood stationary with their thoughts or gathered in small groups to discuss. No one rushed them. Nearly half an hour had passed, and the two sides were even. It came down to a single person.

Pine stood in the middle with his hand gripped lightly behind his back, his eyes focused thoughtfully on the deck at his feet.

"Pine," Sledge urged gently.

Pine nodded, his eyes moving up to meet Caledonia's. On the surface, they were calm, but just beneath an old fury raged. For a moment, Caledonia was sure he would turn the vote against her, but then he sighed quietly and took three steps to the starboard side.

"It's decided." Sledge spoke loudly and without any hint of anger or disappointment, yet his eyes were hard as stone. "Tomorrow, we sail for Slipmark."

CHAPTER TWELVE

The wind cut across Caledonia's cheeks in frigid tracks, pulling tears from her eyes and pressing salt into her skin. The sun was plastered over by a thick layer of puffy clouds, a paler version of the choppy ocean beneath. It was just after sunrise, and the world was a study of milky gray and shadowed blue.

Caledonia stood on the nose of the bridge, her hands braced on two metal spikes. They'd considered clearing the bones from them. Sledge, in particular, had argued that the bodies—whatever was left of them—deserved to rest. But while Caledonia might have agreed, she'd argued to keep their gruesome crown. If they were going to get anywhere near Slip-mark, it would be under the guise of the Bullet ship they'd stolen, and she had yet to see a Bullet ship without a collection of trophies.

It had taken them a full day and night to get underway. While Sledge coordinated a duty roster, Caledonia focused on learning her new ship and crew. She'd come to know each Blade by name, but determining their ship-worthy skills was another matter. To say nothing of the ship's capabilities.

In addition to the *Beacon*'s capacity to emit a tiny shock wave and destroy mines from afar, they discovered a cache of weapons down below, nets, and detachable arms that would allow the ship to trawl for fish. While the food stores would have been enough to keep the Bullet crew fed, it wouldn't have supported the small army of recruits they were supposed to gather.

"He likes to break us down before he builds us up," Pine explained when he saw Caledonia's confusion. "He wants starvation to be one of our most exquisite memories. Conscripts and pledges alike. Everyone learns what it is to starve before he brings you to the table of his glorious goodwill."

Bitterness sharpened every word. He regarded Caledonia with a callous eye, as if she couldn't know what it was to starve. It sparked an anger in her—of course she knew what it was to starve. She was on the edge of responding when he dropped his gaze to the crates of food.

"The casing of any good bullet must be tough and hollow," he said, as though reciting a well-known rule. "So that it might be filled with pure, explosive intention."

It was a glimpse into the lives they'd led, and something of an explanation of the people they'd become. Another piece of the puzzle snapped into place. The younger and hungrier you were when you were introduced to Silt, the less likely you were to question your dependence on it, and by extension Aric. It was a thorough and deadly trap.

Pine stepped in close, his chest brushing her shoulder. "That's how any Bullet is made," he said quietly. Her cheeks warmed, and she suddenly realized that he'd offered all of this because he wanted her to understand—where they'd come from, what they'd endured, and, perhaps, who he was.

The moment passed quickly, swept away by the demands of the day.

The first time they spun up the propellers, Caledonia felt just how different it would be to sail this ship. A tinny hum reverberated throughout the hull, and the propellers cut loudly into the ocean. Water sluiced from them, leaving a churned trail in their wake for an easy half mile. Even the vibration of the deck was more sluggish than she was accustomed to. This ship was nothing like the *Mors Navis*, but she needed to find a connection to it regardless. She needed to focus on its strengths—stability, inertia, heft—so that when the time came, she could wield it like a weapon.

With the Blades divided into teams and given assignments, she took them on a short run along the westward coast. It was like sliding into a coat that didn't quite fit. Each maneuver played out differently than Caledonia expected, and she longed for her sisters.

With her sisters at her side, the task ahead wouldn't feel as daunting as it did.

With her sisters at her side . . . It was a powerful promise. It trilled in her blood, constantly buzzing in the base of her spine. Her sisters. She knew where they were. They were within reach. And she would see them soon.

Finally, she ordered a test of the shock wave. They dropped a single mine attached to a bright orange buoy, and when they were a quarter mile away, Caledonia turned to Harwell, who stood ready at the controls.

"Let's see how this works," she commanded, and Harwell hit the shock wave.

For a few seconds, nothing happened.

"I think it's charging," Harwell explained. "Probably has to—"

Whatever he was going to say next was lost as the entire ship pulsed. Energy and sound ballooned around them, raising the hair on their arms and popping in their ears. The pulse traveled visibly through the water, creating a series of fast-moving ripples with the ship at its center. Almost faster than Caledonia could track, the first ripple slammed into the buoy. Instantly, the mine was triggered, sending up a font of water in a single explosive blast.

Harwell laughed, throwing up his arms in celebration. "I like this button. I'd like to formally request that I get to push this button again sometime," he said, grinning in a way that made his cheeks round and boyish.

It was difficult to keep a smile from her own lips. "I'm certain that can be arranged."

By the end of their daylight hours, the small team of twenty-four Blades, with five still recovering from their injuries, had been transformed into a manageable crew, Caledonia's tow had been loaded onto the deck, and Triple had catalogued the available quarters and distributed assignments. The night had gone quickly after that, and morning arrived with a surprising sight.

Figures stood all along the rocky shore. Adults and children were huddled together, wrapped in blankets and coats of muted colors. Colonists. The missiles they'd fired had complicated the battle in Caledonia's favor. Even if their motivation was only to ensure the Blades left the Northwater, they'd taken a stand.

As the *Beacon* churned slowly toward the open ocean, the colonists raised their hands in parting. The Blades returned the gesture with an air of caution and hope. Trust was a long way from this moment, but perhaps it hadn't been destroyed as thoroughly as Caledonia feared.

Now the ship cut through a restless sea toward the port of Slipmark, and Caledonia's mind had little to do but churn like the water in their wake. There were so many terrible questions she had no way of answering. It had now been three days since her crew's capture. Had they all survived? What was being done to them now? To her ship? What would be left of them by the time she arrived?

And as each question surfaced, her own fear answered it. Only a few survived the fight, and more died every day they were in custody. She imagined them injured, tortured, and drugged.

She imagined Pisces crying out in pain, and then she imagined no more.

"You'll make yourself sick," a gentle voice said from her side.

Caledonia started, realizing suddenly that her tears had become real. She swiped impatiently at her face.

"I don't want to offer you hollow comforts, but a crew like yours, who has defeated more than one of Aric's ships, will be a prize." Triple leaned against the railing, careful of the spikes surrounding them. "They weren't taken to Slipmark to die quickly. They were taken there because that is where the Steelhand made his mark. It's where people go to suffer. And that will take time."

"This ship is too slow." Caledonia dragged her wet palms down her stomach, letting the wind rip fresh tears from her eyes. "Who is the Steelhand?"

Triple's shoulders rolled forward, and she seemed to grow smaller as she sank into memories Caledonia didn't share. "A dark genius with a mind for torturing the body in simple and complex ways. He won't be in Slipmark, but his designs will be."

"What kind of designs?" Horror rose in Caledonia's throat.

Triple stood quietly for a long moment. "Most of it was quiet. Punishments for individuals or small groups who stepped out of line or failed to execute the Father's orders. But also wartech. The worst of it. Like that star blossom in our weapons locker. One bomb, one hundred deaths," she added in a whisper.

When Caledonia didn't press for more, Triple shook her head.

"Don't think of that part. Just remember that enduring is living, and Aric will want their suffering to be long and visible. To him, that's power. To us, it's hope."

"How did you and the others manage to escape?" Caledonia asked. "How is it that so many of you kept your spirits unbroken through all of that?"

Triple nodded. "That was Sledge. He was Fiveson Venn's right hand and oversaw our Silt rations. We didn't even notice the first time he cut the dose. It was such a small reduction."

The strategy unfurled before Caledonia like a great, beautiful sail. The person in control of handing out Silt could, of course, alter how much each person received. And if they were careful, they could wean an entire ship from the drug.

"The second time he cut it, I caught him in the act." Her mouth twisted at the memory. "I nearly turned him in on the spot."

"But you didn't."

"No." She squinted out over the water, clearly uncomfortable. "He convinced me to give him a week, and by then I was a different person. I started helping."

"And Pine? Was he with Sledge from the start?"

"Pine was a bit more . . . difficult."

Caledonia couldn't help but laugh. She was beginning to understand that she might never be able to predict Pine. He always seemed to move in the direction opposite her instinct. Still, he wasn't fickle. Beneath the seemingly disparate choices was a person with a clear sense of himself and the world. Just because she didn't yet understand his compass didn't mean it wasn't there.

"He's loyal and not always quick to change paths once he's chosen one. We gave him that name because he's as sturdy as any tree in the forest we call home," Triple continued. "Sturdy, but not immovable. Those trees bend and grow and so does he."

"That's . . . a really lovely name," Caledonia said, surprised. "Did you all name yourselves?"

"Mostly. It's important to us that we are able to choose who we are and what we will and won't do."

"Because that's what Aric took from you," Caledonia added, understanding settling in more quickly now. "Choice."

Triple hunched her shoulders against the cold wind at her back. "Once you're hooked on Silt, you have no capacity to choose any course of action but the one that will ensure you get your next dose. It sometimes feels like you have a choice, but it all stems from a need so strong you can't fight it. At least not alone."

This was what Caledonia had known about Bullets her entire life. They were dangerous because the thing they needed most in the world was carefully controlled. If you stood between them and that drug, they'd go straight through you to get it. It had always reminded Caledonia of a riptide, running breezily along the shore. If you were in it, you could swim at an incredible pace, much faster than would be possible on your own. But if you needed to change directions, you'd find yourself beating against that same steely tide, unable to make any kind of progress. Soon, you'd be so exhausted that you'd let that current carry you along without a fight. To get out, you needed someone who could reach in without losing themselves in the process.

"It couldn't have been easy for Sledge to break his own addiction without Venn finding out," Caledonia mused.

"Venn knew. They were friends. As much as any Bullet is capable of friendship."

At least five questions surfaced in Caledonia's mind, but she only asked one: "Is that why he didn't kill him?"

Triple flinched at the question, pressing her lips together as though to stop an answer that had come too readily. "He was supposed to give Venn an overdose. Take him out before we made our move."

"But he didn't?"

"Couldn't."

With a sigh, Triple raised her hand, palm facing out. Caledonia raised her own, letting their palms skim so lightly together it raised the hair on the back of her neck. For a moment, they stood that way, their palms barely touching, the wind snatching at Triple's sunny braids, the brisk kiss of sea spray cooling Caledonia's cheeks.

"Sledge couldn't bring himself to do to Venn what had been done to all of us. He couldn't force Silt on anyone, even a Fiveson. He had to subdue him another way, and it nearly got us all killed."

She let her fingers rest against Caledonia's, touching her for the first time since she'd applied that nanopatch. "Pine has never really forgiven him. But to Sledge *how* we got out was just as important as getting out."

It was hard to think past the warm press of Triple's fingertips on her own. She wanted to let their fingers slide together, to share the full warmth of their hands the way she would have with any of her sisters.

"We can resist them as long as we don't become them," Caledonia said quietly. They were her mother's words, but the last time she'd heard them aloud it had been Pisces who said them, urging her to keep Oran alive.

"For us, it's more that we have to *un*become them. We have to become something else, and we have to keep choosing what that is."

The two girls fell into silence. Wind ripped through the tattered clothing still clinging to the bones mounted on pikes, and far behind them propellers chewed up the water. The Blades had chosen to live a secluded life away from Aric's influence. Now they'd chosen to join Caledonia on a dangerous journey straight into one of his strongholds.

Her own quest had never felt like a choice. Fighting Aric, taking down his bale barges, had seemed more like a compulsion. Going after Donnally and Ares also hadn't felt much like a choice. Even going after her crew didn't feel like a choice. These were things she had to do.

But as they drove toward that eastern horizon, she wondered how many other Bullets might choose a different way of being if given a sliver of choice.

Maybe Aric's hold wasn't as ironclad as he thought.

Suddenly, the ship pitched to one side, throwing both girls to the deck. Caledonia's cheek smacked against the gritty surface, feet skidding beneath her as she struggled to stand.

Triple rolled gracefully into a crouch, steadying herself with one hand, confusion widening her eyes.

But where Triple felt confusion, Caledonia felt her blood rushing as though awakening from a long sleep. She knew what that was. She almost grinned when she said, "We're under attack."

CHAPTER THIRTEEN

C aledonia was running for the bridge before a second boom rocked the ship.

They were a Bullet ship in Bullet territory, and that should offer them cursory protection from attack. She and Triple had been stationed on the nose. Whatever hit them had come from the rear. Yet there had been no cry of alarm, no sighting of any ship on the western horizon.

Before Caledonia could follow that thought too far, she was swinging around the hatchway into the bridge, Sledge hard on her heels.

"Report!" they shouted together.

Caledonia scanned the sea and found . . . nothing.

"We don't know," Pine was saying. "We can't—"

Another blast rocked the ship. They pitched sharply starboard. Everyone braced against whatever was nearest.

Caledonia spun, searching again. In every direction, the sea was a clear, flat plane. There was nothing in sight, nothing that could account for the explosions dogging their hull. If it had been a minefield, they'd have hit several all at once. Not these single, separated blasts. There was something else. Something they couldn't see. But what?

"Search the ship!" Sledge was shouting. "We've got a stowaway down there. Find them before they sink us!"

Five Blades raced belowdecks. But as a fourth explosion rocked the ship, Caledonia knew they'd turn up empty.

"All stop!" she cried. "I want us at a standstill!"

Eyes drifted between her and Sledge. He hesitated only a second before nodding. "Do it."

"Harwell!" she shouted as she raced out of the bridge once more. "On my mark, I want you to hit that button again, clear?"

"Clear!" Harwell responded, his joy tinged with mounting concern.

She gripped the ladder leading to the top of the bridge tower and hauled herself up. As the engines quieted and the ship slowed, Caledonia planted herself atop the ghost funnel, eyes trained on the water off the port side. When she'd waited as long as she dared, she stomped three times on the sloped shell and called out, "Now, Harwell!"

A moment later the ship pulsed with that tantalizing burst of energy. Caledonia watched ripples course away from the hull, eyes as sharp as her instincts. And there, not a quarter mile away, a break in the otherwise seamless ripple pattern.

Any vindication she might have felt at being right was swept away in a ferocious current of alarm. The attack had come from below because there was a ship beneath the surface.

A deepship.

They were a thing of legend. A remnant of the old world that had only survived in stories and the occasional photograph or painting. As far as anyone knew, none of the tech still existed. Yet there was no other explanation. Someone had either discovered one or figured out how to construct one. And right now, it didn't really matter which.

For a long moment, she stayed where she stood. The day was clear with a bright sun. The ocean was calm and as blue as the skies. The crew was waiting. If she were in her own ship, she'd tell them to drive the engines to full and outrun this mysterious deepship. But this was not the *Mors Navis*, and it was not built for outrunning anything.

The ship rocked again; the explosion sent Caledonia to her knees, and a sharp spray of water splashed across the quarterdeck. They were targeting their propellers. Caledonia hurled to her feet and leapt to the deck below.

"They're beneath us?" Sledge asked, uncertain and wary.

The entire crew was watching them, their expressions panicked. They'd armed themselves with guns and blades, and every single one of those weapons was useless right now.

"They are." Caledonia was careful to keep her voice firm and commanding. If they saw concern on her face, they'd lose the battle before she'd determined how to fight it.

"Are we running?" he asked, closing the distance between them so he wouldn't be overheard. "Shouldn't we run?"

She curled her fingers into a fist. "We're not running."

"We can't fight something we can't see," Sledge protested.

"Then we'll have to find a way to see it," she countered.

Apprehension pressed at the corners of Sledge's eyes. Caledonia knew he worried for his people more than anything, and she also knew that running was likely to get them all killed. She needed him to trust her.

Holding herself steady and calm, she raised her hand, palm facing out. His eyes flicked to it and back to her face. All around them, the Blades stood locked in place as though the ship were holding its breath. Then Sledge raised his hand and placed his palm against her own.

It was a simple gesture, but it came with a power so palpable, Caledonia felt it shift in the air between them. He stepped back, waiting for her orders, a signal to every other person to do the same.

She was in command.

"Thank you," Caledonia said solemnly, panic spinning in her chest.

"Your orders?" Sledge asked.

She had none. She had no experience fighting a deepship. No

one did. And if she didn't figure out how to do it successfully, she'd waste the trust Sledge had handed her and probably lose this too-slow ship in the process.

If her girls were here, she'd ask them for options. Pisces, Amina, and Hime would circle around her and offer any idea that occurred to them in the moment. They wouldn't all be good ideas, but they'd lead to one. And one was all she needed.

"Caledonia?" Sledge asked again, growing nervous.

They had guns, which were useless; the pulse, which was only good for showing them where the deepship was; and nets, which would be great if they wanted to gather fish, but—that was it!

"Pine!" she shouted. "Get those trawler nets ready! We're going fishing."

The crew leapt into action. Pine shouted orders, and Blades stretched the nets across the quarterdeck. The ship rocked again, but the crew kept working, attaching bright orange buoys along the topside of the netting.

Sledge and Triple took four others down to the weapons locker and hauled up every large piece of artillery they could find, laying each one out on the deck for Caledonia's perusal. There were missiles and cable mines and that deadly star blossom, which ejected hundreds of tiny metal pieces when detonated and could cut a crew to shreds. But the weapons Caledonia focused on were the harpoons.

These weren't made for fishing, but for piercing a hull. Bullets used them to hook smaller ships and reel them in before they took on too much water. They were perfect.

"Net's ready!" Pine called from the quarterdeck.

"Get every last one of those harpoons ready to go," she ordered, turning her steps toward the bridge. "Harwell, I'm going to need you to hit that button again. Stand by."

"Happy to, Captain!" he called, a new eagerness flushing his cheeks.

Caledonia swept her gaze across the deck and her new crew. Ten people stood with the nets at the rear of the ship, another six had loaded the harpoons and mounted them above the port railing. Still others had eyes trained on the surrounding ocean, searching for any new sign of trouble. She hoped this worked.

Another blast rocked the ship, pushing their tail in a partial spin.

"Hold steady!" Caledonia called as the ship regained its balance. "Now, Harwell!"

He hit the button. The air tightened with electricity, and the ship pulsed.

Caledonia watched the ripples, her sight snagging on the place where they bent around the shape of something just beneath the surface. It was smaller than she'd anticipated, smaller than the *Beacon* by at least half. They'd moved in closer, thinking they had the advantage. Caledonia smiled.

"We're going to cut right across her nose, then make it look like we're running," she called to the bridge crew, stepping in to take the wheel. "We need to be fast, but not too fast. Propellers to quarter-power. Let's keep the water as still as possible so Pine can get that net down."

"What happens if they fire on us before we're ready?" Harwell asked.

Caledonia offered a pinched smile. "Then this doesn't work."

The propellers made a terrible noise as they came to life and slowly pushed the *Beacon* across the path of the deepship. Pine and his team lowered the long net over the port rail, letting it slip carefully into the water. When the last buoy dropped, he called up to the bridge, and Caledonia directed the ship away from the net.

It was eerily quiet. The only sounds were the slow splashes of propellers against the water and the soft roar of the engine. Caledonia watched the line of orange buoys shrink in their wake, and the second they were far enough, she ordered the engines to full. The propellers shrieked, but the *Beacon* rushed forward.

The crew stood, waiting with harpoons aimed at their invisible assailant. Minutes passed, and the line of buoys didn't move. Had the deepship seen the trap? Had they cut beneath, in pursuit once more? Panic, insidious and uncomfortable, wormed its way up Caledonia's throat. She couldn't fight what she couldn't see. And she couldn't protect her crew if she couldn't fight.

An order to drop every cable mine they had was ready on her tongue when all at once, the buoys moved. They snapped

together like wings and hissed along the top of the water in a
violent line.

"Those buoys won't last long!" Pine shouted from his position
on deck.

Almost before he'd finished, a single buoy broke away from
the net, bouncing once over the surface of the ocean to settle far
behind them.

"Cut the engines!" Caledonia returned the wheel to her bridge
crew and raced to the deck. They needed to be fast. And they needed
to hit their targets. "Harpoons ready!"

Sledge, Triple, and their small team stood at even intervals
along aft deck, each of them tracking the approaching ship. One
by one, the buoys were losing their grip, flying away from the net
as though shocked. With each missing buoy, the shape of the ship
became less and less clear. They didn't need clarity, Caledonia reminded herself, they just needed direction.

The deepship drew closer, buoys popping off at an alarming
rate.

"Fire!" Caledonia called.

But just then, the *Beacon* rocked under a fresh explosion,
knocking the crew off their marks. Three harpoons flew wildly
through the air, plopping harmlessly into the water nowhere near
the deepship.

The *Beacon* sputtered, one of the propellers spinning out of
sync with the other and arching them directly into the path of the

deepship. Sledge and Triple regained their feet and brought their weapons back to their shoulders.

And just as the last buoy flew from the netting, they fired.

The harpoons hit their mark. Their tethers snapped tight against the *Beacon*'s rail. Then, just as quickly, the harpoons burst out of the water, dragging steel and netting with them and crashing against their hull.

The surface of the ocean burbled once and then again, violently like boiling water. They'd struck the deepship. She was taking on water and would soon be committed to the deep.

CHAPTER FOURTEEN

T he crew cheered, but Caledonia watched until the surface of the water stopped churning with the final gasps of that ship. Sledge stood at her side, solemn even in the face of this victory, while behind them Pine shouted for people to stop crowing and survey the ship for damage.

"Bullets don't have that kind of tech." Sledge's voice had a dark edge.

"It's been a while since you were with them. Maybe they do now?" But even as Caledonia spoke, she doubted her words.

"Maybe," he conceded. "But if no distress call went out, then they had no way of knowing we weren't Bullets. Why would they fire on their own ships?"

That was the question Caledonia had been saving for later. Aric wouldn't allow his ships to fire on their own. And if the deep-ship didn't belong to Aric, then it likely belonged to an enemy of Aric's. Which meant they'd just taken down a potential ally. They'd killed a crew that in all likelihood had been very like her own.

"May the ocean keep you," she said softly. She couldn't help but wonder how many had been on that ship, what their names had been, and whether or not there'd been some other way to resolve the situation. Had there been some option she hadn't stopped to consider? Doubt found all the cracks in her mind, pushing through and making room for regret.

She turned away from the sea to find Sledge watching her with a pitying expression. "We didn't have any other options, Caledonia."

No good options, right, Captain? The ghost of Redtooth's voice was as vibrant as ever.

She nodded, feeling her heart squeeze in response. Not long ago, she'd never had to question her actions in this way. She knew her enemies from her friends, she knew when to attack and when to run, and she never would have found herself in a situation like this: forced to fight the people she should be helping. But everything had become so complicated, and it had all started when a Bullet landed on her ship and convinced her to trust him.

"I know," she said, exhaling all her breath in a rush, trying to release the uneasy feelings of regret and guilt with it.

"Aric did this, remember." Sledge folded his arms across his broad chest and narrowed his eyes. "Not you."

"I know," she repeated, growing irritated.

This was the kind of conversation she should have had with Pisces and only Pisces. The girl was so close to Caledonia's heart, it was impossible to hide these tricky, confounding emotions from her. Pisces knew exactly how to guide Caledonia through the maze of her own worries and anxieties until she found herself on solid emotional footing once more. And in spite of hating everything about that process, she wished her sister were here to pester her. Not Sledge.

"Captain, ah, Captains." Harwell's tentative voice was a welcome distraction. He approached cautiously with fresh grease smeared across the bridge of his nose.

"I think we've established that only one of us can claim that title," Sledge answered without any hint of resentment. He stepped back, relinquishing the title.

Caledonia squared her shoulders, forcing confidence where it had waned. "Damage report."

"Yes, well, it's certainly not good news, though I reckon it could be worse given we took seven hits and it could have gone on quite—"

"Harwell," she interrupted kindly. "Damage report."

"Right." Harwell pinched the bridge of his nose, expanding the grease smear toward both cheeks like little wings. "Do you want me to start with the bad news or the good? Or, I guess, none of it is *good* exactly, but—"

"Harwell."

"Right. Yes. We've temporarily plugged two breaches on level three. One is midship, one stern, both are minor, though we'll want to do something more permanent, of course."

"Of course," she said, encouraging him to continue.

"The bad news is the propeller. One of the blades took a significant blast, and it's bent. If it were only a little bent, I might be able to do something about it, but as is, if we spin up the engines before repairs, we'll do ourselves critical damage."

"Do we have what you need to fix it?" Caledonia asked.

"We do," Harwell answered cagily. "But it's going to take some time."

Time was one thing Caledonia was sure they didn't have. "How much?"

Harwell braced as if for battle before speaking again. "I . . . don't know. Days? I think days, honestly."

Each of Caledonia's fingers curled into fists, and she clamped her teeth together to keep from frowning.

They were so near to Slipmark. A day's sail at most. And now they were going to spend more than that amount of time right here, stamped in place, while Harwell and his team figured out how to fix the propeller. It didn't matter that he knew what he was doing. This was an unfamiliar ship with unfamiliar tools. And every minute they spent here was another minute her crew spent enduring some terrible Bullet torture.

Amina would have known exactly what to do. She would have come to her with the problem and a plan, and they'd have been underway again in no time. Amina and her beautiful mind were made for this kind of problem, and she might never see her again.

Caledonia felt the edges of her nerves beginning to curl like a paper held too close to a flame. Panic would do her no good. Her crew was strong, brave, and together. Whatever they were facing in this moment, they could handle it until she reached them. They had to.

It was a small comfort, but Caledonia's mind cooled, and she cast her eyes over the deck of the *Beacon* where the crew of Blades waited for instruction. From her, she realized. They were all watching her. While she recognized all of their faces, had learned each of their names, it was still shocking to see how much they looked like a clip of Bullets on this ship. It was no wonder they'd been attacked. How was anyone to know the difference?

How was anyone to know the difference!

"Harwell, begin repairs, but only do what is absolutely essential. I want us to look more injured than we are. Can you do that?"

Harwell nodded.

"Sledge." Caledonia spun on her heel to find Sledge waiting there, quietly supporting her from behind. "How do you feel about impersonating a Bullet?"

The mountain raised an eyebrow before answering carefully, "I suppose I thought it was inevitable."

Three minutes later, Caledonia stood in the bridge with Sledge, Triple, and Pine. Sledge's hand was on the radio, his eyes locked on the dash.

"If this works," he began, not lifting his eyes from the controls before him, "we'll have to do a lot more than just sound like a Bullet clip. You're sure this is the way you want to go?"

It was a lot to ask, but Caledonia was certain. "It's our best option," she confirmed.

Triple nodded in agreement, and so did Pine.

Without another question, Sledge lifted the receiver. "Slip-mark harbor, this is *Beacon*, come back." He paused, giving them time to respond, and after several seconds had passed, he repeated his call.

They answered on the third try: "We read you, *Beacon*, go ahead."

Sledge cleared his throat and straightened his spine. "We've encountered a rogue ship and taken heavy damage. We're unable to repair on our own. Requesting a tow, over."

"What's the status of the rogue ship, over?"

Sledge grimaced and delivered the lie. "Unknown. Damaged, but sailing. They fled south."

If Aric wasn't already aware that someone out here had a deepship—regardless of whether or not it had been the only one to ever survive—they weren't about to tell him. That kind of information was power. And if they reported the location of the downed deepship, Aric would send a recovery team before they'd even reached Slipmark. He'd take that tech and make it his own. This way, the ship remained a secret for at least a little while longer.

Silence filled the small room. There was a lag between each

message, but this one stretched longer than the others. If this didn't work, they'd have tipped their hand and the road before them would get considerably steeper.

Finally, the radio crackled to life.

"Hold position, *Beacon*," the voice on the other end replied. "We're on our way."

CHAPTER FIFTEEN

P ine was staring at her.

He had been for several minutes. At first, Caledonia ig-nored him, but as his gaze grew steadily more onerous, she found herself wanting to squirm beneath it. And she would not give Pine the Sullen the satisfaction of seeing her squirm.

"Speak or avert your eyes," she growled.

"We need to do something about your hair," he said from his perch atop a table in the galley, feet propped on a chair, where he'd been supervising the transformation of Blades to Bullets.

It had been half a day since contacting Slipmark, and they expected to be intercepted by Bullets at any moment. When they arrived, the Blades would have to convince them that they were the rightful crew of the *Beacon* and had been sidelined from their recruitment mission by an attack from a rogue ship. From there they would be towed into the infamous Slipmark harbor. But that was only the first stage of their plan. After that, things got a little more complicated.

Though every single one of the Blades had been in Slipmark as children, only a handful had been there in the last two turns. Harwell was the one with the most recent experience, and they'd spent the past few hours listening to him outline everything from port procedures to meal schedules. The more he spoke, the more dangerous this seemed. From the outside, Bullet society was a violent, faceless roar, all chaos and fury. But from the inside, it was the picture of order. A single misstep would raise suspicion.

"The harbor keeps a rigid schedule," he'd said, delivering the only scrap of welcome news in the lot. "Barracks are reserved for stays of more than six nights. As long as we have a crew manifest to hand over, our—"

"Clip," Pine corrected him.

"Right, yes. Our repairs, all things considered, are minimal and should only take a day or two, so our *clip* will be kept on board the *Beacon*. We just need to make sure our papers are in order, which we can do."

"And the prison?" Caledonia asked.

"Ah." Harwell's eyes widened sympathetically. "About that," he said, reaching for a sheet of paper and beginning to sketch a crude map of the city. "There are, or were, three. Here, here, and here."

Sledge had cursed before Harwell placed the third mark. Each of the prisons was separated by a considerable distance. "We can't do anything until we know which one they're in," Sledge nearly growled. "And what if they aren't all in the same one?"

Caledonia had raised a hand to stop his panic before it infected everyone. "One step at a time."

They decided that while Sledge should stay aboard to keep an eye on their ship and their crew, Caledonia, Pine, and Triple would venture off ship to investigate each prison. For that, Caledonia needed to do more than pass as a Bullet.

Choosing a name had been easy. There was no name in the world she'd respond to as quickly as that of her mother, Rhona. It was the next part that was proving difficult.

She resisted raising a hand to touch her red braid. "I'll tuck it under a cap."

"It's too recognizable. They're looking for you, remember?" Pine's eyes pinned her in place with a hard challenge. She found it impossible to look away. "It would be better if you cut it off."

She touched the curling ends of her hair, thinking of her mother standing tall and proud at the bow of her ship, red curls rolling behind her in the wind. In her mind, her mother's hair was a sign of her strength and the last, vibrant connection they shared. She'd never realized how attached she was to her hair until this moment; the thought of cutting it off felt like cutting away a piece of Rhona Styx.

"Or we cover it with grease." Triple was seated on the floor a few feet away. She'd rolled up the sleeves of her thin cotton shirt, baring a single ropey scar on her left bicep. Not all of them would need to show their scars, just enough to maintain the illusion.

"Won't feel great, but it'll get the job done, and you'll get to keep your hair."

Pine's mouth twisted. "We're taking Caledonia Styx—captain of the *Mors Navis*, wanted by Fiveson Lir *and* the great sick fish himself, Aric Athair—into a Bullet stronghold where both her ship and her crew have been for several days, and you want to hide her exceedingly recognizable hair with grease?"

"It only has to work for a little while," Triple answered, sounding less convinced than her words suggested.

"Sure," Pine said with a dash of skepticism. "Great idea. And if it doesn't work, we'll get everyone killed. Seems worth the risk to me." Pine swung his legs off the chair and hopped to the ground, irritation sharpening his movements. "At least do something about that damn tattoo." He pointed at the family sigil on her temple. "Might as well sail into port screaming your name for anyone to hear."

He was right. And hair was a small sacrifice to make in exchange for saving her entire crew.

"We'll do both," Caledonia conceded.

Caledonia and Triple spent the next half hour alone in a bathroom with a pair of scissors and a bowl of pungent bleach. Triple tried to divert Caledonia's attention with stories about how many times Sledge had snapped a bow in half trying to fire an arrow when they'd first settled in the bay, but her anecdotes dried up, and both girls did their best not to wince at each slice of the scissors through Caledonia's thick hair. Soon, the gray floor was littered with bright orange curls.

The bleach was more of a challenge. Harwell had thickened it with a syrupy mixture of flour and water, and even so, Caledonia had to keep her head tipped over the sink and her eyes pinched shut while Triple chased errant drips away from her temples. But when it was done, Caledonia's hair was an explosion of brassy blonde spikes. She hardly recognized herself.

"I won't say it's better," Triple said, brushing a few drops of water from Caledonia's cheeks and neck. "But they'll never think you're the red-haired girl they've been chasing."

Triple circled to stand in front of her, lightly brushing at the short hairs that curled around her ears and scattered along her forehead. She lingered on the tattoo, her fingers feather light and still warm from the water. Caledonia was so starved for the constant affectionate touches of her sisters that she had to force herself not to lean into the caress.

"A family mark?" Triple asked.

Caledonia nodded once, not willing to break the gentle contact between them. "My brother has one like it."

The next question landed briefly in Triple's mosaic green eyes, but she blinked it away before asking.

"I had good reason to believe he sailed on *Electra,* and that I might . . ." Caledonia broke off, suddenly feeling far more vulnerable than she'd intended to be.

"Save him?" Triple supplied. Her eyebrows rose, and her lips quirked in a smile as she grabbed the tin of grease and twisted the lid off, exposing the black cake. "So you *do* think Bullets can change? As long as they're Bullets you've loved."

Caledonia winced. It was a fair comment, but it stung. "I know Bullets can change."

"He's lucky. Most people, when Aric takes someone they love, they let him take the love they feel, too. So it hurts less. All that's left is fear." Triple dipped her fingers into the pot and dragged a line of black grease down Caledonia's face from her temple to her chin. Her breath skated down Caledonia's cheek, ghostly warm.

Caledonia's answer was barely more than a whisper. "I think I'm afraid of him, too. Can that be real? That I love him and am afraid of who he is now?"

Triple sighed, a sad smile appearing briefly on her lips. "I can't speak for him. But I can tell you that before I got out, I was afraid of who I was and who I would be if I wasn't a Bullet. Fear is easy. Don't let it overshadow the love you still have."

Though she hadn't asked anything of Caledonia directly, it felt like a plea. "I won't," she said.

With gentle hands, Triple turned her toward the cloudy mirror. Between the hair and the grease, she was barely the same person she'd been when they started. Her skin was pasty in comparison to the blonde spikes, and the black streak somehow muddied the brown of her eyes. Dressed in the same shades of tan and brown as everyone else, she was every bit a Bullet in appearance, and she had to admit that if she weren't expecting to find a girl here, she wouldn't.

Before she could say anything more, Pine was in the doorway, pounding with one fist as the hatch swung open. "All call. We've got company. Time to test that disguise."

On deck, the transformation of the Blades was remarkable. They'd gone from the bright-eyed bunch she'd grown to know to a group that skulked across with deck with an air of barely bridled aggression, chins tucked and eyes trimmed like sails. They'd layered holsters over their shoulders and hips, and several had sliced their sleeves to reveal the bright orange scars of their bandoliers. Stepping into their midst, Caledonia had to remind herself: *Not* Bullets. Blades. *Not* a clip. A crew. Her crew.

Hanging heavy in the west, the sun burned for the horizon, dripping fire along the dark sea. In the east, a second ship now slowed to make its approach. It was a small ship, more muscle than bite, and it was brimming with Bullets.

Caledonia couldn't stop the shiver that raced down her spine. Her gut told her to run or fight, anything but sit here and wait for them to arrive.

Sledge was standing high on the command deck. Even from a distance his frame was locked and rigid. The length of his braid fell down his back, like a spear between his shoulder blades. Every bit of him communicated strength and control.

But they weren't in control. This entire plan required that

they put themselves in increasingly vulnerable positions and be convincing about it.

Slowly, Caledonia climbed to the bridge where she would be just as visible as Sledge. Close enough to hear what was said without getting in the way of Bullet procedure. The tug ship was approaching head-on with their captain mirroring Sledge's position. He was a short man with years of battle written across a face as flat and broad as the sea itself. The scowl he wore was etched into his bones, as though it hadn't moved in years.

Pine lifted a hand to press once at Caledonia's elbow and directed her even closer to the railing. "We need them to get a good long look at you."

If anyone was going to recognize Caledonia Styx, they wanted it to happen while they still had a fighting chance. Out here, on the open ocean, their chances of survival were significantly better than inside Slipmark. This meeting was the only dry run they would get.

"Not to mention *him*," Triple added with a cutting look toward Sledge.

"What is that supposed to mean?" Caledonia asked, barely keeping her expression steady. When neither of them answered, she rounded on Pine, pushing her face into his. "Pine."

A wince landed so briefly in his features that she wasn't sure she'd seen it. "Sledge was Venn's—"

"Right hand."

Caledonia's mind reeled.

Pine's expression was placid.

"So tell me why it isn't you up there instead of him?!" Caledonia was very near to losing her tenuous control. Furious both that they'd neglected to bring this up before the tow arrived and that she'd forgotten what Triple had shared with her so recently.

The tug was adjusting its heading now, preparing to come alongside port to port.

"Pine?" she asked, nervous and angry. "He's hardly inconspicuous."

"Exactly," Pine answered with a nod. "He wasn't the only hammerhead out there, and he was never stationed at Slipmark, but if they're going to challenge him, we need to know now."

"And you don't think this is the sort of thing you should have mentioned ahead of time?"

He merely shrugged. "What would it have changed? Rig is a wanted defector. If his description is out there, we'll know it soon."

"That was his name? Rig?" Caledonia asked, trying to keep her blood from spinning her toward battle.

"A boy and a ship all at once. But never under his own sail."

The tug's nose was slipping just past their own now. Though Caledonia was still furious at being caught unawares, the time for discussion was past.

"That right there?" Pine ducked close to whisper. "Perfect Bullet face." Her scowl deepened, which only won an approving nod from Pine. "Perfect," he repeated.

Triple came up on her other side, slid her round body between two tines, and hopped up onto the railing. She leaned out over the water, letting her sunny hair flutter like the tattered rags on the bones around her. Caledonia chose to keep her feet on the deck, locking a glower on her face. The moment the Bullets noticed them, however, she struggled to maintain her composure.

The first to see her seemed to stare right through her. Then, suddenly, his eyes focused on her face and widened. He threw an elbow into the side of the Bullet next to him and nodded. His companion's reaction was similar, a flash of shock accompanied by a rip of tension.

Caledonia stared back, her pulse pounding in her ears, a thin sweat cooling her neck. Every instinct telling her to fight, fight, fight. The sound of Sledge greeting the tug captain was lost behind the roaring in her own ears. They'd seen her, they knew her, they were going to come for her. She was sure of it.

A hand landed on her own, rough fingers pressing against her knuckles. Pine casually pushed his body in front of hers, bending so his face was very close to her own.

"Relax," he said, his voice low and warning. "At least take your hand off your gun."

Her gun? Her gun.

Without realizing it, she'd wrapped her fingers around the weapon at her waist. Pine tipped his head forward, waiting while she forced her hand to relax beneath the gentle, constant pressure of his own. She was letting her nerves get the better of her.

"Thank you," he whispered, and she was surprised to realize he meant it. "You good?"

"Steely," she replied, drawing a long breath to ease her nerves. If she pulled a gun on another Bullet clip, it wouldn't matter if she'd been recognized or not. This would be over.

He nodded, stepping away but staying close, a shield on her left side. "You're just another Bullet to them. So just . . . act like it."

She ground her teeth together, letting her discomfort show. The ships were only yards apart now, and their Ballistic was eyeing Sledge with suspicion.

"Why don't you have any recruits aboard?" he asked, a snarl in his voice. "You called in from the Northwater two days ago."

Sledge's answered rumbled across the gap. "We called in a sighting of a rogue ship. We gave chase before gathering the taxes, engaged them, and ended up exactly as you find us now."

The Ballistic narrowed his eyes. To Caledonia it was a gaze of deep suspicion, one that had her hand reaching once more for her gun. But Pine didn't move, and she forced herself to remain still. These were Bullet cues. She needed to let the Blades interpret them.

"And the other ship? How'd she get away from you?" This question was laced with judgment.

"Lucky shot," Sledge answered, voice even.

"Not so lucky for you," the Ballistic's voice carried a breezy warning that sounded slightly suspicious to Caledonia's ears.

But Sledge seemed unconcerned. "Nothing wasted but time."

The Ballistic studied Sledge for a full minute. Each second was more painful than the last. Then he turned to his crew, released a piercing whistle, and shouted an order. "Bring us around and ready the rigging."

In the next minute, the tow had its rear deck aligned with *Beacon*'s nose, and the clip was readying the lines and lashing the two ships together. Their ruse had worked. Barely, it seemed. Now they were cruising steadily toward Slipmark, and it was far too late to change course. Caledonia couldn't bring herself to leave the deck, convinced something was about to go wrong. She wanted her eyes on the tug at all times, so she planted herself in the bridge and stayed there, even as the sun slipped beneath the horizon and the tug dropped its anchor for the night.

At some point, Pine joined her, settling into the comm station with his legs propped up by the radio and arms crossed over his chest. Together, they passed the night in silence, tracking the occasional movements of sentries on the Bullet ship. They were both waiting for the moment their cover cracked and the Bullet clip turned on them, but it never came.

The tug's engines spun up with the sun, and they resumed their slow trek toward Slipmark. And as the miles slipped past their hull Caledonia realized that this was only the first hurdle, and everything was about to get a lot worse.

CHAPTER SIXTEEN

The sun dipped toward the western seas, unsheathing Slipmark like a knife.

Caledonia's eyes fixed on the glittering walls before it. Aric had established Slipmark harbor inside a natural cove with peninsulas that curved toward each other like long arms. That might have been protection enough, but not for Aric, and not for the site that housed his precious recruits. From the end of each peninsula, massive walls extended into the water. They rose forty feet above the sea, locking together in the center to form an impenetrable barrier designed to keep unfriendly ships out and everything else in.

She had done everything she could to imagine this wall, and it hadn't been nearly enough. Staring at it now, she couldn't shake the feeling that Slipmark was a trap and as of this moment, she had no idea how she planned to escape it.

"Not exactly a welcoming sight," Pine said from his position at her side. Though he was slouched against a nearby cleat, ostensibly focused on mending the shirt in his hands, she knew he'd only picked that cleat because it was close to her. He hadn't left her side since last night.

The tug sailed steadily out in front of them, and the Bullets on board took turns keeping watch on the *Beacon*. Even knowing it was a safety measure, to ensure the ships didn't collide, they were left with the nagging worry that their cover had failed and they were allowing themselves to be hauled into the same prison that held her crew.

"What are those?" Caledonia asked, squinting against the piercing shine of Slipmark where a few dark shapes appeared to hover over the ocean. "Fueling stations?"

Even as she asked, she knew it was wrong. The structures were rounded with flat tops and bottoms, and they stood out of the water on tripods. Fueling stations would be anchored but buoyed to rise and fall with the tide. These were fixed in place where the rising tide would nearly cover them, which made them useless for nearly any function Caledonia could imagine.

"Tide cans."

"What does a tide can do?" The shapes gained depth and dimension as they drew near. In the sides of each, narrow slits dripped rust down curving walls.

Pine hesitated, his eyes lingering on the cans. He answered in a flat voice. "You go inside, and they lock the door. When the tide comes in, the cans fill. But not all the way. There's room to breathe, and you'll tread water for as long as you're able. Or until you choose not to."

Words abandoned Caledonia. The tide was racing in, slapping at the bottom of each tide can while water slowly dribbled from the narrow windows. This far from shore, the tide rose and fell by several feet. Easily enough to fill those cans without submerging them entirely. Twice a day, anyone inside them would be forced to tread water for several hours, or drown.

"How do we know—" Caledonia's voice failed her.

"Your crew's not inside them," he assured her. And when her expression begged for an explanation, he left his mending behind and came to join her at the rail. "Flags are positioned along the top when the cans are occupied. And taken down one at a time as they die. Torture only works if everyone else knows it does." Pine's hands tightened on the rail, his knuckles flashing white. "Those were a gift of the Steelhand."

There it was again. The name that Sledge, Triple, and now Pine had spoken with dark reverence. Whoever the Steelhand was had left a mark on her friends as surely as this place. Her own life had been marred by Aric's ever-present shadow, but she'd escaped that particular trauma.

"I shouldn't have asked you to come here," she admitted.

"Maybe we were never meant to leave," Pine murmured, eyes shifting to what lay just beyond the tide cans. "Maybe we'll never leave again."

A shiver snuck down Caledonia's spine.

The crew was as silent as a forest, their bodies tense and rigid as trees, their haunted eyes trained on the wall that had once held them prisoner before sending them into the world as Bullets. Their fear nudged at Caledonia, but she watched that wall with hope strangling her heart. On the other side of it was her crew and her ship, and if she was careful, smart, and lucky, she'd get them all back very soon.

The tug released three pulses of its horn, announcing their arrival.

Caledonia and Pine turned and together made for the bridge. They found Sledge and Harwell ready by the radio, the receiver in one of Sledge's hands and the ship's code book in the other.

The radio crackled. *"Beacon*, send your flag when ready."

Harwell snatched the code book, rapidly flipping through the pages until he found what he was looking for and offered it to Sledge.

"You're sure?" Sledge asked.

"Enough to risk my life," Harwell answered with tempered alarm.

"This is *Beacon*," Sledge began, holding the receiver to his mouth. "Flag reads 'Copper-Eight-Three-Trigger-Nine-Nine.'"

The radio clicked off. Silence followed.

"Are we nervous?" Caledonia asked.

"Yes," Sledge answered in a whisper. "But this is procedure."

Another moment passed before the radio clicked again. *"Beacon*, you're clear to dock."

Sledge beamed at Harwell, who released a shaky breath. It was a small victory, but this entire plan was built on small victories.

"Stand by for outbound vessel before you approach," the Bullet continued.

The radio fell silent just as the massive walls of Slipmark harbor began to bend outward, creating a gap between the two sections.

A ship nosed through the clawlike arms, and Caledonia's stomach pitched. She ran from the bridge to the deck, only stopping when her hands hit the rail. For a second, she held on to her denial, but once the ship sailed fully into view, there was no question.

It was the *Mors Navis*.

Her ship skimmed across the water like a bird gliding across the sky. She was elegantly sculpted and skinned in dark gray metal with paler seams marking past injuries and repairs. At the very end of the quarterdeck, the sun sail shimmered like the scales of a great black fish, soaking up light in flashes of deep red and the brightest gold. Down the centerline, all four mast blocks were closed with the masts safely snapped inside.

She sailed gloriously, and she was covered with Bullets.

No sooner had the ship cleared the walls than the tug revved her engines and pulled the *Beacon* in its wake. Toward the harbor. Away from the *Mors Navis*.

Caledonia stood in place while her thoughts reached across the painfully small stretch of sea toward the ship that had raised her. She'd left her once, thinking she would never see her again, trusting her to carry her girls safely. Now she was being taken from her.

There was no way they could save the *Mors Navis*.

She would be handled by Bullets who would not love her. They wouldn't hear the soft sigh of her transformer with the same fondness, nor would they appreciate the triumph that was the deployment of her masts or keel. They didn't know her history, and they would give her the most violent future imaginable.

There was every chance that the next time she saw this ship, she'd be fighting against it. The thought left her cold and empty, and there was exactly nothing she could do for it.

This was goodbye, the end of the *Mors Navis*.

Caledonia clenched her teeth, grinding them together until her jaw ached, and forced herself to look away. The ship was gone, but her sisters remained.

The tug pulled them between the long arms of the wall and to the harbor within. Several smaller boats darted out to meet them, guiding them along as the great walls of the harbor closed behind them, locking them inside.

Caledonia kept her sights on the knifelike city ahead of her. Rows of low-statured buildings, each gilded with glittering black solar panes, raced to a sharpened point high in the eastern hills while the base of the blade butted against an impressive network of docks in the harbor below. It was the largest town Caledonia had ever seen, and even from a distance the object of its design was visible. This was a city of order, in which hiding would be impossible.

Thankfully, hiding in the city wasn't their goal. Their goal was to remain in plain sight, safely on board the *Beacon*. They would dock, check in with the harbor master, then work on repairing their ship while Caledonia, Pine, and Triple searched for the crew. It was a plan with a deadline. If they didn't find the girls by the time repairs were done, they had to get out regardless.

The gangway hit the dock with a resounding *thump*, firmly connecting them to Bullet territory. From this point forward, everything they did would be face-to-face. It would require a subtle cunning that was as foreign to Caledonia as life on land. She looked out over the town, glittering and teeming with activity, and she felt a shadow of fear slip down her spine.

"This is just procedure," Pine said, taking her elbow in hand. "They're expecting Bullets, so that's what they'll see."

Sledge came to join them with Triple close behind. "Manifest ready to go?"

"Ready," Triple said, raising a thick clipboard in one hand. "We've got names and ranks for everyone."

"Then, if we're ready?" Sledge's focus was already at the bottom of the gangway, where six Bullets waited to receive them.

Once they hit the dock, they'd be all but surrounded. And they'd have done it on purpose. Caledonia's chest tightened, and though there was a determined chill in the air, sweat prickled between her shoulder blades and at her temples. Next to her, Triple clicked her teeth and scowled, reminding Caledonia to do the same. She locked her teeth and fixed her brow in a frown of vague displeasure. There was no going back now.

An older woman stood out from the rest of the Bullets. Her skin was weathered and ruddy and lined with orange scars, her hair shot through with silver and cropped short around her neck and ears, and she carried herself with an air of hardened authority. Behind her was a younger woman, perhaps ten years Caledonia's senior, with eyes a pale, bleached-out brown made even paler by the rich brown of her skin. Like Triple, she carried a stack of papers attached to a clipboard, a pencil clutched in one hand. Next in line were four young men who couldn't have yet earned the first scar of their bandolier.

The older woman watched them approach with a shrewd eye, revealing nothing of her intentions, while the brown-eyed girl studied Caledonia with a heavy gaze. It took every bit of her control to continue walking as though she had nothing to hide.

They had *everything* to hide.

And everything to lose.

"Ballistic Dair," the woman said, taking a single step toward Sledge. Had she lingered on the name? Did she know who he truly was? Panic spiked in the back of Caledonia's throat. Pine should be the one posing as their Ballistic. Why hadn't she pushed the issue? Even Harwell would have been a better choice. "The last time I saw the *Beacon*, it was under Merrant's command."

She paused and Caledonia recognized the trap. It was a test. Meant to weed out imposters. Exactly like them.

Sledge had to answer, and however he did would confirm who they were one way or another.

"Command belongs to those who can take it," he said in the voice of someone quoting a regulation.

The woman's eyes narrowed.

They were caught. They were caught. They were—

"Indeed. I'm Harbor Master Lyall," the woman continued, and now an ill-fitting smile spread across her lips. "Welcome to Slip-mark."

CHAPTER SEVENTEEN

Somehow, in the wake of Harbor Master Lyall's smile, everything felt worse. As though a noose were cinching so slowly around Caledonia's neck so as not to be threatening.

Harbor Master Lyall gathered their manifest and list of requested repairs, reviewing each before passing them off to the girl with the pale brown eyes.

"Your timing is good," the harbor master said, casting her eyes along the length of the *Beacon*. "A full clip just set out so your repairs will take priority, and Barrack D is available for your clip. You'll bunk there."

The noose around Caledonia's neck cinched all at once. She fought to keep her expression blank, to keep the shock she felt trapped inside. Bunking in town wasn't part of their plan. When Harwell was last here, they kept clips on their own ships because they didn't have space to accommodate short stays. Keeping the crew on the ship worked in their favor. It reduced opportunities for discovery. It kept them safe while they carefully and strategically searched out Caledonia's crew. Staying in town was *not* in the plan.

Harbor Master Lyall kept talking. "Bullet Gloriana will give you your assignments, schedule of repair, and the shore duty roster. Any other questions, direct them to her. You may disembark when ready, but once your clip sets foot on my harbor, my rules apply. Clips come off, weapons stay on. Keep to your tides, Ballistic."

"Keep to your tides," Sledge responded automatically.

With that, Harbor Master Lyall spun on her heel and retreated down the dock, leaving Gloriana and the other four Bullets behind. Gloriana busied herself with her clipboard, not speaking to any of them while she methodically completed her work. Caledonia tried to catch Sledge's eyes. The plan that had felt solid on their way in had shifted to sand beneath their feet. Her tenuous bit of control was gone, and all she could do now was follow Sledge's lead, and he wasn't offering even the assurance of a shared glance.

Lowering her eyes to the dock, she drew a deep breath. *Blood. Gunpowder. Salt.*

When she looked up, Gloriana was watching her with a firm gaze.

Caledonia forced herself to return the look in that same steady way, forcing her eyes to relax in an imitation of someone under the influence of Silt.

"Your assignments," Gloriana said, ripping a piece of paper

from her clipboard and handing it to Sledge. "Bullet Cade will lead you to Barrack D. We'll begin shipwork in the morning." She took up a position at the end of the gangway. "Ready when you are, Ballistic."

She was going to stand there and mark every Bullet to leave the ship, check their names against the manifest they'd given her, and look into each of their faces. Caledonia took another deep breath to conceal her discomfort. They had no choice but to act as though this was exactly what they'd been expecting to happen.

"Rhona!" Caledonia's head instantly snapped toward the name, and she was glad she'd chosen something so familiar. Sledge continued with his back to her, a Ballistic giving an order to a Bullet. "Assist Bullet Gloriana."

Caledonia stepped to Gloriana's side while Pine hurried up the gangway to coordinate topside and Triple followed two of the Bullets on a survey of the ship's hull. Sledge turned to Bullet Cade, and with a nod of his head encouraged him to lead the way to Barrack D, where he would prepare for the crew's arrival.

They were splitting up, and Caledonia felt the noose tighten a little bit more.

They know what to do, she reminded herself. Her Blades were once Bullets, and they knew how to play the part even if she didn't. Sledge wouldn't have left her in a position she couldn't handle.

"Bullet Rhona," Gloriana said in her toneless way.

"Bullet Gloriana," she returned, hoping there was nothing else she was meant to say in this situation.

"Are you a shiptech?"

Caledonia reached for the right answer. She had no idea. She'd chosen a name, not a designation. What *were* common Bullet designations?

"I'm whatever they need me to be," she answered evasively.

That won a curious smile from Bullet Gloriana. She gestured to Caledonia's cheek where a smear of grease covered her tattoo. "You missed a spot. Wash up when you get to the barracks."

Caledonia's hand rose instinctively to cover the spot on her temple. She stopped just short of touching it, letting her hand fall away without disturbing the grease. Gloriana watched her, an eyebrow arching with interest. It was only then that Caledonia realized the gesture was out of place. Someone with nothing to hide might have swiped at the smudge, not carefully avoid touching it.

"Thanks for the warning," Caledonia said quickly, sweat beginning to prick along her forehead.

Soon, the Blades were marching down the gangway with seabags slung over their shoulders and not a weapon among them. They reported their assumed names, and Gloriana checked each one against her list until all twenty-six Blades left aboard were accounted for and standing on the dock around them. To their credit, they managed to look irritable instead of anxious that their plans had just been blown to rubble.

"Let's move!" shouted Pine, stepping in close to Caledonia

once more. Then, in a voice that was only for her, he added, "They know what to do."

She knew it was true. They knew how to move within Bullet society better than she did. Yet, as they turned their steps toward the eastern hills, she couldn't shake the sensation that every step took them closer to the moment their illusion would shatter, leaving them exposed and vulnerable. The sun tucked into the horizon, and the city opened before them like a great maw, sunlight dripping from solar panels like blood from teeth. It was going to devour them whole.

Stop it, she chastised herself. She turned her focus to how the town was organized, committing the path they took to memory. Somewhere in this maze her sisters were being held, interrogated, and tortured. The sooner she got her bearings, the sooner she would find them.

This place was nothing like the haphazard press of Cloudbreak, where you could hide as easily as breathing. Here, they were surrounded by neat buildings of blue-gray stone, every bit of which had a dedicated purpose from the solar plates to the funnels at each rooftop corner meant to capture rain for reuse. No space was wasted. Just like on a ship, everything was designed to fulfill multiple functions; every corner was defined, every street swept and tidy, every individual painfully visible.

Especially the twenty-nine intruders now marching toward Barrack D.

The shadows grew suddenly deeper, the air cooler, the foot traffic thinner. Caledonia looked up to discover they'd left the shorter buildings behind and were passing the only structure that stretched higher than one or two stories into the air. This was the tower she'd spotted from the water. The place from which all of Slipmark was visible.

"Sister's tower," Pine said, eyes flicking away from the structure as though it were too bright to behold.

It cast a long shadow, both in town, and in the minds of every Blade. Perhaps without even realizing it, the group stepped up the pace until Sister's tower was firmly behind them.

Barrack D was the last in a short row of identical buildings midway up the hill. Here, the air smelled savory—like freshly baked bread and buttery roasted fish. Caledonia's mouth watered as they were led into a large and impeccably clean foyer.

One of Harbor Master Lyall's Bullets was nearly finished writing their names on individual nameplates and fitting them into a grid along the wall. Across from that were shelves containing stacks of linens and shower kits. Everything they could possibly need, and more than they usually had at their disposal.

Sledge waited in the center of the room, looking like he wanted to hurt something, while the crew filed in and circled up. Next to him, two young Bullets had the clip manifest and stood ready to receive each Blade and issue meal tickets. They were far into this now, and the tension was starting to reveal itself in clenching fists.

They hadn't prepared for this, and every second they spent here was another second they might be discovered.

Sledge, however, continued smoothly as though everything were as it should be.

"Find your name, grab your kit. Mess is two doors south. Be ready for dinner in ten, and I want to see everyone in this hall when the sun rises. No exceptions." He paused. Caledonia felt his discomfort expand to fill the small space. These were orders a Ballistic would give his clip, not orders Sledge would give his crew. When he spoke next, his voice was low and heavy. "The day's ration will be issued each morning with your meal."

No one moved. They'd been prepared to take on the appearance of having Silt in their systems. They knew how to pretend. But this was a dangerous level of exposure. This was temptation.

"Grab your kits," Sledge repeated darkly, eyes flicking to the Bullets around them.

Triple guided Caledonia through the unfamiliar steps of plucking their names from the wall, gathering linens and shower kits, then following the group into the bunkroom and claiming a bed. The mattresses were firm, the bed frames well maintained, and the sheets were made of a fabric so soft Caledonia almost looked forward to sleeping beneath them. When all the beds had been claimed and made, the group headed toward the mess.

"Won't it be suspicious if we keep traveling in a pack?" Caledonia asked, though her stomach twisted as they stepped outside and she was reintroduced to the scent of fresh food.

"It's not unusual for clips to keep together," Triple answered softly, eyes scanning the darkened streets for trouble. "And it's probably best that we don't stray from the pack."

Triple stepped into the crowd of Blades, but Caledonia hung back. Dusk was edging firmly toward night, and the street was lit by perfect rows of solar pips held aloft by slender metal arms attached to each building. Their light was so thin and icy that it turned the few Bullets that passed beneath them into ghosts.

There was a system to this city. It had taken them by surprise, but it hadn't defeated them. They were inside it now and it could work for them if she trusted her new crew to know more than she did. She hated not knowing. But right now, she needed to sit with that discomfort and let her crew hold her up.

Her heart was just beginning to lighten when she noticed a figure walking beside her. He was a dark shadow in the corner of her eye with brown hair hanging low over his forehead and a dull nose. A Bullet. A stranger.

She lengthened her stride, attempting to catch up with the Blades several paces ahead. The stranger matched her, beat for beat. And when she dared a glance, he was looking directly at her. The instant he caught her eyes, he began to smile, lips curling curiously.

Before she could do anything more, Pine was there.

His fist snapped against the Bullet's face, and he curled his body around the other boy in a move that was almost elegant. He spun, dancing them both into a shadowed alley. Pine's hand caught the boy's chin, and before Caledonia had drawn a single breath, Pine slid a blade behind the boy's ear and straight into his skull.

Blood slipped around the hilt of the blade. The boy struggled once and then fell limp in Pine's arms.

Shadows wrapped strong arms around them. The only sounds were the receding footsteps of their crewmates, heading into the mess hall.

"Pine." It was all she could say.

He met her eyes. The Bullet that usually lurked just beneath the surface was here now. Hard, unyielding, unforgiving. He shifted his grip on the boy, holding the blade in place to control the flow of blood. Then he moved down the dark alley in search of a place to hide the body.

Caledonia waited, her vision narrowing to a single drop of scarlet soaking into the pale pavement by her toe.

She killed to survive. She had done so many times, but never like this. Never outside the context of battle. Had he even recognized her? Had Pine seen something she hadn't?

No. He'd seen less than she had. She knew that. He'd reacted to the barest sliver of a threat because that was what he'd been trained to do.

Pine returned to her side. He reached for her elbow, then stopped himself.

She met his eyes, letting her conflict surface.

"Pine," she repeated because she could think of nothing else.

With a sad nod of his head he responded, "Let's go."

CHAPTER EIGHTEEN

The dining hall was cacophonous and too bright after the dark alley. It was filled with ordered rows of tables and chairs, nearly all of which were occupied by Bullets enjoying a hearty dinner. Lines formed at either end of the long room. In one, fresh fruits and vegetables were piled high. In the other, hot dishes of every sort were offered. There was perfectly roasted fish in buttery sauces, tender vegetables drizzled in tangy sweet vinegar, mashed potatoes, fresh bread with seeds baked into a crispy crust. There was butter and gravy and all of it was there for the eating.

Caledonia's mind struggled to release what had happened outside and behave like a Bullet. Over and over, her mind replayed the Bullet's smile. Had it been menacing? Flirtatious? Or merely a friendly gesture? She was horrified to discover she couldn't remember, and each time it replayed she pictured it differently. She would never know if he'd been a threat, or just a Bullet who smiled at the wrong person in the wrong moment.

She was equally horrified by herself. She didn't blame Pine.

He'd seen a potential threat and he'd taken care of it. She couldn't be upset with him for that. But she should feel more regret than she did. Shouldn't she?

Still lost in thought, Caledonia filled her plate until the surface disappeared. With each new addition, she felt her hunger taking over, urging her to add more of everything—grains, vegetables, shredded meat, a scoop of gravy. She topped it off with an additional slice of bread, earning a laugh from the cook behind the buffet. He was an old man, far older than any Bullet she'd encountered on the ocean, with a face that wrinkled and cracked so much around scars that it became a puzzle.

"Must've hit on hard seas this moon," he said. Caledonia nearly smiled in return when he added, "The Father provides."

She felt her expression hardening, her stomach knotting. Suddenly, the food on her plate represented so much more than the temporary end of her hunger. It represented Aric's complete control. Beyond Silt, Aric controlled people by withholding something that should be accessible to everyone. He'd somehow managed to figure out how to clean the soil to grow food and then kept that secret to himself.

How could she enjoy anything that came from him?

"The Father provides," a voice said from behind. Then a hand pressed her elbow and pushed her firmly forward.

She pulled away, irritation replacing every other emotion in a flash. "I don't need rescuing."

"Then move," Pine responded quietly.

They spotted Sledge and joined the Blades at a table on the outskirts of the room. As she slid into her seat, Caledonia couldn't stop thinking that just beyond these walls, the body of a Bullet was stashed in an alley. The instant it was discovered, they'd be in even greater danger than before.

"Eat," Pine grumbled, climbing into a seat next to hers.

"Don't tell me what to do," she snapped, digging a fork into her fish. All around the room, the eyes of other Bullets were trained on them. "They're watching us."

"Of course they are. It's because we're the newest clip in town. Don't watch them back," Pine instructed. "Let it play out."

Teasing scents of salt and herbs and butter rose toward her, and one bite was all it took to reignite her hunger. The first forkful was almost overwhelming, and for a brief second she was arrested by guilt. Her girls were certainly not having a feast such as this, and it felt like a betrayal to enjoy it. But they needed her strong if she was going to free them. And food, as Aric had so rightly determined, was strength.

"And who is this?" a voice called.

Caledonia's head snapped up. A Bullet stood next to their table with a broad, eager grin on his face. Next to her she felt Pine coiling like a spring ready to strike.

The Bullet's smile grew as he said loudly enough for the room to hear, "Is this our limp fish clip? Sailed into port with a broken screw and nothing to show for it?"

Smirks cascaded through the surrounding tables, and Caledonia's pulse jumped. But a light touch on her thigh told her not to panic. Caledonia nodded just enough that Pine would know she understood.

Sledge sat up taller. "I am no limp fish," he announced.

The Bullet raised a hand, dangling a dead fish from his fingertips. It was only a few inches long. Whole, unskinned, and certainly uncooked. "Prove it." He held the fish toward Sledge.

The room was waiting for something. They'd stopped eating and turned to watch the scene unfolding here. Caledonia looked from the Bullet to Sledge, hoping the confusion didn't show on her face.

After a long moment, Sledge stood and took the dead fish. The Bullets surrounding them began to drum their fingers on tables. Then Sledge tipped his head back and swallowed the fish whole.

The room erupted in cheers. Sledge and the Bullet clasped hands, and everyone returned to their meals. Whatever that was, it had worked. They'd been welcomed into the mess hall as if they belonged there.

"That could have been worse," Pine whispered.

Caledonia only shook her head, driving her fork into a piece of salty meat and taking a bite. Between the murdered Bullet and the dead fish, her stomach was uninterested in food, but she ate anyway. There were vegetables she couldn't name, grains she'd only ever had as a dried ingredient in seed cake, and the meat was so tender she could rip it apart almost as easily as bread. This was far more than she'd ever seen growing on Aric's AgriFleet. More often than not, those ships supported primarily baleflowers, not crops, certainly not animals. There was more to Aric's farming operation than she'd ever imagined.

She was just distracted enough that she didn't immediately notice the moment a new tension warmed the hall. Sledge straightened in his seat, seeming to grow by at least a foot as he glowered over the heads of his Blades. In an instant, the chatter in the room shifted from a low, companionable murmur to something more frenzied and excitable.

Panic slicked down Caledonia's spine like a cold sweat. She dropped her fork and scanned the room, sure that the boy in the alley had been discovered and they would be next. But instead of people entering the mess hall, she saw the opposite. Bullets were quickly clearing their tables and rushing from the room.

A knowing glance passed between Sledge, Pine, and Triple, and the three of them slowly rose to their feet.

"What?" Caledonia hissed.

"Time for theater." Triple's answer was grim but oblique, and there wasn't room for anything more.

The hall was nearly empty now. If they didn't follow, they'd certainly be noticed. Even the cook was closing up his trays of food and preparing to leave. Whatever theater entailed, it wasn't optional.

Outside, they were swept along darkened streets until they came to an open square. On all sides, buildings stood with doors flung open to the night. Strains of music floated above the constant chorus of the crowd, and the air smelled faintly of alcohol. The cacophony upended the usual lock-step rhythm that governed the rest of town.

Behind them, more Bullets pushed into the square, forcing the Blades to keep moving. Pine's hand gripped her wrist as they were pushed closer and closer to the front of the square and a raised wooden stage upon which two posts stood tall. There was no fighting the crowd. As more Bullets poured into the square from behind, Caledonia found herself perilously close to the stage.

To one side, two dozen children, each younger than Nettle, stood shoulder to shoulder with a clear view of the stage, still and alert. Whatever was about to happen, these recruits had seen it before. The only comforting thought Caledonia could muster was that this had nothing to do with her or the body she and Pine had left behind. This was Bullet business, and she just had to get through it.

A rhythmic pounding began somewhere ahead of them. It echoed off the buildings, growing louder and louder until it filled the square with an ominous pulse. In another moment, Caledonia located the source: a train of Bullets processed toward the dais, pounding staves into the ground as they entered the square. Before them, a boy, bound and stripped to the waist, walked calmly toward the stage.

The procession stopped, allowing a single figure to climb up the steps. A woman with ropes of silvered hair wrapped tightly around her head turned to face them. She wore robes of orange and the palest cream cinched around her waist by a belt of woven baleflowers. She was as old as the cook in the mess hall, and she was striking.

"Good tides, my siblings." Her voice rose above them like a feather on the breeze, captivating and deceptively fragile.

"Good tides, Sister," came the heavy response.

Deceptively fragile indeed.

"We've come here this eve to celebrate one of our brightest brothers. He has chosen to leave us, and we must cut him from our hearts. Little by little." Her words were sculpted and dangerous, and they clearly communicated more to everyone around Caledonia than they did to her. "Bring him up."

Two of the young guards raised their staves and moved toward the bound boy. Though he was outnumbered and unarmed, they moved with inexplicable caution. Instead of prodding him as Caledonia has expected them to do, they halted just shy of touching him, their nerves evident in the way they choked their weapons. The crowd roared, eager to move things along, and the guards drew new confidence from that anger, driving their staves into the boy's back. He stumbled, but after a long second strode purposefully, even proudly, up the steps and onto the stage. When he turned to face the audience Caledonia nearly gasped.

It was Oran.

CHAPTER NINETEEN

Onstage, Oran was perfectly calm, but Caledonia's heart was racing.

She took in every inch of him, from the warm brown of his tree-ring eyes to the split on his full bottom lip, from the shadow of a bruise on his jaw to the wide planes of his cheeks. He was thinner than he'd been, every muscle in his brown torso cut into perfect relief. His ribs were darkened with cloudy bruises, but it was the old scatter of brilliant orange scars splayed like lightning across those bruises that trapped her gaze.

He raised his chin and looked out over the square. The audience seemed to draw back a step, and an unexpected silence snaked through the crowd. Then their fear morphed into anger and they roared.

Sister took a single step toward Oran and raised a hand between them. In it a long blade gleamed.

"Our brother was once the proudest among us. Fiveson Oran. We all remember the moment he disappointed the Father and fell from glory. But he has fallen farther still!" She paused, allowing space for the crowd to voice its disapproval. "He joined that mutinous radical, the still-at-large Caledonia Styx!" The crowd roared at that. "Attacked us where he once professed loyalty!" Again, the roar rose in the night sky. "And tonight we will give him exactly what he wants. We will cut him away."

Now she brought down her knife, slashing through Oran's bicep and his bandolier.

Blood wept down Oran's arm, dripping onto the stage by his feet, but he made no show of pain. His only movement was the slow turn of his head toward Sister. His gaze was cold and deadly, and the entire audience held their breath with something akin to terror.

With a jolt Caledonia realized that it wasn't Sister they feared. It was Oran.

He was both the same boy she'd met on the deck of her ship and someone entirely new. These Bullets didn't know him as she did. They knew him as something altogether different, and she was beginning to understand that he was still very much a stranger to her.

Sister swept her robes behind her and called out, "Recruits!"

The young children hurried to the ground just below the stage, and now Sister spoke to them over hands cupped delicately before her. "You are the next of us. You will be better than we are, and that begins tonight as you demonstrate your commitment to our family. Remember, we don't want to kill him tonight," she added with a smile that was almost maternal. "Tonight is only the beginning." Now she turned to Oran, her smile transforming into something venomous. "If I recall, this was one of your favorites. I hope you enjoy it as much from the other side."

Beside Caledonia, Sledge, Pine, and Triple clearly knew what to expect. But she couldn't look at them without revealing to anyone who laid an eye on her that she did not.

"Begin," Sister said.

A child stepped forward. He was tall and gangly with narrow shoulders and long fingers, and he reached into a basket on the ground and pulled out a small dagger. He shifted his grip a few times, testing the weight in his hand before, to Caledonia's horror, he took aim, drew back his arm, and threw the blade.

The dagger plunged into Oran's arm. This time he flinched, and a second trail of blood slid down his bicep. The dagger slipped out again nearly as quickly, *thunk*ing against the stage as it landed. The blade wasn't long enough to stay put. Just long enough to wound.

Another one flew through the air. This time sinking into his leg, where it hung for a moment longer before falling away. After that, the blades flew more quickly. The children stepped up one after the other and the daggers flew like bees, sinking their stingers into Oran's exposed flesh. Wounds opened everywhere, from his cheeks to his shins.

Caledonia wanted to stop it and also knew that it was the last thing she should do. But she could meet his eyes. She was close enough to the front of the crowd already. If she could only catch his eyes, he'd know help was close.

Ignoring the tug of Pine's hand on her wrist, she inched toward Oran's natural line of sight, urging him to look up and find her in the unfriendly sea before him. In just a few feet, she was there, exactly where his eyes rested as he waited for another blade to fly.

His eyes caught on hers. Caledonia held perfectly still, certain that he'd seen her. But just as soon as it happened it was gone. Another blade cut into his shoulder, and his eyes closed in pain.

"What are you doing?" Pine hissed in her ear.

But she ignored him, keeping her eyes on Oran, willing them to pull his gaze like two magnets. He clenched his jaw as the new blade slipped from his skin and slowly opened his eyes again, casting fury over the crowd.

Caledonia stared, and then, suddenly, he returned her gaze. The fury fell from his face, and he saw her. He *knew* her.

Pine pinched her wrist—hard—but it was too late. Sister had seen the change in Oran's expression, and now she was studying Caledonia with a careful eye. Pine's hand was a vise on her wrist, his whole body stiff beside her.

"An old friend?" Sister asked, stepping close to Oran.

Oran cut her with a glare. "Aric's sons have no friends."

Sister smirked, turning her attention once more to Caledonia. "Little sister, what is your name?"

The crowd quieted. Though she didn't dare turn around, she felt every eye in the square seek her out, felt Sledge becoming a mountain at her back.

"Rhona," she answered as steadily as she could manage.

"A strong name for a strong Bullet. Would you like to be our first volunteer?"

This was not a choice. This was another test. One she would have to complete without Pine or Sledge or Triple to guide her.

"I'll fight anyone for the pleasure," she said.

Sister laughed. "Then step forward."

Pine released her wrist, and Caledonia stepped toward the basket as all the heat drained from her body. The blades were indeed short, not meant for killing, and just long enough to avoid puncturing anything important. Theater. The word echoed in her mind as she finally understood exactly what they'd meant. This was a show, a demonstration of pain and suffering, and they wanted it to last a long time.

She selected one of the small daggers, testing its weight in her hand. Her fingers trembled. She pressed them more firmly against the cold steel.

"Show us how we must cut this traitor out of our hearts." Sister's voice was crooning and soft, its message exactly the opposite.

Caledonia lifted her eyes from the dagger. Oran watched her, lids heavy with exhaustion. Black hair bent in sweat-soaked locks around his ears and cheekbones, and his lean frame was streaked with dirt and old blood.

He clenched his teeth and held her gaze.

Cold washed over Caledonia. He was giving her permission.

She pinned her eyes to his chest. The dagger was too shallow to actually puncture his heart. At least, that's what she told herself as she drew her arm back. With a flick of her wrist, the dagger sailed through the air.

Oran's cry was like a whip snapping against her own heart. His head bent forward. His arms strained against their bonds as his entire body attempted to curl around the fresh wound. Was he performing now? Pretending her blade hurt more than the others in order to protect her? Or was this pain real?

Caledonia quashed her thoughts before they could betray her. Sister would sniff out any hint of sympathy.

"Beautiful," Sister said with a sigh.

There, perfectly positioned over Oran's heart, was the hilt of her blade. Around it, blood blossomed like a tiny red flower. Caledonia gritted her teeth, hoping the anger in her expression would be interpreted as disgust at the traitor and not herself.

She felt a hand grip her wrist and tug, and she let Pine pull her back into the crowd as Sister's voice asked sweetly, "Next?"

CHAPTER TWENTY

B y the time they left the square, Caledonia was certain that
she would not leave Slipmark unscathed.

It wasn't enough that she'd had to participate in Sister's cruel
theatrics, but she'd been forced to stay there and watch until the
last dagger was thrown. In the end, Oran was so thoroughly sliced
that he was more blood than boy. Still, his eyes were open, his chin
high, and the entire show had done little to dim the crowd's fear of
him, but Caledonia recalled Sister's words, *Tonight is only the beginning*, and knew there was more to come.

If this was what they did to their leaders, she couldn't imagine what was happening to her sisters. Somewhere in this city,
they were trapped and suffering and Caledonia couldn't do a single
thing about it. She had been in Slipmark for nearly twelve hours,
and she hadn't had a chance to determine which prison held them.
After tonight, the thought of freeing them, or getting anyone out
of here, was beginning to feel laughably foolish.

She was so consumed by her own failures that she didn't

realize Sledge was angry until they reached Barrack D. He barged through the doors ahead of her and stalked to the center of the room in silence, where he stopped and waited for her.

"What was that about?" he demanded, voice laced with a venom that took Caledonia by surprise.

"What do you mean?"

"What do I mean?!" Though it was dark, she could see the flush in his cheeks. He wasn't just angry, he was furious.

There was a scatter of disbelieving laughter. Caledonia turned to see that the rest of the Blades had filled in behind her, their scowls and rigid postures loud echoes of Sledge's anger. All of it directed at her.

"We need to know, Caledonia," Triple said, stepping forward. The betrayal on her face was softer, but no less cutting.

"Know *what*?" she demanded, looking from Triple to Pine, who alone among all the Blades looked unsurprised by what was unfolding here.

Before she could turn back to Sledge, he was at her side. He gripped her arm and with a sound that was very like a growl, he directed their steps toward the far corner of the room. The second they stopped moving, Caledonia ripped her arm away and squared her shoulders.

"Sledge, if you don't—"

"Caledonia, we have followed you into a hell fight because you asked us to help you save your crew, and that is a good thing. But you need to tell me right now: What was that back there?"

Caledonia was angry now, her mind on full alert and her breath coming fast. "That was a terrifying display of power is what it was. Hundreds of people gathered to watch the torture of one!"

"Not just any one," he said quickly. "That one deserved what he was getting. He *designed* it!"

That stopped her in her tracks, her mouth dropping open in surprise. She understood anger, but this kind of anger from Sledge was completely unexpected.

"And you," he continued, trembling slightly. "I saw that look you shared with him, and it's just a good damn thing that Sister assumed you were a Bullet. You might have got us caught. And for *him*?"

"Oran?"

"Oran," he said, vehement and amazed. "You call him by his name."

"Oran is a part of my crew," she stated, giving each word weight.

"And you didn't think it was worth mentioning that your crew included a Fiveson? That you were asking *us* to save a *Fiveson*?" He towered over her now, his temper barely contained. "Do you remember who we are?"

"Yes," she stammered. "I do. And he is the same as you: a Bullet who defected."

"No. Not the same as us." Sledge drew a hard line between

them. "And I won't risk a single one of my people to save his life. You want to do that? You're on your own."

"What?" Caledonia asked, and though she feared she already knew the answer, she added, "Why?"

"Because"—Sledge leaned in close—"Fiveson Oran is the Steelhand."

The word was like a flood, swallowing her up before she knew it was there. It filled her lungs, her throat, her nose, her ears, until she was cocooned in its violent embrace.

The Steelhand.

She expected to feel shocked, surprised, somehow deeply horrified by this revelation, but there was only an unexpected kind of understanding. Part of her had always known that Oran's past was littered with the kind of violence that shredded lives and families and minds. Now that it was laid out before her, it was almost a relief.

"Maybe that doesn't mean anything to you," Sledge continued. "But it means a great deal to us. The Fivesons are more like Aric than anyone. And for a while the Steelhand was more terrible even than Lir."

At the mention of his name, an image of Lir ghosted through her mind, and she knew with unrelenting certainty that if anyone asked her to save the boy who had killed her family, she would react just as Sledge had. The only difference here was that Oran wanted to change. Once it wouldn't have been enough of a difference. Now it had to be.

"It does mean something to me," she said, hoping Sledge heard the truth in her words even if they ignited his anger. "And he's still a part of my crew."

The muscles of Sledge's jaw flexed, his eyes narrowed to slits.

Caledonia let his anger wash over her without feeding into her own. "He's part of the reason I came here," she added. "And I'm not leaving without him."

For a moment Sledge didn't say anything. He stood with his back to the corner, shadows draped over his shoulders making him look even more mountainous than usual. Finally, he took one step forward, stopping with his shoulder even with hers.

"We'll help save your crew, but you don't want any of us near the Fiveson." He nodded as though that was as far as he'd go toward an agreement, and then he was gone.

CHAPTER
TWENTY-ONE

C aledonia woke the next morning before dawn after a fitful rest. None of the others stirred, and she moved silently toward the washroom for a quick shower. Dressed once more and with a fresh smear of grease down the side of her face to cover her sigil, she left Barrack D.

Slipmark was quiet so early in the morning. The lanes bore a few figures hurrying in different directions, and the air carried the first yeasty scent of fresh bread. In the distance, the harbor was waking to the soft cries of shore birds. Up and down the streets, solar lights flickered and went out as high in the east dawn light glazed the sky.

Where Slipmark was quiet, Caledonia's mind was a driving storm, and she could no longer stay indoors. She needed room for her thoughts. So she tucked her chin into her chest and turned her steps uphill, away from the harbor.

All night, her mind had tossed out question after question. Where were her girls? What state were they in? How would she get them away from this place that made a show of torture? How was she going to get *any* of them through those massive walls? And how was she going to save Oran without Sledge's help?

Oran. The Steelhand. Architect of suffering and the shadow that still haunted the Blades after so much time. They'd served with Fiveson Venn, yet it was the Steelhand they feared.

It was more than that. Sledge *hated* him. And Caledonia was certain that if he found himself alone with Oran, one of them wouldn't survive. Which would present an enormous problem when they were on the same ship.

She couldn't worry about that right now. Right now, she needed to prioritize each problem and build a strategy. Oran was alive, and he'd stay that way until Sister was done with him. Her first priority had to be locating her girls. Today, they would scout each of the prisons to find them. Once they'd done that, she could figure out how to free them.

Oran was likely being held in a different location, which meant she needed to plan not one, but two rescues. One of which she'd have to complete without the help of the Blades.

Caledonia kicked at the smooth-paved ground, winning a glare from a Bullet passing in the opposite direction. She glared right back and kept pushing up the hill. She needed more time, but every minute they spent here was a fresh risk. Sooner or later, someone was going to figure out the *Beacon* had come to port bearing the wrong crew. That or Pine was going to murder one too many Bullets.

From one cross street to the next, the buildings grew lower to the ground, allowing more light to fill the channels between. Caledonia paused to take in her new surroundings and was surprised to find that the buildings here weren't constructed of the same blue-gray stone as elsewhere in town, but out of endless panes of self-healing glass.

In the first, the glass was so densely fogged that she could see nothing but vague shadows within. The next was more of the same, but the third was clear, and through the windows she saw long rows of tables piled with soil.

Caledonia edged closer, scanning the large room for any other presence. It was empty, as was the street around her. Hurrying to the door, she waited one minute more, then entered.

The air inside smelled overwhelmingly fresh and loamy. Caledonia had only smelled something similar once before after a hard rain in the Blades' camp, when soil and fern and moss all sighed with relief. It made her long for something she'd never had, and made her hope that they could all have it again.

She moved between rows of long tables, noting that the soil on each was a slightly different shade of brown. On the very last table, it was nearly white. It sifted through her fingers more finely than sand, leaving them coated with a ghostly powder. She recognized it immediately. This bleached soil was the reason the northern colonies remained dependent on the coastline for sustenance. It was the reason they all relied on the oceans and what few islands had survived. It was the reason Aric had come to power. He'd found a way to reclaim it and then he kept it a secret.

And that reclamation happened right here.

Caledonia looked over the vast room, understanding exactly what she was seeing. Each table bore soil in a stage of recovery. Whatever Aric did, it required time. And soiltech. It had to be here. Somewhere.

"Caledonia!"

The hushed whisper came from directly behind her.

Caledonia reached for the blade hidden in her belt as she spun, barely stopping herself from cutting the small girl before her. On her cheeks were the pale brown lines of scrollwork scarring. The skin completely free of the burnt orange pigment of Silt.

"Nettle!"

"Noru," the girl corrected her.

"Rhona," Caledonia added.

"I know. How do you think I found She Who Cuts Hearts?" Nettle said with a disapproving glower. "Not a great way to avoid notice. But you made it easy for me to find you."

She was dressed as Caledonia was, in the multilayered browns Bullets wore, and a single orange ribbon bound her dark hair firmly atop her head. It seemed to Caledonia that she'd grown, reaching past her own shoulder now.

The girl rushed forward, wrapping her arms around Caledonia to squeeze her tightly. "I knew you weren't dead. I knew you'd come."

Caledonia's throat pinched in response, and she allowed herself a moment to return the hug before pushing the girl away to ask, "Where are the others?"

"Imprisoned in East Keep." Nettle pointed farther up the hillside.

The news landed heavily. Up the hillside was farther from the barracks, farther still from the *Beacon*. "Noru," she said, suddenly suspicious. "How did you escape?"

Nettle's smile was as smug as it was satisfied. "Trade secrets."

Caledonia had a dozen questions she needed to ask the girl, starting with: "How do we get them out?"

"Not here," Nettle said, pulling Caledonia's hands into her own and dragging her toward the doors. "We have to get you out of here before—"

"Nettle, wait, I need to know how he does this. I need this tech!" She tugged, but Nettle didn't let up until they were outside.

Dawn had flooded the town in her absence, and the sounds of Bullets getting to their daily work were everywhere.

"I caught some chatter," Nettle said, keeping her voice low, her words fast, though there was no one near enough to hear them. "They're moving our crew to the tide cans."

"The tide cans," Caledonia repeated as the blood drained from her lips. "When?"

"I don't know, but I can find out. Just give me—"

"Noru!" The voice assaulted them like the snap of a rifle, and both girls turned toward the sound.

A woman three times Caledonia's age cut toward them with a severe stride and an expression to match. Behind her marched a stream of boys and girls close to Nettle's age.

"You're early," the woman charged, displeasure evident in the bow of her mouth. "And who are you?"

"Rhona," Caledonia answered immediately, feeling herself respond to the aggression in the woman's tone with some of her own. It wasn't a good thing. She needed to keep her head.

"What are you doing in my sector, Rhona? And with one of my Hollows?" The question was laced with more threats than Caledonia knew how to unravel. What did it mean for a Bullet to be found outside their sector? What might bring a Bullet into a sector they weren't assigned to? She didn't know. She only barely knew what a Hollow was.

"She got lost," Nettle supplied. "Their clip only arrived yesterday."

"Lost." The woman repeated, considering.

It was an excuse of incompetence. Caledonia suspected that never landed well among Bullets, but if Nettle thought it was her best option, she wasn't going to argue. The girl was damned resourceful.

"Lanning!" The woman's call dislodged one of the young Hollows behind her. Bringing them to her shoulder in three quick steps. "Get the Hollows inside and to work. You, Rhona, will have to come with me."

Caledonia hesitated, loath to find herself under this woman's charge.

"Bullet Rhona!"

The shout was like a clap of thunder, sharp, familiar, and unwelcome. Gloriana marched toward them, chewing up the distance with long, quick strides.

Nettle's eyes widened at the sight, and sweat pricked between Caledonia's shoulder blades.

"One of yours, Bullet Gloriana?" the woman asked.

"Hardly. She was spotted outside her sector. I came to intercept." She locked her eyes on Caledonia in a way that suggested she knew more than she was saying. "I'll take her from here."

"Take care you keep to your sector in the future," the woman said, turning to usher Nettle toward the greenhouse. "No one gets lost in Slipmark."

"No Bullet," Gloriana added quietly.

Caledonia's stomach pitched.

Nettle dared one last glace over her shoulder as the woman drove her forward. Caledonia gave her an encouraging smile, a promise that they would see each other again. With Nettle on the ground, she didn't doubt it. But with Gloriana at her side, she feared it would be through the bars of a prison cell.

"After you," Gloriana said, and with her next word she cinched Caledonia's fears. "Caledonia."

CHAPTER TWENTY-TWO

S lipmark was alive now, and it was full of clamor and the rhythmic thumping of feet on pavement as Bullets jogged up or down the main street in perfect formation. They chanted to keep the pace, and each time they passed another troop doing the same they roared in unison.

Caledonia watched it all with a distant kind of horror, while a single word stretched across her mind like a cloud covering the sun: *caught.*

"Where are you taking me?" she asked, craning to peer over her shoulder.

Bullet Gloriana didn't answer. She walked with her eyes straight ahead almost as if she'd forgotten Caledonia was there.

There were so many parts of this town she hadn't noticed before. From the regular patrol that traveled in teams of three to the holos posting the time in orange numbers against blue walls. It was time for her crew to report to the mess hall for breakfast, after which they would return to their ship and begin repairs. She would be missed, if she hadn't been already, and once Sledge knew she was gone, someone would come looking. She was sure of it. She just wasn't sure it would do any good.

As they cut toward the middle of town, Sister's tower rose high above them. Its stones were a pale blue and with sunlight painting gold along its edges, it looked like a sword forged from the sky. Toward the tip, a slender balcony wrapped around it in a ring, giving a view of both the harbor and the city itself.

Gloriana turned down a narrow alley and suddenly, Caledonia knew that the tower was their destination. Her mouth turned sour, and for an instant she considered sliding her blade into Gloriana's side. If she were Pine, she'd have done it the second Gloriana said her name. But it was a plan with no strategy behind it. And this way, she stood a chance of seeing her girls again.

If she couldn't save them, she could at least die with them.

They came to a door in the side of the tower. Not the main entrance, Caledonia noted, but one that was so infrequently used its hinges whined in protest of opening. Inside, a dim hallway led directly into a stairwell.

"Down," Gloriana said, pulling the door shut behind them.

The stairs coiled down into another hallway that stretched in two directions. It was unnaturally quiet here with several feet of stonework blotting out the world above. They were very, very alone.

"This way." Gloriana led them to another doorway beyond which was a small, square room piled high with books.

Caledonia momentarily forgot herself, greedily taking a book in her hands and turning it over. The book was unbroken. Whole. A book with a beginning, an end, and all the pages in between. On the *Mors Navis* they'd never been lucky enough to find a book that wasn't damaged in some way, but Pisces used them regardless, teaching the girls to read and fill in the blanks for one another.

This room must contain dozens of books. Dozens of stories trapped down here, uncared for and unread.

"We can talk here," Gloriana said.

Caledonia dropped the book and spun to face her captor. "Talk?"

"About how you're not a Bullet."

Caledonia swallowed hard. She wasn't bound, and Gloriana hadn't pulled her weapon. In fact, she'd gone to some trouble to avoid looking like she was driving a prisoner through town. It all occurred to Caledonia at once, and she felt ridiculous for not seeing it sooner. But whatever Gloriana wanted from her, it wasn't going to be good.

"I'm not who you think I am," Caledonia said.

It was the invitation Gloriana had been waiting for. She leaned in, lips curving faintly toward a smile. "You've missed a spot," she said, raising a thumb and smearing it along the top of Caledonia's cheekbone. It came away blackened with grease. "Curious. It's the same spot you missed yesterday."

The woman was so close, Caledonia could smell the salt of her sweat and the honeyed perfume of Silt underneath. "Not so curious when you work on a ship."

Gloriana wasn't deterred. "Or it's covering something you don't want anyone to see."

Caledonia held herself rigid, preparing to meet aggression with aggression as she'd seen Sledge do, but Gloriana's next words changed everything.

"I know who you are." Gloriana's voice had become a whisper. "And I know you've come for your crew." When she paused Caledonia saw a flash of uncertainty surface in her eyes before she added, "I want to help."

Caledonia hadn't given her a second thought since their meeting yesterday afternoon, but she considered her now: several years Caledonia's senior, fully under the influence of Silt, and in a position of relative power as Harbor Master Lyall's right hand. She was a Bullet. She was a stranger. And she knew enough about Caledonia to end everything right here and now.

But she hadn't.

Run, said her mother.

Trust, Pisces's voice said.

She knew Pisces was right. She had to trust them to change or nothing ever would. But trust was just another word for risk. When she trusted, she risked more than her own life. She risked the lives of all who trusted her.

Aware that her next move could cost them everything, she asked, "Why?"

Gloriana stepped away, leaning her back against the door. "Because I'm leaving with or without your help. And I'd like to hurt them when I go, and because I've never seen anyone stand up to them the way you have."

"And what do you want in return?"

The question startled a smile onto Gloriana's face. For a brief second, she was so much more than a Bullet. "A ride out of here."

"Nothing more than that?"

"Drop me in the first friendly harbor we find."

It took Caledonia a second to understand that Gloriana was offering the help she needed to save her crew and all she was asking for was a way out. She turned toward the unruly stacks of books, letting her fingers run over their cracked covers as she gathered her thoughts.

"Why did you bring me to Sister's tower?" she asked.

"Isn't it obvious?" Gloriana laughed softly. "We needed a place to speak privately, and this is it. No one comes down here. Not even Sister herself." She paused, looking around the room. "Learning to read is required, but books are forbidden. I've never really understood why."

Caledonia turned slowly. These books were a treasure. They were history, information, stories, and Aric knew that collectively, they wielded more power than he ever could. So he locked them away. Everything he did came back to a careful balance of starvation and abundance. Only here, in the roots of Sister's tower, did Caledonia understand that he feared the mind of every Bullet in his army. He fed them Silt to keep them dull, to curb the appetite of their intellect.

This was one more piece of Aric's power. Knowing it calmed her and gave her a sense of possibility. When power revealed itself completely, it could be dismantled.

"All right, Gloriana," she said. "I'll give you a ride out of here if you help me."

Gloriana nodded, trying to contain her relief. She'd been more nervous than she'd let on. "Good. I'll do whatever you need me to, but I hope you have a plan because getting your crew out of East Keep isn't going to be easy."

No, it wasn't.

Now that she knew the layout of town and where the girls were being held, it was easy for Caledonia to let her mind walk through different scenarios. Her previous tensions and fears were still there, but they were quiet now, held down by the familiar comfort of forming a plan.

No matter how they did it, getting the girls from East Keep all the way through town and aboard the *Beacon* would foil any chances of getting out of the harbor. Either they succeeded in sneaking them out of prison and risked a conspicuous mile-long trek through town, or they blasted them out of their cells and were discovered much sooner. Regardless of how it happened, the second an alarm sounded, the harbor walls would lock together and after that, the only way out was on foot, which did them no good.

"I'm not going to get them out of East Keep," she said, feeling certain that she'd found her footing. "I'm going to let Sister get them out of Slipmark for me."

Gloriana's pale brown eyes widened. "The tide cans."

"Exactly. Once they're past the jetty walls, I can get to them without risking so much exposure."

"Then what do you need from me?"

Every one of Caledonia's plans started with a feeling, a small kernel in the pit of her belly that felt like the center of everything. When that feeling bloomed, she knew she was in the right place. She had that feeling now.

"If a ship tries to leave the bay without clearance, will the jetties close?"

Gloriana nodded. "They can close inside five minutes."

"Good. And it will take five minutes for them to reopen?"

"Yes, but a small ship can get through in three."

That was less good news, but Gloriana didn't need to know it. "What about setting explosives? Can you help us sabotage the arms?"

"If you can get me the bombs, I can place them," she said with confidence. "I just need some time."

The plan bloomed a little more. "I'll get you the bombs, and after that all I need from you is to open the jetty walls on my signal."

"That's it?"

"That's it. Open the jetties and get to the ship. We'll take care of the rest."

Gloriana crossed her arms over her chest, and with a shake of her head said, "I've heard stories about you, you know. How you started by picking off bale barges in the south and took on Fiveson Lir in the north. In nearly every story they tell, you lurk beneath the waves like a many-headed hydra and are out there, biding your time before you strike again."

"A hydra?" She laughed at the image.

"I think I see what they mean." Gloriana reached for the door, pausing with her hand on the latch. "And I hope you're as unkill-able as the stories suggest."

She pulled open the door and led the way back through the hallway and up the stairs. It was just as quiet as when they'd arrived, only this time, Caledonia moved with confidence. Everything was falling into place. All except one piece.

"One more thing," she said, stopping Gloriana just inside the door to the alley. "Do you know where they're holding Or—Fiveson Oran?"

Now Gloriana frowned. "I don't," she said solemnly. "Nor do I wish to."

Caledonia recognized the same mix of fear and anger she'd seen in her Blades whenever Oran was mentioned, but she pushed on. "Can you find out?"

The woman's frown deepened, and she nodded reluctantly. "I can try."

"Good. Do it."

Gloriana's frown dug in as she nodded her agreement. She

turned suddenly, ripping the door open and stepping through. They emerged into the same alley to find the day was in its full stride.

"I'll wait for your signal," Gloriana said. "In the meantime, keep to your sector. I can't watch you all the time."

"You were following me?"

"Of course," she answered with true surprise. "Did you think that was luck?" The woman laughed. "There's no luck in Slipmark, friend."

Caledonia hoped that wasn't true. For all that her plan was a good one, she would need a little luck for the pieces to knit together in the right order.

"Meeting you was lucky," Caledonia countered, then paused. "How did you know? It couldn't have just been the grease."

"No, not the grease, though if you're here for much longer, it's going to start to look suspicious to more than just me. You might consider staging a fight and using a bandage," she said with genuine warning. "It was that Ballistic of yours. Dair. He used an outdated code on your manifest form. It made me curious and, well, once I started looking at you I just had a feeling. That, plus your display in the quad last night? I figured it was worth the risk."

"You have sharp instincts, Gloriana," Caledonia said, wondering just how remarkable those instincts would be unburdened by the weight of Silt.

"Sharp enough," the woman answered, continuing down the alley. "Sharp enough."

CHAPTER
TWENTY-THREE

Hope took a firm hold in Caledonia's mind, tumbling quickly toward steely resolve. There were still many details to untangle, but the plan was within reach. All she had to do was pull on the right threads and the remaining knots would unravel.

She followed Gloriana down the alley with a renewed sense of control. And that was key to the success of any plan.

Just before they reached the main street, Nettle raced around the corner. Gloriana squared her shoulders, authority emanating from her in dangerous waves. But before she could reprimand the young girl, Nettle slid to a stop, her wide eyes bouncing between the two of them.

"It's all right," Caledonia said to both her companion and the young girl. "We're all friends. What is it?"

Nettle puffed out her cheeks, clearly still skeptical, but harried enough to move past it. "They're moving the crew."

Caledonia nodded. "You told me already."

"No." Nettle's voice was urgent. "They're moving them *now*."

Nettle didn't wait for a response from her captain. She spun on her heel and raced back the way she'd come. Caledonia followed, her heart already beating rapidly in her chest. Behind her, Gloriana matched her pace. She had just enough clarity to think that if she needed to be stopped, if there were something severely out of place about a Bullet racing toward the site of prisoners on the move, then one of her two companions would stop her.

Nettle led them toward the harbor where the crowd had grown dense and loud. They were all enjoying the sight of the girl crew on parade, all enjoying the thought of what awaited them when they reached the tide cans.

They cut around the press of jeering Bullets and down an empty wharf with a clear view of the crew. There, on the wharf opposite where they stood now, Bullets were driving the girls up a gangway to stand on the deck of a ship. One by one, her girls appeared, each with hands bound before her.

Amina stood at the front of their group with her long black braids falling behind her. She looked thinner than before, but her eyes tracked the skies above, no doubt for signs from her spirits. At her side stood Hime. The smaller girl held her hands tucked against her chest as she counted each crew member to board the ship behind her. There was Tin and her four sisters, Pippa and Folly, Far, and even Ares, each covered in bruises and old blood.

Caledonia's chest squeezed tightly. She was at once desperately relieved to see them alive and fighting the voice in the back of her head that said it was too soon. They weren't ready. Their ship wasn't ready. She had only just settled on a plan.

The last of her crew to board was tall and broad-shouldered with a cap of black hair. *Pisces*. Caledonia clenched her jaw to stop herself from crying out.

Then, a voice rose over the harbor.

"Fiveson Oran!" Sister called. "We offer you a choice."

Caledonia had been so fixated on the sight of her crew boarding that ship that she'd missed the group waiting on the dock below. Now she could see Sister in her cream and orange robes standing before the figure of a boy covered in wounds. Her voice fell on them from above where it was piped through slender speakers.

"Demonstrate your regret and your fealty by putting each of them to rest, or, join them in the device of your own making."

Two Bullets stepped between Sister and Oran, bearing loaded guns. They offered them to Oran, along with an end to his own suffering if he chose to shoot each and every member of Caledonia's crew.

Nettle drew a sharp breath.

Oran stepped toward the boys, pushing his shoulders back with obvious effort. Then he turned and slowly walked up the gangway to stand with Caledonia's crew. *His* crew.

Sister nodded, and the engine of that ship began to growl, preparing to take her crew away and lock them in those dreadful cans where they would be forced to tread water for as long as they were able.

"Hoist your eyes," Caledonia whispered, knowing there was no way they could hear her.

But Pisces turned her head, looked directly at Caledonia. And in spite of the distance between them, in spite of the Bullet clothing and short blonde spikes of Caledonia's hair, Pisces knew her sister.

I'm coming for you, Caledonia signed, making each sign as loudly as she dared. *Hold on.*

For a second, Pisces only stared at her, but then she gave the barest nod of her head. She had seen her, she had understood her, and she would pass that message on to their sisters.

They weren't prepared, but Caledonia would make sure they got prepared. Fast.

"Gloriana," she said, eyes still pinned to the ship carrying her sisters out to sea. "When is the next low tide?"

"Close to midnight."

Caledonia nodded. "That's our mark. We'll get the bombs to you in two hours. Plant them, open the jetty walls at midnight, then get to the ship."

"I'll see you soon, Captain," Gloriana answered, turning swift steps away from the wharf.

Caledonia was filled with a terrible kind of hope as she watched the ship carry her sisters past the jetty walls toward the tide cans. They would be locked inside, and there would be no way to open those hatches again once the tide came in. They would

have to endure a full tide before she could reach them. That would
have been a challenge for many of them when they weren't starv-
ing and weakened by days of abuse. In their current state, this
could kill them.

"Hold on," Caledonia whispered. "I'm coming for you."

205

CHAPTER
TWENTY-FOUR

C aledonia spent the rest of the day aboard the *Beacon* ensuring it was ready for what came next and mapping out the plan for Sledge.

"Say it again," he said, huddled in the small chamber beneath the bridge.

"At midnight, Gloriana will open the jetty walls for us. As soon as they realize what's going on, the Bullets will start to close them again, but we'll already be moving. We have five minutes to take the *Beacon* through, and when the walls close behind us, we blow the arms. The walls stay closed. We free my crew and sail out of here before anyone can pursue."

"You make it sound so simple," he grumbled. "But how can you be sure we'll get through? What happens if we're too slow?"

Caledonia offered a tight smile. "We can't afford to be slow. No delays."

He leaned back, giving her a long look. There was more distance between them now, a prodding staff that pushed them in opposite directions. Oran was out there with her crew. Sledge might not like it, but he wasn't ready to openly defy her. Instead, they let the subject sit silently between them. It was uncomfortable, but manageable. At least, for now.

There was a cursory knock on the door, then Triple slipped inside. A fresh sheen of sweat stood out on her brow, darkening the hair at her temples. She tossed a remote to Caledonia with a confident nod.

"I handed the explosives off to Gloriana," she said. "She'll have them placed inside each jetty tower before she meets up with us tonight."

"Any sign of trouble? From anyone?" Sledge asked, emphasizing the final word.

Caledonia jumped in before Triple could respond, saying, "Gloriana could have taken me straight to Sister. Why go through all of this if not to help us?"

"Because she's heard stories about you and wanted to encourage you to plan something elaborate so she could make a show of taking you down," Sledge countered. "Like we're doing at this precise moment."

Caledonia understood his misgivings, but any room she gave at this point was too much. They needed to trust the plan or it would be too weak to support them.

"I know it's a risk," she said, looking from Triple to Sledge. "Everything we've done here is a risk. But you said it yourself. You have to *un*become them. You have to become something else, and you have to keep choosing what that is."

Triple scowled at her own words being used against Sledge. "How is that relevant right now?"

"Because." Caledonia released a slow breath. "The first time a Bullet told me they wanted out, I believed him, and a lot of people I loved died."

"Lir," Triple said, eyes widening in understanding. "That's why you went after him."

"It is." She paused long enough to catch Sledge's eye. "It's taken me a long time to trust that anyone means it when they say the same thing."

"But you do this time," Triple stated, her unease less than it had been just a moment before.

"I have to." The truth startled her. "The last two times I've heard a Bullet say they wanted out, they've told the truth. And somewhere out there is a Bullet I need to believe would say the same if given the opportunity." Her throat squeezed at the thought of Donnally. Alive and forever out of her reach. "If we stop trusting the people who say they want out, then we'll never believe anyone is worth saving."

"Some people aren't." Sledge strode abruptly to the door, pushing it open. "I'll be ready when you need me."

"Sledge!" Triple called, surprised.

But Sledge was gone. The door closed behind him. When

Triple turned to Caledonia her face was strained with concern, her hazel-green eyes deep with conflict. She held Caledonia's gaze for a long minute, sharing so much with just that expression, and then she sighed.

"Sledge asked us to respect your wishes," she began. "I think you should know that. This is hard for all of us, but when Sledge asks us to do something, we do it. You say the Steelhand is a part of your crew, we'll respect that."

"Oran," Caledonia supplied softly, but the smile Triple returned was rueful.

Caledonia nodded, wishing she could make Triple and Sledge and the rest of the Blades understand that the Oran she knew was not the Steelhand they remembered.

"We trust you to lead us," Triple added. "But this isn't about trust. This is about history. We left him in the past, and you're asking us to make him a part of our future. It is the last thing we expected from you."

At that Caledonia smiled. "It surprises me, too. I tried to kill him the first time I met him." She paused. "And maybe a few times after that."

Triple laughed, tossing her golden braids over her shoulder. "First Oran, then Lir? Fivesons really are the same. Unkillable bloat fish."

An unexpected heat flooded Caledonia's cheeks. "There's an essential difference between the two of them."

"What's that?" Triple asked, raising an eyebrow.

"Oran didn't try to kill me back."

Night pressed thick on the rooftops of Slipmark as one by one, the Blades slipped out of Barrack D. They chose different paths, ghosting their way toward the *Beacon* until most of their crew was secretly aboard.

Caledonia and Sledge were the last to leave, jogging together in unison. The streets were iced in solar light while the sky above collected a scatter of puffy clouds glowing with moonlight. The only sounds were the near whisper of their footsteps and the regular pattern of their breath. Caledonia tried to focus on the plan, but her mind kept skipping out past the jetties to where her crew had endured a full high tide inside those cans. She wanted to believe that every one of them had survived, but she also knew it was unlikely. Improbable, even.

Her girls had survived the improbable before, she reminded herself. They were smart and strong and resourceful. There were ways to survive in the water, and surviving was their job right now. Everything else was up to her.

Caledonia reeled her thoughts back into the harbor. They had precious few advantages right now, but chief among them was the fact that the Bullets of Slipmark had spent so much time protecting the harbor from external threats that they wouldn't be expecting one that came from within.

She and Sledge emerged a hundred yards north of the ship and paused long enough to ensure the wharf was clear. Everything looked bigger without the constant crowd of Bullets. The solar lights were dimmed, their bluish light transforming the wharf into a wintery landscape. Cautiously, they stepped into the open, cross-ing to jog beneath ship hulls where the shadows were deeper.

As they drew nearer to the *Beacon*'s dark hull, the only sign that things were not as they should be was the slack in the lines. They'd been uncoiled from the cleats on deck, ready to shove off the minute Gloriana stepped aboard.

Sledge picked up speed as they approached the gangway. Har-well greeted them on deck with a wide smile that was equal parts eagerness and anxiety.

"Report," Caledonia said in a hushed voice.

"Everyone's on board but Gloriana. Engines look good, pro-peller's in place. We're ready on your signal, Captain."

"Good," she said with a nod. Then, turning her gaze toward the jetty walls, she muttered, "Now we wait."

"I hope this works," Sledge said, echoing her own thoughts.

"It'll work," Nettle answered with complete confidence. "Cap-tain Caledonia is the steeliest on the seas."

"You brought us a guppy," Triple teased, reaching out to flick one of Nettle's ribbons, which had reappeared in all their rainbow splendor.

"Guppy?!" Nettle did her best to look offended. "What does that make you?"

Triple smiled, leaning in close to the girl. "A snapper!"

Nettle laughed, slapping at Triple. The girl had a way of charming anyone, which was probably how she'd survived so long. It was certainly how she'd worked her way onto Caledonia's crew.

"Look!" Nettle exclaimed quietly, bouncing on her toes and pointing.

The group turned toward the jetty walls, where blinking orange lights marked the top of each one. At first, it was hard to tell if they were moving. Then a small slice of black ocean appeared where before there had been only metal. They were opening.

"She did it," Sledge said with some amazement.

A small victorious feeling lodged in Caledonia's chest. She pushed it away. "Now all she has to do is get here, and we do the rest."

"There she is!" Nettle whispered.

A figure appeared on the wharf, dashing between the shadows on her way to the ship. She was still some distance away when three figures skulked out of the shadows behind her. A patrol team.

"She's not going to make it," Triple said, pulling her gun. "Not without help."

"We shoot, we lose our advantage," Caledonia said, eyes pinned to Gloriana, wishing she could do more than wait and watch. "Hold your fire."

Triple's fingers flexed around her gun, but on this point, Caledonia felt her nerves turning to steel. She wanted to help Gloriana and she would, but not at the risk of everyone else under her command. Not at the risk of her crew.

On the wharf, the patrol team had gained on Gloriana, calling her to a halt. She stopped, hands climbing in the air. She was caught and she knew it. Before she turned to face the patrol, she waved her hand once. It was a message: go.

"Spin up the engines, Harwell," Caledonia commanded. "Sledge, get the gunners on the aft deck. But don't fire until you have to."

"What about Gloriana?" Nettle asked, alarmed. "She risked everything to help us. We can't just leave her!"

Guilt and regret made a familiar knot in Caledonia's belly. "She did and we can. Now, I want you on the helm."

"Wait!" Nettle cried, racing down the gangway with something small clutched in her hand. "I can help!"

"Nettle!" Caledonia shouted, but to no avail.

The small girl sprinted down the wharf. She kept to the shadows, running hard, and when she was still several yards away, she threw her object into their midst.

It made no sound, but a light flashed so violently it left a blank spot in Caledonia's sight.

"Dammit," she grumbled, trying to blink away the residual light. "I can't see them. Report!"

"They're down, but—" Triple's voice was punctuated by a single gunshot.

They were officially out of time.

"Is she hit?" Caledonia asked, an image of Nettle lying dead on the ground flashing through her mind.

"No. But Gloriana is cut off from us. She's retreating. And Nettle is . . ."

Another gunshot.

"She's hit." Triple's words were rushed. She darted away from Caledonia, racing down the gangway to help Nettle.

"Pine?" Caledonia called, frustration mounting.

"No clear line of fire," he yelled from his position on the rear deck.

She wanted to ask how badly Nettle was hurt, if there was a chance someone else might reach them in time, but there was no time for distractions.

In the harbor, the blinking orange lights of the jetty walls were moving farther and farther apart. *Beacon*'s engines rumbled beneath Caledonia's feet. Her vision cleared a little more, and now she could see that the Bullets on the wharf were still struggling with their own sight. Gloriana had vanished, and Nettle was running back toward the *Beacon*, struggling on her feet.

Another gunshot.

Triple sprinted straight past Nettle toward the three pursuing Bullets. She fired, striking one of the Bullets in the shoulder. Then she raised her sword.

"My glory is yours if you can defeat me!" She shouted the Bullet challenge, making herself a shield for Nettle.

Caledonia felt her heart spinning up like an engine, her blood swirling like a whirlpool.

The Bullets traded guns for blades. They grinned and howled and moved in close.

"Pine?" Caledonia called again.

"I don't have a shot!" he shouted, anger curling through his words.

Sledge aimed for the gangway but Caledonia caught his wrist in an uncompromising grip. He met her eyes with a furious glare.

"No delays." Her words were like knives.

Once again, Caledonia found herself in the position of having to choose between people she loved. If those Bullets knew the *Beacon* was getting ready to cut and run, they wouldn't waste their time with Triple. They'd sound the alarm, and Caledonia's situation would become much more precarious. Triple was giving them time. It was Caledonia's job to use it.

On the ground, Triple raised her blade. The Bullets stood around her in a gleeful semicircle, their eyes alight at the prospect of taking her down.

All at once, they attacked. Metal clashed against metal as Triple held them off.

Nettle was ten yards away from the ship, her small arms pumping hard.

"Ready on the gangway!" Caledonia shouted, preparing to pull the platform up the instant Nettle's foot landed on the deck. Preparing to leave Triple behind.

Triple spun like a star, pulling the Bullets into her orbit. She drew them into the pattern of her attack beautifully. Once. Twice. And on the third round she had them. She twisted out of the pattern she'd just taught them to expect and drove her sword through a Bullet's chest.

On deck, the Blades cheered. Pine fired, taking down a second of Triple's attackers. Caledonia dared to hope she would make it. That they could wait just a second longer for her to return to them.

But in the next instant, that cheer became a scream. The remaining Bullet retaliated with remarkable speed, forcing Triple to expose her side. The second her arm was raised, he drove his sword beneath her ribs.

She slumped to her knees. The Bullet withdrew his blade, and instantly Triple was on her feet again, lashing out with everything she had.

She fought brilliantly. But the Bullet fought dirty. The next time she turned to deflect a jab, she caught a sword in her back. She stopped, frozen in a perfect arc, like a feather on the verge of being raised by the breeze.

Then she fell.

CHAPTER
TWENTY-FIVE

Caledonia screamed. The air filled with the sound of violent rain as Pine's gunners finally opened fire.

Nettle was on deck, gasping for breath and bleeding from the bullet graze on her arm, but otherwise unharmed. "Captain," she wheezed as Caledonia pulled her upright. "I'm sorry. I—"

"I need you on the helm," Caledonia stated. "Can you do it?"

Nettle straightened, nodding resolutely. "I have the helm, Captain."

Caledonia allowed herself one last glance at Triple, crumpled on the ground where she'd fallen as her attacker fled for cover. She wanted to cry out, to release her tears and rage, but now was not the time. She bared her teeth and turned toward the harbor.

The night was full of sound now; the town was wide-awake, and Bullets converged on the wharf from all directions. There was no time to wait for Gloriana. She had to trust that she would take care of herself now. If they delayed a second more, this would all be for nothing.

"Shove off!" she shouted.

"Get low!" Pine's voice rang out.

They hit the deck just in time for a host of Bullets to race down the dock, firing wildly at the departing ship.

"Clear!" Pine called, when they'd moved out of the direct line of fire. "Gunners stay ready! I want three teams on the aft deck!"

Caledonia headed for the bridge and climbed to the flat roof where she could see the bay ahead and the docks behind. The sound of engines roaring filled the air as clips scrambled to make their ships ready for pursuit.

For now, the *Beacon* was the only moving point in the entire bay, dragging a line of stirred water behind them as they headed for the open jetties. But that would change sooner than they liked. Caledonia studied the scene, letting possibilities spin quickly through her mind.

Of the many ships waiting in that harbor, maybe two of the larger vessels could give chase with enough speed to make a difference. It would take them several minutes to get underway. In the meantime, smaller vessels would dog the *Beacon,* forcing them to engage while the larger ships made ready to move in for the kill. Right now, her best hope was speed.

The jetty walls were moving again, only this time, they were closing. The structures moved much faster this time, creating great ripples as they traveled inward. If they closed before they got through them, there would be no escaping this bay. No way to reach her crew.

Though she'd anticipated this moment, Caledonia's pulse jumped.

"Three ships in pursuit!" Pine called from the stern. "Two buzzers, one mag ship!"

She leapt down to the command deck and charged into the bridge. Nettle was driving them forward with a determined glare.

"Nettle, I need you to slow us down." Caledonia called. "Just a bit."

The girl turned to her in alarm. "This bucket is slow enough as is! They'll catch us."

"I need them to catch us," Caledonia explained. "But it won't be for long."

Now the girl smiled, showing all her teeth. "It's good to have you back. I mean, I guess it's just good to *be* back."

Caledonia gave the girl a tight smile before turning to Harwell. "Ready on the pulse on my mark, Harwell."

"My pleasure," he answered, standing ready at the console.

She moved to the command deck where wind whipped at her cheeks. The buzzers were doing exactly as she'd expected, harrying the *Beacon* along one side while the mag ship approached from the other. All three gained on the larger ship as ahead the jetty walls continued to close.

"I hope you know what you're doing," Sledge said from his post at her shoulder.

"Trust me," Caledonia answered.

The mag ship put on a burst of speed, darting forward and deploying its magnetized harpoons. She heard the *thunk* of each one attaching to the hull of the *Beacon*. Six tethers snapped tight, securely connecting the two ships. Then the mag ship cut its engines and tossed three sea anchors into its wake.

Pine's gunners fired at will, forcing the mag ship crew to take cover. But the damage was done. The anchors sank, opening like canvas sails to fill with water and create enough drag to kill the *Beacon*'s speed.

Caledonia let the scene unfold, let the mag ship think they had her, let the buzzers break their own inertia as they slowed alongside the *Beacon*.

Ahead the space between the jetty walls grew increasingly narrow. In less than a minute, it would be shut. The crew waited on the edge of panic, their eyes measuring the distance between themselves and freedom. Caledonia let the walls close a fraction more, then it was time.

"Engines to full!" Caledonia commanded.

Their engines strained against the force of the mag ship's magnetized harpoons, yearning toward the jetty walls. Behind them, three more Bullet ships moderated their speed, thinking the *Beacon* was thoroughly snared.

Caledonia grinned. And just before the jetty walls closed, she shouted. "Now, Harwell!"

The ship pulsed. Water snapped away from the hull in sharp ripples, and all six magoons slipped from the hull, demagnetized.

The *Beacon* surged ahead, nearly hopping as the propellers churned at full speed. They were fifty yards away before the buzzers managed to swing their noses around and climb back to speed. It wasn't much of a lead, but it would be enough.

Nettle didn't need an ounce of direction. She aimed at the narrowing channel between the walls and held steady.

No one breathed. All eyes were pinned on those closing arms.

Beside Caledonia, Sledge dropped a curse that would have made Redtooth proud. "We're not going to make it."

But Caledonia knew better.

They charged into the channel with only feet to spare on either side, and just as they soared out again, the arms pinched against the hull, igniting a tail of sparks in their wake.

The walls closed behind them, locking all pursuing ships inside. For the moment, they were free. Caledonia hit the remote. Two seconds passed, then an explosion shattered the southern jetty tower, disabling the arm.

The crew turned their attention to the northern jetty tower, but after five more seconds, it was clear that the explosion had failed. There was no time to dwell on it.

"Take me to my crew!" Caledonia cried.

CHAPTER TWENTY-SIX

The tide cans hovered against the night sky like rusted demons risen from the depths of the ocean. On top of three, orange flags fluttered.

"Nettle, get us in close!" Caledonia called. "Pine, I need those steel punchers!"

"Captain!" Shale called from the bow. "Middle can! They're already free!"

Lights flared on deck and turned on the middle of the five cans. There, perched atop the structure, were at least a dozen girls. They huddled together, climbing to their feet and shielding their eyes against the light. Caledonia saw them—Neece, Britta, Pippa, Wen, Amina—drenched and shivering but alive and whole.

Someone had released them. She scanned each of the other cans and found a shadowed figure clinging to the side of another. Shirtless, covered in wounds, and working at the hatch.

"Oran!" she shouted. The boy's head snapped around, spotting her at once. "Move away from the hatch!"

Understanding and relief washed down Oran's face. He climbed to the roof of the can and moved back while Nettle nudged the ship even closer. From within the remaining cans, they could hear pounding on the walls.

"Stay steely, girls!" Caledonia shouted.

"The hatches are too low," Pine said, steel punchers in hand. "They'll have to swim and climb."

Caledonia had reached the same conclusion, and while she didn't like it, there wasn't time to find a better solution. If the northern jetty wall opened behind them, they'd be forced away from the cans whether they had her crew or not. "They can do it."

Pine tossed a steel puncher to Sledge, and when Caledonia reached for the third, he laughed. "Not a chance, Captain. Starling!" He tossed the steel puncher to a boy who'd been named for his song. "In the water."

Starling plucked the steel puncher and leapt overboard. Sledge was right behind him.

"Jetties on the move!" Mint shouted from the aft deck.

Pine dropped to the ocean below as Caledonia turned her steps toward the command deck. All around the sky was dark except for the dagger of Slipmark. The town was now slicked with light, a blue-white blade nestled in the deep black clutch of hills. In the bay, the northern wall began to open.

"Gunners ready!" she shouted.

Behind her, the steel punchers went *pop-pop-pop!* The hatches of all remaining tide cans would be open in seconds, her girls soon in the water. If only they had a few more minutes.

On the main deck below, five Blades rushed to the railing to throw rope ladders over and help the first of her crew on board. Caledonia's heart thrashed in her chest. She wanted to run to them, to throw her arms around them and kiss their cheeks, but she stayed put. She needed to keep her head in the fight.

Almost as if summoned by her thoughts, a missile speared the middle tide can, exploding on impact. Her stomach lurched. Had all her girls made it out of that can?

Behind them, the wall opened even more, and a single ship pushed through. It roared toward them as a second missile sang past another can, exploding in the water some distance away.

"Move, move, move!" she heard Sledge's voice thundering over the water.

Her girls needed little encouragement. They dropped into the water even faster than before, swimming toward the *Beacon*.

Caledonia kept her eyes on the approaching ship. She had a decision to make: bring the rear of her own ship around to shield the girls still in the water, slowing down their rescue by several minutes, or hold steady and rely on darkness to conceal them until the last few climbed aboard.

A second ship zipped through the walls.

"Gunners!" she cried. "Target the first ship! I want constant cover now!"

The air erupted. The gunners fired continuously, spending countless bullets in an effort to prevent return fire.

It wasn't enough. A third missile crashed into their hull, rocking the ship and throwing shrapnel over the girls still swimming. Two ladders snapped and fell into the water.

She was going to have to spin the ship broadside to protect the girls. The maneuver would give the approaching Bullet ship an even bigger target. But she was out of options.

Just as she was about to give the order, the second Bullet ship did something unexpected: it opened fire on the first.

"Gloriana!" Nettle yelled from her post at the helm. "It has to be!"

"Keep firing!" Caledonia shouted to her gunners. "Get those girls on board!"

For another minute, her girls poured over the railing. One after the other, they landed in shivering heaps while the sky exploded behind them.

Another missile struck the ship. They heaved starboard amid sounds of twisting metal.

"Sledge!" she called.

"Let's move, Captain!" Sledge bellowed from his position by the ladders, his strong voice barely audible over the storm.

A third ship pushed through the walls, forcing their protector to flee south. Caledonia hoped it was Gloriana, and she hoped that wherever she ended up, it was better than here.

"Nettle! Get us out of here!" she called without hesitation.

The ship rumbled and roared, driving straight ahead, away from Slipmark, where soon the night ocean would obscure their trail.

Caledonia took one look at the crowd of girls now clustered on the deck below—her girls, her crew, her sisters—and she smiled.

CHAPTER TWENTY-SEVEN

Victory was never simple.

They'd done everything they'd set out to do. They'd done what had never been done before, and they deserved to celebrate that fact, to celebrate the return of her crew. But they'd also lost Triple, and they deserved to mourn her.

Caledonia couldn't make room for either. Not until she was certain they weren't being followed, until she'd put as much distance as possible between them and Slipmark. For an hour more, she kept her eyes on the sea in their wake, searching for signs of trouble until finally, she was convinced they were clear.

"Nettle," she said at long last. "Hand off the helm and go get that arm taken care of."

"Yes, Captain," she answered in a tired voice.

When the girl was gone, Caledonia headed belowdecks. Her steps were rushed and her breath quick as she hurried toward the galley, which was now transformed from dining hall to temporary barracks. Cots hung from the walls; tables and chairs were arranged in a makeshift common space; and the kitchen was serving cups of hot soup.

The girls were dressed in dry clothes and sat wrapped in blankets, cupping soup mugs between thin fingers and murmuring to one another in soothing tones.

Caledonia stopped a few feet into the room. Silence cast a perfect net as the girls all turned to lay their eyes on her. She saw Tin, standing tall in the midst of the Mary sisters, her strong arms wrapped around the youngest. She found Folly snuggled beneath a blanket, a deep gash across her forehead. There was Amina, seated with one of Hime's hands held between hers, wrapped in fresh gauze. There were girls clustered together and gathered around tables, there were girls tending to the needs of others and girls unable to rise from their cots. Ares crouched at Wen's bedside, tying off a row of stiches in her side. There was no sign of Oran, though he'd been so badly injured he was surely in the med bay. And there, in the center of the room, stood Pisces.

For a moment, everyone stared. Then Hime moved, letting her blanket fall away as she crossed the room to stand before Caledonia.

Captain, she signed, tapping her own shoulder briskly.

Relief broke in Caledonia like a dam. A laugh of a sob escaped her lips and she went to hug the girl, but Hime reared back and slapped her hard across the cheek.

The sting of it was as much in her heart as on her skin. Caledonia let surprise linger on her face as she pulled her eyes back to Hime's. The small girl breathed hard.

You left us, she signed. Anger was bright in her accusing eyes, and there were echoes of that same anger all around the room.

Caledonia nodded. "I deserved that."

At this, Hime released a smile like a sunrise. *We knew you'd come!*

Hime stepped forward and wrapped her lithe arms around Caledonia, squeezing her tightly. She was too thin and so cold, but there was nothing more beautiful than hugging her sisters. Caledonia held her just as tightly and let her tears spill against the girl's neck.

Amina was next, pressing her cheek to Caledonia's and a kiss near her ear. "Captain," she said in her quiet, steady way.

After that, it was all of them. Her girls crowded around her, hugging her and squeezing her hands, thanking her for coming or telling her they'd known all along that she would. She named them off in her head, trying to keep track and failing. She was just relieved to find so many still alive.

The only one who didn't come forward was Pisces. She kept her distance, standing back to watch, but not approach. Caledonia understood, and while she was increasingly desperate to pull her sister away, wrap her arms around her neck, and tell her everything, this was not the time and not the place. Their reunion would happen later.

When she'd seen everyone who could walk to her, she made her way to those who were too weak to stand. She knelt by their beds and squeezed their hands, looked into their eyes and spoke their names. They were glad to see her even if they were angry with her, too. She could feel their resentment at war with their relief, and she knew that she'd earned that conflict by abandoning them. It didn't feel good, but soon it would be in the past, firmly woven into the fabric of their lives.

"Whose ship is this?" Folly called, a demanding edge to her usually gentle voice.

"Mine," Caledonia answered simply. "Along with some new friends."

Caledonia turned to Pisces. It was hard to see her and not feel a swell of pride and affection. She was thinner than she'd been, all hard edges and defined muscles on her broad frame, and there was evidence of strain carved into the skin around her eyes. She'd been holding this crew together for months in Caledonia's absence. Now Caledonia was back, and everyone expected a new plan of action.

With a steadying breath, she faced her girls again, and now she traced the missing faces. "Darlo. Kit. Genevene."

"We lost Kit when we were taken," Tin said.

"Darlo and Genevene died in Slipmark," Amina added. "Their wounds were too great."

Folly stepped forward. Her cheeks slick with tears. "Pippa drowned."

Caledonia frowned. She'd seen Pippa on top of the tide can Oran had opened. She'd been one of the first in the water; she should have been one of the first out again.

"She waited for me," Folly answered her silent question. "And she got hit. I couldn't save her."

Caledonia felt her own tears falling in a seamless stream down her cheeks. "Lost," she said.

"But not forgotten," the rest answered solemnly.

Four. They'd lost four girls. Counting the five they'd lost in the Northwater, they were a crew of forty-five, including Ares.

"Eat your soup," Pisces commanded gently, gesturing for Caledonia to join her.

Pisces turned and moved briskly into the passageway, giving Caledonia the sudden and distinct impression that they were going to fight. But that was absurd. Wasn't it?

All their lives, Pisces had been nearly impossible to push into real anger. As younger girls, they'd argued over small things like who was using more than their fair share of paint to practice their letters or who'd taken the best fishing pole. Pisces had always been calm and observant of others, especially Caledonia, and that skill had given her the ability to see rising tensions before they snapped. She was the overwhelming tranquility of the deep ocean while Caledonia was the capricious surface, constantly in motion. But Pisces was angry now. Caledonia was sure of it, and she didn't know how to prepare to face it.

"Lead the way," Pisces said, stepping back to give Caledonia room to pass.

Caledonia's stomach pitched like a tiny ship in a massive storm. She nodded, mouth twisted tightly shut as she drove her heart back into its place. "My quarters," she said, taking the lead.

Her room was small with two berths that dropped away from the wall when it was time to sleep and just enough space for two people to stand. For a moment, neither girl spoke. They were alone, and it seemed that fact made Pisces just as uncomfortable as it did Caledonia.

It never would have been the case before. It never *had* been the case before.

"You changed your hair," Pisces said, gently breaking the silence. "I don't like it."

"Neither do I." Caledonia wanted to laugh, but her throat was too tight. "The red was too recognizable for Slipmark. Didn't want to blow it before I had a chance to find you."

Pisces's own hair was nearly as long as Caledonia's short locks. If this were any other time, Caledonia would offer to shave her head for her. But this wasn't the reunion she'd hoped for, and she didn't know how to proceed.

"Pi, I'm so—"

"I don't want to be their captain," Pisces said, cutting her off. "You have always been their captain and in spite of everything, they'd rather have you than me. It doesn't hurt me to admit that."

Taken off guard, Caledonia stood speechless.

"I don't want to challenge you. That wouldn't do the crew any good anyway," Pisces continued. "And I shouldn't be in charge. I got us caught and imprisoned. Not only do I not want to be captain, I don't *deserve* to be."

"And I do?"

Pisces was silent for a moment, her eyes dropping briefly to the floor. "No. But they—we—deserve a captain like you. It would be selfish and stupid of me not to recognize that. You're my captain. From the very first, you've been my captain, just as you're theirs."

Now Caledonia did smile. All the anxiety she'd felt over this reunion began to melt away. "Pi, I'm so glad—"

"Stop." Pisces's voice was flinty and sharp. She studied the space between them as though it were a book in which she might find the answers she needed. Then, without warning, she stepped forward and pulled Caledonia into a hug, pressing their cheeks together. She pulled back just as suddenly, catching Caledonia's face in her hands and pressing a firm kiss to her lips.

Then the distance was between them again, and Pisces drew a careful breath before speaking.

"You're my captain. And you're my sister. And I am so mad at you." When she looked up, her eyes brimmed with tears. "You're my sister, but you left me. You chose revenge over me, and you forced me into a role I *never* wanted." She paused, fists clenched between them. "I'm sure you rationalized that choice. I'm sure you thought I could handle it, but that's not the point. You didn't ask. So I don't know what 'sister' really means to you. Until you figure it out, and until I can figure out how to forgive you . . . stay away from me."

Pisces turned and left the room, taking all the air with her.

CHAPTER TWENTY-EIGHT

"The damage, all things considered, is minimal. Nothing we can't handle on the move." Harwell trotted along at her side to give his report, and while it was good news, Caledonia couldn't agree that the damage was minimal.

"Thank you, Harwell. Keep your teams on it. I want this ship fit before anyone rests for the night."

This was a terrible order. Everyone needed rest after the long night, but right now they needed to remain alert and get themselves ready to run again when the sun rose.

"Yes, Captain." Harwell hurried away with less enthusiasm than she'd grown used to seeing in his stride. He was tired. And it would only get worse for everyone.

She continued on her rounds, taking every opportunity to steer clear of the mess hall. She wanted to see her girls again, but with every step, she heard Pisces's voice. *Stay away from me.* Those words were like bullets, crashing again and again into her heart, punching holes in her lungs, ripping through her veins, and scorching her skin.

She'd expected the conversation to be difficult. She'd expected to have to defend her actions, to allow Pisces to be angry with her. She'd expected Pisces to be reluctant to give up command. After all, Caledonia had given her everything, and it wasn't fair of her to come back and make demands. She had expected a negotiation.

She hadn't expected this.

This was so much worse. She was a stone falling through water, and as she tumbled faster and faster into the black unknown, she lost her sense of direction. There was no up, no down, nothing except this endless falling. She didn't know how to apologize. She didn't even know if she should.

Had she found Pisces only to discover they would never be close again? Could she be a captain without her sister at her side?

Every question seemed to lead to one more devastating than the last. None of them had answers. At least, none had answers Caledonia wanted to entertain.

She walked confidently through the narrow passageways, ducking where the piping scooped low and stepping neatly over the occasional hatch. This time, she took the lesser used corridors leading to the storage rooms near the nose of the ship. It was there she found Pine.

He stood beside a long table bolted to the floor bearing an odd collection of objects. There were rocks and bullets, a few assorted carvings of wood, scraps of cloth all in shades of gray, even a few small pieces of tech.

Pine didn't look up when she entered, though he knew she was there. His focus was on a bit of metal cut into the shape of a bird, which he polished with an old rag. His movements were slow and methodical, almost meditative. When he finished, the bird was clean and bright. He moved on to the next and the next, setting them down or stringing them together in sets of three.

These were tokens for Triple. They didn't have her body to care for so they were building a memorial to her. One by one, the Blades had come to this room, bringing anything that reminded them of their lost friend.

"We have more of her than they ever will," he said.

Caledonia wasn't sure when she'd started crying. Hot tears splashed against her jacket. She pictured Triple striding past Nettle, protecting the girl, and giving Gloriana the time she needed to escape.

And for that, they'd left her behind. She would be collected and displayed on the crown of some Bullet ship, used to spread fear across the seas.

"We can honor her, put her to rest," Pine continued.

He wasn't angry with Caledonia, though he had every reason to be. She felt her thoughts slipping quickly toward regret and willed her mind to become as still as the ocean. She closed her eyes.

"It isn't your fault." Pine was standing in front of her now, peering down at her as though her thoughts were as clear to him as daylight. "We all consented to be here."

"You did," she agreed. "But every time I ask people to fight, I am in some way responsible. I have to be, or all of this becomes meaningless."

"We give this meaning," he said, holding her with a gaze as steady as the sun. "And when we decide to risk our lives, the only one responsible for that choice is us. Not you."

Always, Pine brought her to this place of uncomfortable honesty. "But I'm still choosing the fight. Putting you all at risk."

Pine stepped closer, taking her in with his eyes. "Caledonia, if you are willing to let us kill for you, you are also willing to let us die for you. You can't have half of that equation."

Her breath hitched in the back of her throat. She was still reasonably sure he hated her, but in this moment, she thought he might see her more clearly than anyone on this ship. Before she could respond, the hallway reverberated with the sound of running.

Caledonia raced from the room with Pine hard on her heels, seeking the source of the noise.

Her name rushed toward them. "Caledonia!"

Nettle.

The girl skidded to a furious stop. Her hair was wild, her cheeks flushed a tawny rose, and her small body was puffed up and ready for a fight.

"What is it?" Caledonia demanded.

"That brick of a boy locked Oran in the hold!" Nettle cried.

"He should be in the med bay, but I just found out he's been in the hold since he came aboard."

Caledonia was already running. She raced straight through the galley and down a level toward the hold, where she found Sledge planted like a tree.

"Where is he?" she demanded.

Nettle was right. He should be in the med bay. He'd been covered in dozens of tiny stab wounds, abused in myriad other ways she couldn't see. He should be resting where someone could give him proper care.

Sledge stared down at her, angry betrayal scrawled across his features. "He's the Steelhand, and he doesn't belong on this ship."

"He just helped save my crew," Caledonia countered. "He had one of those cans open before we even got there. He has as much right to be here as anyone else."

"You want to know why he had that can open?" Sledge shouted. "Because he designed it!"

It was the truth, and it was a terrible one. The Steelhand would know the weakness in his own design. But he'd used his knowledge to free a third of her crew before they arrived. He wasn't the same person he'd been in Aric's fleet. He couldn't be.

"He's my crew," she asserted. "A former Fiveson like you're all former Bullets. Or does that only apply to the people you know?" As she said the words, she heard Triple's voice accusing her of the same, and the air froze in her lungs. "Move aside."

Sledge moved, but only just, forcing her to press between him and the wall.

The hold, deep in the belly of the *Beacon*, was a splinter of a room cut in half by a narrow hallway. On either side, dimly lit cells with barred doorways and steel walls were stacked from end to end. None of the rooms bore a porthole, so the only ventilation was provided by a sluggish fan set into the wall at the far end. It was stuffy and warm and smelled distantly of sweat.

As Caledonia entered, Oran groaned from where he sat slumped against a wall in a cell near the door.

"Oran," she snapped. Irritated, though not at him.

He sat up, revealing a fresh bruise on one cheek. Anger ruffled deep in her chest.

"Caledonia." His voice turned her name into an ocean, rising and falling with a mix of wonder and surprise. He cradled his chest as he struggled upright, everything about him communicating pain. Then his eyes flicked over to Sledge.

Effortless and subtle, his posture shifted, and instead of weakness, he communicated rigid poise. "Tell me your new friend's name."

Caledonia blinked at him. She turned on her heel, facing Sledge. "Unlock his cell."

"No," Sledge stated. "You don't know what you're asking."

"I thought you were in the business of giving Bullets a fresh start?"

Sledge nodded, deep in his signature solemnity. "Bullets. Not Fivesons." His eyes shifted to a point over her shoulder. "Not *him*."

Caledonia tipped her chin up and fixed him with a gaze dipped in steel. This was her ship. This was her crew. And she would let him know it.

"He's my crew, not a prisoner. I want him in the med bay," she said, keeping her voice low, her words precise. "I won't say it again."

Two figures stepped into the doorway. Caledonia didn't have to look to know it was Pisces and Pine. This was the kind of stand-off that could leave these two crews fractured beyond repair. But if she backed down, let Sledge direct this moment, she'd lose all the ground she'd managed to gain with the Blades.

Sledge clenched his jaw. His eyes tightened, and he let his glare drift once more to Oran. He stayed that way for a long moment, old resentments warring with new loyalties. He didn't want the Fiveson on the ship, but he also wanted to work with Caledonia.

"Keys." She held out her hand.

The air warmed with tension. Sledge looked from Caledonia to Oran, his expression clinging to anger, but edging toward something like fear.

Then Sledge released the barricade of his arms and fished the keys from his pocket, dropping them into Caledonia's hand. She immediately passed them to Pisces, keeping her body in front of Oran's cell like a shield.

"Don't leave him alone," Sledge growled, turning to leave the prison.

And as Pisces gathered Oran up and led him out, Caledonia realized she didn't know if the statement had been offered for Oran's safety—or their own.

CHAPTER
TWENTY-NINE

Once again, Caledonia was in the position of needing to keep Oran as close as possible. If Sledge's threat hadn't made that clear, their walk through the ship did.

Every Blade they passed paused to watch him go by. Their expressions went slack or their eyes distant or they stepped back with heads ducked to avoid his gaze altogether. On the air, a single word traveled in a shrinking whisper: *Steelhand*.

For his part, Oran rejected Pisces's support and walked as though he contained nothing but strength in his battered limbs. His torso was bruised and sliced so that his skin was more mottled purples and reds than pale brown, and his feet were bare against the metal floor, yet he walked as though he drew power from the pain and cold. In the presence of those who knew his past, he walked, Caledonia thought, like a Fiveson.

Even she felt the pull of it.

Leaving him in the med bay was out of the question. Instead, they brought him to the room next door to Caledonia's. It was a mirror image of her own, with the cots secured to the opposite wall.

Pisces paused at the door. "I'll find Hime," she said, expression shuttered as she left.

Stay away from me.

The words would haunt any interaction they had. Anything Caledonia said right now would only make matters worse. So she swallowed her heart and turned back to the Fiveson.

The instant the door closed behind Pisces, he collapsed against the lower cot, only Oran again. All the strength he'd shown on their journey through the ship vanished, and his breath came in shallow puffs.

Caledonia crossed the room to kneel before him. "I'm sorry. That shouldn't have happened. And I should have known it might."

"Not your fault," he said with a careful shake of his head, eyes drifting closed. "I just need a minute."

She began to stand, but his hand darted out and caught hers. She froze.

"Caledonia." Oran's voice was low and strained. "I thought you were dead."

His fingers curled around her own, rough but warm and so tempting. She thought of the kiss she'd taken. The thrill of it, the electric current in her blood. She wanted it again.

And maybe she could have it. Her heart was raw, still aching from the loss of Triple and the unexpected rift with Pisces.

Everything was complicated and difficult, but maybe this could be simple.

She threaded her fingers firmly through his, drawing him to his feet with a tug. His eyes flew open in surprise, his lips parted, and she stepped in close. And then she stopped, hovering an inch from him.

"Cala," he breathed, warm air ghosting over her lips.

As her eyelids fluttered closed with longing, she realized what she was doing. Nothing about Oran could ever be simple.

She pulled away. "I thought you were just a Fiveson," she answered.

A doleful smile tilted one side of his lips. "I suppose we were both wrong."

This wasn't the boy she'd left aboard the *Mors Navis*. That boy had been fighting for his life, eager and desperate and not a threat to anyone. This? This was a young man whom she'd seen bring a hundred Bullets to silence and stand boldly in the face of Sister. This was the Steelhand. "You should have told me." She pulled her hand from his and stood back. She missed the contact immediately and chastised herself for the feeling. He was a former Fiveson, and more dangerous than she had time to parse.

Oran didn't back away. His muscles flexed against the cold, and his skin was smeared with blood. A hundred tiny wounds. "Caledonia. I came to you because I needed help. And I've stayed with your crew because I need whatever is left of my life to be better than it was. But I won't hide anything from you. Not ever. I will tell you anything you want to know. Just . . ." He pressed his lips together, the smallest hesitation urging him to stop. "Before you ask, make sure you want to know."

She stared straight into his tree-ring eyes. Part of her wanted to demand he tell her everything—all the things that made Sledge loathe him, all the things that made the rest of the Blades cower from him, all the things she didn't know. But another part? She was afraid.

Caledonia swallowed hard. Her eyes fell to the marks over his heart. Hers was one of several shallow cuts. She wondered if he knew which one. Without Silt in his blood they would scar in the natural brown of his skin. His own mark on her life wasn't visible, but it was just as pronounced.

"I need you to know something about me," she said. "Lir killed my family. I met him on a shore run in the Bone Mouth. Alone. And he asked me for mercy. He said he wanted a different life, and I believed him." She paused, grinding her teeth at the memory. "That was the first time a Bullet lied to me, and I lost nearly everything because of it."

Oran's eyes widened in sudden understanding. "Of course. Of course that was you."

Anger spiked in Caledonia's veins. Lir's words from the night she attacked him on his ship snaked through her memory. *You gave me a great gift that night.* And the gift she'd given Lir? That was his power. He'd risen to the rank of Fiveson on the bones of her slain family. Oran may not have known who they were, but he'd have heard about that night.

And he'd have done something just as horrible to become a Fiveson.

The realization forced her back a step.

"Caledonia?" Oran asked, concerned.

"What did you do?" she demanded. "To become a Fiveson?"

The concern fell from Oran's face. He became a wall, revealing nothing. "Are you asking me?"

"I—" she stopped herself. This was precisely what he'd meant moments ago. Knowing the answer to this would change everything.

"Hime will be here soon," she said.

Oran held her eyes as he nodded once, solemn and resolved to keep his promise to her no matter the cost.

One day she would be ready. But not today.

CHAPTER THIRTY

When dawn threaded the horizon with a single promising band of gold, Harwell moved through the ship with the bell, rousing everyone with its tinny clang. As he went, he repeated the same phrase. "All friends bury the dead." His voice was a sweet, earthy counter to the high note of the bell.

The crew gathered on deck, slipping silently into the brisk morning air. Caledonia watched as her girls emerged. Apart from those who were unable to move easily, every girl was here. Even Far drifted out and clung to the edges of the crowd like a timid spirit. Oran kept his distance, positioning himself in the command tower. It was better that way. There was no point in stirring tensions.

Pine was perched on the starboard railing. Looped around his hands was a string of every trinket and stone the Blades had brought him over the course of the night. He'd collected them like beads in sets of three, knotted tightly together. Sledge stood on the deck nearby, one side of him washed in fresh light, the other still dusted in purple shadow. He was so still, so peaceful, yet sunlight clung to the tears sliding down his long cheeks.

"Captain?" Nettle had come alongside her, her eyes shiny with tears.

Caledonia paused. She knew what was on the girl's mind because it was on her own. "You acted without permission," she said. "But so did Triple."

"I'm sorry," the girl answered with a nod.

There was no easy way through this. Not for any of them, but especially not for Nettle. She would take part of the blame for Triple's death and carry it with her the rest of her life. Caledonia knew it because she would do the same.

With a gentle sigh, she turned to Nettle and placed a hand lightly on her shoulder. "Your actions saved Gloriana. And she saved us."

Her tears spilled over, creating tiny streams along her cheeks. "But Triple—"

"I don't blame you." Caledonia bent to look directly in Nettle's eyes when she said, "Victory without regret is tyranny. When we fight for each other, we win, no matter what."

Nettle's tears came faster even as she frowned against them. "This doesn't feel like winning."

With a sigh, Caledonia answered, "It rarely does."

When everyone was gathered, Sledge raised his booming voice to the young morning. "Our friend Triple has given her life in service to those who still live. We see you, Triple."

All around, the Blades responded, "We see you, Triple."

Harwell chimed the bell. The note reverberated in the air, a sweet, solemn song to accompany the lapping waves below and the gentle breeze above. Only when it had faded completely did Sledge speak again.

"She transformed herself from the tool of an oppressor into an instrument of her own power. We remember you, Triple."

Again, the response, this time with a few more voices. "We remember you, Triple."

The bell chimed, lifting sighs and memories as it slowly faded. Caledonia felt a hand slip into her own. She didn't know when Hime had come to stand beside her, but she was glad to have her. She squeezed her fingers in her own.

"She was here of her own consent; no other controlled her. We honor you, Triple."

This time, the entire ship answered him. "We honor you, Triple."

Again the bell. And this time it came with the sounds of tears.

Caledonia's free hand was taken between two rough palms and gently pressed. She knew before turning that the hands holding hers belonged to Amina, but she was surprised to find that she was now surrounded by her crew. Her sisters.

"And we gift you to the deep, where you will transform one final time. In peace."

As Sledge spoke these final words, Pine turned with his bundle, letting it slip from his hands to the ocean below. Harwell rang the bell one last time, holding the instrument aloft so the sound followed in Triple's wake, so that she didn't leave them in silence.

Now Pisces stepped forward bearing four glowing sun pips secured to dishes of blue foam.

"Kit," she stated, and as one, the crew repeated her name. "Darlo. Genevene. Pippa." She paused after each name while the crew echoed them. "Our hearts go with you. May you keep us from below."

Turning, Pisces let each sun pip fall against the waves. Caledonia watched, recalling sharply the moment they'd given Lace to the sea. Lurking just behind that memory was a sharp stab of guilt, a reminder that she had not been there to see Redtooth's funeral. Or that of any of her other girls who had given their lives in the fight against *Electra*: Alesa, Quinn, Thatcher, Maddy.

She had missed those important moments, and those gaps had loosened the weave of her crew's fabric. They were here. They were inviting her back into that tapestry. But she couldn't simply rejoin their pattern. She needed to create something new. Something stronger.

Releasing Hime's and Amina's hands, she stepped into the center of the gathering. The sun was warm against her tearstained cheeks, the wind chilling her fingertips. She let her sadness, her anxiety become a slender core of steel extending from her crown to her toes. She let it hold her up instead of drag her down.

The eyes of dozens of boys and girls landed on her, and for a moment she felt tacked in place. They were a marked ship on the edge of the Bullet Seas, they were the people who'd taken more than Aric cared to give, and they were waiting for her to give them a way forward. Several of them were waiting for her to make good on the promise to get them on the other side of the Net. Before she could give them what they wanted, she would have to give them what they needed. Right now, that was one another.

"Friends," she began in a low voice, commanding the space without volume. "You don't know one another yet, but you will. We have decisions to make and seas to cover, and to do that well, we must work together."

Unease ruffled through the crowd. There were two distinct sets of people here: the Blades and her crew. And even though every single Blade had been essential in freeing her crew from Slip-mark, they had precious little reason to trust one another.

She couldn't force trust where there was none. So she would show them where it already existed.

"Sledge," she called.

He stepped forward, masking his uncertainty beneath a stony exterior. He was still angry with her, but anger didn't erase trust. At least, she hoped it didn't.

"Pisces," she called.

Pisces moved to the front of the crowd, crossing her arms over her chest. She, too, was angry with Caledonia. At least they had that in common. Caledonia took a steadying breath and reminded herself that it wasn't her job to be liked. It was her job to keep them alive.

"I want you to each select one person and join me in the box. Hime, you're with me."

Speaking in a single voice, Sledge and Pisces answered, "Yes, Captain."

CHAPTER
THIRTY-ONE

The box was the small, windowless chamber beneath the bridge. When this had been a Bullet ship, it had served to collect their records and accounting of how many conscripts came from which colonies. One wall was covered in drawers, snapped firmly into place and filled with papers. A small ledge extended along the wall opposite, just wide enough to use as a sort of desk, and in one corner was a single chair, now occupied by Sledge, who only barely fit in these tight rooms to begin with. Sitting put him closer to their eye level and made him somewhat less imposing.

The rest stood around the room in a semicircle with Caledonia at the center. Amina waited with one hand braced against her hip, her long braids spilling behind her like a cloak. Hime was next to her, hands folded quietly in front. Pine leaned against the back wall with a generous scowl pulling at his lips. Sledge had his elbow braced against his knees, an air of calm expectation about him. And Pisces stood directly across from Caledonia.

They weren't going to like everything she had to say.

"You are all used to commanding your own people," she began. "And we need to stop thinking of ourselves as two crews on one ship. I want clear lines of communication and reporting. We have seventy-five people on this ship, sixty-nine excluding the six of us, and I want every single one of them to know who they're responsible for and who they report to."

"I want Tin on Operations," Pisces started.

Pine pushed away from the wall, ready to stake his own claim, but Sledge held up one hand and he stopped.

"This isn't a discussion, not yet." Caledonia kept her tone even and decisive. She'd spent the rest of her sleepless night bringing her own thoughts into order, and now it was time to do the same to this crew. Given the opportunity, Pisces and Pine would fight to put people they trusted most into authoritative positions. They would argue for their own immediate comfort. It was understandable, yet shortsighted. This wasn't about reaffirming trust where it already existed, but about building trust to cement this new crew.

"What is this then?" Pisces asked, looking nervous.

"Our command crew."

This time it was Amina who reacted. Her body stiffened as though shocked, and she cast her angry glare across the room. "What about Tin? Or Nettle? The people who have commanded in your absence are no longer welcome?"

Caledonia had prepared for this; she'd told herself it would happen and that it would feel like tumbling in a massive wave.

But she'd been wrong. It was so much worse. The full impact of Amina's anger felt like trying to draw breath only to discover a massive weight was pressing her lungs flat. The girl took a step toward Caledonia, eyes narrowing shrewdly. Amina had not expressed much of her anger since Caledonia's return. She'd fallen so firmly back into place that it was tempting to think she wasn't angry at all. It would have been foolish to believe it. She was angry, and it was surfacing now because she was protecting her crew.

"Captain, we should be the ones to discuss this with you."

In the past, that's precisely what Caledonia would have done. In a different situation, perhaps, it was still what she would do. But their current circumstances were too fragile. They were all afraid of what the others might do. Caledonia alone trusted both her original crew and her new one. It was up to her to make the hard choices right now, not cater to individual fears.

She held Amina's iron gaze and answered, "No."

Caledonia waited, letting her authority linger for just a second longer. This was the point on which she would hold her ground no matter how painful. She could understand Amina's anger without folding beneath it, and if she wanted to pull this crew together, that's exactly what she was going to have to do.

"Our job is to turn seventy-five people into a single crew. The only way we can do that is if we look united. You can disagree with me and you can let me know, but when we're in front of them, what is decided in this room is law." This time, she didn't pause, but pressed on. "Pi is my second-in-command; that will remain unchanged. Sledge, I want you in charge of readiness. We may not have bows, but use what you can find and keep everyone in fighting form. Pine, you're on weapons. Know what we have and who can use what. Amina, shiptech. I want your eyes on every piece of this ship; I want to know what we have that we aren't using. Hime, keep your finger on our pulse as firmly as you can. Tin is operations; I want Harwell on engineering; and Nettle stays with helm."

It wasn't much of a shuffle in responsibilities, and she didn't expect to see much upset surface in the larger crew. But here in this room, these five people strained against the discomfort.

"Pisces will oversee the division of teams among the crew. Sledge, I want you to work with her. Let her know which of your people have what skills or where they might fit best. I don't want to find ourselves in a situation where we don't know the shiptechs from the divers." Now she paused, giving herself room to breathe and survey the room once more. "Steely?"

Pine and Amina nodded, but Sledge leaned in. "What about the Steelhand? Where will you keep him?"

Caledonia settled her hands on her hips and treated the question as though it were like any other. "I want Oran with me on bridge crew. He has intelligence we can use. When he's not there, I want him on shiptech with Amina."

Pisces asked, "Is this a discussion now?"

Whatever bomb waited behind that question, Caledonia felt prepared for it. "It is," she answered.

"I request that you make Amina your second-in-command. Put me on engineering and Harwell on shiptech. From what I've seen, he'll have a knack for it, and engines have always been mine."

It wasn't a terrible suggestion. In fact, it was one Caledonia had considered. She and Pisces had always operated as a completely united front. Knowing that a rift existed between them was painful, but it wasn't a reason not to keep her at her side. Every single day, she'd have to confront the uncomfortable new reality between them; she'd be forced to remember all over again exactly what she'd done to change who they were together. It would be a constant, agonizing chorus in her head of *your fault your fault your fault*.

"Request denied," Caledonia said, letting some of her tender feelings for her friend soften her voice. "You may have lost your trust in me, Pi, but I haven't lost my trust in you."

Pisces's eyes shone, and for a flash of a second it was her old friend standing before her, full of complicated feelings and things she wanted to say to her sister and best friend. Then she blinked, and Caledonia saw the mask fall back into place.

Resisting the urge to sigh, Caledonia continued. "I know you're good with engines, but our crew is nearly twice what it used to be, and I need you to know who they are, what they can do. Can you do that for me?"

This time, Pisces didn't hesitate. "Yes, Captain," she said.

If they'd been alone, Caledonia would have said more, but this was her command crew. They needed to know there was strain between their captain and their second, and they needed to know that it wasn't going to keep either of them from doing their jobs. Anything beyond that was personal.

"Good." Caledonia took a step back. "I know you're all tired. I know our people are injured and hungry and anxious to know what's next. And the only way we're going to make it through this is if we work together."

All five retreated into silence as they considered her words.

Finally, Sledge stood, looming as he said, "I'm with you, Caledonia, though I haven't forgotten your promise."

"What promise?" Pisces asked abruptly.

"To punch the Net," Pine supplied. "That was the deal. After we got you out of Slipmark, she'd help us punch the Net, Tassos be damned."

Pisces turned to Caledonia, eyes wide with a subtle surprise. "What about Donnally?"

Caledonia swallowed hard.

"I promised to get the Blades through the Net, and that's what I'll do," she said, knowing that Pisces would see it for the evasion it was.

We can't punch the Net now, Hime signed. *The crew is too weak.*

"I know," Caledonia agreed.

"Ah." Pine leaned forward, eyes passing from Hime to Caledonia. "How do we communicate with you? With her? If she doesn't hear?"

"She hears," Amina answered. "She just doesn't speak with her voice."

"She says the crew is too weak to punch the Net," Pisces said, emphasizing where her words matched her signs. It was an imprecise alignment of the two languages, but it was how they'd all started. "It's taken us years to learn. We can teach you, if you want."

Pine nodded, eyes so hungry for more it was almost endearing.

"So where are we going, if not the Net?" Sledge asked.

They were interrupted by a fierce pounding on the doors.

They opened it to find Harwell, eyes wide with alarm. "We've got towers," he announced. "They've found us."

CHAPTER
THIRTY-TWO

Three ships. One in the west and two in the east.

Caledonia climbed to the command tower. Oran glanced in her direction, but before he could report, one of Amina's Knots called out, "Two towers in the west!"

Caledonia cursed. She had a disjointed crew, and now she had four ships to outrun or outsmart.

The Bullet ships resolved themselves quickly, sailing near enough that their profiles were visible from deck level. But there they stopped. Sizing them up from a distance.

"Those are Venn's ships," Oran stated with easy confidence.

"Agreed." Sledge's expression darkened and his teeth clashed together, rocks rolling beneath the surface. "What are they waiting for? Why don't they attack?" he asked, eyes darting nervously from one set of ships to the next.

"They're trying to draw us out. Get us to do their work for them." Caledonia understood Sledge's urgency, but it wasn't useful to her right now. "I'd prefer not to. Nettle! Let's tack a few times on this bearing. Give them something to look at." *And react to*, she thought.

Nettle drummed up the engines and took the ship back and forth a few times without driving toward Venn's position. It gave Caledonia a few new vantage points on the waiting ships, but elicited no response from the notorious Fiveson Venn.

What was he doing?

"Crew is armed and ready, Captain," Pisces called, climbing up to the command deck.

Caledonia nodded. Something was off here. All four ships were holding steady. They had every advantage, so why not engage while Caledonia was in the weakest position?

"Do you think there are deepships?" Pine asked softly. "I know you don't think they were Aric's, but isn't it possible they were?"

"Deepships?" Pisces repeated. "I thought those were legend?"

"Not anymore," Caledonia answered. "We encountered one on our way to Slipmark, but they thought we were a Bullet ship and attacked. Aric doesn't like to waste his own resources like that."

"Maybe he was trying to make a point," Pine suggested. "And who else could have that kind of tech? It's not the sort of thing you just stumble upon."

It was a good question and a good point; a mystery they would need to unravel at some future time. Right now, the only relevant concern was whether or not a deepship was in these waters. Every instinct Caledonia had told her there wasn't, but there was *something* she couldn't see.

"The deepships aren't Aric's."

Nettle had slipped up behind them, quiet as a cloud. She smiled with a brilliant mixture of contrition and gratification.

"Explain," Caledonia commanded.

"Hesperus," the girl piped. "The Sly King is the only one who has them."

"Of Cloudbreak?" Pisces asked, frowning. "He doesn't have any ships. He's not allowed."

Nettle nearly rolled her eyes. "Well, he's also technically not allowed to aid anyone Aric has an interest in, but . . ."

"How certain are you?" Caledonia asked.

Nettle lifted her chin, the paler skin of her scrollwork scars like the curling path of a wave in the ocean. "I'm certain."

That was enough for Caledonia. But that didn't explain why Venn was being so coy. His ships still hadn't moved. It was starting to put her on edge.

"What's wrong?" Pisces asked, stepping in close.

"Something feels . . ."

"Captain," Oran called, a warning in the tenor of is voice. "We have a problem."

"What is it?"

"Venn doesn't sail four ships—"

"He sails five," Sledge finished in alarm.

"Captain!" Amina called from her position on the roof of the bridge.

The girls spun. Behind them, a crusher ship was in pursuit and much too close for comfort.

Caledonia ignored the way her heart squeezed as she raced toward the bridge. "Engines to full!"

The ship roared, moving sluggishly for a few seconds before it gathered enough power for real speed. Once more, Caledonia's body anticipated a faster transition than this ship could provide, leaving her out of sync for a disorienting second.

She was furious with herself. Venn had kept her focused on him while he sent a smaller ship to flank her. Its low profile made it nearly invisible to her Knots until it was too late. Now they were on the run, and he was in control.

"Incoming!" Amina shouted from above.

They were too slow, too heavy, too far behind the momentum of the crusher. Pine had his gunners positioned to open fire on the incoming vessels, but this wasn't going to be a fire fight.

"Strap in!" Caledonia shouted. "Brace for impact!"

The crusher was on them in a second. It held its course and speed, and as their own engines struggled to push them faster, the incoming ship rammed them, bruising their starboard hull with its punishing metal wedge.

Caledonia slammed into the side of the bridge, her knee cracking against the wall with a spike of pain.

The crusher's nose was still pressed into their side, yet no Bullets rushed to board them, and none fired from the deck. Instead, the crusher was revving its engines. They were pushing them. But where?

In two steps she was on the nose of the ship, scouring the surrounding plane for any sign of Venn's other four ships, but she found none. Ahead, it was just them and the ocean.

"Captain!" Pisces called, darting up the ladder to the command deck. A bright smear of blood marked her green top and the palm of her hand. "Captain, we've got a breach."

"How bad?"

"We've got a split on level two, above the waterline. It hit the galley." She paused for just a second, fingers curling into her bloody palm. "Far's hurt."

Caledonia clamped down on her specific concern for Far. Hime would have her. "Can we contain the breach?"

Pisces frowned. "Not until they let us go."

"Don't let up on those engines, Nettle!" Caledonia called, moving once more toward the bridge. Venn wasn't moving in. It didn't make any sense, but she'd take whatever space he gave her. "We won't make this easy for them."

The girl was a fixed point at the wheel, her features set and determined. Behind her, Harwell was a spear of panic. He looked out the windows at the western sea over their port side.

"Captain," he said, voice thin.

Ahead, the water had changed. It was no longer a smooth black plane, but full of chop. It was almost as if thousands of scales flashed along the surface.

Caledonia frowned. "What is that?"

"A whirl." Sledge was braced in the doorway.

Caledonia had heard stories of the part of the ocean where a storm opened up beneath you and sucked ships down to the deep. She'd thought they were only stories.

"It's real," she said, turning her astonished eyes forward once more and finding the paler ridges that marked the edge of the vortex. They extended in rings just below the horizon, stretching at least a mile wide, possibly more. As they drew nearer, a thin, screeching wail rose from within the whirl as though the ocean itself screamed.

"It's about to be a little too real." Harwell's voice trembled. "But it's not on the map!"

Oran was at her shoulder, eyes pinned to the torrential water ahead. "That's because it's not always here. It appears once in a ten-moon."

That was why Venn wasn't moving in. He was keeping his distance because he could. And because he had to. The whirl would do his work for him, but if he got too close, it would take them all into its treacherous rings. That was her only advantage. With Venn holding back, all she needed to do was get free of the crusher. Then she could put the whirl between her and Venn.

"Gunners! Starboard!" Pine's commands were accompanied by gunfire.

"They've come along the hull, Captain," Sledge reported. "They're going to try and—"

An explosion sent a short plume of fire up the starboard hull, nudging the ship hard to port. The deck tilted, the hull groaned, and one propeller rose above the waterline, smashing uselessly against the ocean.

Sledge and Pisces vanished into the belly of the ship. The gunfire faded, and Caledonia knew without being told that it was because the Bullets had accomplished their work. They'd put another hole in their hull and retreated into the protection of their reinforced ship. Why waste lives and ammo when you didn't have to?

"Captain." Pisces returned soaked in seawater, her breath quick. "They punched a hole in level three. In the hold and forward storerooms. We're taking on water."

CHAPTER THIRTY-THREE

With a hole in their side, the whirl would pull them under as easily as if they were a flower petal. Panic sang a single piercing note in Caledonia's mind, warning her that there was no way out, that she was about to lose her second ship and kill her entire crew. It reverberated through her body, freezing her in place.

And then she quashed it.

"Oran, tell me why it appears here," she said, letting her world narrow on him for a moment.

"We think there's a deep trench here. The whirl shows up when two opposing currents pass over it. That's our—their—best guess."

She nodded, returning her sights to the whirl, her thoughts to the task ahead.

"Pi, take a team. Get everyone off level three and do what you can to seal the breach." Pisces nodded once and was gone in an instant. "Harwell, tell everyone to strap in; Nettle, kill the engines," she said calmly. "And give me the wheel."

Nettle was all too happy to comply. The engines faded. The ship tilted more firmly into the crusher. The ocean roared around them, fore and aft. Caledonia placed her hands on the wheel. She let her palms rest firmly against the worn wood, her fingers curled loosely there so that she could feel the rumble of the ship in the pads of her fingertips. She adjusted her stance, placing her feet firmly beneath her hips, letting the ship become an extension of her own body.

Then she waited.

The scream of the ocean grew nearer, the rings of the vortex stood out creamy white against the muddy blue of the surrounding waters, and the air was dense with salty mist.

"It sounds hungry," Harwell said, not even bothering to hide his fear.

"She sounds furious," Nettle added with considerably more wonder and admiration in her voice.

Caledonia thought it sounded like a warning, but it was one she didn't have the luxury of heeding.

"Everyone's off level three," Pisces reported. The edge in her voice conveyed that the damage was tremendous, but no lives had been lost. "We've sealed off the forward quarter. Still working on the breach."

The ship was still taking on water. It would make them bottom heavy, front heavy, and even more difficult to maneuver in the rough waters ahead. But there was nothing to be done about it.

It was up to Caledonia now.

After another long minute, the pushing stopped. The crusher reversed so suddenly that both ships jerked as it released its bruised prey and screamed in the other direction to avoid the vortex.

The *Beacon* twisted, pulling itself upright and sweeping along as the ocean willed it. Caledonia held the wheel with a careful hand as she studied the current now controlling her ship.

The water will tell you where it's been and where it's going, her mother had said. *If you know how to speak its language, you will always know what to do.*

Ridges of water swirled in long arcs toward the center of the pool, where the water tucked down as though someone stood beneath the surface and tugged. Not a single current, but two, traveling in opposite directions alongside each other, forcing the water to bend and pull in this pattern.

As fascinated as Caledonia was, she had no time to consider it. The ship listed hard to starboard, spinning as the stern was snatched by the opposing current. From one breath to the next, the ship was in a spin. Their nose swung wildly around, and they pitched steeply from port back to starboard.

Caledonia could feel the sluggish climb of her ship as the water trapped on level three weighed them down. The starboard side dipped perilously low, allowing water to slosh over the gash into level two. Every single drop they took on made them heavier, less buoyant.

The bridge was silent. Her crew standing at the ready to complete any order she might give. But there was none. Not until she found her opening.

The spinning slowed, but did not stop. They rocked and spun and rocked and spun until it felt as though her own belly had been transformed into a whirl like the one on which they sailed.

She felt her internal balance adjusting to their new heft, forced herself to keep her breath even and slow, to match the new rhythm of the current around them. And as the ship spun around once more, she steered directly into the opposing current. The spinning stopped.

"Oh, thank you, Captain." Harwell's voice was green.

"Don't vomit in my bridge, Harwell," was Caledonia's only response.

She kept her eyes on the sea road ahead, her hands firm on the wheel.

"Nettle, I need those engines again."

"Yes, Captain."

The engines roared and they flew, propelled both by their own power and the power of the whirl. Faster and faster, they climbed to speeds this ship wasn't capable of on its own. The ship bit more deeply into the ridged water. And for a moment, the sea dragged at the open gash in their side, trying to pull them sideways into the center of the whirl. But Caledonia held firm.

She kept their nose aligned with the rushing water as she

read every ripple and ridge and—there!—a smooth sash of water cutting toward the center of the whirl.

Caledonia aimed directly for it, letting the ship travel at an angle. While their propellers drove from behind, the water hammered against their broadside, pushing them sideways even as they traveled forward. She felt the ship bucking, stuttering as it struggled to resist its own heavy belly and the drain of the whirl.

Sweat slipped between her shoulder blades, her jaw clenched tight. She could sense the eyes in the room moving between her and the whirl. There was Sledge and Oran, Nettle and Harwell, and Pisces standing nearest of all. Each of them held tight to their trust in her, and she, in turn, held the other end of that same trust, letting it tether her in the midst of so much chaos.

The ship dipped ever lower, listing harder and harder toward its wounded side. Caledonia held the wheel steady. The edge of the whirl was visible now. She could see the place where the current transitioned to smooth, flat waters.

But they were slowing down, tipping even farther to starboard.

"Kill the engines, Nettle."

Caledonia had no choice but to steer back into the whirl, letting the banded currents sweep them around the wide circle, ever closer to that perilous center. Though still listing, the ship regained some of its balance. They needed speed.

"When we come back around, drive the engines up." Caledonia didn't dare take her eyes off the roiling plane before her. If she missed a single shift, they could find themselves careering toward the center once more.

Her shoulders bunched tight, her palms began to sweat, and her arms trembled. Doubt crept in around the edges of her focus. What if this didn't work?

A slender hand pressed against her shoulder blade. "You have us, Captain," Pisces soothed.

The simple gesture was charged with energy. Caledonia felt her muscles settle, and the instant that sash of smooth water came into view once more, she ordered the engines to full.

With one final burst of power, they broke away from the whirl, limping out like a beached whale. Far across the whirl, Five-son Venn's ships were small shapes against a tired afternoon sky. If they pursued, they would have to sail around the whirl, giving Caledonia an even bigger lead than she already had.

"Engines are struggling, Captain," Harwell warned.

Caledonia nodded. "Just keep us going until we can't."

The ship rocked slowly back and forth like a bell, far too heavy on the bottom, far too low in the water. But they were out and they were alive, and that was a small piece of victory.

"No signs of pursuit," Amina reported.

"Nice sailing, Captain!" Nettle cried.

It sparked an even larger outcry of relief and approval from the rest of the crew, still mostly gathered on deck. Right now, it didn't matter that they were taking on water or that they were still mostly strangers. It only mattered that they'd worked together and survived.

"We might be afloat right now, but we won't stay that way if we don't start patching those holes!" Caledonia cried, bringing the crew back to the problem at hand.

"Divers! I want you port side!" Tin was shouting.

"Shiptechs, follow me!" Pine added, heading belowdecks.

Oran stepped out of the bridge and slid down the ladder to follow. The second he was out of sight, Caledonia felt a twist of tension in her gut.

"That was a bright piece of sailing, Captain," Pisces said, coming to stand at her shoulder.

The compliment tugged her thoughts away from Oran, straight into the hopeful pool of Pisces's affection. "Shouldn't have had to do it to begin with."

"Maybe not, but you got us out of it. All of us. Like you always do."

She was speaking to Caledonia, but there was another layer to her words. They carried small knives, all pointing inward.

"I should've seen that crusher coming," Caledonia admitted with as much ownership of her mistakes as possible. "But I didn't. And now we have new problems."

Pisces nodded, clearly unsatisfied. Whatever it was she came to say, she hadn't said it.

"Pi." Caledonia reached across the space between them to place her hand on Pisces crossed arms. It lasted for a second, then Pisces pulled away.

"We'd better get down there."

Caledonia nodded, holding her breath tight in her chest. Yesterday, she'd been sure that her relationship with Pisces was breached beyond repair. Today? They may have taken a direct hit, but they were still afloat.

CHAPTER
THIRTY-FOUR

E verything inside the ship was wrong. The air smelled heavy and dank, sounds were uncharacteristically muted, even the bulkheads seemed to bend in ways they shouldn't.

Pine flew ahead of Caledonia, trusting her to follow. She stayed on his heels as they barreled through the corridors, past crew members flattened against the walls to let them pass.

"The hold and forequarter of level three are sealed, but there's a second breach in the desal room!" Pine called over his shoulder. "The pumps can't keep up!"

Caledonia kept her eyes ahead, but there were signs of distress everywhere, and it was hard not to take stock as they passed.

Level two was unrecognizable. The crusher had pierced the wall of the kitchen, driving straight into the mess. Steel curled viciously toward the interior of the ship, destroying the pantry, stoves, sinks—everything required to feed a crew of seventy-five. The ground was littered with fallen chairs and tufts of green vegetables. It was hard to imagine anyone had survived, especially if they'd been in the kitchen at the time.

A breeze laced with smoke and the promise of rain drifted through the gash beyond, which the sky was darkening with clouds. Caledonia caught it all in a flash. Whatever they were going to do, they needed to work quickly.

"Make a hole!" Pine barked, as they passed out of the open galley and dove down the narrow stairwell to level three.

They landed with a splash. Several inches of water covered the floor in all directions, and there was a rushing sound that seemed to emanate from the walls.

Every ship was compartmentalized for just this reason. Small breaches might be stopped early, but large breaches—fast breaches— could sink a ship in an instant if you didn't patch them or seal the chamber. The water rushing past Caledonia's ankles told her neither had happened yet.

Voices sounded from directly ahead. Pine led them into a room on the starboard side where the crew was madly shifting equipment away from the wall and sealing off the adjoining chambers. Water poured through splits in the hull where the metal was frayed like fabric.

Caledonia's gut pitched.

If this were any other room, they'd have closed it off and left it to fill while they protected the rest of the ship. But this was the desal room. Everything in this space was dedicated to purifying seawater for drinking, bathing, and cooking. Without it, they'd have what remained in the tanks, and then they'd have nothing.

Sledge and Pine leaned toward the wound in the hull, their muscles straining as they attempted to slide a metal sheet toward the hole. There were sheets like this one all over the ship. They rested flat against the walls and when needed could be shifted one direction or another to cover a breach. But this one wasn't moving. And the water was rising.

Water lapped at Caledonia's shins, seeping up the fabric of her pants. Sledge and Pine were still pushing at that stubborn metal sheet. Water crashed violently around them, proving that the strength of the ocean was effortless and terrible. It was very clear to Caledonia: they were not going to save this room. All that remained was saving as much of this level as possible.

"Everyone out!" Caledonia pitched her voice to be heard above the roar. "Move!"

Everyone moved toward the hatch except Sledge. He stayed put, smacking a fist against the plate with a growl before yanking at the handles once more.

"Now, Sledge!" she shouted.

The water was climbing past her knees. It wasn't going to be long before sealing this chamber became impossible. If they weren't careful, they could lose so much more than a single level of the ship.

Caledonia counted each crew member who moved past. A

small pocket of dread wedged itself in the back of her mind as the number climbed. There would be no way to know if they'd trapped someone down here until it was too late.

Pisces was pulling the interior hatchway shut. "Forward chambers clear, Captain!"

"Sledge!" she shouted.

"I can get it!" His voice was thin from exertion, his face reddening with the effort.

"Hatch is getting heavy, friends!" Pine called from his station by the doorway.

"We can save the ship or your life, Sledge," she called. "You know which one I'll choose!"

Something snapped. The metal sheet popped away from the wall, smacking into Sledge. He stumbled. A bright red smear appeared on his head and then he was gone, his broad shoulders consumed by the dark water.

Before any of them could respond, a figure dove past Caledonia into the room. Oran.

Caledonia held her ground. The water was climbing quickly now, inching past her thighs toward her hips. Inside the room it was even deeper. With every second that passed, the danger to the rest of the ship increased exponentially.

"Captain!" Pine called. The warning in his voice was clear: if they didn't close that hatch now, they never would. "I hate to give you orders, but I'd like to request you get the hell out of there!"

"Caledonia!" Pisces shouted. "Now!"

Anger spun in her chest. At Sledge. At Oran. At the decision they were forcing her to make. It was them or the entire ship, and she didn't have the luxury of waiting, of saving two people who meant so much to her when the lives of so many others rested on her shoulders. Her chest squeezed and her eyes burned, but she turned and pushed through the water toward Pine's extended hand.

Her fingers brushed his, and then his hand was a vise on her forearm. With a single tug, she was through the hatchway, crashing into Pine as she struggled to regain her feet.

"We have to seal it," he said, face beaded with sweat, eyes pinched with the same pain she felt.

She nodded, a rock settling in her stomach as she gave the order: "Close it."

Behind him Pisces kept her expression steely. They'd come this far by making hard decisions. Even when they didn't agree, those decisions hadn't come between them until Caledonia had made one on her own.

Together, they placed their shoulders against the heavy hatch and pushed. The door began to move, but slowly. Then it stopped. No matter how hard they pushed, the water was stronger than all of them.

"We need to seal the level!" Caledonia called, saving her panic for later.

Then, just as they were ready to release the hatch and flee to level two, Sledge's head appeared around the lip of the doorway. Bright red blood spilled from a gash on his forehead. He rose from the water just ahead of Oran, and the instant they were both through the narrow opening, they turned and pushed. The door shut and Caledonia spun the wheel, locking every bar in place.

When she pulled her hands away, they trembled. She tucked them beneath the water and drew a deep breath before turning to face her four companions. Pine and Pisces stood to either side, breath coming in quick puffs. Sledge leaned against the wall opposite her, blood coating the left side of his face. Oran was hunched over. His shirt stuck to fresh blood all along his torso, and old orange scars were visible through the wet fabric.

She let her gaze fall solidly on Sledge and Oran. Anger trembled beneath every inch of her skin. They were alive and for that she was glad, but their actions had forced her to make a terrible choice. And she'd made it. She had killed them both, and it didn't matter that they'd survived. She would always know that it was a choice she would and could make.

"If either of you disobeys an order like that again, I'll put you in the hold and let you kill each other." Even to her ears, her voice sounded heavy, ominous.

Sledge blinked in surprise, but Oran's lips tightened with contrition.

"Do you understand?" she pressed.

"Yes, Captain," they answered together.

"Good. Sledge, get to med bay," Caledonia commanded.

"I'll take him." Oran reached out to steady the mountain as he swayed again.

Pine stepped in front of the two boys. "I'll take him." He reached for Sledge almost as if asking permission of the former Fiveson.

Oran nodded, somehow maintaining a sense of command as fresh blood darkened his shirt.

"You too," Caledonia said to Oran.

His lips bent in a subtle frown. "Yes, Captain."

When the boys had gone, Caledonia and Pisces leaned on opposite sides of the wall to catch their breath. They heard the moment the desal chamber filled completely; the rush of water was replaced by the whir of the water pumps as they struggled to lower the water level in every other chamber along level three.

The danger of sinking had passed, but an unstable hull was a bomb waiting to explode, and a ship with as much standing water as they'd just taken on was one storm away from the bottom of the ocean.

"If we hit rough water, this could capsize us, drag us down, maybe," Caledonia said, feeling the heavy roll of her ship.

"I need to get in the water." Pisces ran her hands over the walls as she spoke, her chin tilted toward the steel as though listening to its secrets. "Help with the repair and check over the rest of the ship. Make sure there aren't any surprises waiting."

This was far from the worst the two of them had faced. Four years ago, they'd patched their family ship with so much less at their disposal than they had right now. For a moment, Caledonia felt the same rush of possibility she'd felt on that beach. They'd taken their stubborn rage and sorrow and dreams for revenge, and they'd convinced themselves that two girls with nothing but their broken hearts could repair a ship. It was strange that a memory so steeped in terror and blood could feel like innocence. Yet as Caledonia felt the weight of responsibility—for her ship, her friend, and her crew—settle against her shoulders, a small part of her longed for the ease of that moment.

She resisted the urge to reach for her friend. Instead, she nodded. "Get in the water, but I want people tracking you. Don't get stuck anywhere we can't find you. I—" She halted on the edge of something tender. "Your tow's up there. I don't know if you saw it."

Pisces pursed her lips, dissatisfied, maybe even disappointed that Caledonia had stopped herself, but she was still too angry to push. "Right away, Captain."

Captain. Not Caledonia. Not Cala. The title was a wedge. And as Pisces left to organize her team, Caledonia felt the distance between them settling firmly into place, mortar between two stubborn stones.

CHAPTER THIRTY-FIVE

After a full night of rain and repairs that took everyone to the point of exhaustion, Caledonia gave Tin the order to send all who could be spared to their berths for rest.

Though the rain wasn't severe, it added chop to the sea, making everything more challenging both on the *Beacon* and beneath it. Their divers had to use mag grips to follow the slow roll of the ship as they attempted to spotweld flexible steeltech patches in place. When that was finished, Amina and Harwell turned their attention to the engines. Everyone did their part to ensure that when the sun rose once more, the ship would be ready to soak up those powerful rays and set sail.

The command crew had gathered briefly in the box, much as they had before the attack began, only this time, they were in desperate need of a heading. As it was, they were out of fuel, nearly out of food, and their water would soon be gone.

Caledonia settled her hands on her hips. "We're going to Cloudbreak," she stated.

"Cloudbreak?" Amina's eyes flicked briefly around the room. "The Sly King is no friend of ours. He will certainly not be happy to see us."

That was an understatement. He was going to be furious and anxious, and those two things would make him dangerous. But better a danger she knew than the alternative.

"You let me worry about that," Caledonia said. "I want the rest of you worried about getting us there."

The hit to the galley had destroyed almost every bit of food they had. All that was left was enough seed brick to go around once. Nettle estimated it was a two-day journey to Cloudbreak at full power and capacity. For them, it would take at least four. But as long as the sun reappeared in the morning, and as long as nothing else went wrong, they would make it work.

Though the command crew wasn't excited by the prospect of sailing into a place where they weren't exactly welcome, they could find no better alternatives. They dispersed, each prepared to present a brave face to the crew, and each eager for a bit of rest. Soon, the ship was at rest.

The crew shuffled belowdecks a few at a time, in threes, or in pairs, and Caledonia sat alone in the bridge as the ship rocked steadily back and forth. It was an uneasy way to end the day, but for now, the wind had carried the rain farther east, and the air was cool and crisp.

Sledge was restless. He paced the deck until the sky was dark and the deck ringed in the cool blue glow of sun pips embedded around the edge. He continued in that way until Pine appeared, stopping Sledge in his tracks and then raising his hands in the sign of consent.

They stood a foot apart, their edges glazed in blue light, the space between them cast in shadows. Then Sledge raised his hands first to Pine's and then past, sliding his fingers along Pine's jaw and pulling him close. The kiss was brief but powerful and Caledonia felt a twinge of jealousy that they could so easily find comfort in each other when she found the lines between friendship and command so immovable. Pisces had told her many times that it was possible for a captain to be intimate with her crew if she desired it, but Caledonia couldn't imagine taking someone to her bed one day and sending them into danger the next.

For years, she'd quashed every fledgling spark she'd felt for any of her girls, convinced that it was irresponsible. It had definitely been irresponsible to kiss Oran. But here was Sledge making the choice she'd never been confident enough to make.

Pine took Sledge's hand in his and pulled him toward the hatch. Then they vanished belowdecks together.

Caledonia was left alone with the night. For some time, the only sounds were the distant chugging of the water pumps and the laughter of ocean waves as they splashed against the hull. Then a whisper of sound announced Hime's arrival. She treaded quietly through the bridge hatchway followed closely by Amina.

We knew you'd be awake, Hime said, still signing with one hand. *You shouldn't be.*

"You should be resting," Amina added.

Caledonia smiled, chest warming at the sight of her sisters coming to keep her company. "I am resting," she countered.

Amina laughed ruefully. "I believe you think so."

Hime came forward, producing a fourth of a seed brick from a sack.

Caledonia looked up, startled. "Hime, no. I appreciate the gesture, but you need that just as much as any of us."

Hime didn't move. Like the rest of the girls, her cheeks revealed how little she'd had to eat in recent weeks, but she regarded Caledonia like a hawk regarded its prey.

With a sigh, Caledonia took the portion from Hime's hand. "We'll split it."

Hime rolled her eyes and to Amina said, *Didn't I tell you?*

Amina laughed again, drawing Hime to her and kissing the back of her hand lightly. "You know our captain well, Princelet."

Amina took a seat on the floor, and Hime settled between her legs as the three of them slowly chewed on their food. It was dry and unappealing but they took their time, tricking their stomachs into thinking it was a full meal.

It was hard to believe she was sitting here with them again. For so long, she'd imagined them sailing past the Net, free and finding new ways to thrive. Then, when she knew they'd been captured, she imagined them suffering. In all that time, she hadn't imagined this kind of quiet communion, and she found she didn't know what to say. She had too many questions to choose from.

"Pisces was a good captain," Amina offered. "Though she will probably tell you otherwise."

"I have no doubt," Caledonia answered quickly. "Just as I'm sure you were an incredible second."

Amina shrugged the compliment away with grace. "It will take her too long to tell you herself because she feels so badly about getting caught, but it wasn't her fault."

It was a trap, Hime added. *They were waiting for us.*

Caledonia's chest tightened as they unraveled the tale.

"When we left you, we were caught up in the Perpetual Storm again. We couldn't stay in the western seas, so we cut east, hoping to skim down the coast of the Rock Isles. One morning, there was a ship in our path. Seemingly in distress."

Immediately, Caledonia understood what had happened to them. Pisces had seen their distress and wanted to help because that was the kind of person she was. It made her—and all of them—better, but in this case, it had been their downfall.

"They let us draw so near that we could not maneuver easily around them. Then the Bullet ships were upon us, and that was that."

She thinks you would have seen it coming. Hime paused, a compassionate frown bowing her lips. *She's right, isn't she?*

Now Caledonia frowned. "I can't judge without having been there and I shouldn't. Whatever she did kept the majority of our crew alive. And that makes it the right choice."

Amina nodded, stifling a yawn with one hand. "You should tell her that."

"I will," Caledonia answered softly, knowing that anything she said to Pisces right now would only fuel her resentment. "Maybe."

Hime rose, pulling Amina after her. *You should get some rest, too, Captain.*

Caledonia nodded. "I promise."

She was tired, but she couldn't sleep. Not while her ship required attention. She needed to hear every sound, to feel every roll and pitch. If something were to happen, she needed to know that she was completely connected to the current state of the *Beacon*.

As the girls took their leave, her eyes strayed from the eastern horizon to the sun sail. Her stomach tightened around its meager contents as she considered all the possible ways this could go very wrong very quickly.

Venn was almost surely in pursuit, though unlikely to sail at night, especially near the whirl. In spite of having a radio of their own, the Bullets had jumped to a new channel, preventing them from listening in. If Venn had called for assistance, there could be dozens of ships in pursuit already. If the *Beacon* didn't make it to Cloudbreak, it would be because they were dead in the water or in Fiveson Venn's hold.

And if they did make it to Cloudbreak and Hesperus refused them aid, how would she ensure her crew didn't slowly starve to death in those sparse waters?

All she wanted was to keep them alive. She would find a way. She had to.

She pulled every strand of fear that wove through her gut and her lungs, or coiled in her belly, into a single cord. Taken altogether, her fears would be her strength. She would make sure of it.

The cabin of the bridge felt larger than usual without additional bodies packed inside. The space was cool and dark with a few lights illuminated on the dash, letting her know that they were perilously low on power and that the pumps were active down below. The wrap of windows gave her a full view of the deck, where a reduced dead watch of two patrolled fore and aft beneath moonlit clouds. Even knowing how quickly this situation could go from precarious to desperate, it was peaceful.

A scratching noise fluttered from one of the bridge stations, filling the air with an erratic staccato. Caledonia narrowed her eyes on the radio, still resting on the same channel they'd used to radio Slipmark. She slipped out of her seat, moving closer to investigate. It crackled again, and this time she heard a voice.

"Caledonia."

She froze halfway between her chair and the radio. The room was suddenly very cold.

"Caledonia." The voice was silk behind static, a smile beyond a fogged windowpane, and it slipped beneath her skin like a thin sheet of ice.

Again, static punctured the air. It sounded like water rushing into her ears, and for a second she forgot to breathe.

It was Lir.

"Was that you in Slipmark, Bale Blossom? Coming after your crew? You who so deftly evaded Venn today?" He paused, and Caledonia couldn't help but picture the delighted smile on his lips, curled as artfully as a flower petal. "Caledonia . . ." Her name was a song and a taunt on his tongue, the notes offered in complete faith that she was there to receive them.

He was goading her. Daring her to reveal that she was alive. Until now, all he'd had was the absence of her body and perhaps a tantalizing sliver of hope that they would meet again. If she responded, all of that would change.

She knew this, felt it on every level, and yet some part of her yearned to pick up that receiver and prove that he'd failed to kill her.

"I think it was you. In fact, I hope it was," he continued. "We left things on such a disappointing note. But look, the moons have gifted us with a new opportunity."

Walk away, Caledonia. She raised a hand to switch the radio off. One flick of a switch. That's all it would take. He would be gone and she would be free. So why couldn't she do it?

"You continue to impress me. You have nothing. Only yourself, and yet you survive." She heard him exhale before following another dreadful thought. "You took your crew back, of course, but you also took Bullet Ares and Fiveson—well, he was once Fiveson Oran." The intrigue in his voice was thick and dangerous. "I'm surprised at your interest in my once-brother considering all he's done. But then, perhaps you're more complicated than you've led me to believe."

There it was again. The implication that the Oran she'd come to know was not the one he'd been in the Bullet fleet. In spite of knowing that this was Lir's precise intention, the words lodged a firm spear of doubt in her mind: What had Oran done?

"Didn't manage to reclaim your ship, though. I promise you we've put her in good hands. She is a treasure we will guard well."

Another long exhale. "Caledonia. I know you will come for me again, but I must admit, I don't know how. Whatever it is, I know it will be magnificent. And it will change us both. The world, even. You and your surprising capacity for endurance."

His voice was aggressively casual, as though they were in the same room and his eyes rested on hers. He was so sure she was listening to every word. And it was true. Of all the moments he might have chosen to speak to her, he picked the time she was alone in this cabin. But she didn't have to give that to him. She could walk away and leave his voice to the night. "Just like your brother."

The receiver was suddenly in her hand, her mouth so close

to the speaker. She pressed the button and spoke: "What have you done with Donnally?"

The pause that followed was so self-satisfied, Caledonia felt her gorge rise in her throat. He'd baited her and he'd won.

"Caledonia," he nearly crooned. "I knew you could hear me."

Biting down on her anger, she drew a deep breath and repeated herself. "Lir, what have you done with Donnally?"

"Come to me and I will show you."

Caledonia opened her hand, letting the receiver rest in the center of her palm. It quaked back and forth, responding to the tiny, agitated movements in her muscles. She raised her eyes to the plane of the ocean and was almost surprised to see it was still there. As Lir spoke, her world had narrowed more and more until the only thing in focus was that receiver and the sound of his voice.

She drew a deep breath, casting her mind out over the black chop, letting her world expand once more. This was yet another ploy. A trick to convince her to make a poor choice at her weakest moment. It wasn't possible that he knew the full extent of their situation, but he must have a sense of it. Why else would he call to her now?

She brought the receiver to her mouth and pressed the button on its side. "You won't draw me out so easily."

"Ah, Caledonia." He sighed his way through her name. "I would be disappointed if that were the case."

Finally, Caledonia felt her mind settle into focus. She saw Lir seated far away, a receiver clamped in one hand, all arrogance and that strange charm that clung to his smile, the shattered crown of his hair. She saw just how desperate he was to find her, to defeat her. And she stood taller as she lifted the receiver once more.

"I will disappoint you one day, Lir. That is my promise to you."

Before he could respond again, she snapped the receiver back in its holster and flipped the switch on the radio, cutting the connection between them.

CHAPTER THIRTY-SIX

She knew it was true. One day, their paths would cross again. But she'd learned something else in the course of this deep night conversation. When the day came, she intended to be ready. She wanted to be able to strike back without running the instant the battle was won. She wanted more power than she'd ever thought to possess. She wanted to *fight*.

She would never sleep now, not with Lir's voice so fresh in her head, but she needed to leave the bridge. When her fingers had stopped trembling, she turned toward the door and jumped at the sight of a figure.

He was too tall for the doorway, yet he'd stopped there, head bowed over his broad shoulders. Though he was both tall and broad, he was also slender, his skin a warm, sunny brown that denied the cool light of the moon. She knew him. Or, more accurately, she'd known him. Once.

"Ares," she said, voice tipping with surprise.

"I didn't mean to." He paused, eyes passing guiltily from her to the radio. "Well, I didn't mean to overhear."

A selfish irritation rose in her throat. She'd been caught. She hadn't meant to get pulled into Lir's orbit, but once again, she had, and this time, there was a witness. Shame warmed her cheeks.

"I heard his voice," Ares continued when she didn't speak. "It's not one I'm likely to forget. I thought I was dreaming. I've, ah, had some trouble knowing the difference between dreams and waking."

"Of course," she said quickly. And now there was guilt worming its way through her already flush bouquet of emotions. He'd been on her ship since Slipmark. She'd grown up with him, and not once had she gone to check on him. Or even to express her relief at seeing him again. She told herself it was because she'd been busy, which was true. But there was more to it than that.

Looking at Ares, and especially looking at Ares and Pisces together, reminded her of Donnally. He reminded her of how she'd failed to save her brother. And beyond that, looking at Ares reminded her that there was someone on this ship who knew exactly what her brother had become. She could ask, and she was sure he would answer. And that certainty drove a tremor straight down her spine.

"You look like you're doing better," she said. "I'm glad to see it."

"Sometimes," he said with a shrug. He carried himself at odd angles, like he couldn't get comfortable in his own body. Oran's withdrawal had been easier, but so had his experience in the Bullet fleet. "Hime is a tyrant. I understand why they call her Princelet."

Caledonia laughed. "And we are all the better for it."

He nodded, but his lips never moved toward a smile. They seemed set around a permanent meridian, carved there by too much—pain, hardship, Silt. Whatever it was that had left Ares in this fragile state had also siphoned his capacity for mirth, leaving him with a friendly sort of melancholy. It struck a chord of regret deep in Caledonia's heart. This boy had once been full of passions, a trickster, roving the *Ghost* on the lookout for any opportunity to cause mischief.

"He won't hurt Donnally."

At first, the words made no sense. Her mind refused them, scattering them like a puzzle she slowly pieced together again: Lir wouldn't hurt Donnally. "Why not?"

"He's—they have some kind of connection. I think he likes him. As much as a Fiveson is capable of liking anyone." He paused there, then, seeming to sense Caledonia's next question, he continued. "He's always looked out for Donnally. Like a little brother."

Brother.

"He's *my* brother," Caledonia growled. Her stomach clutched violently around sudden nausea.

Ares watched her with the pitying expression of someone who understood what they were witnessing and saw the futility of it.

"I know why you won't ask me about him," Ares said softly.

"And I won't tell you if you don't want to know, but I will say that he's not like some of the others. He's never forgotten you or where we came from."

She didn't know how to feel. There was too much possibility packed into those words. Donnally was still her brother, he still remembered his family, but he was different. Someone else called him brother. The boy who'd taken everything they loved. Had he also taken her brother's heart?

The nausea in her belly churned and churned. She couldn't speak, could only lean one hand against the console behind her.

"Were you in Lir's fleet?" she asked.

"I was," he answered with a nod. "Until we were placed on *Electra*. Conscription falls under Decker's purview. I suspect it was a means to an end, though. Lir always wanted bigger things for Donnally. Giving us to Decker was the best way to move him into command. Putting me on his crew ensured he had some support. The rest he had to fight for. They expect all their Fivesons to demonstrate some kind of unique aptitude for that kind of thing."

"What?" Caledonia's voice stretched thin over the word.

"I—I thought you knew." Ares stood up straight, his shoulders even for once. "Lir was sponsoring Donnally to compete as a Fiveson. To replace Oran."

A quiet storm started in Caledonia's ears, like the distant promise of thunder. Questions formed faster than she could properly consider them. "My brother is a Fiveson?"

"No. At least, not when I left. There were only four: Decker, Tassos, Venn, and Lir. Each of them was allowed to sponsor a candidate. That's when Donnally was pulled from *Electra*. To undergo the trials. And before you ask, I don't know what they entail."

"Oran does." She felt numb even as the idea occurred to her.

Ares only nodded, but once again, Caledonia had the impression that it was with a sense of futility. Whatever Oran had done to become a Fiveson, he knew exactly what it was. Whatever he'd done to lose that same status? That was the question that gave her hope. It carved just enough room around Oran in her mind to make him worthy of the trust she'd already given him.

"But every Fiveson must prove he is more ruthless than the others competing for that power. If that had happened, we'd have heard of it in Slipmark." He exhaled slowly, calmly, as if none of this disturbed him on any level.

It wasn't much of a comfort, but in light of all she'd learned in the course of this unexpected conversation, it was enough. Donnally was not yet a Fiveson. She would believe it until she no longer could.

"Lir became a Fiveson the night he killed our families. He was the youngest boy to claim the destruction of an entire ship as his own. And Aric had been after us for much longer than our parents let on. I guess we had some important people on that ship, some people Aric wanted dead." Ares shrugged. "Lir's victory made him famous and invaluable in the eyes of the Father."

"Ares," she began, thinking she would ask him to stop. It was too much to think about, and too much to fold into her already painful understanding of the past. But instead, she asked, "How do I get to Donnally? Before he becomes a Fiveson?"

Ares only shook his head slowly back and forth. "I'm sorry."

"It's all right." She gave him a small smile. "You should get some rest."

She moved to his side and gently placed a hand on his shoulder. The night sky was inky and pricked with starlight, the air dry and cool. In spite of the persistent chill, Ares wore short sleeves and his skin was hot and damp to the touch, almost feverish.

He let her lead him out of the bridge, down to level two, and all the way to his quarters.

"Caledonia," he said just before entering his room. "Fivesons will do anything for the Father. They will go after whatever the Father most wants in all the world. After what you did for us in Slipmark, I have to think that thing is you."

When the door was shut, Caledonia let darkness and silence wrap her in a welcome cocoon. Her mind was brimming and her heart was, too. It was almost too much for one night.

But if Ares was right, then her surest way to Donnally was through Aric himself.

CHAPTER
THIRTY-SEVEN

Caledonia lay on her back beneath the sun sail studying its black plates. They flashed in the sunlight, luffing ever so slightly in the breeze, and when there was no breeze, they trembled with the vibration of the ship's engines. One alone was virtually useless, but taken together, they were the most powerful piece of equipment on any ship.

Even with power restored, they couldn't do anything about the water on level three, and it was going to take four days to reach Cloudbreak. Four days of reduced rations, a diminishing water supply, and a web of tension strung between Oran and nearly everyone else on the *Beacon*. Even her own crew seemed to move around him with more care. Whether that was because they'd heard the name Steelhand or because he had changed so dramatically around the Bullets, she wasn't sure.

She had to admit that his ability to transform was unnerving, and it made her recast him in her memory. He'd come aboard her ship to escape, and then he'd become exactly who he needed to be to survive. If it was true of the Oran she'd first met, it was certainly true of the Oran the Blades knew. And it left her with a question that hummed quietly in the back of her mind: Which was the true Oran?

They were in day three of this journey, and the crew was showing signs of exhaustion. Caledonia was no exception. She'd been in the rigging of the sun sail when her head flooded with a disorienting lightness. She'd climbed down at once and lain here where she could catch her breath.

A hand landed lightly on her wrist, fingers pressing flat against her pulse.

"I'm fine, Hime," she protested, but she was too tired to resist.

Hime shook her head and kept counting. After a quiet minute, she sighed and dropped Caledonia's wrist. *Stay out of the rigging. Expend no—*

"Unnecessary energy, I remember."

Do you? Because I saw you up there, she signed, and when she pointed into the rigging it was with exaggerated frustration. *Didn't look necessary to me.*

Caledonia scowled softly. Even facial expressions were taxing.

"Need me to take her to her rack?" Amina kneeled next to Hime, her hand automatically reaching for the other girl.

"How's the rest of the crew?" Caledonia interjected.

Showing signs of dehydrating. Headaches, disorientation. Things will get much worse before the day's through.

"Great." She pushed her way to sitting, squeezing her eyes against the dizzying rush of blood.

When she opened them again, Hime and Amina were scrutinizing her with looks of irritating concern. She ignored them both, letting her gaze drift across the deck. Pine and Pisces were settled on the port rail, their hands raised in signed conversation. Pine seemed determined to learn Hime's language, and Pisces was a patient teacher. Higher up on the forequarter, Nettle sat atop the ghost funnel with Harwell and Glimmer to keep watch. They sat in a triangle with their backs pushed together. Usually, they'd have one person in each post, but with everyone's energy waning, Sledge had recommended three people positioned fore and aft.

Amina leaned forward. "We'll make it, Captain. Don't worry about us. Just make sure you're ready to do what needs doing when we get to Cloudbreak. Now, let me take you to your rack before you alarm the entire crew."

It always amazed Caledonia how naturally Amina moved between being her crew member and her commanding equal. She gave Caledonia her hand and pulled her to her feet, taking care to steady her without making a show of it.

The light buzzing in her ears accompanied her all the way to her quarters, and the sight of her bed was more welcome than she'd anticipated.

I'll come by to check on you in two hours, Hime promised.

"Don't let me sleep for more than one."

"You'll sleep as long as she tells you," Amina countered.

The two girls ducked out of the hatchway just as Oran appeared. He made room for them to pass, holding out a cup for Hime's approval.

Hime smiled as she disappeared down the corridor with Amina. Caledonia frowned.

Oran stepped into the hatch with her. "I know you've been cutting your own rations," he said, voice low. "Take it."

"You can't know that," she murmured, even as her throat ached for a drink.

"Am I wrong?"

"Oran," she breathed.

He shifted to put his shoulder against the frame of the hatch, the gesture so casually powerful that Caledonia was struck again by the difference in him. Or the difference in her perception of him. He was self-possessed and confident in a way that communicated a quiet and deadly strength.

She liked it.

But Lir's voice twisted through her mind, drawing questions close behind. She'd considered asking several times in the past few days, *What have you done, Oran?* She didn't like that Lir knew more than she did, but she wasn't ready. Not yet.

Oran's gaze held steady. "You keep putting your crew ahead of you and you'll get us all dead."

The cup sat in his hand, the water clear and glistening within, not more than a single swallow. And she wanted it.

As she reached for the cup, her fingertips brushed his, landing for just a second longer than they should. They locked eyes again. She took the cup and drank. The water was a balm to her dry throat. It seemed that every bit of her body cried out with relief, and just as quickly she wanted more.

"Thank you," she said, her voice raw.

He didn't answer. He was watching her with that same mixture of wonder and admiration he'd had when they first met. Only now, she saw it with a difference. He understood power. He'd had his own, relinquished it, and now he'd willingly placed himself in her path. It was her power he admired.

"Stop," she said.

"Only if it's an order. Is it?"

She considered him for a moment. His arms were folded across his chest, and shadows caught in the planes of his shoulders, the lithe muscles of his arms. Though his eyes were intent on hers, it was that kiss she thought of, and her gaze slid to his pressed lips. Was it an order?

Caledonia needed strength right now, not distractions. She pressed a hand to his chest and pushed him firmly into the passageway.

"Yes," she said. "And thank you."

As she swung the hatch closed, he never moved, his eyes drinking her in until the last second.

CHAPTER
THIRTY-EIGHT

"We're out of water," Pisces reported. "Last rations are being distributed now."

It was the fourth day and everyone knew that they should have made land by now. The ship was slowing down, all systems pushed to their limits.

"'Rations' is a generous word for what we've been getting," Pine nearly growled.

It's keeping us alive, Hime snapped back.

Pine's frustration grew. His eyes flicked to Pisces.

"It's keeping us alive," she repeated.

"Are we sure we can't get more out of the engines?" Caledonia asked. The command crew was huddled on the quarterdeck where their words were obscured by the churn of the propellers.

"If we push them any harder, we might lose them altogether." Amina's answer was measured and calm, but only on the surface.

Caledonia turned hungry eyes westward. As their thirst increased, their tempers shortened and tensions were most keen between Blades and the crew of the *Mors Navis*. They needed to find a source of fresh water. It was out there. They were so close now her mind filled in the faint impression of cliffs where the Rock Isles should be.

"Divert all unnecessary power to the engines," she ordered. "Water pumps, air filtration, anything else we don't need to move this ship forward."

The team nodded, motivated by an immediate plan of action, but Caledonia felt it only dimly as she turned her steps toward her cabin.

Exhaustion hung from every bone in her body, and she tried not to dwell on the hollow feeling in her belly as she readied herself to see the Sly King. Last time she'd been in his town, she'd had the scales of their destroyed sun sail to trade and he'd proved untrustworthy. Aric's bounty had been too much to pass up, and the Sly King had come very close to handing her over. It was the *almost* part of that equation that gave her hope now. Hesperus Shreeves might obey Aric's law most of the time, but he didn't like it.

In the mirror, Caledonia's cheeks curved toward the corners of her lips and her nose was as sharp as the prow of her ship. Her brown eyes were wide beneath rusty eyebrows, and her hair looked like little flames with red roots pushing up from beneath brassy blonde locks. Her skin was unevenly tanned across forehead and the bridge of her nose, marking her as a girl of the sea. She might feel tired, but she looked hard-edged.

She swapped her travel-soiled clothes for her only fresh garments, a brown close-fitted top and black pants. To complete the look, she tied Triple's abandoned gray sash around her waist, letting the knot sit low and the fabric swing to her knee. Even knowing weapons wouldn't be allowed in the presence of the Sly King, she strapped on her gun belt and sword. The second they spotted Cloudbreak, she intended to be ready.

A knock sounded on her door. When she opened it, she found Pisces. Instantly, the lethargy in her limbs was replaced by a nervous kind of hope. The two had been in constant contact over the past days, but rarely alone.

"Time?" Caledonia asked.

"No. Sorry."

Caledonia waited, hoping there was more and a little worried that there wouldn't be.

Pisces opened her mouth, then thought better of it and closed it again. Caledonia could see the resolve falling back into place as she'd seen a dozen times already. Next, she'd see the expression that confirmed they were sisters in name only. And she broke.

Caledonia stepped forward and pulled her sister into her arms, hugging her tightly. At first, Pisces seemed primed to resist, but then she returned the hug, wrapping her long arms around Caledonia's shoulders.

"I'm so sorry I got caught," Pisces murmured.

"Pi!" Caledonia cried, pulling away and taking the girl's face in her hands. "You kept them alive. That's what matters."

"I was trying to be you," she said, voice harsh. "I was furious with you for leaving us and I was trying to do what I *thought* you would do and it got us caught."

"What do you mean?"

"I've never seen you pull back from a fight. Not once. It never occurred to me that you would do something like that, but back there at the whirl, that's exactly what you did. You didn't turn and engage, you ran."

"Because it was the right thing to do," Caledonia answered, guarded.

Pisces's mouth flattened. "I've blamed you for all of this. For getting caught, for losing more girls, for leaving me behind." She paused to pull Caledonia's hands away from her face. "I don't want to keep blaming you."

"I understand why you do."

"I'm not saying it isn't justified," Pisces snapped. "But there are more important things between us than injury and blame."

"What are you saying?" Caledonia held perfectly still. If she moved, she was convinced she'd destroy whatever was happening between them right now.

"I need to know you aren't going to leave me like that again."

"I'm not," Caledonia promised, feeling dizzy from hunger and hope all at once. "I won't. I—Pi, I don't want to lose you again."

"Caledonia," Pisces said with a sigh. "That's what you don't understand. You will always fail to lose me."

"Thank you." They were the most precious words Caledonia had ever heard. If she had any water to spare, she'd have cried with relief.

"Cliffs!" The excited call rang throughout the ship. "Cliffs!"

"There's never any time, is there?" Pisces nodded, tucking her smile away for later. "Let's go."

White cliffs broke against the blue sky, and the entire ship released a sigh of relief. All except Caledonia. Getting here was only the first hurdle. It was what came next—getting inside Cloudbreak, and then getting her entire crew fed and watered—that worried her. That was going to require as much strategic thinking as any battle.

"Keep a steady course, Nettle," she called. "Remember this is a Bullet ship."

Soon, the archipelago of metal islands guarding the port of Lower Cloudbreak came into view, their jagged edges pointing out of the water like deadly icebergs. Beyond them, the wharf of Lower Cloudbreak nestled against chalky cliffs, at the top of which the market town of Cloudbreak perched in a mountainous nest. The only way in or out was by treacherous rope lifts.

Nettle slowed their approach. Caledonia couldn't help but be reminded of the last time they'd come here. Her crew had been so different then. Half as big and not yet fractured by loss and anger at their captain. Redtooth had been alive.

It was getting easier to think of the girl, of her red-tipped braids and her beautiful battle cry, of her incredible strength and her soft, soft heart; Caledonia could hear her voice now, grumbling about no good options as they'd threaded those protective breaker islands in the *Mors Navis*.

They'd been a marked ship and come in under cover of the morning fog, but this time Caledonia didn't want cover. She wanted Hesperus to see her. The fastest way to do that was to appear like a threat, and for that, all she needed to do was take her Bullet ship right up to the breaker islands and wait. On the main deck, Sledge and Pine positioned teams to port and starboard. Their numbers visible, but unarmed as a sign of peace. Far on the aft deck was Oran. While the rest of them had turned their eyes west, he kept his on the eastern horizon.

It took even less time than she'd anticipated. No sooner had they cut their own engines when they spotted a boat zipping away from the wharf. It was barely more than a dinghy, but its engine growled against the water and it aimed directly for them.

Pisces and Caledonia stood high on the command deck. Amina joined them, the crest of her braids freshly knotted in place. Then came Hime, her injured hand tightly wrapped in cloth instead of bandages. They circled Caledonia out of habit, and she realized with a sudden pang that this was the first time they'd all come together like this. Her stones; flint, granite, agate. It was a smaller circle than it had once been, but in many ways it was stronger now. Memories of Lace and Redtooth would always weave between them; their sunny citrine and stoic marble girls would never be entirely lost.

"Looks like company." Amina tracked the approaching boat.

"I don't see any weapons," Pisces added.

They don't know what we are, Hime offered smartly.

With a nod, Caledonia strode forward so that she would be visible from the water. Behind her, she felt the girls fan around her, readying weapons.

The small boat cruised alongside the *Beacon*. A figure stood on the prow dressed in deep grays and bearing the cerulean blue capelet of the Sly King's guard. She had cool, brown skin and a shorn head.

"Caledonia Styx!" the woman called in reluctant admiration. She casually rested one hand on the hilt of a gun holstered high on her thigh. "You're not what I expected."

"It is good to see you, Mino," she called back, surprised at how easily those words came to her. She *was* glad to see her, if only because it would make getting to Hesperus that much easier.

"Is it?" The woman slid her gaze down the length of the ship where several of Caledonia's crew had gathered. "You look more like a Bullet than the last time I saw you."

"Captain." Amina's gentle voice was in her ear. "I see gunners on these islands. This could very well be a trap."

Caledonia nodded once to indicate she'd heard the warning, then she smiled and stepped forward. "Sometimes the best disguise is the uniform of your enemy."

"Why have you brought Bullets to my port?"

"They aren't Bullets," she called, and when Mino raised a skeptical eyebrow, she added, "Not anymore."

"And your ship?" Mino frowned at the *Beacon*, dissatisfaction scrawled across her face. "Looks like one of the Father's."

There was no point in lying, though Caledonia's stomach twisted. "It was. It's mine now. And it needs repair. I've come to trade with your brother for that and more, if you'll let us pass."

"You have something to trade?"

"I believe I left a collection of very valuable solar scales in your possession last time I was here." She raised her chin and gestured to the line of her crew. "We've come to collect on that debt. But in addition, I have an offer I think he's going to want to hear."

Mino's expression dipped toward suspicion, but instead of pushing back, she nodded. "All right, Captain, but you can't dock that here. Follow me."

The woman disappeared into the protected cabin of her bridge, spinning up her engines. She led them through the breaker islands and past the wharf where several ships occupied the docks and figures could be seen loading goods for trade onto the rope lift pallets. Mino bypassed it all and led them straight into the canals.

Like last time, the entry was difficult to detect, but unlike last time they were sailing at a reasonable speed. Making the turn was decidedly easier, and soon the sheer canal walls rose on either side of the *Beacon*. The purr of their engines filled the air, accompanied by the rush and splash of water against rocks.

"This is not a good situation." Sledge was on the command deck now. His shoulders were hunched and his eyes bounced nervously from one wall to the other as though he saw something they didn't. "Not a good situation at all."

"We've sailed these canals before," Pisces soothed, always so intuitive.

"Yeah but . . ."

"He doesn't like small spaces," Pine explained.

"We've been living on a ship." Amina sounded incredulous.

Pine only shrugged. "Never had a problem with ships. Just—" He gestured at the narrow slip of sky above them. "Anything that makes him feel small, I think."

Sledge shot Pine a dark look, and he stopped talking.

"Hold it together, Sledge." Caledonia made it sound like an order.

"I'm fine," he growled. "You should all be just as worried as I am about these walls."

As if on cue, a rumble sounded far above them. Rocks crashed against the nose of the ship and the water below. None was much larger than a fist, but they hit the deck with tremendous force.

Sledge skulked off, muttering to himself as he went.

Caledonia stayed exactly where she was, marking every fork they took in her memory. Even without the map they'd used to navigate these canals a few months earlier, she knew they were headed into the northern passages. The ones Hesperus had told her unconditionally to avoid if she wanted safe passage. Cloud-break was more than it appeared to be.

Which was exactly what she was counting on.

CHAPTER
THIRTY-NINE

"L et's go," Caledonia called.

They'd followed Mino's boat for several twisting miles through the canals to a hidden harbor deep within the mountain range. Though Caledonia was sure Nettle had marked every fork as well as she, getting out again wasn't a task she wanted to attempt under any kind of pressure. The *Beacon* was thoroughly woven into these canals. Trapping her there would require very little effort on Hesperus's part.

The harbor was a natural bowl in the canals, tucked around a bend with a long dock carved into the rock walls. Currently, the water was low enough to reveal two sets of stone steps leading toward the dock. Mino kept the *Beacon* in the center of the harbor and pulled her smaller boat alongside to ferry them across the short distance to the stairs.

Caledonia gathered Pisces, Amina, and Hime and for a moment considered taking only them. Then her eyes fell on Sledge and Pine and Oran. Three former Bullets standing by her side would speak more loudly than anything she could say to the Sly King of Cloudbreak.

"Tin! You're in command," she told the girl with a firm nod.

"Yes, Captain."

Caledonia and her team of six moved to the rail, where a ladder draped over the side to the deck of Mino's boat.

"Wait!" Nettle came rushing across the deck, her rainbow hair ties flashing in the sun. "Let me come. I know how he works. I can help."

"Nettle." Amina stepped in to chide the girl. "The last time you saw the Sly King, you stole from him. Our task is hard enough without negotiating your past. Much as we're glad for your clever actions."

"But I have something he'll want! Something we can bargain with!"

Every single person in that small circle sighed.

Nettle only smiled, devious and delighted, as she produced a small device from a pouch at her waist. A long, slim rectangle that at the touch of a button transformed into a handheld sifter. "Soiltech," she said proudly.

"Nettle!" Caledonia reached for the contraption.

"I knew you wanted it. And who better to figure this little barnacle out than Hesperus, the Slyest Fish in the Seas?"

Caledonia's mind reeled with myriad possibilities. If they could crack Aric's soiltech, find a way to reproduce it even, they could change everything. Nettle was right. She was even right about Hesperus being the one with the resources to do it, but his loyalties were still in question.

"This is precious," Caledonia said, pressing the device back into Nettle's hand. "But now isn't the time for it. Keep it safe."

"But you can't go to him empty-handed," she protested.

"I have something he'll want even more than goods for trade." A smiled played on Caledonia's lips as the rest of her team waited for the answer. "A secret you gave me."

Nettle couldn't help but give a knowing smile at that. "That'll work. But don't let him put you off. He's better than he wants people to believe."

"And how do you know that?" Caledonia called, moving toward the rail.

Nettle's mouth snapped shut. Her chin tipped up and she smiled.

"More trouble than you're worth!" Pisces teased.

One by one, they descended the ladder with Amina insisting that she go first and Sledge dropping in last. Mino watched them arrive in silence, sizing them up with unnerving solemnity. Caledonia was sure the woman had accurately marked each gun and blade and had a reasonable idea of what it would take to disarm or overpower them. But Mino gave no indication that she found them at all troubling, and the boat sailed swiftly toward the stone stairs.

"Up" was the only word she offered as she herself disembarked and climbed onto the slick stones.

Amina kept herself at the fore, always ready to place herself between Caledonia and danger. The rest filed in behind, and together they treaded carefully up the slick stairway. They followed Mino to the narrow lip of a dock and from there toward rounded openings in the canal wall.

"I feel like I know what's waiting for us in there," Pisces muttered miserably.

Soon, they found themselves in a small chamber with a metal grate at the far end. Pisces's fears flushed into her cheeks as they boarded the lift and Mino secured the grate behind them. In seconds, the lift was off the ground, zipping up the dark shaft as though unbothered by the eight bodies it carried. Wind rushed past their ears, smelling of rock and cold sky. Far above them, metal gears clicked as they turned, providing their journey with a distant rhythm.

The trip was fast, though not fast enough for Pisces, who shut her eyes and leaned a shoulder against Caledonia. Caledonia relished the contact. Her instinct was to slip her hand into Pisces's, let their fingers twine together to offer comfort. Instead, she held herself steady and still for her sister, making herself a stone while Pisces needed the support.

Too soon, the metal grate snapped open, and they were herded through a narrow chamber onto a flat plane of packed earth and scuffed, pale grass. While they'd been down in the channels, the sun had fallen from view. But up here, it was still visible far to the west, making a slow dive toward a ring of snowcapped mountains. To the east, a sloping valley fell away toward a ridge of cliffs and the ocean beyond. It was a breathtaking sight. They were high on the western wall of mountains overlooking the network of merchant tents and family homes that made up the constantly shifting city that was Cloudbreak. From here, the chaos looked almost welcoming, a tangle of threads holding the community together.

And it was cold, a drastic difference from the warmth of the sheltered canals. Caledonia's breath came in small white puffs and her skin prickled. She shivered, yet her hunger-dulled senses came alive at the shock, and she felt more prepared to meet the Sly King. He would not be tired and hungry and parched. Nor would he be distracted by the thought of an entire crew withering away or worried over the state of a ship. He would arrive with a single goal in mind: to get the best possible deal out of the exchange. And he was going to be disappointed.

The path soon dipped into a valley brimming with short trees bearing needles of the deepest green. The center of the valley had been cleared to make way for a dozen cabins. Each was made of reddish wood, their roofs gleaming with solar panels and their walls lined with small gardens.

"Wait in here," Mino said, showing them into a large cabin near the center of the compound. The main room seemed to be a dining hall, though it was empty and cold at the moment. There were rows of sturdy wooden chairs and long narrow tables all pushed against one wall. At the back of the room were two doors, one on either side of the kitchen. "There's water. Help yourselves."

The door shut behind her, and the seven of them stood speechless for a moment. Water.

Pine was the first to break. He hurried toward the door Mino had indicated, disappearing behind it for several minutes. He re-emerged with a pitcher, a stack of seven glasses, and a near delirious grin pushing at his hollow cheeks.

He passed the cups around as quickly as he could fill them, and they all but inhaled the precious liquid. Caledonia downed three full cups before she stopped, her stomach tightening around its sudden contents.

"I almost feel full," Sledge mused, wiping an arm across his mouth. "Too full."

"You're not," Pisces said with a frown. "Just take it slow."

Hunger was something every child knew. There were times when the fish wouldn't come, when scavenging turned up nothing but dry fruits and nuts that cracked to dust almost as soon as you'd plucked them. But watertech was so plentiful that thirst was practically foreign.

"The rest of the crew needs just as much," Amina spoke. "If we can convince the Sly King to give us any."

"I trust water isn't the only thing you've come to ask for."

The voice took them all by surprise. They'd been so focused on quenching their collective thirst that they'd left the door unguarded.

"Hesperus," Caledonia said, turning to face the man as Amina slid into her protective position.

He was just as imposing as he'd ever been in her memory. Tall and broad-shouldered with skin the cool black of moonlit waters, he moved with an air of command that challenged Caledonia to do the same.

"I must admit to some surprise, Captain," Hesperus continued. "I'd heard you were dead."

He stood three steps inside the room with two guards at his sides. He was dressed in grays and blacks, his billowing great coat falling nearly to the floor. A thin sheen of sweat stood out on his brow. He'd hurried to meet them.

Caledonia smiled. "Only a little."

"I suppose if you're going to be dead, being only a little dead is preferable to the alternative. I am glad to see you alive. And you, Amina," he said smoothly. "But I'm afraid I haven't had the luxury of meeting your other companions."

"Crew," Caledonia corrected him.

At this, his eyes narrowed. "I understood from our last encounter that your crew were all girls."

Amina and Pisces stood close at either side. They had chosen her long ago because they had nowhere else to go. But behind her stood Hime and Oran and Sledge and Pine, every one of them a former child of Aric. They'd chosen her over Aric. The deep power and trust of those choices filled her up now, making her tall and strong.

"My crew has grown. Aric wants us to believe that no one leaves his service. Even I believed it. But it isn't true. I have many former Bullets among my crew. Sledge and Pine and Oran all—"

She made it no further. Hesperus burst forward, his sword hissing out of its sheath. "Fiveson!" he shouted, pressing his blade along Oran's throat. A small red line appeared there, blood beading along the blade.

Oran held perfectly still. His eyes rested on Hesperus as though he were of little concern. "Captain," he said, as though requesting another cup of water.

Caledonia's chest tightened. "Stay steely," she said with every bit of control she possessed.

It had the desired effect. Hesperus's grip shifted on his blade. "You brought a Fiveson into my city." Hesperus kept his eyes on Oran while he spoke, every word pitched to cut. "And not just any Fiveson. This one's as bad as Lir."

Uncertainty pricked at Caledonia's mind, reminding her she didn't know all that Oran had done in service to the Father. Telling her that one day she would discover what those things were and she would never see him the same way again.

"Oran fights for me now."

The two guards had moved closer and removed guns from holsters, but neither had taken aim. Behind her, she was certain Pine and Hime mirrored their actions. Caledonia felt a thread of tension coil around her spine.

"You are always bringing danger to my steps, Caledonia Styx." The man finally stepped back, passing the sword over his pant leg before returning it to its sheath. "A Bullet ship and a Fiveson? You are too bold."

She took a step forward. "I think you're more bold than you let on."

He raised a single eyebrow in response and waited for her to explain.

"A few weeks ago, we came across a strange ship. It sailed entirely beneath the surface and attacked from below." She watched his expression carefully as she spoke.

"Deepship tech doesn't exist anymore," he said swiftly.

"Except that it does. I saw it. I fought it." Here she paused, making sure that he met her eyes when she said, "I *sank* it."

There it was. The flash of a response, the nearly imperceptible rise of his eyebrows. Irritation.

"Aric has been after deepship tech for years," he said, evading her implied accusation. "It must have been his."

"I thought so, too. At first. But this ship attacked us because they thought we were Aric's. I feel certain that if we'd been able to communicate, we might have avoided the fight." She lowered her voice. "I am deeply sorry for that."

His jaw clenched, and he blinked hard. He cared about the loss of the ship, but there was genuine sorrow written into the lines of his face. The concern he'd shown for his family during their very first meeting extended to the rest of his people. He mourned their lives in a way she recognized, as someone who felt responsible for sending them into danger.

"If you're building deepships, then you're more willing to resist than you want me—or anyone—to believe." She took one final step forward and felt her team brace themselves around her. "I need your help, Hesperus, and in exchange, I'll keep your secret."

"Hell." Hesperus bowed his head with a shake. When he lifted it once more, his eyes were narrow, his mouth pinched. "Of course that was you. Even though you were dead, I knew it had to be you. Dammit all, Caledonia Styx."

"And you have others?" she pressed. "Show me."

She knew she was asking him for everything he had to offer. Maybe a few months ago she would have demanded less. She would have created room in her world for a man who wanted nothing more than to keep his small corner of it safe. But the only way to change things was to make demands.

"Hesperus," she repeated. "Show me. Or I take what I know with me."

The man frowned. His eyes skated over her companions, lingering on Oran a little longer than the others. He ran a hand down his mouth and finally said, "Only you. Your crew stays here."

She heard Pisces draw a slicing breath, felt Amina bristle, knew that the other four clenched fists and jaws and resisted the urge to speak over their captain. She understood their hesitation, she felt it herself. But she had just changed the game, and she needed to play by these new rules. There was no more room for hesitation.

"Lead the way, then, Hesperus Shreeves."

CHAPTER FORTY

The sun was sinking fast when Hesperus and Caledonia roared out of the clearing on two four-wheeled rovers. They dove beneath the trees, traveling down a path that led more deeply into the mountains at a rushing pace. Cold wind bit at their cheeks and knuckles so harshly it was as if the air was laced with thin sheets of ice.

Caledonia had assured Pisces that Hesperus was trustworthy, but as they careened through the darkening wood, she doubted herself. She was still tired and weak from hunger, in no shape to fight a grown man. Even now her fingers struggled to keep their grip, and strength leached from her thighs until she thought she might slip from the back of this foreign vehicle.

Just as she thought she could no longer hold herself on the back of this machine, Hesperus turned sharply and drove toward the mouth of a cave, where they parked the rovers side by side.

An ominous silence surrounded them. It was hard to gauge just how far they'd traveled, but they were well out of earshot. If she called for her crew, screamed for them, there was no chance they'd hear her.

Caledonia's machine ticked once while the battery discharged, and her ears filled with a sudden, disorienting absence of wind. She swung one leg over the seat and wasn't entirely sure her feet were on the ground when she saw Hesperus pull something swordlike from the back of his rover.

"If we go down this road, there's no coming back," he said, skulking toward her. "I can't just let you leave here with what you know. You do understand that, don't you?"

His threat rode the back of a strange wind that gathered in her ears. Her skin warmed and her limbs seemed to float. She was losing focus, losing all sense, and Hesperus was still coming toward her.

"Stop," she said, voice alarmingly weak.

His laugh seemed to come from very far away. "Oh, it's far too late for that."

Her vision narrowed to a point on his black coat, and then there was nothing but comfortable, smothering blackness.

She opened her eyes to find the face of Hesperus Shreeves hovering just above her own, his brows knit firmly together.

Her body felt light and filled with fluttering birds. Her ears rang with a hollow whistle, and slowly she came to understand that Hesperus's mouth was moving.

"I can't hear you," Caledonia said, or at least, she thought she said it out loud. Even her words felt different.

Hesperus frowned again, then he gently shifted her to the ground—which was the moment she realized she'd been cradled in his arms—and left. He returned a moment later with a canteen and a sack of dried, salted meat. Her mouth watered hotly, and she consumed the first strip of meat before she registered its flavor.

"Slowly," Hesperus chided, holding the sack away when she reached immediately for another. Instead, he offered the water, waiting until she'd had several swallows before allowing her another piece of meat. "I take it water isn't the only thing your crew needs. I should have known. You're as thin as two threads spun together."

Caledonia let him talk, choosing to focus on the meat. Now that she'd had a taste, her body was ravenous. If she could have chewed any faster, she would have.

Hesperus was shaking his head. "Good thing you waited until we stopped to faint. That, at least, shows some reason. Why didn't you ask—?" He stopped himself, knowing the answer to his own question. She didn't ask for food because she had nothing to offer in trade for it. The Sly King of Cloudbreak didn't trade something for nothing.

When the meat was gone, she reached for the water, draining the canteen in one long pull. Her body was beginning to feel cohesive and less like it was filled with a flock of fluttering birds all trying to move in opposing directions. The ringing in her ears receded like the tide. She was still hungry, but the desperate vibration in her blood was gone.

"Thank you," she said.

Hesperus grimaced. "I should start a tally: all the ways Caledonia Styx owes me."

"If you don't intend to let me leave, I'm sure you'll find a way for me to pay you back."

Though it was unsaid, they both knew his threat had been an empty one. Caledonia regarded him coolly, daring him to admit that he wasn't the callous business-man he professed to be.

"Caledonia, you don't really want me as an ally." Hesperus took the canteen from her, screwing on the lid and dropping it into a compartment on his rover. "I'm no better than Aric."

That surprised a dry laugh from Caledonia.

"The only reason I've remained in power for as long as I have is because I keep him happy. I make deals. I protect the people who are useful to me by taking advantage of the ones who aren't." He fixed her with a hard look. "I meant to hand you over to him, keep your solar scales, and take whatever boon he was willing to offer for your capture. I don't want you deciding that I'm better than I am. I would have turned you over and never looked back."

He wanted her to believe it, and part of her did. But there was another part that knew Nettle was right. He wasn't as terrible as rumors would lead them to believe. Of course, those rumors were a layer of protection. He had every reason to see that they traveled well.

"I believe you," she said. "Mostly."

"You should believe me completely."

"The only people I believe completely are my sisters."

He laughed. The sound was loud and joyful; it rolled in his throat and brightened his dark-sky eyes. Caledonia couldn't help but smile in return, and Hesperus let the laugh rumble in his chest before receding into his gruff exterior. She liked him. Always, in spite of herself.

"If you're feeling ready, we should move." He rose to his feet and retrieved two lanterns from his rover, handing one to Caledonia. The swordlike shape she'd seen before gracefully passing out was nothing more than the slender roll he kept them in. "We'll need these inside, and it'll be dark by the time we make it back up."

"Up?" They'd traveled straight into the woods with mountains rising ahead of them. The only way down was back the way they'd come.

Hesperus gave her a tight smile. He flipped on his lantern and made for the opening of the cave, pausing to ensure Caledonia followed.

Inside the cave was deep sea black but for the bluish bands of their lanterns. The passage bent immediately around a corner and from there narrowed so severely that Hesperus had to turn sideways to squeeze through an opening in the wall. Without him, Caledonia might never have registered the small gash as an opening at all.

Beyond that point, the corridor widened, while the mossy air pressed in close, absorbing the sounds of their footsteps. It was warmer here, and soon a layer of sweat covered Caledonia's arms and chest.

"Sharp left here," Hesperus said after a long while. "Keep your left hand on the wall and you'll be fine."

Hesperus rounded the corner, keeping his hand flat on the wall as he went. With a steadying breath, Caledonia followed. Her light showed that the path did indeed turn sharply left, continuing down the wall of a massive cavern. Beside the path was nothing but a long drop.

"Keep your eyes on the stairs." Hesperus's voice carried in the wide space of the cavern, fraying around the edges as it found the far reaches of the room. "If you get dizzy, stop and sit. I don't want your crew thinking I killed you unless I actually do."

If it weren't for the gaping maw beside her, Caledonia might have laughed. As it was, she clenched her teeth and cautiously maneuvered around the corner and onto the hewn stairway. She wasn't afraid of heights the way Pisces was, but this made every muscle in her body contract.

To distract herself, she returned to the question of Hesperus and his ambiguous loyalties. "Would you turn me over now?" she asked.

There was a slight hitch in his step. He thought for a moment before responding. "No."

"Because of what I know?"

Again, a span of thoughtful silence. "Because I have a feeling you'd find your way back. You'd keep pestering me until I gave in and helped you on this damn foolish aim."

She smiled at the words and the gruff manner in which he'd spoken them. "I may make an ally of you yet."

"Caledonia." He stopped three steps below her, spinning to place his right hand against the wall. "You are clearly a girl of vision, and it seems I am destined to help you in spite of my better judgment. But I have an entire city to consider. I won't put them in danger to foster a small war that will likely get the smallest players killed. *We* are the smallest players. And I don't intend to die tomorrow or anytime sooner than many long years from now. I'd also rather you didn't die. But better you than me. You should know that will always be my final reckoning: better you and yours die than me and mine."

She considered the man before her. He was several years her senior, though still quite young. And in spite of his thirst for power, every word he said circled around to a desire to keep people other than himself safe. He was a caring man even if he didn't want to admit it.

Caledonia took one step forward, her eyes level with his. "I'm not interested in a small war, Hesperus. I'm interested in a smart one. I've taken down one of Aric's deadliest ships, interrupted his conscription routes twice, stolen my entire crew out from beneath his thumb at Slipmark. I command lost girls and Bullets and even a Fiveson. I will command more before long, and one way or another,

I'll have more than a single ship to my name. I will stand against Aric Athair and anyone who supports him. You want to protect your people? So do I. And I'll do it with or without your support, though I'd much prefer to have it. It's your choice, of course. We don't have many in this world, but that one belongs solely to you."

As she spoke, a feeling of calm washed over her from brow to boot. Just a few months ago, she'd never have dreamed of making this kind of declaration. Now, though, it felt inevitable. As though the course she'd adopted after losing her family had been this one all along, slowly but surely leading her toward a fight she could only win with the help of her crew and the people of the Sly King of Cloudbreak. Maybe it seemed foolish to someone like him, but it was always going to seem foolish. Right up until the moment someone believed it was possible.

All at once, she recognized a change in herself. She was still the same Caledonia who wanted to keep her girls safe. But she'd discovered that she was also the Caledonia who wanted to take risks and change the world. She wanted to fight.

Still standing before her, Hesperus nodded, then spun around and continued his downward climb. "You have a good sense about people, Caledonia," he called over his shoulder. "I can get my hands on almost anything you can imagine. And if I can't, then I can probably get what you need to build it. That's what I do. I build things—relationships, cities, economies . . ."

Caledonia watched as he reached a ledge and paused there,

fiddling with a panel on the wall. There was a snap, and the cavern filled with light. They'd come much farther than she'd been able to determine in the dark. Overhead, the treacherous stairway crawled along the wall in a wide spiral, disappearing into the net of darkness from which they'd come. But below them . . . that was what snatched her breath.

They'd come to a wide pool, an inland cove buried deep in the heart of a mountain fed by the canals. The pool was ringed by wooden docks all lined with steel, dismantled shiptech, and building materials. And in the water were the rounded tops of nearly a dozen deepships.

"I can even build ships that shouldn't exist anymore. But when it comes to using them, well, that part I'm not as well versed in."

With one hand still pressed firmly to the wall, Caledonia joined Hesperus on the ledge overlooking the hidden pier.

"You've made yourself a fleet," she said, nearly breathless.

"I thought that's what I was doing," he said, annoyed by some unspoken failure. "But I was wrong."

Caledonia turned with the question ready on her lips.

Hesperus swept one hand out, gesturing to the collection of ships before them and said, "I've made *you* a fleet."

CHAPTER FORTY-ONE

Hesperus made himself a consummate host. Every member of Caledonia's crew was bunked in one of the many cabins, and the next day they were greeted by the scents of an incredible feast drifting through the crisp air. It drew everyone outside of their bunks with guarded yet hopeful expressions as they sought the source of the delicious smells.

Caledonia emerged to find the grounds transformed. Tables were arranged in the common space. On each, plates, silverware, and glasses were set in neat rows, and bottles of the Sly King's renowned cherry wine sat uncorked, ready for pouring. From the kitchen where Caledonia and her command crew had gathered the previous evening came a string of Hesperus's people all bearing steaming plates of food, each more enticing than the last.

"My end of the bargain." Hesperus strode toward Caledonia, the early morning sun warming his black skin. "The first bargain."

Their conversation had ended without resolution last night. Caledonia wanted to fight. She wanted to take the fleet Hesperus was offering her and carve away at Aric's power. But for all of that, she'd made a promise to Sledge and the Blades to see them through the Net, and she didn't see how she could have both.

Instead of accepting what Hesperus offered, she'd asked for exactly what they'd come to ask him for: food and shelter while they repaired their ship.

"Thank you." Caledonia wouldn't let him push her into a negotiation on his terms. He could wait. Especially when there was food to be had.

Caledonia stepped up to the head of the central table. Her crew had collected in an anxious semicircle around the tables, their hunger slowly overcoming their resolve. She reached for the nearest wine goblet and raised her voice. "Claim your cups!"

They didn't require a second invitation. They moved in, reaching for the wine-filled cups until every person had one. They held them ready, eyes on Caledonia.

"First, to the Sly King for his hospitality and this very fine food." She tipped her glass toward the man himself and paused while her crew repeated in a single, hearty voice, "To the Sly King!"

Everyone took a sip of the tart liquid, murmuring in appreciation.

Caledonia continued, "You've all worked hard and well. We are not the same crew we were at the beginning of this journey, and I am grateful to have you all fighting by my side." She smiled and raised her glass. "To the good fight and to this fine crew!"

The cheer that rose from the crowd was even better than the wine. They slipped into their chairs and began filling their plates with meat and vegetables and bread. Even Far joined the line, and it was a delight to see her taking her fill for once.

Caledonia's head was light from a few sips of wine, her stomach roared and her mouth watered, but she waited until everyone had a full plate before them. Then she piled her own plate high. Even after filling her mouth three times, there was still food on her plate. She was reminded so sharply of the few meals she'd taken in Slipmark, but where there had been plenty of food in the Bullet camp, each bite had been a reminder of Aric's power. This meal was different. This was food he didn't control, and it was food that would fuel resistance.

The sun rose in the morning sky, adding warmth to their gathering. There was teasing and negotiating and trading, and in the end, Nettle appeared to announce that there were sweet breads for everyone.

"You get one!" Nettle shouted. "And if you take more than your fair share, I'll take your hand in return!"

The breads were distributed, more wine poured, and soon the stories began. They started quietly, one group of Blades swapping tales with some of the crew of the *Mors Navis*, but it wasn't long before the group leaned collectively toward them, their ears eager. The Blades told stories of their magnificent hunts and the girls of defeated bale barges. These were the kinds of tales that would build a network between the two crews, and before long, their stories would overlap, weaving them into the same fabric.

"Tell us how you met the captain!" Tin called out, swept up in the spirit of things.

There was a pause as the Blades turned toward Sledge. He nodded to Pine, who sat up tall and began to tell the story.

"We kept our distance from the conscription ships, but we always watched them." Pine spoke in a voice Caledonia had never heard; he spoke the way someone might when they enjoyed telling the story. "One morning, a conscription ship sailed into the bay and was attacked by a ship skinned with gray and sleek as a shark. The battle was a beauty to behold—a force of girls foiled *Electra*'s tech and stormed the ship, besting every Bullet on board. They fought well and then they left, all except for one."

Caledonia suddenly worried that this would remind everyone that they were upset with or still hurt by their captain's actions, but her girls were riveted. They wanted to know what had happened to her.

"This girl waited for a small fleet of Bullet ships to arrive, then she climbed aboard the flagship and fought valiantly against none other than Fiveson Lir. She held her own, but she was outnumbered and he fought dirty. He used the pikes of his own ship to spear her through the back and would have left her there to die if her own bomb hadn't gone off at that moment. We watched her. Her red hair burned like fire against the black sky as she struggled off that pike and got herself overboard. She should have died, but she held on to her tow and washed up on our shores. How could we let someone so bold bleed out on the rocks?" Pine paused, looking toward Caledonia with a flame of respect in his eyes. "We couldn't."

He returned to his seat, but the tables were still and quiet. Confused, Caledonia turned to Pisces, finding a look of awe on her sister's face. This, Caledonia realized, was the first they'd heard the full tale of the night she left them.

"Cala." Pisces pressed her palms to the table as though holding herself up. "You almost died."

It was the first time she'd used that name since her return, and the sound of it hummed along Caledonia's skin. She smiled. "Only a little."

"You—you didn't tell us," Pisces said, sorrow tugging at her mouth. "Oh, Cala."

She reached for Caledonia's hand, understanding what Caledonia didn't have to say aloud. That she didn't know how to share anything with Pisces mad at her.

In the moment that followed, Hime rose from her seat. She looked at Pine and signed: *Thank you for saving our bull-headed captain.*

Pine smiled. "I think I understood that. And she didn't make it easy."

Everyone laughed. They'd found perfectly common ground at the expense of their captain. And Caledonia couldn't even begrudge them their joy because it wasn't anger or resentment that lifted their laughter, she realized. It was something closer to love.

"You should have seen her the day Pi went overboard!" one of her girls shouted.

"Or when she ran from Pine, bleeding all the way through the forest!" a Blade added.

Sledge stood, his mountainous form commanding silence in an instant. "Our captain's foolish bravery is only tempered by her incredible head for battle. I've never seen anyone able to keep her head in demanding situations quite like her, and I am honored to fight at her side." Here, he paused and raised his glass. "To our captain!"

The crew echoed in a thunderous voice, "To our captain!"

From across the spread of tables, Hesperus raised a cup in Caledonia's direction. His smile was barely there, and his eyes pushed his question forward again. Would she take what he'd offered? Would she command his fleet and fight Aric head-on?

She would. She already knew that she would accept and that she would ask her crew to join her. Most of them would. She was as sure of that now as she was of anything. But commanding a fleet of her own would change the fight. More of her people would die, and she would be the one sending them to their deaths. Trading the lives of some for the lives of many.

She had everything that she wanted: a willing crew, powerful ships, and her sister's hand in hers. And she hadn't expected it to feel so heavy.

CHAPTER
FORTY-TWO

The drowning dreams were back.

Every night, Caledonia dreamed of clear blue water. For a moment, all was calm. She was cradled in the arms of the ocean, rocked gently back and forth in the current. She was warm and calm and when she tipped her head back, she could see the sun winking against the tips of little waves. Her mind was still, her heart quiet. It was like taking a deep breath and feeling it fill you all the way down to your toes.

Hoist your eyes, my brave girl.

She opened her eyes to find the water cast in shadow and so much colder than before. It surrounded her, gripped her ankles and wrists with watery hands and held her five feet below a burning surface. Flames danced over her head, swirling their vicious orange skirts across the water again and again, trapping her there. She opened her mouth and screamed, letting air rush out in furious bubbles, letting panic overwhelm her reason. Her lungs constricted, empty and desperate.

Then all at once, the watery hands released her. She was free to rush for the surface. Her future was up to her and the choice was dismal: to drown or burn.

She woke eager to tear something apart. Usually, she could satisfy that kind of desire by sparring with Pisces or Amina or joining Sledge's training sessions. But this morning, she was too irritable for any of that.

Over the past few days, the crew had settled into a new routine, which looked a lot like their old routine minus the ship and the broad ocean. No one seemed quite as bothered by the change as Caledonia felt. In fact, they were thriving.

Every morning, she watched them smile and eat their fill of something hot and far from any stage of rot. They kept to their duty schedule. They were healthy, well rested, and the ship was improving by the hour. It should make her happy, and on some level it did. But still, she woke feeling like she was trapped, suffocating, and heading toward the moment when she would once again find herself without her crew. She wanted to take everything Hesperus was offering and fight, but the task of asking the others to do the same was an ever-present weight on her chest.

She cut through camp toward the high canal ridge. Wind burned against her cheeks, and she pulled her thick jacket—yet another gift of the Sly King—more tightly around her waist. Her blood began to race and her thighs burned as the land tilted sharply upward. She reached her destination just as a band of the thinnest gold appeared on the horizon.

The overhang sat high on a sharp protrusion of stone that lunged over the canals below. As sunrise coaxed the world back to life, Caledonia felt her breath come more easily. She felt less trapped when she could see the ocean. When she could cast out her thoughts and let them settle.

The wind was layered with the scents of chalk, moss, and dry earth, and Caledonia took her fill of the rising sun as it set fire to the wide ocean. It wasn't the same as standing atop the mizzenmast of the *Mors Navis*, the sun sail winging out beneath her boots. But it was closer than she'd come in a long while. She stood there, letting the quiet of the world before her fill her up completely.

Pisces was waiting for her when she finally left the overlook. She stood at the base of the path with steam curling away from the mugs in her hands. They smelled earthy and bright and the slightest bit sweet. Caledonia took one and brought it to her lips.

Pisces waited while she sipped. "You're still not sleeping well." It was a statement, spoken with a barely concealed undercurrent of concern.

"I'm sleeping enough."

"Hmm," Pisces replied, rolling her mug between long fingers. She opened her mouth, shut it, frowned. All within the space of a few seconds.

"Pi."

Her frown plunged more deeply, then lifted away as she resolved some thought. "I want you to know that we trust you. We're all with you."

"But . . ." Caledonia began.

Pisces took a bold step forward. She placed a palm flat against Caledonia's cheek and leaned in to kiss her lightly on the lips. "Cala," she said. "Whatever is keeping you up at night, whatever it is Hesperus said to you while you were alone out there, it's time. You need to let me in."

Caledonia's throat squeezed. She blinked fiercely and nodded, reflecting her friend's gentle strength. "I want to fight."

Pisces's eyes narrowed. "Yes," she said suspiciously. "You have always wanted to fight. Why are you saying it like it's something new?"

"Hesperus has a fleet of deepships," she admitted. "He wants me to command them."

This time, Pisces's mouth opened in soft surprise. "What does that mean? A fleet?"

"He has eleven deepships," Caledonia continued in excitement. "Do you know what we could do with eleven deepships Aric doesn't know exist?! We could change things, Pi. We could destroy the Net, take Slipmark, defend the colonies!" Hot water sloshed over her hands as her excitement grew.

"We could take a stand," Pisces said in wonder.

"Yes! We could do so much more than we've ever done, but . . ."

"But what?" Pisces pressed, an echo of Caledonia's passion lighting her eyes.

"But I made a promise to Sledge and the rest of the Blades. That I would get them through the Net if they helped me free you." She paused, uncomfortable with what she was going to say next. "And you—I left you once. How can I ask you and the girls to fight for me again?"

Pisces studied Caledonia with a puzzled expression, as though she couldn't believe her friend didn't know the answer to that particular question. "Caledonia, we've never asked you to be perfect. We've only ever asked you to be *ours*. To fight with us and for us. And that's what you do. Even when you stumble, you come back to us. That's what matters most."

"I don't like making mistakes," Caledonia grumbled, linking her arm through Pisces's as the two turned slow steps toward camp. "And I wouldn't blame them if this kind of fight was too much."

Their boots crunched softly over fallen pine needles, and the strains of a lively camp called them forward.

"You know the crew will fight for you," Pisces said after a moment. "What is this really about?"

She should have known Pisces would see straight into her heart. And she should have known that it would help her clarify her own thoughts. Pisces was right. She wasn't afraid that her crew wouldn't follow her. Not anymore. She was afraid of something else entirely.

"What if I can't command a fleet?" she asked. "What if I make a mistake and it gets us all killed?"

Pisces nodded as though that was the answer she'd been expecting. "Nothing about this is going to be easy. Just remember that we're fighting to change the world that forces us to make choices like this. And we're choosing you because you keep showing us that you *can* do this. We trust you to keep us safe, but more than that, we trust you to help us fight well."

The squeeze in Caledonia's throat went from tight to painfully tight. She wanted to say something, but it wasn't possible. There was a tremor that moved from her lips to her jaw to her lungs to her fingertips. She nodded shakily.

"Pi," she managed after a long swallow. But there was nothing else to say after that.

"I love you, Caledonia Styx. You make me furious and proud, and I will always love you and follow you," Pisces said, placing herself mercilessly inside the bounds of Caledonia's heart. "There are no perfect decisions for us, no easy choices. But it's important that we keep making them. And right now, you have to give Sledge a choice and trust yourself to make the best of his decision."

Finally, Caledonia laughed. "You're a hell of a girl, Pisces Amar."

"Don't think you can sweet talk me into anything," she returned with a smile. "But you're also a hell of a captain."

The warmth of the moment was passing, swept away by the reality of what awaited her. Uncertainty, frustration, anxiety all warred for space in her gut, but as they came into camp and spotted the mountain of Sledge seated with Pine and working on a hearty breakfast, Caledonia gave a determined nod. "No point in putting this off."

The instant Sledge spotted Caledonia, he straightened, pushing his plate away. Pine looked up with a glower, begrudgingly doing the same.

"This is not your good morning face," Sledge said. "This is a bad news face."

"Good morning, Sledge." Caledonia set her mug down. "Morning, Pine."

"I hope you're here to settle a private matter between us," Pine said. "I say you're going to revoke your promise to get us through the Net. Sledge says you wouldn't do that." He leaned back with a thin smile. "Prove one of us right."

Caledonia did not fidget. She stood tall and held on to Pisces's words. She could give them a choice, and even if it wasn't what they wanted, it would matter.

"I'm not going to the Net," she began, ignoring the triumphant flip of Pine's mouth. "The Net is a dream and a distraction. We have no guarantee that what's on the other side is better than what we have here. And what's here is worth fighting for."

She expected another jab from Pine, but when she flicked her eyes to his, she was startled by the encouragement she found, the subtle shift in his smile from triumphant to admiring. He moved his head in an almost imperceptible nod, and she continued.

"I made a promise to you, and Pine's right, I'm not going to fulfill it as intended. But the *Beacon* is yours. Take it and punch the Net if that's still what you want. I won't stop you. Hesperus will give you everything you need to make the journey."

Sledge pulled a hand across his forehead, leaning broad fore-arms on the table. "And what will you be doing, Caledonia Styx?"

"Hesperus is giving me command of a fleet of deepships," she said, standing tall and confident. "I'm going to take them and what-ever crew wants to join me, and I'm going to give Aric a hell fight."

Sledge glared. "How many ships?"

"Eleven," Caledonia admitted, knowing it was a paltry number compared to Aric's forces. "But it's a strong eleven. Stronger with a good crew."

Sledge shook his head in dismay, and Caledonia pressed on.

"I know this wasn't the plan. I know the plan keeps chang-ing. But every time we let him convince us to run away from his power, he wins a little bit more. I think it's time to take some of that power away from him. I could really use your help to do it," she said. "But the choice is yours."

When she finished, Pine's smile was wide. "I'm with you," he said, pounding a fist on the table.

Sledge nodded, rising to his feet as though the weight of this choice had filled his veins with lead. He turned to Pine, letting his eyes rest there with more tenderness than he'd ever revealed before. Then, turning to Caledonia, he raised his hands, palms out.

Caledonia, met him with her own palms, still unsure if this was goodbye or something else.

"It wasn't the plan," Sledge agreed. "But I think you were the plan we needed. I'm with you, Captain, as I suspect most of the Blades will be."

Now Caledonia let her smile unfurl. Her team was coming together, and it was growing. "With their consent."

CHAPTER
FORTY-THREE

By midday, Hesperus and Mino arrived with six rovers ready to take Caledonia's chosen team to the deepships. There weren't enough for everyone to have one of their own, so they rode double; Amina and Nettle, Pisces and Ares, Sledge and Pine all moved toward their rovers, which left only Caledonia and Oran.

Caledonia took the driver's position, gesturing for Oran to climb on behind her. "You're going to want to hold on," she said over her shoulder.

His hands settled against her waist, fingers curling into the fabric of her jacket so that it brushed her skin. She resisted the urge to shiver when his breath tickled her neck.

"Captain?" Hesperus called, the sound of his voice clearing her head in an instant.

"Ready!" she shouted back.

They traveled in a line into the woods, down the same path toward the hidden cave. The trip was easier and shorter when she wasn't withering away from starvation, clinging to the handles with her last drops of strength. And this time she noticed that the path was less an established channel through the woods and more a series of trees marked with a dab of cerulean blue at a level just higher than she would naturally look. It would take a certain amount of luck for someone to follow it unwittingly.

When they reached the cave with the harrowing stairwell, Hesperus took the lead. Mino followed at the rear, and in between, the eight of them took every single step with great care, Pisces muttering the whole way.

Finally, they reached the dock, and their real work began. Light flooded the air, winking against the rounded tops of all eleven deep-ships. They were each roughly ten feet long and only half as wide with a hatch in the roof as the only way in or out. The rest of the ship was hidden beneath dark water, where they would all soon be.

It wasn't until this moment that the full scope of what they were about to do really settled in for each of them. Caledonia saw the same twisting tension she felt in her chest pull at the corners of Sledge's wide mouth and drain the color from Oran's warm cheeks. The only one of them who didn't look as though they'd take an invitation to travel right back up those stairs was Nettle. Her eyes shone at the sight of the ships.

"We won't all fit in one," Hesperus explained, as Mino hopped from the dock to the roof of a deepship and pried open the hatch. Inside the cabin was dark and terribly small. "I'll take one group and Mino the other."

"Will Sledge even fit?" Nettle asked with a laugh as she crouched to peer inside. "I think he could wear this ship like a skirt."

Sledge frowned at the small girl, but she had a teasing gleam in her eye.

"Pi," Caledonia said. "You take Sledge, Amina, and Ares and go with Mino. Nettle, Pine, Oran, you're with me and Hesperus."

"The thief, the Bullet, and the Fiveson," Hesperus grumbled. "What could possibly go wrong?"

It was everything Caledonia hated about being underwater. The cabin was cramped, long, and barely wide enough to accommodate two people standing abreast, or a single Sledge. Either end was cupped in thick bulbs of self-healing glass beyond which pressed black water. Once the hatch above them was sealed, the entire world narrowed to what they could see in those two directions. Which at the moment was absolutely nothing.

The room smelled like metal and salt and the electric burn of energy. The container dampened every sound so that even a breath was stifling. None of which seemed to bother Oran; he moved to a control panel, fingers grazing the switches affectionately. Then he spun to Hesperus.

"You've pressurized the chamber," he said with appreciation. "But how did you solve the problem of water pressure?"

Hesperus narrowed his eyes. "Two hulls," he answered, as though that explained anything. Which, to Oran, it clearly did.

Hesperus quickly oriented them to the mechanics. The ship could be controlled from either end, allowing it to change directions without having to swivel or turn. It could be loaded with four dozen missiles and had a reliable range of fifty yards. Of course, the constant challenge was visibility. Even with the self-repairing glass and flexible maneuverability, if the water was cloudy, there was little to be done about navigation.

"What about lights?" Nettle asked, already perched behind the small wheel at one end. "How long does their power last? How deep have you taken them?"

Hesperus paused in his explanations, his expression caught between annoyance and . . . was that fondness? It was as if, in spite of himself, he couldn't help but be impressed by Nettle's gumption. Caledonia could certainly relate to that, but this felt like something more.

"Lights are controlled here," he said, reaching above her head to flip a series of switches, illuminating the dark bowl of the cove ahead of them. Which was somehow worse than the darkness that had existed there a moment earlier. "At full charge, each ship can travel four hours at top speeds. And we've taken them to a depth of seventy feet. They'll go deeper, though."

"Hmm," Nettle answered in the most critical way possible.

Hesperus loomed over the girl, drawing Caledonia closer. "If you had better ideas, you might have stayed to implement them."

This brought a flush to Nettle's tan cheeks, the paler scroll-work of her scar standing out against it. Her eyes darted between Hesperus and Caledonia, mildly alarmed, but not for the reason Caledonia thought she should be. She raised her hands in surrender, and Caledonia reached out to snatch her left one.

There, nestled in the soft webbing between her thumb and forefinger, was a small tattoo, the exact match to Hesperus's own.

Caledonia felt her jaw drop open. "You're his daughter?"

"No!" Nettle protested.

"Niece," Hesperus answered. "And a willful one at that."

"I know I should have told you." Nettle let her hands fall to her sides, her shoulders slumping. "It's just . . . I didn't think you'd take me on if you knew, and your crew—it's just the most amazing thing I've ever been a part of."

Caledonia knew she should be annoyed, irritated, full of fresh doubt about this girl who'd joined her crew under false pretenses. But she found instead a still pool of understanding. She'd always admired Nettle for her daring and bravado. That had not changed.

"Please don't kick me off the crew," Nettle said in a small voice, her eyes wide and pleading. "I'm too good for you to let me go."

Hesperus barked a laugh. "Until you have something she wants, then she'll rob you and leave without a word."

Caledonia let a smile warm her cheeks. "Maybe you didn't give her enough to do," she chided.

"Ha!" Nettle clasped her hands into victorious fists. "That means I get to stay, right?"

"You get to stay," Caledonia confirmed.

Hesperus shook his head and continued his lesson. There were controls for ascent and descent, for thrusters, which were positioned all around the small ship, for pressurizing the cabin as they descended and the weight of water increased. There was even a scope they could use when they were near enough to the surface to gauge the distance to any ships. It was a complicated system designed to keep them all breathing in the very bosom of the ocean. The more they learned, the less Caledonia liked it. This was so much worse than relying on a blue lung and swimming beneath the ship as Pisces often did. This was intentionally trapping yourself inside a metal canister and dropping it into the deep ocean.

Caledonia leaned on Hesperus's every word. She needed to know exactly how these worked even if she wasn't destined to pilot one. And she needed her crew to believe she had faith in the ships even if they became fodder for her nightmares. She couldn't ask half of her crew to do something she wouldn't do herself.

"Pine, release the cables," Hesperus instructed, calm and confident. "Nettle, be ready on port thrusters."

The ship bobbed as Pine detached the clamp holding them against the dock, then the cabin filled with a gentle vibration as Nettle initiated the thrusters and began to move the deepship into open waters. Caledonia curled her fingers more firmly around the wheel, her palms already damp and too hot.

"We're going to take her out slow and steady." Hesperus stood at her shoulder, his eyes glued to the glass bowl before them. Beams of light swept across the gleaming metal hull of six other deepships as they nosed away from the dock. "The others haven't moved, so we're all clear, but stay on your guard down here."

Caledonia glanced up where the bowl of glass joined the steel husk of the ship. Water splashed along it in shallow waves, proving they were not yet fully submersed. The surface was still within easy reach. It wasn't much of a comfort.

Under Hesperus's direction, they skimmed the surface until daylight brushed the water around them, casting it in shades from pale blue to bruised purple. Nettle shifted from thrusters to propulsion, Pine was ready on cabin pressurization, and Oran had taken the ballast station nearest Caledonia, ready to force the ship into the deep.

"Ready to take her down?" Hesperus asked, and when his eyes landed on Oran, he added, "Kind of a redundant question for a Fiveson, I suppose."

She'd grown so accustomed to how the Blades regarded Oran with a twisted kind of reverence and apprehension that Hesperus's disdain continued to surprise her. He wasn't afraid of Oran in the least. Or if he was, he was doing a hell of a job hiding it.

Oran didn't react except to say, "Ready on your command, sir."

"Then do what you do best." It was spoken with specific confidence. Hesperus knew more about Oran than Caledonia, and it was starting to become a problem. Oran the Bullet. Oran the Fiveson. Oran the Steelhand.

Ignoring the fresh tension in the room, she kept her slick hands tight on the wheel and focused on keeping her breath even.

"Hey," Oran said softly, placing a hand over one of her own. "We can turn back. There's no need for you to do this part."

Her cheeks flashed hot and cold at once and she scowled. "I don't run away from things."

Oran pulled away in surprise. "Of course not, Captain."

Everyone else in this too-small container was watching. She'd been harsh. Perhaps harsher that she'd needed to be, and she didn't quite know why herself.

"When you're done with this lover's quarrel, we're ready to descend to thirty feet." Hesperus's voice fell around them like a fog, curtailing any further discussion.

From the back of the ship, Caledonia heard Pine shift loudly. Nettle, however, made no sound. Oran nodded, turning his attention back to his controls and keeping it there.

"Beginning descent," he announced.

"Pressurizing the cabin." Pine's voice was taut as a bowstring.

The air in the small room tightened around them, adding a pressure deep inside their ears, and the small bit of surface visible through the top of the glass vanished. As they descended, Caledo-

nia let her discomfort replace any misgivings she had about snapping at Oran. Her nerves were too frayed, her control too strained
to give any thought to the boy and all the things she didn't yet
know about him.

It seemed only a minute had passed when Oran announced
they'd arrived at their intended depth. Caledonia's ears popped
once, and they shifted to thrusters only. They floated serenely in
the wake of their own lights.

"We never want to take the ships any deeper than this in the canals." Hesperus walked from one end of the cabin to the other, craning
over their shoulders to check various gauges. "The canals run a little
deeper than this, but not by much. Thirty feet keeps us low enough
to avoid any keelers and high enough to avoid gouging our own belly
on the bottom. It's a little easier in the open ocean, of course. Better
light all around, for one thing; more space, for another."

"How far are we going today?" Caledonia asked, doing everything in her power to keep the tension in her voice invisible.

Hesperus paused before answering, "Not too far." And even
though Caledonia strongly suspected he'd adjusted his plans based
on her, she didn't challenge him.

He guided them down the winding channel until they entered an area he called the pool. Even without having a full view
of the space, Caledonia sensed the change around them. The walls
opened wide, pulling away on either side and letting more light
filter through.

"Now we have room to play." Hesperus was brimming with a new energy Caledonia almost didn't recognize in the man. He was *excited*. "Let's give her some power, and I'll show you exactly how she moves."

Within moments, they'd gone from their serene, almost dreamy pace to barreling through the water like a shark. Their engines hummed so loudly through the cabin they had to shout to be heard.

Caledonia slid her palms over her thighs one at a time, then gripped the wheel tightly. Ahead, the water was clear for a mere thirty or forty feet, and they rushed forward with incredible speed. There was no way to read the water down here. There was only the sweep of the ground beneath and the flat blue ahead—right up until the moment there was something else in their path, of course. She kept her gaze alert, pinned to the spaces where rocks might suddenly appear or fish, anything that could crash against their hull and cause trouble. Or drowning. Which seemed the more likely outcome of any encounter.

"Getting the feel for it?" Hesperus asked. Without waiting for an answer from anyone, he continued, "We're going to back off propulsion and get ready to reverse control. Nettle, take the wheel. Pine, jump on thrusters. Fiveson, don't touch anything."

The ship eased out of speed and for a moment, they cruised smoothly forward. Then Hesperus gave the order to reverse control. There was a loud groan as gears complied with the request;

the propellers at the rear folded into the base of the ship while the propellers at the fore unfolded. The light indicating Caledonia had control blipped out, and her wheel locked into position. There was no way she might accidentally resume control and compromise the ship's course from here.

"All right, let's spin her back up."

With another loud groan, the ship came to a shuddering stop, then slowly chugged back in the direction they'd come, with Nettle holding them steady this time.

"What do you think, Captain?" Hesperus couldn't hide the pleasure in his question. He had good reason to be pleased with himself. These ships were unlike anything Caledonia had ever experienced.

"Impressive," she said, climbing out of her chair to stand next to him. "But what happens when something enters your path? Reversing control took a full minute, changing directions another minute still; how do you ever avoid anything down here?"

"We designed them this way initially because of the canals— we can go backward without having to turn around. But do you feel up to a demonstration?" he asked, a spark of genuine concern flashing in his dark eyes.

"That's why I'm here, Sly King." Irritation welled in her chest like blood from a wound.

Grinning, Hesperus stepped forward, calling for Nettle to relinquish her seat to him. "Hop on thrusters, and Pine, propulsion if you would. Caledonia, next to me."

"What can I do?" Oran asked.

Hesperus shrugged. "That is a question I won't lose sleep over."

"Hesperus." Caledonia made her voice a warning. He might not like Oran, but he was her crew and she wouldn't stand for the mistreatment of any of her crew.

"Apologies, Captain." Hesperus gave her a hard look that suggested those apologies were as thin as the air in the cabin. "Everyone ready? Good. Pine, take us to maximum."

Caledonia felt the ship rumble in response. Quickly, she settled into the station nearest to Hesperus and watched as the floor of the pool whipped by at greater and greater speeds.

Stay steely, she reminded herself, even as her breath quickened and her palms grew sweaty again.

"Nettle, when I say, I want you to burn our port thrusters at ninety degrees as hard as they'll go. Don't let up until I tell you. Pine, I want you to cut propulsion when I say, but be ready to bring us back in an instant."

"Ready!" Nettle called.

"Ready," Pine stated.

Caledonia didn't feel ready. She felt decidedly *un*ready.

The ship rumbled around them. Hesperus grinned, leaning forward in his seat. It was unsettling, and also strangely comforting. Whatever he was about to do, he'd done it before, and he was still alive.

Suddenly, the water ahead grew darker as though the sun had set unevenly, sipping light from the ocean in long stripes. No, it wasn't light. It wasn't even water. In the next second, her fears were confirmed.

Wall. There was a wall directly ahead. She wasn't in command, yet it was on the tip of her tongue to order her crew into a hard turn.

"Now, Pine!" Hesperus shouted, gleeful even as the wall rushed at them. "Nettle, you're up!"

Hesperus pulled the wheel, and the ship swung in an arc, rolling toward the wall for three painful seconds before the thrusters pushed her upright. Again, Hesperus shouted for Pine, and this time the engines roared, shoving them back in their seats as the ship drove forward.

Caledonia couldn't keep her eyes off the wall. They traveled along it now, not four feet away. It would have taken so little to send them careening into it.

"Captain?" Hesperus asked, his hand landing heavily on her shoulder.

When she turned, she found all four of her companions were looking at her. Each of them wore expressions of concern, as though that hadn't been the first time Hesperus called to her.

She nodded once, swallowing her heart, her lungs, her guts, everything that had jammed into her throat during that terrifying maneuver.

"What about firing capacity?" she asked, ignoring every ounce of their concern. "Your ship damaged our propeller but didn't take us down."

"Each deepship carries four dozen stable missiles. They pack a decent punch against smaller ships, but I've got my people working on something that will hit harder," he admitted. "We're building our stores as we speak."

Caledonia gazed through the rounded window. So little of the vast ocean was visible beyond it. They would need a clear day, a skilled crew, and some degree of luck on their side to use deepships to their full effect.

Still, a submerged attack was one no Bullet would ever see coming.

"I can fight with these," she confirmed. "But it's going to take some time to train the crew."

"I can give you time," Hesperus said, solemn. "But work fast."

CHAPTER FORTY-FOUR

I t was strange to feel rested. For a week, they'd had regular meals, comfortable beds, and now they had a mission.

Every member of the crew had been given the chance to stay in Cloudbreak or join the fleet. And one by one, they'd come to Caledonia with their support, commitment, and consent.

Harwell had come to her first, his shoulders hunched so even his ears looked nervous as he raised his hands in the sign of consent. Nettle had been next, delivering a commitment that sounded nearly like a threat. And then all the others, filing into her cabin one at a time.

Last was Oran. He stood in the doorway of her cabin, dusk light caught in his dark hair, and with a slight bow said, "I am yours, Caledonia. Whatever you need."

When it was over, she sat in her cabin and named them all in her head, knowing that after this there might be too many for her to remember. Knowing that after this, she would lead people she might never meet. Pisces had been right to question her fears.

Caledonia wasn't afraid that people wouldn't follow her. Not anymore. Now she was more afraid that so many seemed ready to do so.

She'd been fighting for years. She knew how to pick her battles and keep her people safe. But this wasn't going to be a battle. This was going to be a war. And people were going to die.

The morning was still dim and cold, the sun not yet burning on the horizon when Caledonia rolled out of her bunk and laced into her boots. She pulled her cabin door shut behind her, waved to the crew on dead watch, and snatched a few strips of dried meat and a small block of cheese from the kitchen. Then she strode down the dusty path toward the cherry orchard.

Her mood constricted slightly as she passed beneath a stand of tall pines. The forest always made the world feel so small and close. She was overwhelmed by the desire to get out.

Balling her fists, she began to run, kicking her heels up and pumping her arms as hard as she possibly could. Soon, sweat kissed her neck and brow, and her muscles began to burn with effort. She followed the road as it curved this way and that, leaping over the occasional fallen branch and letting herself breathe loudly.

Finally, she burst from the cover of trees, skidding to a stop on the crest of a hill that overlooked the sleeping cherry orchard. She pressed her eyes closed and tipped her head back. Her heart was wild in her chest, and she relished the feel of it knocking against her ribs, reminding her that she had not yet drowned.

"Caledonia?"

Her breath hitched in the back of her throat. She'd assumed she was alone. She hadn't even taken a moment to glance around.

Reckless girl, she snarled inwardly.

"Oran."

His pants were dusty from sitting and his shirt damp from his own run. Behind him, cherry trees extended toward the horizon in long rows, their winter brown branches bare and twisting coarsely in every direction. Hesperus said in the spring they erupted with blossoms of the softest pink that rained down like snow when the wind blew. It was hard to imagine such distressed-looking trees could produce something so beautiful.

"Good morning," Oran said.

Caledonia nodded, swallowing her annoyance at not being alone. It wasn't his fault. And he'd clearly been here before her. He didn't deserve her anger simply by virtue of proximity.

"I didn't think anyone would be here."

A dry smile turned one corner of his lips. "I'll go."

Every time she looked at him, she recognized herself less. Her heart fluttered and her lips warmed with the memory of their long-ago kiss, while her mind screamed, *Bullet, Fiveson, Steelhand.*

He'd done so much for her and her crew. But there were things in his past she still didn't know. And there was no more time for secrets.

"No, stay." Her voice carried the weight of command. She heard it, and he heard it. He raised an eyebrow, and it was almost as if she could see the protective veneer of Fiveson Oran slide into place.

"As you like, Captain."

He remained standing just six feet away and slightly lower than her on the hillside. He was dressed in a dark blue jacket tied close around his waist, the cut of it perfectly accenting his lithe body. His wounds had healed for the most part, and he'd slowly worked to rebuild his strength. In the early morning light his brown hair shone with highlights of copper and rust. One side of his face caught the rising sun, leaving the other cast in shadow.

Her midnight conversation with Ares lurked in the back of her mind. She'd done her best to keep it there, and not consider it too closely, but it was time to let all the questions she'd formed that night come out.

"Who are you, Oran?"

The skin around his eyes tightened. "You know who I am. Your crew. Your friend. Yours." He added the last softly, sadly.

She let her fingernails bite into her palms. "You told me once that you wouldn't lie to me. Is that still true?"

"It will always be true."

She hurried forward, afraid she would lose her intention in the deep pool of his brown eyes. "What made you a Fiveson?"

"Caledonia." He said her name with such gentle remorse.

"I've waited as long as I could."

"I understand," he said.

A sudden inexplicable fear squeezed in her chest. "Wait," she commanded.

She closed the distance between them in three long strides, sliding her fingers along his jaw and into his hair. She paused just long enough to see surprise widen his eyes. She opened her mouth to ask for his consent, but it was there. They crashed together without a word. His lips were warm and welcoming, his tongue sweet against her own. His arms circled her waist and pulled her flush against him. She kissed him hungrily, fiercely, and then slowly, as though it were the last thing she might ever do.

She let her fingers twist through his hair, skate along his jaw, and slide down his neck as her kisses grew further and further apart. His breath was warm against her lips, and the tips of their noses brushed. Then she leaned her forehead against his and closed her eyes.

"Caledonia," he said again, like the most personal of prayers.

"I'm sorry," she answered. Then she pulled herself out of his grasp, putting only air and sunrise between them. "I need to know."

He turned away from her, pinning his eyes to the orchard as though speaking his past to the trees were somehow easier.

"It was years ago," he began. "Lir was already a Fiveson, and Aric held up Lir's feat to all of us as the kind of offering any potential Fiveson should aspire to. And I did."

Unbidden, memories of that night crashed around her like waves. Lir had used her to get to her family, then he'd taken her brother under his wing, all to please Aric.

"There were no Fivesons before us. It was new. The fastest way to the top. And we all knew that whoever succeeded Aric would be among them. We went a little wild with it. One day, we were young Bullets. We trained, we followed orders, we served knowing eventually, if we proved ourselves, we'd be rewarded; taken off rotation and sent to the Holster to raise children for Aric." He glanced up at the sky, steadying himself there before continuing on. "The next day, we were each competing to be more dangerous than every other Bullet we knew. We trained harder, but we also looked for opportunities to prove we could be dispassionate in the service of the Father." He paused there, searching for the exact words that would drive his point home. "We looked for opportunities to practice cruelty."

Caledonia's stomach knotted. Her mind spun through so many terrible possibilities. She'd heard many tales of Bullet cruelty from her girls. She'd believed each and every one. There was no reason for them to lie.

But this time was different. This time, she wanted none of it to be true.

"When Bullets are still coming into their prime, they're assigned to the AgriFleet. I was there longer than some because I was given—no, I *took*—the opportunity to command. I was responsible for all the youngest recruits, and I was hard on them. I saw the way people feared Aric, the way they talked about Lir, and I knew if I wanted to stand with them, I had to do something worthy of their notice. Something *more* than Lir had done." His lips pressed flat in a private sneer. Every muscle in his body was tense. Caledonia wished she could reach out and soothe him, but her body was just as tense.

"One night a dozen recruits . . . a dozen children tried to steal a prowler in the middle of the night and escape. But I knew it was going to happen, and I was waiting for them. I let them take the ship. I let them think they were getting away." Sunlight spilled through the orchard and over them, glinting off a sheen in Oran's eyes. The apple of his throat plunged up and down as he worked to gather himself and keep telling the story. "When they were a half mile from the barge, we circled them. Five ships to corral one. It was more than we needed, but I wanted everyone to see how futile it was to try and escape Aric. How dishonorable.

"I remember how perfect it was that night. We'd gone north to avoid some summer storms, and the air stayed heavy and humid. We were always uncomfortable. But in the middle of the night, under the light of the Sheering moon, there was just enough of a breeze to make everything pleasant. I almost needed my jacket, but I was so proud of my first band." He raised a hand to his bicep, clutching at the place where his scars marked his skin.

When he dropped his hand again, Caledonia caught the echo of a tremble. The sight nearly brought her to call this off. She didn't want him to share this pain. She didn't want to carry any piece of it.

But it was already there. And closing her eyes to it wasn't going to help anyone.

"I brought the rest of the young recruits out on their barge. I made sure they could see their former companions." He drew in a long breath, exhaling sharply. "None of them were full Bullets yet. Their punishment was up to me, and it certainly wasn't the first time someone or even a group tried to escape. There were many options available to me. But I wanted to make a statement. I wanted to demonstrate, for all of them and for Aric, just how deserving I was."

A tear rolled down his cheek. It winked in the sunlight, then plunged to the dust at his feet. Caledonia looked away, bottom lip clamped firmly between her teeth.

"I told them that the only way they would survive was to jump overboard. Relinquish the ship and prove they still wanted to be here. They did. All twelve jumped into the water. And then I told them that their ticket out of the water again was to kill one of their peers. To drown them or be drowned themselves."

Before this moment, Caledonia hadn't given herself room to consider the tortures of the Steelhand. In her mind, the tide cans and the small blades existed in the realm of Slipmark. But that wasn't exactly true. They were the designs of a single mind: Oran's mind.

"For a minute, all they did was tread water. They were these wide-eyed boys and girls not ready to believe the world was that cruel, but all it took was one. One boy to realize this was the only way he would live. In an instant, they went from working together to escape, to trying to kill one another." His voice grew hard again. "Two of them survived."

She couldn't look at him. She filled her eyes with the sun and with the blurring field of cherry trees. Her lips were cold and numb. The kiss that had warmed them moments ago was a distant memory. Part of her past now. The Oran she had kissed was not the boy standing next to her. He was changed and so was she, and she didn't know if they would ever fit together again.

She held him in her memory: The boy who'd saved her best friend, the boy with tree rings in his eyes, the boy who watched her with such hope, and such admiration. The boy she'd slowly come to trust. She still trusted him, that had not changed, but everything else had.

"That was what made me a Fiveson, Caledonia. And it was only the first thing that distinguished me as the Steelhand. After that, Aric wanted more." He paused. "And I gave it to him."

Warm tears slipped down her own cheeks, falling silently to the ground, and she let them. They weren't for her. They were for the children who had died to make a point, and they were for the child who had killed them for the same.

Without another word, she turned and left the hill, letting the dark trees of the forest wall her in.

CHAPTER
FORTY-FIVE

Put it from your mind, Caledonia urged herself as she rushed back through the woods toward camp. There were far more pressing things to consider, and she felt selfish for letting herself wallow over Oran's past deeds.

She had an army to train and a war to plan. She shouldn't let herself be distracted by her feelings for Oran.

She was so lost in her brooding thoughts that she didn't see the approaching figure until she'd collided with him. Hands landed on her arms to keep her upright, and she heard Pine's voice calling her "seagirl" with amusement.

Then, suddenly, he wasn't amused.

"What's happened?" He ducked his head to gaze fully into her face, dark eyes tracing the tears on her cheeks. "The Steelhand," he growled, moving toward the wooded path.

"Do not call him that," Caledonia answered quickly, putting a hand on Pine's arm. The last thing she needed was Pine, or any of the Blades, thinking Oran had done something to her. "And anything that happens between him and me is my business."

Pine's arm flexed beneath her hand. His eyes were pinned to the woods, waiting for Oran to appear. "And anything that happens between him and me is mine."

"Pine." She made her voice a sword. "I know what he's done. I know who he was. And I also know who he's becoming. Maybe Bullets don't come back, but you do change. Doesn't he deserve a chance to change, too?"

When he turned to face her, his eyes were hooded. He stepped in close, and when he spoke, his words were laced with old pains. "Are we fighting Bullets or saving them?"

Caledonia answered almost without thinking: "Both. It has to be both."

It was at once the simplest truth and a tremendously complicated one. The fight ahead was going to cost lives, and it was ironic that in order to save Bullets they were going to have to kill them, but there was no other way. At least, none Caledonia could see.

"This is going to change you, too," he said sadly, brushing his thumb so lightly across a tear on her cheek she almost didn't feel it.

"It already has."

A dreadful understanding passed between them in that moment. In order to do a good thing, they would let a piece of themselves change into something hard and dangerous and irrevocable.

"Captain! Pine!" Harwell's cheery voice rang out behind them. "We have good news."

Caledonia gave Pine's arm a squeeze before turning to find not only Harwell, but Hime and Amina approaching.

"The ship is repaired," Amina announced. "Seaworthy and sound and ready for you, Captain."

"That is good news," she said with an approving nod. "Good work."

"Not only that, but we've cleared all the Bullet markings and laid the bodies to rest," Harwell continued merrily. "Desal tanks are repaired, hull is patched, she's almost good as new."

All she needs is a new name, Hime signed. *We thought you might want to do the honors.*

They needed this from her, from their captain. And she wanted to be able to give it to them, but her thoughts were still tethered to Oran's past, Pine's future, and what it meant for all she was trying to do. What it meant for Donnally.

None of us comes back, Pine had said.

When he'd first said those words, she had needed them to be true. She needed to believe that there was no way to save Donnally. Now she understood that they were complicated. Maybe you didn't come back from being a Bullet, but you also didn't have to stay one. If a vicious tide pulled them away from themselves, surely something brighter could return them. It gave her an idea.

"Let's called her the *Luminous Wake.*"

》 《

Sitting high on the hill overlooking the cabin village, the sleeping cherry orchard, and the winking city below, Caledonia tracked the telltale puffs of dust as Mino's rover chewed up the mountain path. There wasn't much to see, but she was learning how to read the air in much the same way she'd learned to read the waves. Subtle changes in either spoke volumes.

Mino's trail swung around the cherry orchard, hitting the straightaway that would bring her right into the cabin village where Caledonia's crew had gathered in the main mess for dinner. Even high on this hill, the air carried the promise of a hearty stew with fresh meat and vegetables.

After the conversations of the morning, Caledonia had come to a decision. The crew was adept with the deepships, their flag- ship was repaired, Hesperus had prepared stores of ammunition for their disposal. They were an army in want of a fight, and it was her job to find the right moment.

Mino's trail disappeared inside the band of trees that wrapped around the eastern edge of the cabins. She'd arrive in a few more minutes. Caledonia abandoned the hill and made her way toward camp. As soon as she was in the open, all attention turned to her. On the western edge, a group paused their sparring, straightening to nod their heads even as they puffed for breath; those waiting in line for mess nudged the person next to them, offering hasty nods of their own. Any who passed near enough said simply, "Captain." She nodded, feeling the pressure of their respect both lift her up and push her away.

Most unsettling was the fact that Hesperus's people—men and women who were all older than her—treated her exactly as her own crew did, with deference and admiration. She had changed in the eyes of everyone around her, and she felt like she should be able to put her finger on the part of her that was different. Every time she tried, however, she found herself panicking that she'd tricked everyone, including herself, into believing she could stand up to Aric Athair.

To Caledonia, it seemed the change had occurred overnight. But Pisces knew better. She said it had everything to do with how Caledonia had confronted Hesperus in their first meeting; that she and Sledge and Amina and especially Pine had told the story of how small, young Caledonia Styx stood up to the Sly King, that everyone had noticed how resolutely he'd deferred to her.

"That's not how it happened," Caledonia had protested, perched on her bed. "We negotiated. That's all."

Pisces's laugh was bright and joyful and reminded Caledonia that she rarely had a clear vision of herself.

"Well," Pisces said, dismissive and amused all at once. "That's not how the story will be told. But I don't think you should worry about that. You worry about everything else. Deal?"

Caledonia grumbled. "It's hard not to worry about it when they look at me like ... Like I'm ..."

"Like you're their leader?" Pisces offered when Caledonia failed to find her own words. "Well, get used to it fast, *Captain*."

Mino drove into camp a minute after Caledonia arrived. As always, she was dressed in layers of dove and leathery brown that hugged her lithe form, with guns and blades holstered to every available part of her from her calves to her forearms. Yet, somehow, she managed to make it all look like seamless extensions of her body. Her head was shaved smooth and her smoky brown skin was gilded in dusk light. Every time Caledonia looked at the woman she was struck by her unassuming beauty and strength. This was a woman people underestimated only once.

"Captain." Mino clipped the word around the edges.

"Mino," Caledonia said in greeting. She'd asked once if Mino had a title she should use instead of her name, but the woman had only responded by narrowing her elegant eyes. "It's nice to see you."

Mino brushed past the pleasantry. "We're sending more rations up tomorrow. Another three days' supply."

"It's more than generous, thank you."

When this exchange had first begun, Caledonia felt nervous at every turn. Now she'd come to understand that was Mino's intention—to put Caledonia on the defensive with her own brusque nature. It was so opposite to Hesperus's charm that for a while, at least, it had worked exactly as intended. But no longer. Caledonia held her ground and refused to let Mino set the tone of the exchange.

"Training is going well," Caledonia continued. "We're taking the ships through the western portal tomorrow. It's time the crew got some experience outside the canals."

Mino's eyes grew wide at that.

"We've accomplished as much as we're going to in the canals. The teams need practice responding to a dynamic ocean. And target practice, which we're not doing where a bad shot might bring a ton of rock down on their heads."

"What do you need from us?"

"Only to keep the western portal clear. I'd prefer if we didn't stumble into battle prematurely."

Mino nodded thoughtfully. The western ocean wasn't Cloudbreak territory. It wasn't really anybody's territory, and even Bullets avoided straying too far into its stormy waters. But that meant there were plenty of rogue ships around: Gulls, Slaggers, crews like Caledonia's.

"I'll take care of it." Mino didn't sound pleased about it, but she was the kind of person who didn't lie because she didn't have to.

"Thank you. And what of the Bullet fleet?" she asked, moving through their usual routine.

Now Mino frowned. "The Fivesons are mobilizing. All moving north."

"Are there still only four of them?" She heard the note of desperation at the end of her question and hoped Mino had missed her moment of weakness. She needed information, not a heart-to-heart.

But understanding misted down Mino's face, softening her

features. "There are still only four of them," she confirmed. "But we've had news of the trials to find a fifth."

The relief Caledonia had expected remained just out of reach. Donnally wasn't yet a Fiveson, but whatever he was going through—whatever he was *doing*—was terrible enough to dampen even Mino's stoic exterior.

"Mino." Caledonia couldn't keep the fear from her own face. "What is it? What have you heard?"

The woman shifted. She regarded Caledonia with a knowing kind of pity. She didn't want to hurt Caledonia, but neither did she want to keep her in the dark.

"The Fiveson Potentials are making for the Northwater colonies."

Caledonia's heart thumped painfully in her chest. A cold knot of dread tightening around it. "Why?" she asked.

"They avoided conscription twice. Both times by your aid. They might have escaped punishment if they'd complied, but—" Mino's lips pinched before she continued. "The third time, they resisted. They waited for the Bullets to make land, and then they fought back. That hasn't happened in, well, not since Aric came into his power. The truly amazing thing is they won. They beat the Bullets back and by the time they retaliated, the colonists had fled. They took their victory and their stories and they fled to the other colonies. Some of them even made it to Cloudbreak. Our port is uncomfortably full."

The colonists were fighting back. It was the sort of story that should have left Caledonia elated. A sign that Aric's grip had become too tight. Yet, as she listened, she grew colder and colder.

"They fight because someone showed them it was possible: Caledonia Styx, the Wayward Daughter."

"And the Fiveson Potentials?" Caledonia asked. She could guess. She *had* guessed, but she needed to hear it confirmed.

"They're sailing north to offer Aric a demonstration. To quell the uprising before it really begins."

Mino was gentle with her words, knowing each one was heavier than the last. But she didn't spare Caledonia this truth.

"Me," Caledonia said. "This is my fault."

"Your fault?" Mino's shoulders moved in a graceful shrug. "It wouldn't have happened without you, that's true."

The woman's eyes were not unkind, though her words offered no comfort. Caledonia made herself a stone. Pisces would remind her that Aric was the one at the center of all this. Aric was the one who terrorized the colonists, who stole their children and then forced them, in turn, to steal their own brothers and sisters. Disrupting that system came with consequences.

But the real truth of the matter was that Caledonia had disrupted that system for her own selfish gain. Saving Ares and facing Lir had nothing to do with the colonists, yet the consequences had landed squarely, unfairly on their shoulders. They were fighting now because of it; they would die because of it.

"Are they already on their way to the colonies?" Caledonia pressed a fist to her stomach, pushing her thumb right up under the bridge of her rib cage. "Do you know?"

"Our information is always delayed," Mino answered, apologetic. "But they were waiting until they could all come together. To make a production of it. A show for Aric."

Nausea weakened the back of her throat. "How many days? I know you don't know, but I need you to guess."

Mino frowned hard. "I don't like to guess."

"Please."

The woman drew a deep breath as she considered the obstinate, desperate girl before her. Her desire to refute the question once more was evident in her frown, but something she saw in Caledonia's own expression must have changed her mind. With a sympathetic sigh, she answered, "Three days, Captain. If you're going to do something. You have three days."

CHAPTER FORTY-SIX

That night, Caledonia lay awake in her bunk unable to quiet her mind or her heart. All she could imagine were dozens of ships racing north, hundreds of colonists watching the horizon with wary eyes—and Donnally. Was he truly capable of the kind of act that lay before him? Had he lost so much of himself that he could become a Fiveson in Aric's army? Become the thing that had destroyed his own family?

As if she could hear Caledonia's quiet desperation, Pisces arrived in the earliest morning hours when the sky was still dark and cool with mist, long before the rest of the camp would begin to stir. She slipped inside the room and padded over to the bed, seeming unsurprised to find Caledonia awake.

"What's wrong?" Pisces asked.

She climbed onto the bed, taking Caledonia's hand in her own. Their fingers wove naturally together, and the pressure of her warm touch was comforting.

"How did you know?" Caledonia asked in return.

They both looked up when the door opened again, revealing a star-stained sky and the radiant moon of Hime's lovely face. Behind her was Amina. And behind them both, Nettle and Tin.

We always know, Hime signed. Her right hand was still stiff but finally free of its bandage.

"Well, that's unsettling. Come in. Before you attract any more attention." Caledonia sat up, giving Pisces room to join her with their backs against the wall. While Tin and Nettle took the two chairs, Amina sat on the floor, letting Hime lean back against the strong wall of her chest.

"We saw you leave," Nettle explained to Pisces. "But we already knew something was amiss."

"Amiss?" Pisces asked, amused.

Nettle grinned. "I told you I could use it in a sentence."

"She won't quit." Amina's cheek rested against the crown of Hime's head, but she was smiling as she sniped at the young girl.

"She talks enough as it is. I keep saying teaching the girl new words is a hell of an idea," Tin added with a shake of her head, her pale brown spikes bobbing softly.

Nettle beamed, and the rest of the room pulled in closer around that smile. Seeing the five of them together still fit strangely. It wasn't the team Caledonia had grown to expect, and it was impossible to look at Tin and Nettle and not long for Redtooth and Lace. Yet as the five girls jabbed at one another and laughed over bonds Caledonia had missed, a strange sensation came over her. She felt warm and safe and relaxed. She felt relieved.

She was responsible. Always responsible. But she wasn't just responsible *for* them, she was responsible *to* them. Sitting here wrapped in their friendship, she realized that it was that simple thing that lightened her own burden. She could share it with them, and they would carry it with her.

"Tell us, Captain." Amina's voice was silky and warm.

This was how she'd failed them last time. She had kept her troubles to herself, tried to manage them alone, and in the end, she was wounded, and they'd been captured. Once again, she was hoarding her worries. But it was time to trust them to her sisters.

"There's something I need to tell you," she began.

Holding tight to her courage, Caledonia told them everything: her reasons for going after Lir, all she knew of Donnally, the current plight facing the colonists, even her radio conversation with Lir. They listened. Each one alert and intent on her words. Amina scowled through much of it, her chin perched lightly atop Hime's head. Hime, for her part, held a placid expression on her face. Tin's expression matched whatever emotion was currently roiling inside her, making it difficult to watch her for very long; Nettle listened with the tip of her thumbnail clenched between her teeth while Pisces stayed at Caledonia's side, head bowed slightly, fingers curled through her own and resting there without demanding attention.

By the time she finished, she felt both hollow and light, as if by giving them everything she'd been tossing around inside, she'd created room to think again.

"So, we need to find a way to stop them before they reach the colonists," Amina said, as naturally as the sun rose every morning.

"How can we do that from here?" Tin leaned forward in her seat, elbows planted on her knees. "We're hundreds of miles away."

"But we have three days?" Nettle asked, looking to Caledonia for confirmation.

"If Mino is correct. So let's assume her conservative guess isn't conservative enough and go with two."

Nettle nodded smartly. "Okay, then we need to distract them."

"We're still hundreds of miles away," Tin cautioned. "Even if we set all of Cloudbreak on fire, they'd never see it. Much less care enough to change course."

We need something they want more *than the colonists.* Hime sat upright. Her long hair dragged behind her, keeping her connected to Amina.

"Well, we've only got one thing they could possibly want more than a few dead colonists." Amina met Caledonia's gaze, her dark eyes as solid as a ship's deck. She'd reached the same conclusion Caledonia had, and nearly as quickly. Caledonia nodded.

The room quieted as each girl came to understand Amina's meaning.

"Oh," said Nettle, deflated. "But you can't."

"I can," Caledonia insisted gently. "And I will. But if we let them know I am here, they'll know you are, too."

Pisces inched forward on the bed, folding her legs beneath her and sitting closer to the edge. "They won't only come for you."

Caledonia shook her head.

"They'll come for all of us."

Caledonia nodded.

Pisces paused, thinking through all the implications. "It will be the biggest fight we've ever been in."

"They'll send a fleet." Tin's voice was awed enough for all of them.

Caledonia gave them a beat to let it sink in. She'd had all night to consider this outcome, to let her mind work through dozens of possible strategies, to anticipate all the ways Aric might come at her.

"Can we win?" Pisces asked.

Here, Caledonia moved to the edge of the bed, pushing her warm blankets away and letting her feet rest on the cold floor. "We can win," she said. "With Hesperus's ships and the advantage of Cloudbreak, we'll see them coming and have time to prepare. Even if they outnumber us, I know we can win."

"So what's the problem?" Tin asked.

It will only be the first fight. Hime tucked her legs beneath her, kneeling on the floor in the center of them all. *We will win, but it will enrage him. He'll know where we are and who helped us. It will be the start of a war.*

"And we cannot win an all-out war against Aric," Caledonia finished. "Not with the ships and crew we have."

Amina leaned in, a new light filling her eyes. "Then this has to be the start of something even bigger. We fight and then we grow. I know there are those among my people who would join us, perhaps would even share their tech with us. The colonists merely lack the means to take to the water. And the Slaggers surely have the resources even if they aren't inclined to fight."

"That's hardly enough people to fight a war." Nettle's voice was thinned by fear. "Who else is there?"

"Bullets."

They all turned to Pisces. She sat at Caledonia's side, one knee tucked up against her chest. Her eyes were tired and serious.

"Bullets," she repeated. "The Blades left. Oran left. Ares left. There will be others. We just have to keep showing them they have a place to go."

"It's a good hope, but it's not a plan." Caledonia spoke softly. "The plan has to be this: we call Aric here and we take him down. We kill Aric Athair and his entire empire crumbles behind him."

"How?" the five of them asked at once.

Caledonia paused. They weren't going to like this plan. She didn't like it either, but it was the best option. The trick would be to make sure Aric had no choice but to come to them himself.

"We know what he wants," she said, echoing Amina's statement from earlier.

Now they protested. All five rose up against Caledonia, telling her it was a terrible plan, a bad plan, a plan that could never work.

When they quieted, she held her voice steady and repeated: "We know what he wants."

The only sound in the room was the pulse of their breath. Caledonia turned to each one of her girls, meeting their eyes and holding them long enough to convince each of them that she was committed to this course. Instead of making herself a stone, she made herself a flame, burning in the middle of them, fed by their breath and their steady friendship, stoked and fueled for the fight ahead.

"On the back of the seas, who do we trust?" Caledonia held out a hand, palm up.

One by one, five hands found hers until they'd formed a tight circle, shoulder to shoulder. Dawn light ghosted over their faces, lighting their eyes as they answered together, "Our sisters."

A chord of deep trust rang among them, louder and stronger when they were together. For the space of a breath, it was overwhelming.

"We have a lot of work to do, and not a lot of time to do it in," Caledonia said. "Let's get ready to draw fire."

CHAPTER
FORTY-SEVEN

After weeks locked on the side of a mountain or in a metal tube far beneath the waves, it was a relief to once again stand on the deck of the *Luminous Wake*. As the ship cruised smoothly away from the canals and out beyond the breaker islands, Caledonia breathed a little easier in spite of what she was here to do.

The ship was in excellent repair and lightly crewed. Only a dozen in all, including the command crew. They wouldn't be out long. They sailed until Cloudbreak was just a strip of white cliffs against the steely gray sea and then they let the ship drift with the tide.

They'd spent the previous day readying for battle. The deep-ship crews trained in the open ocean until the very last drop of sunlight fled the sky. Weapons were checked and rechecked, oiled and loaded. As promised, Hesperus outfitted each deepship with more powerful missiles. The underside of the hull of the *Luminous Wake* had been marked with plates of polished bronze to distin-guish her from Bullet ships and prevent the deepship crews from firing on her accidentally. The whole atmosphere of camp shifted to the gently frenzied energy of a looming fight. By the time the sun rose again, they were prepared to make the first move.

Caledonia had gone to wake Sledge and Pine immediately after her conversation with the girls, expecting it to be a challenge to convince them that this was the right move. But they'd merely stood there, shaking off sleep as quickly as they could, waiting for whatever order would follow.

"So . . . you're on board?" she'd asked, doing her best not to appear nervous.

"Tides, Caledonia." Pine shook his head in disbelief.

Sledge cleared his throat and tucked his chin to bring his eyes level with hers. "We wouldn't still be here if we weren't on board."

"You don't need our approval," Pine added, dressing quickly to follow her. "You're not just the captain anymore. You're our commander."

With that, Pine had given her a small but firm nod, effectively ending the conversation.

Now Caledonia stood in the center of the bridge, surrounded by her command crew, Oran, and Hesperus. Pisces was at her shoulder, her fingertips brushing the back of her arm to let her know she was there. Sledge hulked at the back of the room, leaning carefully against the small map table. Amina and Hime were near, hands clasped between them. Pine had assumed a spot near the wheel, one hand resting on the spokes, though they weren't in motion. Oran was a dark shadow in the doorway, as far as he could be from Caledonia and still keep her in his sights. And Hesperus was right at her side.

They were poised on the brink of pushing their small rebellion into something decidedly larger. Once they did this, there was no going back.

"How long do you think this will take?" Caledonia asked, positioning herself near the radio. It wasn't a real question because she knew it had no real answer. But it got her moving past her nerves.

"Depends on who's listening," Pine answered.

"Ready?" she asked Hesperus, who had been deathly quiet since boarding.

He nodded heavily. He had been slightly less enthusiastic about the plan but agreed it was the best way to try to lure Aric himself even if the prospect of *that* was far from appealing.

Reaching out with one hand, Caledonia flipped the switch. The radio scratched to life, filling the cabin with static. Oran brushed past her shoulder, twisting one of the knobs on the dash until the channel cleared just a bit.

"He monitors that one." Oran met her eyes and held them. In them, she saw a man who was as solid and as committed as any of her crew. Every time he looked at her, he was promising to always fight at her side. "They keep it open for Fivesons."

He stepped back and left her there, suddenly so much closer to Aric and his Fivesons.

Her nerves returned in a crush. But then there was Pisces, pressing a hand to her shoulder. And there was Amina. And Hime. The three of them held her up, told her with their touches that they were with her. They were offering her courage, and she took it.

Then she lifted the receiver and handed it to Hesperus.

"This is Hesperus Shreeves. I have welcome news for the Father." He paused, his tongue passing over lips to wet them. "About Caledonia Styx."

He released the button. Static filled the air once more, and a chill raced through Caledonia's fingers.

Then, after several long minutes, the static cut away, and a voice growled in its wake.

"Hello, Sly King." Around the room, Sledge, Pine, and Hesperus all shifted. Only Oran remained still. There was no question that this was the voice of Aric Athair. "Speak your news."

"I have her," he began, eyes locking on to Caledonia. "She limped into my harbor with one of your ships and a skeleton crew, but I have her."

"Good. Hold her there," Aric said, the smallest strain of gratification roiling through his tone. "I'll send one of my sons to collect her."

"No." The room grew smaller around that single word. No one breathed while Hesperus pressed on. "As I understand it, she's already escaped your sons, and I want to ensure I get my bounty. I'll give her to you and only you."

This time, the silence that followed was torturously long. Hesperus's reputation for gathering wealth and power was in their favor, while Caledonia's for trickery and strategy was not. No matter what happened, they would soon have a fight on their hands. Whether it was the fight they wanted was still in question.

Finally, after several moments of silence, Aric's voice returned. "See you soon, Sly King."

CHAPTER
FORTY-EIGHT

The observatory of Cloudbreak was as impressive as Caledonia remembered. Perhaps even more so now that she could take the time to consider all it had to offer. The room sat atop the layered fortress like a cap. It had no walls, just four stone columns dressed in cerulean blue curtains that supported a domed roof gilded in luminescent paint. At each quarter, telescopes perched on sturdy tripods, and in the center of the room a fire burned inside a pit carved into the floor.

The last time she'd been here it had been under markedly different circumstances. She'd had a wealth of solar scales to trade, a bounty on her head, and the promise of finding her brother still shining before her. When Lir's fleet closed in, Hesperus had come very close to trading Caledonia and her crew for the bounty. Instead, he'd given her the map she needed to escape through the canals.

"Any other time and I'd offer refreshment." Hesperus settled himself on the eastern ledge, where he had a clear view of the ocean. "But with the Father on the way, I'm afraid I've run through my generosity."

Caledonia was beginning to understand that Hesperus liked to complain, even when he'd been a willing partner in what ailed him. It was how he soothed his nerves.

"You've been generous enough, Hesperus." Caledonia stood by the telescope, intermittently pressing her eye to the scope to survey the horizon.

They expected a swift response from Aric. Indeed, Caledonia was hoping for one. Anything else, and the colonies to the north would suffer immeasurably.

"Correct," he snapped. "I have been more generous than I should have been, and now I will suffer for it."

A week ago, his anger would have put her on the defensive. She would have worried that inciting anger in someone with as much power as Hesperus would create an enemy where there should have been an ally. Today, it paled in comparison to what was on its way meet her.

"You expected me to take the fight to him. To leave you here in relative safety while we assumed all the risk."

Hesperus didn't have to answer for Caledonia to find the truth in his face.

"I promise you, if that had been the best option, it's what I would have done." As Caledonia answered, she marveled at the authority in her own voice. "If the tides turn against us, I will do whatever I can to keep Cloudbreak safe. In return, I need you to do something for me."

"Caledonia Styx, only you would ask me for more at a time like this."

Caledonia produced Nettle's piece of soiltech from her pocket and held the device up for Hesperus to see. The slender rectangle glimmered in the soft light. She pressed the button on the side, and it smoothly transformed into a handheld sifter.

"Is that . . . soiltech?" Hesperus asked in a shocked whisper.

She nodded. "You said you can build anything, right? I need you to figure out how to build this. No matter what happens here, you crack this, and we'll weaken Aric's hold on the world."

Hesperus took the device, holding it reverently. He held it up on flat palms, eyes already lost in its gears. "You've just given me something more dangerous than a war," he muttered, quickly sliding the bit of tech into his own pocket.

"It isn't yours," she warned. "It belongs to all of us. I want you to figure it out, not keep it."

The horizon was an open promise in all directions. The mist had pulled away as soon as the sun rose, and the only clouds were far to the west. It was a good day for a fight.

"Have you thought about what you'll do when you've supplanted the Father?" His voice had changed. It was no longer coated in irritation but anchored with a new kind of regard. "How will you rule the Bullet Seas?"

The question jolted her. "I will never rule the Bullet Seas."

An eyebrow arched sharply on Hesperus's brow. "Then what are you doing here, Captain?"

She'd told him exactly what she was doing here: drawing fire from the colonists and taking Aric down if possible. All she'd ever wanted to do was remove the tyrant. Had she somehow given him the impression that she wanted to reign over these broken seas?

"Captain." Pine rounded the corner of the stairway, ducking his head in a slight bow and meeting her gaze openly. "Our deep-ships are ready, and Kae has rallied the rogue captains, all awaiting mobilization."

Once the call had been sent to Aric, Hesperus and his other sister, Kae, solicited any willing volunteers with boats capable of battle and sent the rest on their way. The deepships were now in the wharf below, ready and waiting for the signal to crew up and move out. Just beyond the islands, the *Luminous Wake* was at anchor. A clear signal to anyone approaching that Cloudbreak was tempo-rarily closed for business.

"And the crew?" Caledonia asked.

"Making ready on the wharf. Mino's made sure we have every-thing we need for the day." He said this last with a grateful nod to Hesperus. "If they don't show by then, we'll reevaluate."

"Seems as though everything's in place, Captain," Hesperus said, the lightness in his voice at odds with the severity of the situation.

"Except Aric," she added, turning again to study the horizon. "Oh, he'll be here."

As if summoned, a shape appeared on the horizon. It was a dark speck against the brilliant blue sky, but to be visible at this distance, it had to be large. Through the telescope, the ship took on a vague outline, its tower rising into the sky like several vicious animals clawing toward the top of a mountain.

"Do you know this ship?" Caledonia asked, relinquishing the scope to Hesperus.

The man bent to study the approaching vessel through the narrow lens. His fingers curled lightly around the cylinder, barely brushing the smooth metal, and his lips pursed. He remained this way for several seconds, breathing evenly through his nose as the ship drew nearer.

Finally, he straightened, turning a pinched gaze on Caledonia. "Well, Captain, you've done it."

"What, exactly?"

"You've drawn the man himself. That's the *Titan*. I never thought I'd have the misfortune to see it again." He swept a hand across the ocean in a grand gesture. Appearing behind the ominous ship of Aric Athair were dozens of other smaller ships, all racing toward Cloudbreak. "Welcome to your war. Please, keep it out of my harbor."

CHAPTER
FORTY-NINE

T he wharf was fully alive.

Pisces stood atop her deepship, surveying the scramble across the wharf as fifty-three of their crew found their ships and vanished inside. At the other end of the wharf, Ares did the same, waiting for Pine to join him. The remainder of Caledonia's crew were already aboard the *Luminous Wake*, awaiting her arrival.

"Report, Pi!" Caledonia called.

"All crew present and accounted for," the girl responded. "Underway in two minutes!"

"Send them to the deep, Pi!" she called.

"With pleasure, Captain!"

Pisces's hair was freshly shorn, and she studied the dashing scene around her with an air of complete calm and control. Caledonia allowed herself a brief second to admire her friend and sister before she had to move on.

She and Pine strode down the wharf toward the tender that would transport her to the *Luminous Wake*. She looked into every face she passed. There was Tin, corralling her sisters into a single deepship; there was Harwell, vibrating with his perfect blend of anticipation and anxiety; and there was Folly, going off to fight without Pippa at her side.

She'd prepared herself for this moment. Her crew was so large and the scale of this battle so dispersed that there had been no time for anything other than giving orders for the battle to come. She'd said no goodbyes and hardened her heart against the part of her that wanted to stop right now and pull everyone close, to return to a life of hitting hard and running fast in an effort to keep everyone alive. To go back to the moment in time when she didn't know all the terrible pieces of Oran's past.

"Here, Captain." Pine spoke in her ear to be heard over the din.

They'd arrived at the very far end of the wharf where the small collection of volunteer ships nestled together. There were seven ships in all; some large, some small. They were outmatched against Aric's fleet, but it was better than nothing.

The captains stood on deck, eyes tracking Caledonia as she approached her own small boat. They were an odd assortment of men and women in all stages of life, though none was as young as she. Given the time, she'd have liked to speak with each of them, to know what it was that compelled them to agree to this plan. To know for herself that they would follow her. But she didn't have the luxury of time. Instead, she nodded to each in turn, hoping at least a portion of her gratitude came through in the small gesture.

"They're with you, Captain," Pine assured her softly. "Trust me."

Pine guided her down the dock to where Mino's boat waited to take her to the *Luminous Wake*. The tender's engine was already growling when she stepped aboard.

"Pine," she said, catching his eyes. "Stay steely."

"Keep to your tides, Captain," he said, as he turned and jogged toward his deepship.

The second Caledonia took her seat, the boat rushed forward, zipping quickly out of the harbor and through the channels of the breaker islands. In their wake, the seven volunteer vessels made ready and followed while the deepships snapped their hatches shut and sank beneath the surface of the ocean. For a few precious moments, Caledonia could read their trails in the water as clearly as if they sailed atop it, but as they descended, they grew harder and harder to track until they were gone altogether. She smothered the pinch of panic in her lungs with a reminder that this was exactly what would give them an edge over Aric.

The *Luminous Wake* now carried a crew of only twenty, and the deck felt nearly empty with so few bodies. After spending weeks with a crew of seventy-five, it felt almost lonely. But there was Nettle at the helm, and there were Amina and her Knots perched on all the highest points of the ship, and there was Hime standing ready with the deck crew.

"Nettle!" Caledonia called as she came aboard. "Take us out at half speed! Make sure we give those deepships time to get between us and them."

"Yes, Captain!"

Nettle had them moving in an instant. The engines purred and the propellers churned, and they pulled away from the breaker islands at a moderate pace with the seven volunteer ships fanned out on either side of them like wings. The power of that promise was bolstering. This was what it felt like to go into battle with more than a single gun at her hip, a single ship at her call.

Caledonia climbed the command tower to the bridge, where she found Oran. He stood with eyes trained on the horizon, a scope clutched in his hands. Without a word he handed it over. She lifted the scope to one eye and surveyed the approaching fleet. Aric's ship charged out in front, dead center, black as coal with bands of green and orange ripped down its nose. Each of the surrounding ships bore the symbols of his four Fivesons; some streaked with green like blades of grass, others smudged with purple starbursts, or yellow crescents. And there, bringing up the northern edge, were steely gray ships marked with orange bale blossoms.

They were all here. No matter what else happened, she'd lured them away from the colonists. She'd bought time. And if Hesperus's messenger managed to get out with a warning, it would be enough.

The wind rushed against her cheeks, bringing with it the

howling cry of a dozen ghost funnels. It grew louder and more insistent with every second that passed until it seemed the entire sky cried out in that haunting, cacophonous tone.

A shiver slipped down Caledonia's spine, landing firmly in her toes. With the scope pressed to her eye, she counted three dozen ships flanking Aric's monstrous vessel. Its bow was broad and blunt, like the head of a great whale, and on its back a tower rose at least six levels into the sky. Strung from each side were slings carrying large guns. And on the deck sat a cannon, its deadly mouth positioned on a swivel in order to track their targets.

It was like no ship Caledonia had ever seen, and for just a moment, she doubted every decision that had led her to this point.

"Slow us down, Nettle!" she called, returning the scope to Oran, who remained beside her like a pillar.

There was no way for her to know where her deepships were by this point, and right now, taking her eyes off the approaching Bullet fleet was a mistake.

It was a good plan, she reminded herself. She just needed to give it time to work.

The ship slowed to quarter speed. She hoped Aric would mistake her reduced speed for fear and not the ploy it was. The approaching ships fanned out, exercising some degree of caution as they sized up Caledonia's own motley fleet. Surely Aric expected her to have some other trick up her sleeve, and surely there was no way he might have anticipated her deepships. She only hoped that whatever he'd prepared for, it wouldn't matter in a few minutes.

"Captain!" Amina's voice pierced the heavy winds. "They're breaking off!"

Caledonia turned to see that on both sides of them now, the volunteer ships faltered. They slowed, and then one by one, they peeled away, leaving the *Luminous Wake* alone, friendless on the back of the cold sea.

Ahead of them, the Bullet ships growled, charging forward faster now that she was alone.

"Captain," Sledge called, jogging toward her from the bridge. "He's on the radio."

The feeling that landed in the pit of her stomach wasn't fear. It wasn't even dread. It was a bald, untarnished anger; a fury she'd tucked away long ago and forgotten lived somewhere inside her. By the time she reached the cabin, she wasn't sure she'd be able to speak past the explosive feeling building in her chest, but the second her fingers closed around the receiver, that changed. A cold wash of focus slipped over her like a coat. She raised the receiver and pressed the button.

"This is Captain Styx," she said smoothly.

The voice that came back to her rang clear as a bell. "Looks like you're having some trouble, Captain."

The volunteer ships were moving in either direction down the coast of the Rock Isles. Abandoning the fight before it had even begun.

Caledonia licked her lips, giving Nettle the signal to pull them out of speed entirely. "Just a change in plans."

Aric laughed. It was a radiant sound, and his voice filled the entire cabin, tugged on every ear that heard it. But where Caledonia was entranced, she saw Sledge's shoulders stiffen against the unwelcome onslaught. "I recommend you change your plans a bit more. This is the time for surrender, my girl."

"I think you've misread this situation," she countered.

His ships were closing the gap between them. In another few minutes, they'd be surrounded.

"Have I? The Sly King is nowhere to be seen, and you've been abandoned by your friends. It seems your conspiracy has left you both at my mercy." His voice darkened like a stormy sky. "These are my waters, my seas. There is nothing that happens here that I do not know about or control, but I will make you a deal. Surrender now, and most of your people will live."

Aric's ships pulled more tightly together, aiming for her as though they were a spear and she a target they would tear through without a hitch in their pace.

Exactly what she wanted them to do. All she had to do was keep Aric distracted, focused on her.

"Have I given them enough time?" Aric asked, voice dripping with satisfaction. "Your deepships?"

Caledonia stopped. Her fingers were suddenly cold, her voice small, and for just a breath she dared to hope she'd misheard him.

"This won't take long," Aric gloated. "I have new tech, too."

On the side of his ship, the broad barrel of a gun swiveled. For several long seconds, there was only silence.

The gun fired.

Caledonia's sights landed on the shrinking ocean between her ship and Aric's. Her breath caught in her throat as she waited. Then the water exploded. Her deepships were under attack.

CHAPTER FIFTY

"Mag bombs," Sledge said in horror. "Submersible ones. He can target the deepships."

It didn't matter that Hesperus had taken every precaution to keep these ships a secret. Aric had such perfect control over these seas that he'd learned of them anyway. Who was Caledonia to think she could stand against him? She was no one. Just a girl wounded by his reign the same way every other child had been. She'd fooled herself into believing she was something more, and that folly was going to get the rest of them killed.

She needed her sister, but Pisces was down below, taking fire.

We need you to lead, she heard Pisces's voice urge. *We need you to be ours.*

A cold shudder drifted down from her shoulders to her fists. She let it settle there, trembling in each finger. Her sisters were what made her more. Her sisters made her exactly what she needed to be.

Caledonia quashed her horror. One bad turn wouldn't cost them the battle.

"They know what to do. And so do we."

Caledonia surveyed the ships before her. She didn't have the numbers they did, but every single one of those Ballistics and Fivesons would want the personal glory of capturing her and presenting her to Aric. Would they risk destroying her ship and killing her in the process? She didn't think so.

"Nettle, take us in. Let's give them something else to shoot at," she commanded. "Sledge, I want gunners on the port rail. Amina, target that mag gun!"

A wall of water shot up between the *Luminous Wake* and the Bullet ships. For a second, the entire fleet vanished behind a violently churned ocean. Their deepships were on the attack.

"Nettle!" Caledonia cried, but the engines were already spinning, the ship breaking south before the Bullet ships had a chance to regroup and open fire.

A second round of explosions rocked the line of Aric's ships as far below them Pisces orchestrated the attack.

"Two down!" Amina called, her voice ringing with early victory.

"Incoming!" one of her Knots shouted, and the air filled with the pop of gunfire as they sniped at the heavy artillery now singing their way. The missiles exploded in the air before they neared the hull of the *Luminous Wake*.

The deepships struck again, throwing the Bullet fleet into near complete chaos. A third ship listed heavily to one side. The

Bullets aimed their guns and missiles at the water and fired ruth-
lessly, while five ships broke away from the group to pursue the
Luminous Wake.

"Time to run!" Caledonia cried, shifting to the next phase.

The *Luminous Wake* raced from the thick of battle, dragging as
many Bullet ships from the fight as would follow. Nettle brought
them alongside the Rock Isles and tucked the ship in close to the
cliff wall. This far south of Cloudbreak, the wall was pocked with
skinny, sharp coves and unexpected peninsulas. Sticking close
wasn't easy, and that was exactly what they were counting on—
Caledonia wanted these Bullets looking at her and not the minefield they were sailing through.

She heard the first gentle plunk of metal on metal as a mine
snapped against their own hull, and her heart lurched involun-
tarily.

"Damn," Nettle cursed softly. "Sorry, Captain."

"It's all right," Caledonia reminded her. "We expected to pick
up a few. Just make sure it's only a few."

They'd laid this field themselves. Each mine was connected
to a remote, and when triggered they could punch a hole in nearly
any hull. Preferably not their own.

Nettle gave a tense nod, focusing on the way ahead. Oran
stood at her shoulder, gently reminding her where the path
through them was without directing her movements.

"Incoming!" Amina's voice announced the arrival of eight

pursuing ships just as the first spray of gunfire shattered against their hull.

"Don't rush it, Nettle," Caledonia said, standing firmly in the center of the bridge. "We want them right on our tail."

Above them, Amina gave the order to return fire. Beneath it all, Caledonia heard the subtle plink of another mine connecting with their hull. Nettle heard it, too, shoulders hunching in disappointment.

"Stay steely, girls, this is the plan." Caledonia caught Oran's wry grin at being folded in with her girls. She returned it, then swiveled to survey the field behind them.

The eight pursuing vessels were fanning out, perhaps having realized they'd stumbled into a minefield. Farther behind them, the bulk of the fleet struggled against the deepships. They'd dispersed in an attempt to better understand the attack, and from the looks of it, they'd lost more than a few ships already.

How many of her own had she lost? It was a question she couldn't afford to pursue.

"Captain, we're coming up on the cove." Oran pulled her attention forward once more. The cove was hidden just ahead. It was time.

"Do you think—" Nettle began.

"We're not here for speculation, Nettle. Full speed," Caledonia said.

The engines roared, and they pushed ahead of the ships on their tail. Caledonia watched their lead grow, and the instant it was long enough, she retrieved the remote and ordered Oran to hit the pulse.

That familiar electric sensation danced along her skin as energy radiated from the hull of the ship. This was a moment of trust. The mines that had attached to their hull should have fallen away, demagnetized by the full blast of that pulse. They should be drifting swiftly into their wake where they would explode the instant she hit the button.

Harwell had explained it. Had promised her that the mines would fall away and that if she hesitated too long, that same pulse would release the mines from whatever ships pursued her. There was no time for doubt. Only trust.

She hit the button.

The sea erupted in a long trail behind them. Each of the eight ships pitched as explosions bit into their hulls. The force sent one careening directly into the side of another, crushing both beyond repair. Two more slumped deep into the water with no hope of recovery. The remaining four pushed through, gunning for the *Luminous Wake*. Just at that moment, four ships roared out of the cove, charging the Bullet ships with a battery of fresh explosives.

Caledonia grinned, Nettle whooped, and even Oran looked more alive at the sight of the rogue ships coming to their aid. It had been the plan all along, but none of them had been foolish enough to pin their hopes on crews they'd never met. Yet here they were. Guns raised, engines throttled, fighting back at their side.

"Let's use the diversion while we have it. Bring us around, Nettle," Caledonia ordered.

"Prepare for a tight turn to port. Starboard prop on full, kill the port side on my mark."

Nettle expertly led her navigation team through the turn, bringing the ship around without losing all of their momentum. By the time they were reoriented toward the battle, the volunteer ships had made quick work of the remaining four Bullet ships, spearing them with harpoons and dragging them onto their sides. One was capsized entirely, its fractured hull bobbing on the ocean's surface.

Far in the distance, the fight raged on. The great tower of Aric's ship loomed large, and the eighteen remaining ships of his fleet were regrouping. Her deepships had taken a bite out of Aric's numbers, but it wasn't enough. Not with that damn gun in play.

"Amina!"

"Captain." The girl was at her side in a breath. "Once those mag bombs are in the water, they'll seek out the nearest metallic surface before they ignite. With that much inertia behind them they're deadly. But from what I've seen, the gun requires a lot of power. It's fired only three times, which means it has a recharge period."

Her heart beat furiously in her chest, haunted by the feeling that the tides were turning against them.

"Can you disable it?" she asked.

Amina turned thoughtful eyes on the faraway ship, then nodded. "I can. But I need to get close."

"How close?"

Amina lifted her eyes to the sky, tracking a thin slip of clouds that skated high in the blue. Then, returning her gaze to her captain, she said, "Inside the *Titan*."

CHAPTER
FIFTY-ONE

The roar of the engines was thunderous on the aft deck.
Amina crouched over the tow, securing explosives in water-
tight pouches. Her long braids were twisted together, bound tightly
with ribbons, and she was dressed in a slick black wetsuit.

"We'll give you as long as we can," Caledonia called, raising
her voice to be heard above the din. "But once you're in the water,
you're on your own!"

Amina nodded.

"Captain," Sledge called. He jogged to Caledonia's side, a wetsuit like Amina's stretched across his broad shoulders. "One minute to the drop."

"What do you think you're doing?" she asked.

"Permission to accompany Amina and watch her back," he
called.

Sending any of her people to Aric's ship was bad enough.
Sending two? Caledonia's fists clenched. But Sledge was right.

She nodded. "Keep her safe."

"Of course, Captain," he said with a smile.

"Amina!" she called. "Keep him safe!"

Amina gave a salute from her perch on the back of the tow as Sledge climbed on behind her. They pulled the masks of their blue lungs over their faces, Amina raised her hand in a countdown, and then the tow shot off the stern. Together, they sailed into the churned wake of the *Luminous Wake*, and then they vanished beneath it.

Caledonia turned her steps toward the bridge. More than half her crew was beneath the water. A distant part of her mind acknowledged that some of them were dead already. She had to assume that Aric's gun had destroyed at least one of her deepships, if not three. That left her with eight deepships, the four volunteer ships following her now, and if the other three volunteer captains kept their word and returned from their hiding place in the north, she'd still have a fighting chance.

The rest of Aric's fleet was scrambling. They sailed with no strategy, afraid of what lurked beneath the waves while the volunteer ships moved to flank them. It was exactly what Caledonia had envisioned when she mapped out the plan. All except for what she was about to do.

She arrived in the bridge to find Aric's ship looming before them. The rail gun fired again, sending another deadly bomb toward her deepships. The rest of *Titan*'s guns turned on the *Luminous Wake*.

They fired. The *Luminous Wake* lurched and stuttered in the water. Caledonia's crew had no hope of returning fire, and if they took another direct hit like that one, they wouldn't last long.

She needed to keep Aric's focus on the port side, and she needed to do it without encouraging him to give chase.

"We can let her grapple us," Oran suggested.

Caledonia was momentarily stunned. This was no ordinary ship. Getting grappled by an assault ship was bad enough, but the *Titan* could wrap her arms around the *Luminous Wake* like a giant squid. Letting themselves be caught would put them in the greatest danger.

And it was precisely the right move.

"Let's do it," she said decisively. "Nettle, you know what to do. Oran, you have the bridge."

"Where are you going?" he asked in mild alarm.

"To get a surprise for Aric."

Nettle adjusted their approach, and the crew raised heavy shields along the starboard rail, providing cover from gunfire as she drew nearer. It wouldn't be long before they were fully alongside *Titan*.

Caledonia raced to the weapons locker. The belly of the ship smelled faintly of smoke, and the sounds of the battle were muffled by the dense hull. Sweat cooled against her brow as she reached the locker she was looking for and removed the one weapon she thought she'd never use. The star blossom.

It was a heavy sphere with a carbon shell. Inside were hundreds of pieces of metal shaped like stars. When the bomb exploded, the shards would rip into flesh with lethal force. It was a terrible, cruel kind of weapon. And right now, Caledonia didn't have any other option.

Cradling the device in her arms, she hurried topside where the *Luminous Wake* was drifting very near to *Titan*. Nettle had done her job perfectly. She'd sailed with bravado, tricking the Bullets into acting on instinct. They readied their grappling hooks, shouting orders across the deck, raising their voices in an intimidating roar.

Caledonia took a steadying breath. *Blood. Gunpowder. Salt.* And she watched the gathering force with a growing sense of dismay. There were more of them than she'd imagined. Her crew was nothing compared to so many. But they'd stopped firing, which could only mean Aric wanted her alive.

"Captain," Oran said, once again coming to her side. "Do you mean to use that?"

She looked down at the bomb in her hands and swallowed hard. This was one of the Steelhand's creations, designed for cruelty. None knew that so well as Oran himself.

"I do."

Oran hesitated as though he wished for a better option than the one she held. He studied the device as though it pained him to see it and for a moment, Caledonia felt certain he would ask her not to use it. Then he said, "Let me do it."

"Oran, no," she said instantly.

"Please, Caledonia, you don't know what this will do," he said with a deepening frown. "I don't want this for you."

The temptation to hand over the bomb and all that came with it fluttered in her chest. She didn't want this, but she could see no other way. Oran would take this responsibility from her. He would protect her from it by adding to his own wounds. But that was no way to lead.

"Tell everyone to grab their shields and stay as close to the starboard rail as possible," she said with a nod, holding the bomb against her belly.

Oran's expression drew tight, but he nodded and then he moved to complete her orders.

Both crews were in motion, making ready for the fight. And as the grappling hooks came down to lock the *Luminous Wake* in place and gangways followed, Caledonia climbed atop the railing.

"Hold!" a voice growled from the deck of the Bullet ship.

Caledonia found him at once. Aric Athair. The Father himself.

He stood far from the railing with a contingent of Bullets to protect him. With one hand resting on his gun, he was the picture of confidence and command. Sunlight spilled over his shoulders, casting his face in dark shadow, yet his hair was just long enough to catch the light breeze, ruffling around his head like the leaves of an old oak tree.

"Caledonia Styx," he said.

She knew she must look unimpressive—short and slight, her cheeks and nose sharpened by the sun and wind, her hair too short to do anything but twist away from her head like truncated tentacles. She was no comparison to the man of vine and rock standing amid a hundred Bullets.

They were two points on a map that were never meant to meet. Yet here they were: the tyrant and the rebel, the man and the girl.

"Hello, Aric," she said, raising the bomb above her head as she depressed the ignition.

He followed her movement, eyes widening in surprise as Caledonia thrust the bomb high, throwing it in an arc that would place it in the dead center of Aric's deck.

"Shield!" he called frantically.

In an instant, twelve Bullets gathered around Aric in a tight cluster. With horror, Caledonia realized *they* were the shield. They were going to die to protect this brutal man.

And it was too late to change anything.

Behind her, the crew raised a wall of plate metal shields as they ducked low beneath the starboard rail. Caledonia leapt. The bomb exploded. And as tiny stars ripped into the railing, Oran hooked an arm around Caledonia and pulled her close.

It lasted less than a minute. The bomb ejected its lethal stars amid violent cries of pain, and the air cleared. Caledonia was on her feet at once, ready to rally her crew and take advantage of the lull. She climbed atop the rail, gun ready, eyes scanning for a sign that Aric had survived, but the scene that greeted her was so much worse than she'd imagined it would be.

The deck was slicked with blood. Bodies slumped against one another, curled in on themselves, or laying with eyes wide open. Where there had been a hundred Bullets, there were now only a handful.

Nausea twisted thick and ruthless in her stomach, crawling quickly toward her throat and down toward her toes. A Bullet weapon in her hands was just as deadly, just as terrible as in any other hands. Standing there with the sun in her mouth and a dry wind in her lungs, she didn't know what that made her. Not anymore.

"Caledonia." A darkly familiar voice called to her from among the wreckage.

She spun, gun ready, hoping that she was wrong even as she found him in the midst of his fallen sons and daughters. She aimed directly at his head. Her finger curled against the trigger. But Aric shifted, pulling a boy before him and pressing a gun to his head.

The boy was tall with hair that fell around his ears in sky-black curls, and a long, slender nose that tipped just slightly away from his upper lip.

It had been five long years, but she would know that boy anywhere.

"Donnally," she breathed.

CHAPTER
FIFTY-TWO

"On your knees." Aric's voice carved a treacherous path in the air. Donnally knelt with his back to Aric, and though his eyes landed on Caledonia, there was no recognition in them. The boy she knew was buried beneath layers of Silt and years of practiced obedience.

Behind her, the crew fell quiet, their attention snared in the web strung among Aric, Donnally, and Caledonia.

"Surrender," Aric said to Caledonia. "Or your brother dies."

Caledonia stood motionless. Her mind cleared of everything except the sight of her brother. He was alive, he was here. She wanted nothing more than to go to him, to wrap her arms around his neck and hear his voice in her ears. He was her brother, and he needed her right now more than ever before. But she couldn't surrender. Not with so much at risk.

"There is no surrender where you are concerned," she responded, irritated at the weakness in her voice. She shifted her grip on her gun but did not lower it.

Aric laughed. "You would have made me a good Fiveson," he said, thoughtful now. "How about a trade. You for your brother."

She thought she saw a frown flash across Donnally's face. But it was there and gone before she could be sure.

"I will never serve you." Caledonia nearly choked on her response.

A thick sneer twisted Aric's lips. "Then the choice is made."

Caledonia willed her mind to come up with some way out of this, some unexpected turn that would give her the leverage she needed to save both her brother and this battle. But there was nothing. And now her brother was going to die.

Suddenly, Oran was beside her, standing tall on the rail in full view of Aric Athair.

"Oran," Aric snarled, the muzzle of his gun driving into Donnally's head. "Ready to come home, *son*?"

Beside her, Oran was rigid. "Aric," he said, voice deadly.

Caledonia looked from Donnally to Aric and back again to her little brother. Panic pricked at her skin. Sweat greased her palms, and she remained frozen there on the rail, her indecision wrapped around her like a fog for all to see. They were out of time, out of distractions.

"Very well," Aric said, preparing to shoot.

"No!" Caledonia screamed.

The gun went off. Blood splashed across Donnally's cheeks, but he stayed upright. He was still looking at Caledonia. Behind him, Aric's head snapped to one side, and he fell to the deck.

Aric Athair was dead.

And out of the long shadow of *Titan*'s looming tower stepped Lir, gun in hand.

"Rest in glory, Father." Lir's voice sliced across the ship.

No one moved. The Bullets still standing gaped at their fallen leader while Caledonia's people pulled in a long breath. Even Caledonia froze on the rail. This had been her goal, to cut off the head of the snake. But it came with no swell of triumph, no signal to the rest of the Bullets that they were defeated, only a resounding sense of uncertainty.

Because she hadn't done it. Lir had. And the Bullets turned to him now, waiting for the command of their new leader.

He moved to Donnally's side, resting a hand on the boy's shoulder. Donnally stood at the touch, sharing an affectionate glance with Lir that left Caledonia cold.

"You always seem to know exactly what I need, Caledonia," Lir said, turning to her. His face was full of angles, and his hair sharpened around his cheeks like knives. "But I'm afraid your usefulness has come to an end."

Her attention clung to the sight of Donnally standing at Lir's side, so much that she nearly missed the moment Lir raised his hand again. This time, he pointed his gun at her.

It was already too late. She knew that in her gut. Still, her muscles tensed, preparing to jump, when an explosion ripped into Lir's port hull.

Lir ducked, his shot going wild. Caledonia clung to the railing.

"The gun! They've hit the gun!" someone yelled, and the scene devolved into chaos once more.

She searched again for Lir, but he was on the ground, knocked out by the blast.

Turning to her own crew, Caledonia called, "Get these grapples off my ship!" Then she ran across the gangway, landing on Aric's ship with her gun in hand.

"Caledonia!" she heard Oran cry behind her, but there was no time to lose. If this was her only chance to save her brother, nothing was going to stop her from taking it.

She closed the distance between them in a sprint, stopping herself before she threw her arms around his neck. He watched her with a quiet kind of interest, but there was no sign of the desperation she felt.

"Donnally," she said, raising her hand and reaching for the sigil on his temple. He flinched, reminding Caledonia that while she craved human contact, Donnally was more like the Blades. He must be given the choice. She waited, hand poised between them, and when he finally nodded, she pressed her fingertips to the tattoo they shared.

"Caledonia." He said the name as though it were new to him. Then a frown pressed briefly on his brow, and he added, "Nia."

It had been nearly five years since she'd heard that nickname. Five years since she'd thought of it even, and hearing it now strummed a painful chord in her heart.

"Donnally, we have to go," she said, taking his hand in hers. "There's not much time."

She tugged him toward the railing, but he stood firm.

"Donnally?" she asked.

"I can't go with you." He pulled his hand from hers with a slow shake of his head, stepped back. "I can't abandon my brother."

The battle sang in Caledonia's ears. She stumbled back, uncertain she could do any more than that. The world came to her through a cottony press in her ears.

She heard her name in Amina's voice. She saw Lir emerge from across the deck. She knew he held a gun. She knew she should run. But nothing made sense.

Then one thing did.

Donnally looked directly into her eyes and said a single word: "Go."

He turned toward Lir, putting himself between Lir's gun and Caledonia.

"Move!" Lir shouted. "Donnally, move now!"

But Donnally stood firm. He looked directly into Lir's eyes and shook his head. "Not this time, brother."

To Caledonia's amazement, Lir didn't fire.

Her senses returned in a rush. Amina was suddenly by her side, gripping her hand and pulling her into a run. Ahead, the grappling hooks exploded from the rail of the *Luminous Wake*. Oran stood there, furiously waving them over, shouting for them to "Jump! Jump! Jump!"

They leapt together, flying onto the deck as their crew opened fire.

"Where's Sledge?" she demanded of Amina the instant they'd gained their feet.

"With the tow," she answered.

The *Luminous Wake* pulled away, putting space between them and the Bullet fleet. Caledonia pried her eyes away from Aric's ship. The battle rolled on for a few minutes more, but only long enough for Lir to extract his remaining ships. A black flare erupted in the sky, glittering and signaling retreat.

Caledonia had won.

CHAPTER
FIFTY-THREE

All along the wharf of lower Cloudbreak, a celebration continued well into the night. Fires tripped down the rocky shore where groups clustered with skins of tart cherry wine and twisting loops of sweetbread. There were fiddles and pipes, dancing and laughter, kisses and so much more as those who had fought against Aric's forces today and won reveled in this unprecedented moment of victory.

High above the wharf, tucked into the dark bowl of the observatory, Caledonia listened to the strains of their joy. She'd tried to smile with them, to raise her hopes and release her fears for just a moment, but she couldn't. She was a part of them and also apart from them. And she was beginning to understand that was how it had to be.

Wrapped in a blanket of thick fleeced wool, she sat curled on a bench, eyes turned east where Lir's fleet—*Lir's fleet*—had disappeared hours before. She had won the battle, but so had he, and believing differently would be a mistake.

She'd lost, too. And she didn't know how to open her heart to thoughts of Donnally just yet, so she pushed him away. He was alive. That was enough.

Of course, she'd lost more than Donnally. Aric's gun had taken down two of their deepships, and one of the rogue ships had been overwhelmed. Altogether, they'd lost sixteen people. Pisces had been the one to bring her the report, thinking it would land more softly if it came from her. But in Caledonia's mind it remained a number, a representative figure instead of individuals. She'd offered Pisces a gentle nod of understanding and then asked to be left alone. Perhaps a deeper sorrow would follow this moment of shock, but Caledonia worried that this was the new shape of her heart.

Every time a quiet moment settled among her thoughts, she pictured the deck of that ship after the star blossom ripped it apart. She saw the moments of agony frozen in place on the faces of children younger than she, she saw the ring of soldiers twisted around Aric's feet, and she saw the bomb in her own hands. She felt the click of the button beneath her fingers, and she wanted to claw her throat open.

This battle had changed her. She had used Aric's terrible weapons against him, and she knew she would make the same choice again if the situation called for it.

From the doorway, someone cleared their throat. She looked up to find Oran standing there, glazed in the luminescent glow of the golden dome above. The soft light made his eyes shine. It settled on his shoulders like a mantle sculpted to fit his lithe figure. She drank him in, and then she pulled her eyes away.

"Is something wrong?" she asked.

Oran strode into the room. She knew he shook his head, though she still avoided looking at him. "Not out there."

She nodded, and though she'd come here with a severe desire for solitude, she didn't ask him to leave. After a moment, he moved farther into the room, kneeling before her.

"Whatever you need, I am here."

Again, she nodded. Of everyone, he alone had been in this position before. If not exactly, then close to it. "I don't need anything right now. Just . . . to breathe."

A sad smile tilted his lips. Boldly, he slid a hand inside her blanket and found her hand, pulling her fingers between his own. She let her fingers twine with his, gasping a little when he lifted her hand and pressed his lips against her knuckles.

"No one knows what this is like until they do it," he said. "And even if it's different for everyone, it's also a little bit the same. Tell me what you need, Caledonia, and I will do it."

His promise was like a strong ocean wind, bolstering and swift and everything she needed. She slipped down from the bench, letting him catch her in his lap, and then their lips were together. His arms circled her waist, tucking her against his chest as her tongue parted his lips. His mouth was warm and giving, letting her guide the kiss.

She pulled away, resting her forehead to his, sharing his breath and running her thumbs over his bottom lip. If she could, she would stay here forever, in the protective circle of his arms, where they were warm and no one would live or die on her decisions.

But it was a dream, and if she dwelled on it too long, it would become dangerous.

She sat back so she could see his face again, and so that he could see hers. If she was going to become a monster, she would make sure someone saw it happening.

"I didn't see it coming," she admitted. "Battle makes sense to me. I can feel it changing and growing and folding back on itself. I know how to anticipate its movements. But I never expected Lir to kill Aric."

"It didn't surprise me. Lir has always wanted Aric's power. He was just waiting for the perfect opportunity to take it." Oran winced softly. "There was a time when I might have done the same."

She knew what she needed from him. It was a terrible thing to ask, but if she was going to lead her people into a war with Lir, then she needed someone who could think like him, someone who could anticipate what she could not.

"Oran, I need you to be the Steelhand again," she said, tears warming her eyes. His mouth opened in protest, but before he could speak, she added, "Not like you were before. Not an instrument of torture, but something else: *my* Steelhand."

ACKNOWLEDGMENTS

I have learned many things in writing this book, some of it about ships and what it means to build a fantastical world, and some of it about what it takes to publish a single book. And I have one piece of advice: if you're going to set out to write a trilogy, make sure you have a team as tremendous as mine by your side.

I am deeply grateful to the talented people at Razorbill and Penguin Books for Young Readers for continuing to buoy up this adventuring crew. Endless thanks to my editor, Marissa Grossman, who kept me on course through many rounds of revision; Chris Hernandez, who has taken up the cause with such excitement; Lindsay Boggs and Felicity Vallence, who keep me on target throughout the year; Shari Beck, Samantha Hoback, and Marinda Valenti, whose combined efforts give me the appearance of knowing how to appropriately use a comma (which is only true part of the time); Jessica Jenkins, Theresa Evangelista, and Deborah Kaplan for creating yet another amazing package for this series; Cliff Nielsen, whose art brought Caledonia and Pisces to life brilliantly; Ben Schrank, who brought *Seafire* into the fold, and Casey McIntyre and Jen Klonsky, who continue the tradition; Venessa Carson, Carmela Iaria, Emily Romero, Summer Ogata, and the entire School and Library team, who have introduced these books to new readers;

Caitlin Whalen, Kara Brammer, Jennifer Dee, and everyone at Penguin Teen, whose enthusiasm never wavers; Alex Sanchez, Gretchen Durning, and Alex Garber, whose support I see even if we're rarely in direct contact; Jill Bailey, who travels forever in the name of books; and Jen Loja, who captains the ship with grace and compassion. And to all the people who have worked behind the scenes on these books, thank you.

None of this would be possible at all without my colleagues at Alloy Entertainment. I will give you a thousand thank-yous now and a thousand more later. Lanie Davis, who makes me better than I am. Josh Bank, Sarah Shandler, Laura Barbiea, Romy Golan, Matt Bloomgarden, and Josephine McKenna, who all make this work possible, and the entire team at Rights People, who have worked to take this ship overseas. I'm over the moon for you all!

To my agent, Lara Perkins, thank you. In the seafaring metaphor of my career, you are the one who makes sense of the stars, drawing maps in the sky when I've lost my way or need a new one.

To all the booksellers and librarians who put *Seafire* into the hands of readers across the country, thank you! And an extra thanks to my local bookstores, The Raven Book Store and Rainy Day Books, who have been the best champions I could have asked for.

My friends are legion and I will say thank you, but probably owe them so much more than words. Julie Murphy and Bethany Hagen, who keep me honest even when it's rough; Zoraida Córdova, Dhonielle Clayton, Justina Ireland, Heidi Heilig, and Miriam

Weinberg, who give me a place to argue, whine, and brag; my twin, Adib Khorram, whom I met through *Seafire* and who promotes it better than I do; Becca Coffindaffer and Christie Holland, whom I definitely owe dinner; Dot Hutchison and Amanda Sellet, who meet me every Thursday to write; Sarah MacLean, Sophie Jordan, Louisa White, Carrie Ryan, and Ally Carter, who helped me through the whirl; and the entire Kansas writing crew, who inspire me every day—thank you!

Once again, my father endured several phone calls about ships—how to sink them and how to save them—and I am indebted to him for all the ways in which the ships of the Bullet Seas ring true. Thanks for always picking up the phone, Dad.

Many thanks to my family for always asking about my writing and for generally being the best. And especially to my mom for always reading the advanced copy to catch final typos.

And finally, to Tess. We say thank you to each other every day—thank you for doing the dishes, thank you for reading my chapter, thank you for reminding me to eat. If I could build us a castle of thank-yous and set it down in the middle of a wide prairie, I would. Thank you for asking hard questions and for all the ways you make me a better storyteller.